THAT MISSING PIECE IS KILLING ME

Books by Roz Noonan

PUZZLE ME A MURDER

THAT MISSING PIECE IS KILLING ME

Published by Kensington Publishing Corp.

THAT MISSING PIECE IS KILLING ME

ROZ NOONAN

KENSINGTON PUBLISHING CORP.
kensingtonbooks.com

This book is a work of fiction. Names, characters, businesses, organizations, places, events, and incidents either are the product of the author's imagination or are used fictitiously. Any resemblance to actual persons, living or dead, events, or locales is entirely coincidental.

To the extent that the image or images on the cover of this book depict a person or persons, such person or persons are merely models, and are not intended to portray any character or characters featured in the book.

KENSINGTON BOOKS are published by

Kensington Publishing Corp.
900 Third Ave.
New York, NY 10022

Copyright © 2025 by Rosalind Noonan

All rights reserved. No part of this book may be reproduced in any form or by any means without the prior written consent of the Publisher, excepting brief quotes used in reviews.

Without limiting the author's and publisher's exclusive rights, any unauthorized use of this publication to train generative artificial intelligence (AI) technologies is expressly prohibited.

All Kensington titles, imprints, and distributed lines are available at special quantity discounts for bulk purchases for sales promotion, premiums, fundraising, educational, or institutional use. Special book excerpts or customized printings can also be created to fit specific needs. For details, write or phone the office of the Kensington Special Sales Manager: Attn. Special Sales Department. Kensington Publishing Corp., 900 Third Ave., New York, NY 10022. Phone: 1-800-221-2647.

KENSINGTON and the KENSINGTON COZIES teapot logo Reg. US Pat. & TM Off.

Library of Congress Control Number: 2025934266

ISBN: 978-1-4967-4674-0

First Kensington Hardcover Edition: August 2025

ISBN: 978-1-4967-4676-4 (ebook)

10 9 8 7 6 5 4 3 2 1

Printed in the United States of America

The authorized representative in the EU for product safety and compliance is eucomply OU, Parnu mnt 139b-14, Apt 123
Tallinn, Berlin 11317, hello@eucompliancepartner.com

For Emily Slavin
Champion of humans who need help
Guardian of the Constitution
and a sweet dog named Leydi
I'm honored to be your auntie
And grateful that you will always fight the good fight

Chapter One

The place was lousy with mice.
Mice of the munchkin persuasion.

Pink-bellied, felt-eared, fuzzy gray mice with pink tutus and snazzy little tails that resembled red licorice whips. They bopped and pranced about the "fairgrounds," a mixture of grassy lawn and macadam that on most days served as the parking lot for the West Hazel Library.

"And the day was going so well," Alice Pepper said, peeking out of the book tent to take a gander at the outdoor stage. Mice were swarming the area, climbing onto the apron, dancing on the steps, chasing each other in the grass.

The pixie rodents—kindergartners, perhaps—were ready to take the stage and dance their little hearts out as their part of the annual children's book festival. The popular event—which included games, face painting, music and dance, a few alpacas for petting and photo ops, and plenty of books—was admittedly Alice's own brainchild. As head librarian, she knew it was necessary to bring children to the library for fun and expose them to the joy of reading.

So far today the stage had held two marching bands and

a Bubble Baby story time with strollers wheeled onstage and encircling Nancy Savino, their animated children's librarian. A dozen or so teen ballerinas costumed in flowing purple skirts and white blouses had performed a piece called "Willow Dance." And Alice's granddaughter, Taylor Denham, had led some sing-alongs with only her guitar and her strong voice. Taylor was also playing emcee, giving new life to some dry old kernels of jokes. "Sir, is that your car running? You'd better go catch it."

All had gone well, until the mice invasion.

"And this had to happen when Julia stepped away." Alice's right-hand manager and strategic genius, Julia Abe, had headed off to take her daughter to a soccer game. Parental duty called. "Be right back," she'd promised.

But not soon enough.

"Someone needs to wrangle the beginning ballerinas." Beto, one of the assistant librarians, bit back a laugh. "Though they are cute. Where's their teacher?"

"It's Michelle Chong, but I haven't seen her around this morning." Come to think of it, Michelle hadn't been here earlier when her older students performed on pointe.

"And their parents?" Beto asked.

"No doubt taking a well-deserved break." Alice wasn't surprised that moms and dads had scattered. Having hosted various kiddie events, she knew that caretakers tended to fade off for a cup of coffee, a chat, or a deep dive into the stacks once they handed over their little darlings. Against library policy, but who could blame them, craving a minute to themselves?

With mice in her sights, Alice left the book tent in the capable hands of her staff and crossed the field of colorful tents and food trucks that gave the area a circus feel. At the moment the stage was occupied by the high school orchestra in the throes of "Weekend in New England," a fitting piece for an October day, but the rodent invaders were beginning to distract the young musicians, who turned away from their conductor to point and grin.

She wove among the toddlers and parents and high-school–age musicians in their brightly colored band uniforms. Royal blue and white for West Hazel High, and the St. Katherine's musicians were decked in raspberry with silver-spangled trim. She was forging ahead when she came to a lone mouse, a dark-haired girl with a lipstick-pink nose, who sat on a folding chair sipping a juice box just beyond the mayhem.

Alice bent down to her, not wanting to intimidate the poor thing with her six-foot stature and ghostly pale hair. "Where is your teacher?" she asked.

The girl's lower lip jutted out in a pout. "I don't know."

Alice rephrased. "*Who* is your teacher?"

"Ms. Chong, but she's not here."

Alice scanned the crowd. "It's not like her to be late, is it?"

The little girl shook her head and went back to her soothing juice box.

Michelle Chong wasn't just a teacher. She was the proprietor of West Hazel's martial arts and dance studio. A former dancer and actor in a few martial arts films, Michelle still exuded a star aura mixed with the wisdom of a practical sixtyish woman. She was usually on top of these things. Where the heck was she?

One thing was for sure, Alice was in sore need of a mouser.

Chapter Two

Arms folded at her waist, Alice turned to assess the swarming mice. There had to be thirty or more of them, but she could hardly holler to round them up in the vicinity of the stage. That would be rude to the current performers.

Scanning the crowd for help, she spotted Kamaria Richardson, a teacher from the dance studio, hurrying down the street. The young Black woman had launched into a jog that set the wooden beads around her neck bouncing. Moving like the dancer she was, Kamaria loped toward them, graceful as an antelope, despite her three-inch cork heels. Her scarf-hemmed, navy-and-gold-print dress was a wrap, thrown on over a leotard and tights. Studio garb, but Kamaria had the grace to make a casual dress resemble a goddess's gold-spun threads.

In seconds, Kamaria was at Alice's side. "Phew! I just got a frantic call from one of the moms. I'm so sorry! I thought Michelle was here with the dancers, but she's not answering her cell. I lammed out of my tap class and ran right over."

"And in the nick of time. Your mice need a pied piper, and I haven't seen Michelle all day."

"She should have been here with the earlier batch of dancers, but I got this. Apologies. We'll be fine from here." Kamaria raised one arm, three fingers extended toward the sky, and turned to scan the stage area.

Some sort of secret sign, Alice surmised. And it worked. Whiskers in the air, the little mice sniffed the summons, poked their cohorts, and lifted two tiny fingers to the sky.

Kamaria gestured them to come to her, and without a word or squeak they responded. Little dancers removed themselves from the stage, lifted themselves from the grass, and formed a loose semicircle around Kamaria.

"Amazing." Alice smiled. "Thank you."

"Discipline is the backbone of dance," Kamaria said. "And crucial when dealing with dozens of four-year-olds."

"I'll leave you to it."

And with the elegant wave of one hand, Kamaria led the mice to a section of grass beyond the stage, out of the way of the other events.

Crisis averted, Alice headed over to check on her sister, who was running the games. "I love a good field day!" Violet had been enthusiastic when she'd learned of her mission. You could always count on her to find the fun.

Alice worked the crowd as she moved, directing patrons to the restroom, coaching a boy with fat sneakers on how to tie the fluorescent laces. "That's right," Alice said. "Two loops, like rabbit ears . . ." She chatted with Friends of the Library, personal friends, and patrons who'd lived in West Hazel all their lives. People talked most about their selfies with Ginger or Alphie, the alpacas, who'd been brought in by a local family. "We'll have to bring them back next year," Alice promised.

Back onstage, Taylor commanded the microphone, thanking the orchestra. Someone in the brass section let out a low toot, which evoked laughter.

"Was that the trombone?" Taylor asked, turning abruptly so that her long, honey-brown hair swung round behind her. "Shout out to the brass section. I've got some Tums if you need them." That girl possessed stage presence and musical talent, too. Alice wondered if that might be a path for Taylor, when she finally launched. Sooner than later, please. At twenty-two Taylor was eager to fly but stuck on the ground, living with her gran.

Dodging two strollers and a gaggle of boys in a bean bag battle, Alice headed toward the festively colored tents. She passed the blue tent designated for face painting, a red tent for finger painting and spin art. At the end of the parking lot, the lawn events were cordoned off by a portable picket fence.

Inside the game area a cluster of children hopped and yelped in unison, apparently on cue from Violet, who was explaining the rules of a game. Strict on the surface, Violet looked every inch the schoolmarm with her auburn hair twisted into a bun and a navy blazer broadening her shoulders. She had a knack for drawing kids to her. Maybe they sensed her innate kookiness, or perhaps they knew she could be trusted. For whatever reason, kids had flocked to the game lawn all afternoon, thrilled to toss bean bags, shoot a Nerf gun at empty cans, or chase someone around the circle in duck, duck, goose. Alice's favorite event was the go-fish pond, a chance to snag a prize in a kiddie pool full of water. It was the perfect exercise for Alice: low impact and a perennial reward.

Content that all was well in game land, Alice turned and spotted her childhood friend Ruby Milliner. Back in the seventies they'd been neighbors in Queens Village, New York. "Friends 4-ever!" they'd inked on a tree in Ruby's backyard. More than fifty years later, here they were on the West Coast, neighbors and friends in West Hazel, Oregon. Alice had found her sweet spot in this charming town with the most utilized library in the state of Oregon.

"Let me tell you about my day," Ruby said. "Oh, I did that shift this morning at the lost children's table."

"I saw you working your magic there," Alice said. "Drying some tears."

"Sweet little things. No one was really lost, just misplaced. I've got the grandkids now—two of Ada's. She's off getting a pedicure. That girl needs it! But you've got to see this temporary tattoo." Ruby motioned toward her granddaughter. "Beebee, tater, come here. Show Alice your arm."

Summoned from the picket fence, which she and her brother had been trying to climb, Beebee traipsed over and stuck out her arm.

A colorful butterfly seemed ready to spring from its spot on Beebee's smooth brown skin. The kaleidoscope of colors on its wings were thrilling, but Alice was sold on the animation. It had personality.

"It's gorgeous. Beebee. I think it's winking at me. It must be enchanted. You can never wash your arm again."

"Okay," Beebee promised politely.

"Don't tell her that." Ruby swatted Alice's arm. "Hard to believe this was done by an art student," she insisted.

Alice agreed, but their conversation was cut short when Trevor whimpered that he needed someone to paint a truck on his arm. "Here we go again," Ruby said, letting the boy drag her away by the hand.

"Make sure it's got big wheels," Alice called after them.

Seeing that the mice were taking the stage, Alice found an empty chair at the end of one row to take a momentary break and watch the performance. As the music started, the mice stood in three groups, stepping to the ticktock rhythm of the music. Happy mice were they, until they were invaded.

Three lithe cats pranced on the stage, sending the mice fleeing to the back of the stage. The cats were girls of twelve or thirteen, Alice guessed, noting how they raised their arms gracefully and rose onto the tips of their ballet slippers. She knew that dancing on the toes could cause permanent damage in immature bones. Experts suggested that most girls wait until they were at least eleven until they danced on pointe.

It had been this restriction that had prompted her daughter Lauren to stomp out of the local dance studio at age eight, never to return to formal dance instruction.

Ages ago. And all these years later, Lauren was just as hardheaded.

Alice let out a breath and smiled at the children onstage. It hurt not to have Lauren in her life, but then again, it hadn't been her plan to cut off relations. At least she'd had Lauren's daughters, Taylor and Madison, over the past several years. Important years for a young woman, middle school and teen years.

Then again, each season of a woman's life had its turning-point moments.

Onstage, the three clever cats had hunkered down so that they resembled large rocks. And there they lingered, watching, waiting to pounce, as the fleet of small mice came frolicking back onto the stage. Some seemed locked in concentration as they moved through a prescribed dance routine. Others stumbled, tumbled, and rolled like ants spilling out into sunshine.

"Kids," she murmured. You never could predict how they'd behave in any given situation. Alice tore herself away from the ballet and headed back to the book tent. The meese-kins were the final performance of the day, and, as it was pushing four, the crowd was thinning. Dinnertime.

Noticing a cluster of abandoned chairs near the food trucks, she began to fold them up and load them onto a rolling cart. The air was cooling, stirring the leaves, and brushing Alice's hair from her cheeks. Silver hair that Ruby insisted was gray. "You want silver, honey?" Ruby had pressed her, more than once. "I can put you in a hair piece that sparkles! Our platinum series." A generous offer from the owner of Ruby's House of Wigs and Hairpieces. But Alice chose to stay natural. Sixty-five years she'd spent earning this battleship gray. That ought to count for something.

Alice stacked another chair as the music faded and Taylor announced an end to the festival. "We've got one more song to send you on your way," she said, strumming a chord on her guitar. Alice smiled as Taylor's bright voice filled the area. Yes, Alice was biased, but the girl warmed her heart. The song had a tempo she could match with her task, and soon the remaining chairs were folded and stacked.

By the time the song ended, and Taylor wrapped up the event, it was clear that the day was done. The mice had exited the stage area, and there was now an exodus of families and small groups crossing the grounds and dispersing into the neighborhood. The food trucks were still serving, but the lines had dwindled.

At the edge of the parking lot Alice alerted to the sight of a police vehicle. What was that about? Shielding her eyes from the sun, she scanned the departing crowd and noticed the one person walking toward her.

Madison. Her granddaughter, the rookie cop. Paying a friendly visit as the festival wrapped up? Alice hoped that was the case, but from the purposeful way Madison strode forward, she had her doubts.

"Did you catch the last song of the festival?" Alice asked. "Your sister closed the show."

"She was awesome." Madison nodded, and for the zillionth time Alice marveled at the lovely features she shared with her sister. Madison's hair, eyes, and skin tone mirrored those of her twin sister, and yet, Madison's grounded, decisive personality shone in a different light. Identical twins, antithetical personalities. "But I came to talk to Aunt Vi. A police matter."

"Is Violet in trouble?"

"Vice Principal Violet Pepper? Pillar of the community?"

"Everyone has a few skeletons in her closet." For Violet, that included a pursuit of astrology and tarot cards and Wiccan rituals in the forest. Extracurriculars that some conservative parents might frown upon. And those were the "hobbies" Violet had shared with Alice.

"Do you know where she is?" Madison asked. "I have some questions for her about a missing persons case."

Missing persons. The very phrase made Alice's belly ache, her body clench. She'd filed one of those once. The agony of waiting and worrying had imprinted on her psyche. It remained in her DNA, ever present, ready to ignite like a match.

"Is she here?" Madison asked.

"Yes, yes, she's running the games. I'll take you to her." Alice started walking toward the green without checking to see if Madison was with her. She had to walk, shake this off. Madison didn't know. The twins had been too young, and the story would only bring them pain and doubt.

"Gran, are you okay?"

"Fine." Most of the children had left the green, and Ruby and Taylor had found Violet in the game area. They were chatting, storytelling, laughing. When they caught sight of Madison, merriment fled their faces like a scattering flutter of butterflies.

"Oh, Lordy, it's bad news, isn't it?" Ruby scowled at Madison. "You know I love you, honey, but when you wear that uniform you're the harbinger of bad news."

"We've had a report of a missing person. I'm wondering if you've heard from Michelle Chong in the past twenty-four hours?" Madison asked.

Alice pictured Michelle, owner of the dance and martial arts studios. Roughly Alice's age, fit, and, with her martial arts background, prepared to defend herself. Creative and generous, smart and clever. There had to be some mistake.

"We've been checking with friends," Madison said, "and you're on the list, Aunt Vi."

"I just saw her this week, Wednesday night." Wide-eyed, Violet shook her head. "She hosted our book club. But I haven't talked to her since then."

Alice stepped forward, feeling a personal attachment. "I was there Wednesday." She'd been a visitor at that book club meeting. "Her students were performing for us today." She nodded toward the stage. "I should have known something was amiss when Michelle didn't show. She's usually so reliable."

"That's what I've been hearing. People say it's not like her to head off without checking in." Was Madison's face unusually pale? Sometimes her job as a West Hazel police officer put her in difficult situations.

"How long has she been missing?" asked Ruby.

"According to her husband, Lars, Michelle went for coffee yesterday morning and didn't return home. We've been calling Portland-area hotels and hospitals, but there's no sign of her."

"That doesn't sound good," Alice said.

"I'm sorry, Aunt Violet." Technically, Violet was a great-aunt to the twins, but the family didn't dwell on those titles. Madison squeezed the gold star on her collar, a nervous habit. "Her husband seems to think she was kidnapped, but—"

"Kidnapped!" Violet gasped. "Who would do that to Michelle?"

"Mr. Olsen has no suspect in mind, and the theory is a little light on evidence. Olsen gave us a list of friends to contact for information, and I wanted to talk to you personally. Have you heard from her in the past day or so?"

"I have not," Violet said. "But we're not normally in touch every day."

Madison nodded. "Of course. It was worth a try."

"What can we do to help?" Taylor asked.

"We're signing up volunteers for a search of some public areas tomorrow," Madison said.

"Count me in," Taylor said, hands on hips. "But maybe she'll come home tonight."

Ruby clasped her hands together. "I'll say a little prayer."

"Knowing Michelle, I think she's safe. She's one of the most competent people I know," Violet said, staring off over the trees. "I've seen her in action. She's not a woman who would be easily overcome by an attacker."

"We don't know that she was attacked," Madison said.

Violet touched her chin, thoughtful. "I just can't fathom that something bad could happen to her."

Or maybe Violet didn't want to consider that possibility.

Alice squeezed her sister's shoulder; she understood all too well the scourge of worry. "Any clues about where she might have gone?"

Madison's eyes were warm with sympathy. "I wish we had some leads to follow. So far, no one has a clue about where she might be." She cast a sympathetic look toward Violet. "She just disappeared."

Chapter Three

"This is just awful." Violet pressed her palms to her cheeks and stared down at the ground. "I don't know what to think."

Alice slipped her arm over Violet's shoulders and drew her close as a wariness descended on their group. Without speaking, their circle tightened up, and the distractions of the festival faded.

"What exactly did Lars say?" Violet asked. "I mean, maybe she flew to see her family in LA. Or she could have booked a getaway spa weekend. Isn't that possible?"

"The husband claims that nothing was out of the ordinary."

"But she's gone," Alice said. "And the fact is, humans leave a trail wherever they go. Breadcrumbs and footprints. We need to find Michelle's trail."

Violet took in a breath, strong, resolute. "I'm going to stay positive and believe that Michelle is okay," she said. "After all, she's an athletic dancer and a martial arts expert. She's a woman equipped to defend herself."

Taylor tucked a swath of shiny hair behind one ear. "I've had classes with her. If someone crossed Michelle, she would totally kick their—"

"Let's just agree that she's tactically fit for defense," Alice said, interrupting her granddaughter. She refrained from pointing out that even the best martial arts experts could not stop a bullet. This was a time to remain positive. "And it's quite possible this is just some misunderstanding. But it's not something we can solve here in the parking lot amid the leftovers of the festival."

"And I've got to go," Madison said. "There are a few more people I need to contact."

"When does your shift end?" Alice asked, catching herself before she could call her granddaughter "honey." It was important to respect Madison's professionalism, but she was eager to squeeze more information from her. The puzzle of Michelle's disappearance was already tugging on Alice. "Can you join us at the house and help fill in some of the details?"

"I'm off at six. Later if something breaks."

"Keep us posted, and we'll put some dinner aside for you," Alice promised as Madison headed off.

"And you can sign us all up for the search party tomorrow," Ruby called after her.

"Will do."

"I have a date with my masseuse," Ruby admitted, "but I'll reschedule."

Violet's eyes opened wide as she turned to Ruby. "That's huge! You, giving up Mischa?"

"I know, and my shoulder's been killing me, but . . . this is important," Ruby said with a nod.

"We'll meet back at the house. I've got some barbecue sliders ready to go. Homemade coleslaw, too," Alice said.

"Sounds delicious," Ruby said. "But first I need to get horizontal. My boudoir beckons."

"Thank you all for helping out today," Alice told them

before they turned away. "Couldn't have done it without you."

"It takes a village, Gran." Taylor took a few steps on the grass, did a cartwheel, and stuck the landing. That girl followed her own rainbow.

"I'm going to check with some of my book club peeps," Violet said. "Maybe someone knows something."

Alice suggested her office for privacy, but Violet wanted to remain outside. "Right now I need the fresh air."

"You know, I'd like to talk with them, too. Feel free to invite anyone over tonight. Maybe we can arrange for a meeting tomorrow or the next day."

Violet nodded. "Thank you for taking this on." She retrieved her cell from a pocket of her blazer and walked off to make her calls.

Watching her sister retreat under the orange-leafed oak trees at the edge of the library block, Alice was glad she'd had her introduction to the book club ladies this week. Michelle's friends might be a valuable resource. She wondered which of the women was closest to Michelle.

"Someone called the cops on us?" Julia Abe exclaimed as she bustled in from the side street and caught up with Alice.

"A noise complaint," Alice said blandly. "The loud, raucous library."

"You're kidding." Julia shoved her glasses, the transitional lenses now amber, onto her head. "I know you're joking because Madison told me about Michelle. It's very scary. I mean, it gives me a bad feeling. What gives? Are you scared, too?"

"Worried. Once I finish up here, we're going to meet with Madison at the house and puzzle things out."

"Puzzle out the mystery over a jigsaw puzzle, right?" Alice smiled. "I knew you'd like that."

"Such a wordsmith." As Julia tipped back her head to look up at Alice, the late-afternoon sun caught the fuchsia pink in her hair, the same color as the speckles in her glasses. A deliberate color match, and one that suited her. Julia's original highlights had been the outcome of a challenge to her son, Riley. If he got his math grade up to a C, she would dye her hair. She'd been thrilled when he'd been victorious and had chosen a lime-green dye. "It's the real me!" she'd announced.

"Okay, we need to get this operation buttoned up." Julia squinted, rubbed her nose with the back of one hand, and then pushed her glasses on as she scanned the scene. "I'll deal with the vendors, and we've got people coming to dismantle the tents and stage tomorrow. Not to play boss, but if you can just make sure the books make it inside, we're golden."

"I'm on it, boss," Alice said. There were a few staffers ready to help. The task would be quick.

"But first I've got to find my darling son. He's out there, somewhere. I hope he's behaving, though I doubt it."

"A model citizen, I'm sure." Alice got a kick out of Julia's ten-year-old twins—reminders of her twin granddaughters who'd spent many of their growing years under Alice's roof. "The last time I saw Riley he was over by the ice cream truck."

"That boy!" Julia huffed. "I told him no more."

"I might have given him a few bucks. He was out of dough."

"Alice! You're such a sucker." Julia squinted toward the concession area. "There he is!" She waved toward the far end of the lot, where the hot dog and ice cream trucks lingered, serving the stragglers. "Riley! No more ice cream! How many is that?"

Riley glanced over and held up one hand. "Five?"

Julia's mouth dropped open as she turned to Alice. "Can you believe him?"

"At least he gave you an honest answer."

"Stop! No more!" Julia ordered. "No more."

"But I'm hungry."

"Fine. One more and then you can help us move books," Julia called. "And don't tell your father you had five ice creams."

Leaving Julia to manage the big picture—and her son—Alice headed back to the book tent aware of the departing pizza truck and the alpacas being led toward their truck. Otherwise, a relative quiet had overtaken the area, driven by the click and clack of collapsing picket fencing and chairs. Most of the people who remained were either vendors or staff.

When a familiar laugh snagged her attention, Alice turned to the source. Taylor was onstage, chuckling with a woman as they collapsed the microphone stand and packed up the audio system. *Careful, ladies,* Alice thought. The pricy sound system that had put a crimp in their budget three years ago. She was glad Taylor was taking care of it, but who was that other woman, a Marilyn Monroe clone with a well-coiffed platinum hairdo, though she was dressed down in a hoodie and sweatpants? A friend of Taylor? Alice couldn't place her.

Back at the book tent, the staff seemed concerned.

"We saw the police," Fiona Cohen said, "but Beto said it was just your daughter."

"Her granddaughter," Beto corrected, straightening some

books on a cart, then turning thoughtful brown eyes on Alice. "Everything okay? Do you want to sit down?"

"I'm fine, but we were told of a missing person. Michelle Chong, owner of the dance studio."

"Oh, my gosh." Fiona raked back her blond hair. "She was my ballet teacher when I was little."

Probably just a handful of years ago, Alice surmised, as Fiona was one of their teen hires.

"That's so disturbing." Beto was folding up a plastic tablecloth. "No wonder she wasn't here to reel in her dancers."

They discussed the situation, the search planned for the next day. "At this point, there are more questions than answers, and we've got to finish up here." Alice surveyed the tables—now empty. That morning they'd toted a third of their children's book collection out to the tent for children to check out. Decades as a librarian had taught her that books served no one when they were tucked onto a shelf, gathering dust. "You've packed everything up. Nice job."

"Well, a lot of books were checked out, making our job easier," Beto said humbly.

"Even better. Time for these chickens to come home to roost." Alice pulled on a loaded cart, causing two books to flip to the ground.

"My aunt has chickens in her backyard." Beto reached down to pick up the books. "They do seem to like their little hut."

"Can I help you with that, Alice?" Charles Wayland suddenly appeared in the tent entrance, filling the space. A veteran and retired cop, Charles was a tall, large man who possessed a calming manner that everyone was drawn to. "We can handle this if you need to go do some follow-up with the police," he offered.

"I've got this one," Alice said, pulling the cart out of the shadows of the tent. "I want to do my share but thank you. A million thanks to all of you. It takes a village to run a book event, and you folks are the best." Wheeling the cart along the pavement, she was glad for the menial work, eager for a quiet moment to parse through what she knew of Michelle Chong.

The missing woman.

Chapter Four

Engaged in the menial task of moving books, Alice thought back to the book club meeting at Michelle's house.

A few images of the isolated house on Dragonberry Lane had stuck in Alice's memory. First was the house itself, an aging farmhouse that had been expanded decades ago in a ramshackle design. A builder had added an A-line, windowed wing to the front of the original structure—a two-story home with a sloped mansard roof. The results were unsettling.

The new wing seemed to have windowed eyes and a deck that curved into a grim smile so that it resembled the head of a beast. The old, curved farmhouse, its roof covered in moss, was now the creature's body.

"Looks like a sick dragon," Alice had said as she and Violet rolled toward the house down the very secluded, private lane. "Do you see it?"

"I do. But maybe you're influenced by the name—Dragonberry Lane. I always considered it to be more of a decaying armadillo."

"Yup. I see that, too. It's certainly private." Alice had

been determined to say something positive as she backed her car onto the gravel lot near a fat tree stump. "I think their driveway is about ten miles long."

"Maybe a mile," Violet said. "You do like to exaggerate, Alice. Just be careful not to go too far. There's a ravine along that end of the property."

Although Violet had visited Michelle's house before as a member of the book club, Alice had been a special guest that night, brought in to explain the procedure the library used to choose its books and to suggest some interesting titles slated for publication in the coming year.

Alice stepped onto the gravel and closed the car door. The front of the house had no lawn, only an expanse of packed earth and gravel that was bordered by an overgrown ravine on one side and woods on the other. A narrow gravel drive snaked around to the left of the house, and then meandered up a slope beyond the house.

"What's up there?" Alice shielded her eyes from the low sunlight for a better look, but the ground just seemed to drop off.

"Michelle calls it the pond, but it's no day at the beach," Violet said, then lowered her voice. "Emerald says it's an old quarry, and God knows what's buried in there. Cars and trash and junk."

Alice nodded. "Not a waterfront property." She turned to the house. The closest wing was a wall of glass. "But the front of the house has plenty of windows. I bet that gives them lots of light. Perfect for an artist."

The unique house wasn't that unusual in the suburbs of Portland, Oregon, where Victorian mansions, gingerbread houses, or contemporary cubes could be found tucked in the woods or on hillside stilts or hanging over the edge of a freeway. In fact, Alice's home was its own oddity, with a bunch of en suites built into the hillside below the original craftsman house. Weird, but she loved it.

Greeting them at the door, Michelle had shimmered in an embossed teal tunic with swishy black pants. With her auburn hair, broad smile, and brown eyes that transmitted wisdom and mystery, Michelle still exuded a movie star quality. Her voluminous aura filled the cold, empty spaces of that old farmhouse. She had been a gracious and charming hostess, though it had been awkwardly apparent that her famous husband, Lars Olsen, was a bit of a grump who needed his wife to calm the beast within.

Was that always the dynamic of a celebrity couple? One lion and one lion tamer? Although Alice had seen Michelle and Lars around town, the book club event had been her first glimpse into their relationship's chemistry.

Their living space seemed to be more of an art studio, with paintings stacked, six-deep, against most walls and spaces. There was plenty of light from the windows, but Alice felt exposed and lost in the many canvases and easels under the handful of cold track lights mounted on the ceiling. She was grateful to discover a sofa, two upholstered chairs, and half a dozen folding chairs in the adjoining room, but they faced a giant brick fireplace with an opening large enough to house a Jeep, as if the place were a grand ballroom or lodge. The lack of proportion was dizzying, and Alice was grateful that nothing was burning in the open incinerator.

The artist himself had been a disappointment. Perhaps she'd expected a more upbeat man, having seen the painter's colorful, bright work. Although Lars Olsen had been in town only six years or so, citizens of West Hazel enjoyed claiming him as their own resident artist. His work was romanticized and celebrated around town, as if his depiction of the trees, flowers, grass, and waterways of West Hazel were a love letter to the town.

To her dismay, Lars Olsen was anything but cheerful, bright, and warm. At first, he seemed pleasant enough, six feet tall, broad-shouldered, and holding on to most of his wavy tawny blond hair. But a conversation with Lars left a bad aftertaste, a sour note in the finish. Ten minutes with the artist and you would expect him to be churning out dark, terrifying paintings like Goya as he contemplated his descent into madness and old age in the 1820s. A fine example of the way *not* to handle the golden years.

Those dark paintings had scarred her for life. Most of Alice's art education had transpired when she'd volunteered in the grade school's art literacy program when the twins were going through. In the Goya lesson, she would never forget how the boys in the class had marveled over the depiction of a bony, white-haired beast chewing the head off the small, bloody corpse of his son. "Gross!" the boys had proclaimed in a chorus of disgust. Alice had sided with the girls in the class, who were convinced that Goya had gone off his rocker.

But Lars Olsen was not in his seventies like the Spanish artist. In fact, he was some twenty years younger than Michelle, somewhere in his early forties. Too old to be so petulant, too young to be so disenchanted.

According to Violet, the first thirty minutes of book club were meant for snacking and mingling—a time to catch up and catch a canape. But their reception had been dominated by the husband.

"Shell, did you show them my art?" he had demanded, calling her by a nickname she later admitted she didn't like.

"He knows it bothers me, but he can't help himself.

Shell, like a broken shell on the beach," Michelle had confided to a few of the gals that night. "That was my fourth-grade name, what the bullies called me in school." She shuddered. "Not a good memory."

"Show them the paintings. Come, ladies. You're among the first to see some of these pieces. All for sale, by the way. A good investment for you. But in high demand, of course."

The ladies of the club had humored the distracted artist who wanted everyone to appreciate his unique home, his numerous paintings, his artistic genius. With paintings leaning against every wall, nearly blocking the way to the restroom, you couldn't help but view his art.

Compelled to join the group tour, Alice had kept mum. She was no art critic, but she found his recent work to be a bit too red—suggesting blood or crimson crayon or great balls of fire. But many of the women in the club oohed and aahed, and Michelle played up to him, indulged him, smoothed over his sharp edges. With charm and grace, she finally made him disappear so that the women could have their discussion.

As the evening went on, Alice was charmed by Michelle. Though most folks thought Lars was a celebrity, Alice considered Michelle to be the true gem. When the couple had moved to town six years ago, everyone was eager to meet Lars, who proved himself to be temperamental and unfriendly. It was Michelle who developed friendships with folks in West Hazel.

"Ladies, please take a seat," Michelle had instructed, "and give a warm welcome to our guest of honor, Alice Pepper."

The group had been attentive as Alice went through her spiel about the library's methods of book selection and the exciting new fall and winter titles. After she fielded some astute questions about inventory, budget, and fines (people loved to talk about fines), her piece was done, allowing her to sit back and enjoy the conversation.

"And now for this month's book." Michelle had held up the fat novel, hoisting it like a brick. "It was a hefty one!"

Chapter Five

That night's book discussion had been brief, as the month's selection had proven to be a dud for most readers. Although the bestselling book had appeared on many reading lists, it was more than six hundred pages, loaded with subplots and unnecessary details, and male oriented.

"It's too much!" Emerald Shanley had proclaimed, pushing frosted curls from her forehead. "I read the whole thing, and I'm sorry I did."

"I stopped reading after a hundred pages," Violet said. She was wearing her customary navy blazer with sleeves rolled up over a white T-shirt and jeans. "I wanted to love it. A good book can enrich our lives in so many ways. This simply wasn't that book."

Spoken as the sister of a librarian, Alice thought.

"The way the author droned on, so tedious, he seemed to be in need of an editor," Violet went on. "And life is too short to waste on something that doesn't grab you. There are so many other good books to read."

"I couldn't finish it," Juanita Clarion said coolly. "Just not my jam." Dressed in sleek business attire with large, square black glasses, she'd come straight from the office. A legal secretary, Juanita insisted she would never retire because her job defined her days so perfectly.

"I finished it, and I loved it," Michelle said definitively.

An awkward silence fell over the group.

"What were the highlights for you?" Emerald asked.

Michelle's eyes opened wide as she surveyed the group, then broke into a smile. "Just kidding. I couldn't finish it either."

Laughter bubbled up as people started to voice random complaints about that month's selection.

"But I did relate to most of the characters," Rachel insisted. "I think this novel would have succeeded as four separate books."

"Oh, I can't believe this." A petite woman in a flowing black shirt and pants with a metallic gold-threaded black shawl picked up the book from the mosaic coffee table and then tossed it back with a thud. She'd been quiet through the meeting, but now seemed ready to pop. "Guys! I read the wrong book! I read the one about the handyman who helped everyone in the neighborhood. No wonder the conversation made no sense to me."

There was a moment of quiet as people drew in a breath, and then comments and laughter filled the room.

"Oh, that's hysterical!"

"You read next month's book, Merrilee!"

"I was wondering why you were so quiet!"

"You are so lucky not to have wasted your time on this opus!"

"Well, now that we've gotten that dog out of the way," Emerald boomed, rolling her eyes, "we can talk about something more interesting. Michelle, maybe you want to tell everyone a little bit about your background."

Michelle waved her off. "You ladies know me."

"But only for a few years, and some of our members haven't had the privilege of being in your unique home before," Emerald said. "You have a rich history and such an interesting background. Like your childhood in Malaysia?"

"And after that, in Hollywood, maybe?" Holly prodded. Blond, even-keeled, and ready to laugh, she was a retired schoolteacher, much beloved by her students.

"The inside scoop, like who was your favorite costar?" Rachel asked.

"All right, I'll tell you a little." Michelle clasped her hands together. "But no Hollywood secrets. I've always tried my best to stay out of gossip columns. So I was born in Malaysia, and I grew up speaking English and Malay. My parents were both Hok-lo people from China. They've both passed now, but I still have family down in Los Angeles. A few aunties who still tell me what to do during our weekly phone calls." She pressed a palm to her heart.

"Any brothers and sisters?" asked Violet.

"Two sisters and three brothers. And it was my brothers who challenged me to learn martial arts back when I was a little thing. They pushed me, and I loved to fight them."

"Yeah, I still fight with my brothers," Emerald said, "except that now it's over Scrabble words."

Michelle was grateful to her brothers for pushing her to learn martial arts. When she was ten, the family moved to Los Angeles, and once she turned eighteen, she began appearing in action-adventure films. "Minor roles," she said, "but enough to make my car payments." Her career received a boost from Chinese superstar Maxie Tao, who recognized her martial arts skills and comedic acting talent. "Maxie fought to get me parts in his films, and I'll always be grateful to him." When the acting roles tapered off, she began to teach dance and martial arts in LA, and then purchased the academy here in West Hazel. She still had some beloved aunties and cousins in Southern California. "I visit them all the time."

"And West Hazel is your happy ending?" asked Holly, always a fan of a feel-good story.

"Lars and I are very happy here," Michelle said. "But it's no ending. The journey continues."

Those words had stuck with Alice. *The journey continues.* If we're lucky, she thought.

"But you've had great success with the dance academy and the martial arts studio," Violet said.

"I've been fortunate to find success." Michelle rose from the folding chair. "But I was getting bored with the same old, same old. So let me show you what I started." She went to a cabinet beside the monstrously large fireplace and removed a large sketch pad. "You know, I've always been a doodler. I'm happy when I can scratch things out with a pen." She placed the pad on the footrest and opened it up to reveal a storyboard of illustrations.

The women oohed and aahed.

"Wow, Michelle!" Violet was impressed. "This is more than a doodle."

Alice smiled as she scanned one page. "This girl with the dark hair and glasses is adorable. And she's a helper. Talking to the kid who's alone in the lunchroom."

"Her name is Jing, which means clear, sparkly clear. It's her magical visions of people's fears that allow her to help others."

"My students would love this," Holly said.

"Are you kidding me? I would love this." Merrilee pressed her hands together and nodded to Michelle. "You're amazing."

Michelle was glowing with pride. "You're too kind."

"How did you decide to turn to illustration?" asked Juanita.

"I did some research." Michelle looked at Alice. "The reference librarian was quite helpful. He turned me on to the graphic novel. And that's what I'm attempting."

As the women were gathered closer to look over the illustrations, Lars passed through the room and paused at the periphery.

"Oh, that. She's skilled, of course, but I'm the real artist in this family," he said.

Alice gave her sister a "Can you stand it?" look, and Violet rolled her eyes. But no one else seemed to notice the husband as they paged through the tablet. When no one responded, he veered off.

After he left, Michelle admitted she'd had interest from a friend in publishing. But whatever the future held, she was enjoying the process and welcoming this exciting new phase in her life.

"To new chapters!" Emerald toasted, and wineglasses clinked.

As most of the book club members were in their sixties, the conversation turned to new endeavors, third acts... having the courage to venture down a new path. The meeting ended on that high note: a future chockful of possibility.

And now, Michelle was gone.

Had she set off to begin a new chapter? Or had someone ended her story abruptly?

One way or the other, Alice was determined to find her.

Chapter Six

When Violet texted that her friend Emerald would be joining them for dinner, Alice responded with a thumbs-up. *The more the merrier,* she thought as she flung off her flowing librarian tunic and pants and changed into joggers and an oversized Portland State T-shirt. Any fatigue she'd felt from hosting the festival had dissipated amid the taut energy of Michelle's disappearance.

A woman was missing, and Alice was on the case.

She washed up quickly, then hurried downstairs to set up the dinner spread.

Within minutes, Alice's kitchen was ready for a light supper.

Pulled pork simmered on the stove in its honey barbecue sauce—just a quick reheat. Small potato slider rolls were stacked in two baskets lined by red-and-white-checked napkins. Baked beans simmered on low heat in the Crock-Pot, and coleslaw, pickles, carrots, and celery tempted her from platters under the pendant lights.

Where would folks sit?

Alice went to the windowed nook that looked out over the rooftops and green trees of the Willamette Valley, and the white-capped mountains looming from Washington State in the distance. Such a beautiful place. Every day she took a moment to be grateful to live here in West Hazel.

To think, she'd almost lost this zany, delightful house in the divorce. Thank goodness for Violet, helping to save the day by moving in and paying room and board, not to mention a loan between sisters. And now that Ruby, recently widowed, had found security and joy renting her "happy-place suite" downstairs, Alice no longer had to sweat the monthly bills.

"Dinner smells great." Taylor cruised by, perused the fixings on the counter, and snitched a spicy pickle. While Madison had her own apartment, twenty-two-year-old Taylor lived in one of the many en suites on the lower level of Alice's house. A squatter, Taylor called herself, a way to glamorize living in your grandmother's basement. "Want me to put that puzzle back in the box for you?"

"Don't even say the words." Alice gave a mock gasp, looking down at the unfinished puzzle on the table in the kitchen nook. For Alice and her friends, jigsaw puzzles offered therapy and sport. Taylor had grown up tolerating her grandmother's habit, but over time she'd softened a bit and actually joined in on the puzzling. "You know better. In this house, no puzzle gets swept away before its time," Alice said. "It's two-thirds of the way finished."

"But the fun part is all done."

"We need to finish the sky." It was the hardest part, now that the pieces with color and detail—the gardens, rock walls, windows, and turrets of the French palace—had been completed.

"Just put it back in the box," Taylor said. "No one wants to figure out where all those blue pieces go."

"I will not give up. When you get to this stage of a puzzle it requires a different skill set. You need to focus on shape and size."

"Boring," Taylor sang, grabbing a carrot.

"We'll finish it tonight, and you will celebrate every piece snapping into place," Alice said, though Taylor knew she was teasing. She picked up a puzzle piece, mostly blue, with a brush of white cloud on one peg. "I meant to tell you, everyone seemed to enjoy your performances today. Don't know if you could hear, but some of the kids were singing along to the rainbow song. You played well to the crowd."

"Thanks. If I ever get a yearning to put on a purple dino costume and bang a few out, I might have a future in music."

"Nonsense. You could be a pink frog. But seriously, you were good."

"Thanks, Gran. It sure beats a shift in the kitchen." Recently Taylor had been hired by her grandfather, Alice's ex, to help out at Jeff's restaurant. Alice had been careful not to ply Taylor with questions about the job, as she didn't want to jinx it—Taylor's first real employment in months.

For the moment, Alice kept mum on the topic. "So, I saw you talking to someone at the festival. A woman I didn't recognize." Alice kept her eyes on the puzzle, trying to appear casual. "Who was that woman? The blonde with the Marilyn Monroe vibe."

"Some library patron? I thought you knew everyone in town, Gran."

"Apparently, my popularity status is sinking." Alice looked up at her. "Do you know who I'm talking about?"

Taylor shrugged. "Not sure. Why does it matter?"

For a plethora of reasons, Alice thought. *Because I worry about you. Because I want to keep watch over you.*

Because I don't want what happened to your mother to happen to you.

A thousand reasons that Alice couldn't say. Taylor was twenty-two years old, and she did not owe her grandmother explanations of her daily interactions.

"Just wondering," Alice said.

"So when can we eat?" Taylor asked. "I'm starving."

Aware that her question had gone unanswered, Alice looked up and gestured to the spread. "Everything's ready so dig in. Violet's bringing a friend, and Ruby will be up any minute. I might just grab a plate myself. Let's make it casual tonight."

Alice had put out a stack of plates when the doorbell rang. Expecting Violet's friend, she went to the door and beheld a wonderful sight.

"Stone... you're here." She grabbed the neck of her slubby T-shirt, remembering their standing date.

"Not for long," he said, tilting his head to one side, apologetic. "I know it's our night, but I've been dispatched to work in the morning, so I'll have to take a pass tonight."

"Of course," Alice said. Stone Donahue was the manager of West Hazel's senior center, where he kept things running on an even keel and somehow managed to keep most of the customers happy. Everyone fell for Stone's broad smile, warm, gravelly voice, and sincere manner. Tall, lean, and handsome, with the grizzled seasoning of a cowboy and the patience of a saint, Stone was quite a catch.

Alice wasn't quite sure if she'd caught him, as she hadn't been out fishing for a mate. She'd sworn off the addiction of romance after things went south with her ex-husband, Jeff.

And yet, here he was, most Saturday nights, for a standing movie date.

"How about some dinner? We've got barbecue sliders." When his eyes brightened, she ushered him in. "Come in, come in. I admit, I lost track of our plans for tonight in everything that's going on. We just learned that one of Violet's friends is missing, and we're having a quick meet to try and piece things together."

"You mean Michelle Chong?" he said evenly, taking a plate. "That's my job for the morning. Chief Cushman called and asked me to run the search tomorrow. He knows I have experience in search and rescue operations."

"You do?" Alice spooned a portion of coleslaw on his plate, then hers, ever impressed at the diverse jobs Stone had mastered in his life.

"I'm meeting with the chief and Detective Bedrosian in the morning, but I've got a map of the search area ready, separated into grids. We'll make copies for the volunteers. Divide the folks into small teams to search different sectors. We're starting in River Bend Park. Her friends say she liked to go walking on the trails there."

"It's true, I've walked there with Michelle," Violet said from the doorway. "Eavesdropping. Guilty. But I'm glad you're in charge of the search, Stone. We're in good hands."

"I'll be there," Alice said.

"We all will," Ruby said.

"Glad to have your help," Stone said, taking a seat beside Alice at the dining room table. As he went over the details—the walking sticks, the reflective tape—Alice felt a twinge of memory over the earlier search, so many years ago. She let out a breath and lost herself in the delicious, soft slider.

"You know, Violet," Stone said, "the police don't seem to have a lot to go on, and I feel lucky to be talking with someone who knew Michelle. It'd be great if you could fill me in on your friend. Profile her a bit?"

"She's lovely." Violet sat down with her plate and sighed. "A strong but delicate woman." The group ate quietly as Violet shared a few anecdotes about her friend. Their book club getaway to Emerald's cabin in Sunriver when Michelle had tricked them into a twelve-mile hike. "And we thought we were walking a four-mile trail!" Violet said. The tap-dancing class five of the book club gals had taken at Michelle's studio. "I tied my hair back into a ponytail and it was drenched! Dripping with sweat by the time each lesson was done. What a workout!" And the surprise birthday party Michelle and Emerald had thrown for Violet's sixtieth birthday at her favorite restaurant, Andre's. "Michelle is a very special person," Violet surmised.

"Amen to that," Ruby said.

"You've painted a beautiful portrait of your friend," Alice told her sister.

"Um, actually, the artist husband should be the one painting the portrait," Taylor said, tapping her cell. "Says here that Lars Olsen will be on the news at seven giving a live press conference about his missing wife."

"We'll have to check it out," Alice said, clearing a few plates.

"Thank you for sharing, Violet," Stone said. "We're going to do our best to make sure Michelle is safe," Stone said. "I know area searches seem like a drastic measure, but I can assure you the police are out, doing their due diligence in following leads that might help track Michelle down."

"Spoken as someone who has conducted a missing person search before," came a voice from the back room. Madison, still in uniform, had come in through the sliding door on the deck. She nodded at Stone. "Bedrosian told me you were going to be running the search tomorrow. I didn't know you had that kind of experience."

Stone gave a slight shrug. "I've done a few things."

So modest, Alice thought. It made her knees weak.

"Do you want overhead drones for the river search?" Stone asked Madison. She hooked a thumb in her wide black belt, considering. Alice was constantly awed that her trim, athletic granddaughter was able to carry twenty pounds of gun, flashlight, and other equipment on that belt every day. "Drones would be a huge help at the waterfront, if you can get them by tomorrow."

"I know a guy. Shouldn't be a problem." Stone put his napkin down and stood up from the table. "I'd best head out. I know Bedrosian is working on the press conference with Mr. Olsen there, but I'm meeting him later, along with the chief. Got a few things to coordinate before then."

"Thanks for stopping by," Alice said, walking him to the door. "We'll see you tomorrow."

He stepped toward the door, then stopped and turned to take her in.

Did his eyes twinkle, just a bit, when he looked at her? Or was she seeing stars? Or was she getting cataracts?

"Always good to see you, Alice." His voice was low, sonorous, inviting. "Always good."

It seemed that he was lifting her up, though he actually wasn't touching her at all. And then, he was gone. Walking away.

Watching him leave, Alice moved to the open doorway. Was she imagining that cowboy swagger? "Bye," she mouthed, staring after him as he exchanged a greeting with a woman coming down the driveway in the opposite direction.

Passing him, Emerald gave a dramatic lift of her head, braced her container with one hand, tossed back her curls with the other, and approached Alice to whisper. "He's gorgeous!"

Alice breathed a quiet sigh. "Yup." Without taking her eyes off him, she gestured Emerald inside.

Chapter Seven

"You made it!" Violet said, looking up from the open dishwasher. She introduced Emerald to Taylor and Ruby.

"I brought lemon squares." Emerald placed the covered tray on the edge of the puzzle table in the nook. "I was baking when the police came by, that nice officer—oh!" She straightened when Madison came in from the dining room. "It's you, dear Officer..."

"Denham," Madison said. "But you can call me Madison here."

"She's my niece," Violet said. "Here to give us the inside dope on the investigation."

Madison frowned. "Actually, I wouldn't compromise any investigation."

"Of course you wouldn't! Emerald knows what I mean." Violet took a seat at the puzzle table beside Ruby, who leaned over from the banquette to try to fit different pieces into the sky border. "So sweet of you to bring something, Em. I love lemon squares."

"Have a seat," Alice said. "I'll make some tea to go with your dessert. Herbal, of course. Caffeine at this point will keep us up all night." Alice put the kettle on and took a china teapot down from the shelf. Although she lived for coffee in the morning, there was something so civil and soothing about sipping tea later in the day. The warm brew smoothed the edges off any discussion.

"Look at this puzzle!" Emerald seemed impressed. "You're almost finished."

"This last blank patch of sky is slowing us down," Ruby said. "Are you a puzzler? We'll take any help we can get."

"I used to do them with my sisters on holidays. A puzzle every year at Christmas, and then a spring scene at Easter, too."

"African rooibos tea," Alice announced, having surveyed the tea supply. "It's tasty, and good for the health, they say." She put small dessert plates on the table, then delivered tea to all takers. "So, Madison," she said, sliding onto the banquette beside Ruby. "I have a question for you. Not that I pretend to know Michelle well, but when I visited her home this week for the book club meeting, she seemed content and happy. I mean, she voiced some issues with her husband, but overall I wouldn't say she was a woman who appeared to be in crisis. Isn't it possible that Michelle simply went off on a trip? A retreat that her husband forgot about?"

"It's possible," said Madison. "Her wallet and car are missing, so she could have easily driven somewhere. A getaway, or even a trip to visit family."

"But her sisters and aunts are either in Malaysia or LA," Emerald pointed out, "and the drive down to Los Angeles is a long one. Like fourteen or fifteen hours, right?"

"It's long, but doable. So far, we've been in touch with her relatives, and no one has reported seeing her." Madison paused, folding her hands. "We've checked hospitals for her, and airport manifests, but at this point we can't restrict her travel. Lars insisted we put out an alert on her car, and the chief agreed to do that, but reluctantly. She's committed no crimes. We're walking an odd line, trying to do a wellness check without violating her First Amendment rights."

"I can appreciate that." Violet swirled her tea, studying the cup. "I can see her striking out on her own. The inconsistency is that she didn't tell anyone who cares about her. There was no note for her husband? No e-mail or text to Kamaria at the studio?"

"No goodbyes or explanations of a trip," Madison confirmed.

Violet shook her head. "That's not like Michelle. That's why I worry."

"Well, I don't know about you guys, but I just have this feeling that Michelle's okay," Emerald said. "I mean, I'm worried, of course, but she's so capable. A woman with backbone. She built that business single-handedly while Lars had mixed success selling his paintings."

"Sounds to me like she skedaddled," said Ruby. "Probably got fed up with her husband and had to get away. It happens."

"If I was married to Lars Olsen, I'd probably skedaddle, too," Violet said darkly.

"But he's a celebrity. Isn't he a famous artist?" Taylor asked.

"He certainly plays the part." Alice turned a blue puzzle piece to alter her perspective. "And Michelle is a celebrity, too."

"I do think he's talented," Violet said. "But I would find

it hard to live with a man like that. Needy, always seeking praise." She wagged a puzzle piece in the air. "Quite similar to many of our third-grade boys."

"Minus the adorable charm," Alice said.

"He's younger than her, and kind of hot." Taylor held her phone out, revealing a headshot of Lars Olsen. His strong-jawed face was half in shadow, his high cheekbones bold, his cerulean eyes the only vivid color in the shot. "Says here that he's forty-three. That's like, twenty years difference."

"A pretty package," Ruby agreed, "if you go for those moody types."

"The man is a workout," Alice said. "In the short time that he interacted with the ladies of the book club, he couldn't stop talking about himself. Sucked all the energy out of the room."

"But I thought Michelle seemed quite content that night," Violet said, holding up a lemon square. "Not like a woman on the verge of disappearing."

"Maybe something changed," Ruby said.

"Whoa, really?" Taylor said, wincing at her phone. "Now they're saying that Lars won't appear at the press conference. Aw. I wanted to get a look at him."

"Too distraught?" Alice asked.

Taylor shook her head. "Says he's setting up something for tomorrow."

Madison put her teacup down with a frown. "But it's important to disseminate the information immediately so the public can be aware."

"Looks like the police chief is going on," Taylor said.

"Let's watch." Alice led the group into the family room and turned to the news station as the other women took to the cushy sofas.

With somber faces they observed the news conference, staged at the old farmhouse surrounded by trees, overgrown bushes, and brambles.

"You know, I'm a gal who's comfortable amid nature in the woods, but that place always gives me the willies," Violet said. Arms crossed, she stood watching the TV, apparently too agitated to settle into a sofa like the other women.

"Same!" Emerald admitted.

"We're here at the home of the missing woman, Michelle Chong, on Dragonberry Lane," Maya Leona reported in a low voice. "It was here that police began their search for evidence that might lead to the whereabouts of the West Hazel dance academy owner and martial arts expert. As police have found no sign of a struggle, and Ms. Chong's car and wallet are gone, friends are holding out hope that the missing woman has simply chosen seclusion for the time being."

Next the West Hazel police chief, Dave Cushman, made a statement recapping the details of Michelle's disappearance. "Ms. Chong's husband, Lars Olsen, was unable to appear here tonight, but he has asked me to read this brief statement." The chief put on his glasses and held up a paper. "Mr. Olsen says, 'Please, if you know anything about Michelle's whereabouts, call the West Hazel Police. My wife is a beautiful person, inside and out. She's my muse, my artistic inspiration. Please, if you're holding her, let her come home.'" Chief Cushman nodded. "That's it for tonight. We're not taking any questions at this time."

"That was weird," Taylor said, muting the TV.

"Lars seems quite convinced that his wife has been kidnapped." Defiant, Violet put her hands on her hips. "Why is he thinking the worst?" She turned to Madison. "Are you holding out on us, Maddie? Is there something we don't know?"

All eyes turned to Madison, suddenly in the hot seat, no doubt wishing for an invisibility cloak.

Chapter Eight

Alice remained silent as Violet put the rookie cop on the spot. In the past Madison had been guarded about divulging information about an investigation, but Alice doubted that she would stonewall her great-aunt Violet.

"I wouldn't lie to you, Aunt Vi." Madison held up her hands, a contrite concern in her eyes. "As far as I know, we don't have any evidence pointing to foul play or kidnapping."

"That Lars Olsen is stirring the pot!" Ruby said.

"I don't know how she puts up with him." Emerald pressed a hand to her heart. "Please don't think I'm judging, even if I am, but I find Lars to be a selfish poop. Granted, he's not my husband, and I think Michelle likes taking care of him. But I don't trust that man."

"This seems to be the theme of the night," Madison said. "In this group, Lars Olsen would be first man voted off the island."

"So true," Alice agreed. "So what's this man's history? After all, he's only lived here for six years or so. What's the story of his life before Michelle?"

"I've got him on Wikipedia," Taylor said. "He's forty-three, it says. Went to art school, that fancy one in Connecticut."

"Bridgeport College of Art," Ruby said. "My nephew studied design there. Kind of hoity-toity."

"Hoity-toity?" Taylor's nose crinkled. "What are you, a flapper from the twenties?"

"Listen to you, vernacular police." Ruby waved her off. "That expression reminds me of my grandma, and you have to admit, it's fun to say."

Alice was already searching Lars Olsen on her iPad. "It says here that he was part of an American art movement fomented with some colleagues from school, Marco Santino and Solomon Mensah. Anyone recognize those artists? No? They called it Unfiltered Art. Apparently the movement involved getting in touch with childhood instincts, including distorted renderings of people, and focus on primary colors and simple subjects. Earth, sky, trees, sun, and stars. Paintings that depicted the world without the distorted filters of adulthood."

"Ooh, like finger painting." Taylor smiled. "I could do that."

"The challenge is making the painting match the image in our minds," Violet said.

"Well, I'm encouraged to learn that our Lars had some legitimacy," Alice said, still scanning the Web site. "Apparently he knocked around on the East Coast for years, Philadelphia and Brooklyn." Alice scrolled to the end of the entry. "Nothing here on his personal life or family."

"He was hatched in art school," Emerald said, then let out a giggle. "I can just picture the giant egg."

Ruby chuckled, and soft laughter rippled through the group.

"We're getting punchy," Alice said. "It's late, but I want

to know more about Lars Olsen." She turned to Madison. "Does he have a criminal record?"

"Nothing. No arrests or charges in the national database. He hasn't even had a parking ticket here in Oregon. But when I dug deeper, I couldn't find any history on him back east. He didn't have a driver's license or credit history in Connecticut or Pennsylvania twenty years ago. Something about that doesn't add up."

"Hmm." Alice searched "Bridgeport College of Art." "Let's look at the art school. Since Lars became famous, maybe he's on their Web site."

"But he's not mentioned there." Taylor squeezed onto the sofa next to Alice and tilted her phone screen. "See? He's not listed as an alumnus. When I dug deeper, I found some yearbooks online. Lars isn't there, but his artist friends are. The two guys you mentioned? Santino and Mensah graduated in 2003."

"What does that mean?" Ruby asked.

"Perhaps Lars didn't actually graduate." Violet tapped her chin. "But he uses the school in PR profiles."

"Well, it's not a mistake," Taylor said. "All his online profiles mention Bridgeport."

"It's definitely fishy," Alice agreed.

"And if we're looking for reasons why Michelle may have wanted to escape her life, don't forget about Dragonberry Lane." Emerald folded her arms across her chest and gave a shiver. "I used to feel sorry for her, stuck in that quirky, aging farmhouse. She claimed it was enchanted, but I think she was just trying to stay positive."

"More haunted than enchanted," Violet said.

"It sounds so charming," Taylor said. "Dragonberry Lane . . . like a house in a fairy tale."

"A Grimms' fairy tale," Alice said.

"Have you noticed that the structure seems to emerge

from the ground like a fallen mole?" Violet pointed out. "Its roof is covered in moss, as if it's being swallowed into the earth. Inside it's cold, drafty and earthy. I just feel sorry for my friend, living in some sort of purgatory."

"And that fireplace!" Emerald shuddered. "Not that I believe that anything bad happened to her. I can't let my mind go there. But the house is creepy."

"Did you check the fireplace?" Alice asked Madison.

"Detective Bedrosian went out to the house with another cop. I wasn't brought into the investigation until after they took the report. But let's see." Madison tapped her phone, then frowned. "I can't access the report from here, but I'll check later. What's special about the fireplace?"

"It's huge!" Violet answered. "Big enough to roast a large animal or . . . worse."

"A killer could dispose of a body there," Alice said, following Violet's train of thought.

"Ew." Taylor winced. "That's gross and disturbing."

"Oh come on, the husband?" Ruby asked. "Is he really that much of a monster?"

"He can be a beast," Emerald insisted.

"We know he had the means and opportunity," Alice said. "Still working on the motive, but that's two out of three."

Wincing, Ruby hugged herself. "But disposing of the body in the fireplace?"

"I admit, it might seem over the top," Alice conceded. "But it's still possible." The image of Lars with his chockablock horse teeth and meager golden ponytail flashed in her mind. Neigh!

Okay, so he wasn't her type. That didn't mean he was capable of such evil.

"Ladies, I'm glad no one's sugar-coating the venom,"

Madison said, jotting down a note. "As I said, Lars is not winning any votes with this group. But I don't see the fireplace mentioned in the forensics report. I'll find out if Bedrosian checked the giant hearth."

"And if it's not the husband that drove her away, maybe it's the house," Violet said. "Let's face it, that place is depressing. I want Michelle to come back, but no one should have to return to that medieval lair!"

"For that you need a Realtor, not a cop," Madison said, "but your concern is duly noted. And I'm dying to get a look at that fireplace."

Chapter Nine

River Bend Park, one of the crown jewels of West Hazel situated at a bend in the Willamette River, promised lush shade, leaves beginning to speckle with gold, yellow, and red, a cool breeze on the riverfront, and a cerulean sky above it all.

If only Alice were in a state to enjoy it on that sunny Sunday morning. Instead, she was embarking on a mission of hope and dread. She wanted to telegraph to Michelle: *We're coming for you; help is on the way.* She imagined finding her, fallen and unconscious. Saved!

But she couldn't ignore the other possible outcomes.

"You okay, honey?" Ruby asked as Alice turned her car into the park entrance. "It's not like you to be so quiet after two cups of coffee."

"It's just such a somber mission," Alice said, angling cleanly into a spot.

That wasn't the whole truth. Yes, it was bad enough that she'd brought walking sticks to poke undergrowth in search of a body. Not an ideal way to spend a Sunday morning. But on top of that, her anxiety was compounded by a memory of a different search, different park . . . same terror burning a hole in her stomach.

It was not something she could talk about right now, not even with Ruby. So she shrugged on her stoic armor and led her friend down the trail.

With a wide-brimmed canvas hat dangling around her neck and walking sticks in one arm, she guided Ruby to the pavilion that would be the center of operations for the search. It was hard to miss, with the large motor home that would function as the police mobile command center parked nearby.

Just another reminder that this was serious business.

Madison and Stone stood together at a picnic table, handing out maps and fluorescent tape and chatting up volunteers. Alice greeted two teachers from the dance studio, who told her Kamaria wanted to come but she needed to supervise dance classes at the studio. When Ruby and Alice went to sign in, Madison ushered Alice over to the side, to the privacy of a small rustic overhang that featured maps and information about the history of River Bend Park.

"You might be relieved to know that the fireplace was swept clean when Bedrosian brought the forensics team in." Madison tapped her iPad a few times, then showed Alice photos of the gigantic fireplace at Dragonberry Lane. The cement and brick surfaces were charred and dusty, but empty of debris.

"Yes, it does appear to be well swept," Alice agreed. "But that doesn't mean there wasn't a body in there the day before."

"Gran, come on." Madison flicked a glance to the side, making sure no one was listening. When she spoke again her volume was lower, her tone firmer. "It takes three or four hours to burn a body in the superheat of a crematorium. Don't you think an open fireplace like this would take a few days?"

Alice let out a heavy breath. "Sorry. You're right, of course."

"I just thought we'd all feel better to rule out the most gruesome of possibilities." Madison was right, and in her police uniform with its shiny badge, she sparkled with professionalism. Her confidence cheered Alice up.

"True," Alice said. "Good to know." Over by the picnic table, volunteers were forming groups. Taylor and Violet had arrived, along with a handful of book club ladies. Alice wanted to coordinate a time to meet with them to discuss Michelle. Alice wanted to get to them before the operation began. "Thanks, Madison," she said. "We'll talk later."

By the time nine o'clock rolled around, and orientation began, Alice had a date, of sorts, with the book club women. She would meet the ladies during an intermission at an outdoor concert Monday evening. Though the meeting had required some negotiation.

The club had made plans to attend the Last Notes of Sunshine concert at Waterfront Park, but with Michelle missing, people felt ambivalent about attending.

"It's only once a year," Rachel had said, "and I hate to miss it. But I do feel guilty."

"I think Michelle would want us to go," Violet had said, speaking quietly in the small circle of friends. "More than anything, she'd want us to be together, to support each other."

That had persuaded the group. Score one for Violet's motivational speaking skills.

"If I can have your attention here, we'll share a few tips and get started on our search for our friend Michelle."

Stone's gritty, warm voice garnered the attention of the group as he explained that each group of three or four volunteers would be assigned a sector, which they would search, primarily from the park trails. "If there's an area you can't examine or anything suspicious, we ask that you mark it with tape and phone it into the number on the bottom of your map. Officer Denham will take your call. Return to this area when your search is complete, and, depending on time, we'll—"

"Hello, hello, all! Sorry I'm late." A tall man in a safari hat, khakis, and a puffy white shirt swaggered from behind the police trailer and swaggered to the front of the small crowd. It was Lars Olsen, channeling Hemingway on steroids in a most unattractive way.

"Mr. Olsen—" Madison's voice made it clear she hadn't been expecting him.

"Lars." Stone shook his hand. "Folks, this is Michelle's husband, Lars Olsen. Are you going to be participating in the search?"

"Oh, no. Sorry, but I can't do that." Lars thumped a fist against his breast. "Too painful, and I have a press conference to prepare for. I'm sure you understand." Despite his words, Lars did not seem to be a man in pain. He stood tall, eyes bright, high cheekbones pink with cheer. Or was that a touch of rouge? In fact, with his trim physique and curly blond hair, he could have been a middle-aged model—if only he cut off the ridiculous little ponytail at the nape of his neck. "I just wanted to thank everyone here for volunteering your time. It means so much to me that you would spend your time in search of Michelle." He paused a moment and turned away from the group, gesturing toward the trees leading down to the river. "I know she's out there, somewhere. Somewhere. I just . . ."

His voice cracked with emotion, and for a moment he covered his eyes with one hand.

"Mm-mm." Ruby grunted in Alice's ear, muttering, "It may be Sunday morning, but this ain't no church, and we're not here for the gospel of Lars."

"I just hope we can find her before it's too late," Lars went on, teary eyed. "I can't imagine going on without her. My world, my art . . . everything hinges on her." Lars hung his head for another dramatic pause, but Stone stepped over, slung an arm over his shoulders, and took the opportunity to end the sermon.

"Thank you for those encouraging words, Lars. I know everyone here is eager to begin the search. So without delay, let's head out to our sectors. . . ."

As the crowd dispersed, a few searchers came forward to offer sympathy to the distraught husband, who had taken a seat at the picnic table, slumped over in grief.

"Lord have mercy." Turning away from the distraught husband, Ruby folded her arms and scowled. "So dramatic. The queen is dead, long live the king."

"That's kind of harsh, Ruby," Taylor said.

Violet pinched her chin. "I saw real tears in his eyes."

"All the better to get sympathy and attention," Ruby insisted. "His wife is missing and somehow, he manages to make it about him. He's unable to go on and create his art without her. Hogwash."

"I'm with you, my cynical friend," Alice said quietly. "He may be a renowned artist, but he's a lousy actor." After his hollow speech, she was more convinced than ever that Lars had contributed to his wife's disappearance in some way. She needed to know more. A dive into the foul mouth of Dragonberry might reveal something. But how to finagle her way into the place?

Alice approached Lars, and waited as a man with silver hair consoled him. Two dance teachers from Michelle's studio waited in the queue in front of Alice.

"How's it going at the studio? Is it closed?" Alice asked.

"Still classes as usual," said a long-legged woman with two long braids. She wore a long sweater over tights and Doc Martens. "Because Kamaria stepped in. She knows the deal, and she's doing a great job."

Alice nodded. "Good for her." She would have to stop in and chat with Michelle's assistant.

When Alice moved up to Lars, she had to spin off something fast. She decided to be neighborly.

"I'm Alice Pepper, the librarian here in town. We've met briefly, but I wanted to tell you how sorry I am for what you're going through."

His blue eyes seemed to penetrate her skin. Were those colored contacts? Fortunately, he closed his eyes, as if in a wave of pain, and thanked her.

"My sister Violet is in a book club with Michelle," Alice said, averting her eyes from his gaze, "and she's worried sick about her."

"As am I," Lars said, sighing.

"We'd like to help, in any way we can. I'm a pretty good cook, and I'd be happy to drop by with a meal for you. Or Violet and I could come by and help you with any household chores." When he put up a hand to stop her, she quickly added, "I know you're busy with your painting, and we'll be unobtrusive, I promise."

"Well, you see, I have my assistants to help with the studio and house. But I guess everyone could use a good meal, right?"

"A good meal can feed the soul," Alice agreed, hoping she didn't sound as fake as she felt. "Should we stop by tonight?"

"Come by this afternoon. I've promised local reporters an update and a glimpse inside our home, and I just wasn't prepared yesterday. But join us around three, if you—"

His attention was caught by something off to the side—one of the volunteers. She followed his gaze to a tall man wearing jeans, boots, and a suede blazer in a rich shade of burnt umber. Quite fashionable for a hike through the woods. He had well-trimmed brown hair, sleepy brown eyes, and a mustache that accentuated his broad lips.

Lars moved away from Alice and stepped up to the fashionable man, who met Lars's gaze and smiled a cold, leery grin. Alice wondered why the two men were facing off like gunslingers in a western movie.

"That's Santino," Madison whispered in Alice's ear. "I recognized his name when he registered for the search. He's Lars's colleague from art school. Remember? With the art movement?"

"Santino." Lars hissed the name, stretching his neck back like a snake poised to strike. It was clear that the two men were not friends anymore. "What are you doing here?"

"I came to help in the search, of course." There was a trace of an accent in Santino's voice.

Lars's frown hardened into a scowl. "I meant, what are you doing in West Hazel?"

"Coyote is showing my work in a group show at his Portland gallery. Perhaps you've been invited? It's called *The Colors of Argentina*. A large exhibit. And while I'm in town, I'm also a featured artist in a small gallery here in West Hazel."

"Right in my backyard," Lars said. "That's nervy, even for you, Santino."

Alice watched as the two men squared off. Showdown at the West Hazel Corral.

"Michelle did not tell you? I suppose she had her reasons. But of course, my shows matter little, when your wife is missing." Santino's voice was thick with compassion. "What can I do? I want to help in any way I can."

"We don't need your kind of help. In fact, now that I know you're in town, I might have the police here keep an eye on you." He nodded toward Madison, who winced at the attention. "Funny that my wife disappears when you come to town."

"This is where we differ. I don't find it funny at all." Santino lifted the map and pretended to study it. "I came here today to search. I came for Michelle."

"Just go," Lars rasped.

"Right now, we could use every volunteer we have," Madison said.

"He's in our group," Taylor said, "with Aunt Vi and me."

"Yes, indeed." Violet stepped forward. "I know a spot by the river Michelle used to like. That little stretch of sandy shore. That's our sector."

"Very good," Santino said. "Today I am all eyes and ears, in search of Michelle." With a cold smile for Lars, he followed the women down the trail toward the river.

"He doesn't belong here," Lars said, staring after Santino.

Maybe so, Alice thought, but she was intrigued by the newcomer. Watching the threesome head off, she was annoyed that she wasn't on Santino's search team, though Lars would have seen that as a betrayal. At least her sister and granddaughter knew enough to pump Santino for information about Michelle, and Lars, as well.

"So, Mr. Olsen." Madison faced the artist, trying to smooth things over. "We'll be launching drones to search the waterfront as soon as the truck arrives. We're expecting them within the hour."

"Very good." His mood deflated, Lars swatted at an insect near his face. With the volunteers scattered, he must have sensed his waning audience.

"We can show you the images, once they're launched, if you want to stick around," Stone offered.

"Too much to do." Lars smacked the side of his jaw in annoyance. "I'm heading out but keep me posted."

"Will do," Stone said, nodding as Lars strode up the trail toward the parking lot.

"That is one high-maintenance dude," Stone said.

Alice picked up her walking sticks from the picnic table and turned to Ruby. "Looks like we're a two-person team. Do you have our sector?"

"Actually, all the sectors are assigned," Madison said. "So we thought you and Ruby might stick to the trails and support any other searchers you encounter. Sort of a roving problem-solver. You're good in that role, Gran."

"You're the boss, Officer Denham," Alice said, forcing a smile. She suddenly felt a heaviness, a sense of dread as she adjusted her hat and faced Ruby.

"I'm going back to the car to get some supplies I left in the trunk," Madison said, stepping away. "Be right back."

"Ladies, don't hesitate to call if you need us." Stone propped one foot on the seat of the picnic table and scrolled through his phone. "I'm gonna check on the drone ETA."

"Ten-four, over and out," Ruby called to him, pretending to boogie down the path.

Alice wanted to laugh, but her throat was suddenly tight, and dread clung to her. The greenery seemed to close in around her as she plodded down the crushed stone path. They were still surrounded by open fields, but she felt claustrophobic, trapped. The repetitive movements of her walking sticks clicked her back in time, to the search on that terrible day.

How she'd stopped to poke at a bush, relieved when nothing solid caught her stick.

Spotting a corpse-sized log at the edge of the woods. Leaves crunching underfoot as she cautiously approached. The tension as she stabbed at the object—a body? No, a weathered log.

Not her daughter.

Not Lauren.

Chapter Ten

Alice stopped walking, unable to go on. She'd hit a loaded wall of memories.

One more pebble on the cement, one slight stumble into the bricks would send the whole structure tumbling down.

Ruby paused but continued to natter on about the outdoors. The insects and mud and grass stains. The exercise, healthy but annoying. She hated to sweat. And did she mention the bugs? Those creepy, crawly insects . . .

"I need a minute," Alice said, staring ahead but seeing nothing.

Ruby swung around cautiously, her mouth agape. "Oh, honey, what is it? Did you get bitten by a snake or something?" She brought her hands up to her chest and cautiously checked the ground around them.

"I'm sorry," Alice said. "I just keep thinking of Lauren. When she was missing for days, and we were searching with the police, and I was so, so afraid that something . . . something terrible had happened to her."

"Yes, oh dear God, yes, I remember that awful time." Ruby touched her shoulder gently. "That was so traumatizing for you. Of course it was. It's no wonder all this is stirring up that painful ordeal."

"But it was decades ago." Before Alice could steel herself, tears flooded her eyes. "I should be over it, but I just can't. I can't do this search."

"Alice . . ." Stone's voice came from behind her, smooth, low, soothing. "Sometimes events trigger us. Post-traumatic stress is a real and terrible thing."

"I'm so embarrassed."

He pressed a palm to her cheek, his hand cool on her hot skin. "Nothing to be embarrassed about." Suddenly she was in his arms, drawn into the comfort, shade, and strength of his body. A resting place. Consolation.

"It's okay," Stone said. "There are other ways to help."

Alice pressed her face to his brushed denim shirt and let it all happen. There was no holding it back anymore, no chance of easing out of this gracefully. She was crying in public, and now she might as well take the moment of calm comfort he offered and let the solace soak in.

"Honey, I feel so responsible," Ruby said. "What kind of a friend am I? Here you've been struggling with all this, and I didn't even have a clue? When I should have known all along this search would be a problem for you. I do remember that search for Lauren. I remember it like it was yesterday. We were all so torn up. She'd been missing for so long, and the police had brought in that man who'd been holding that other poor girl hostage, and he said he knew your daughter. And everybody was just assuming the worst. But not you, honey. You didn't give up on your girl."

To hear Ruby tell it, you'd think Alice had been a hero, championing her daughter.

Not exactly. Alice had been like any distraught mom trying to straighten out her kid. Trying and failing.

But somehow, Ruby's nutshell version had put some distance on the memory. An encapsulated trauma that was deep in the past.

Alice breathed deeply the sweet detergent of Stone's shirt, the citrus scent of his skin. She felt the tickle of his hair, and then, reluctantly, she stepped back. "Thank you." She looked up at his lined face of compassion and nearly started crying again. It had been nice to be held, after so long.

He squeezed her wrist. "Anytime."

"That was embarrassing," Alice said, wiping her cheeks with her fingertips. "It's just not like me."

"Happens to the best of us," Stone said.

"Now, Alice, let's just sit down a minute and reassess." Ruby took charge, pointing Alice over to the nearby pavilion, where wooden tables and chairs sat empty in the shade. "We'll sit for a bit and figure out what you want to do from there. And I'm perfectly happy to leave if that's what you want to do."

"Let's stick around here for a minute till I get my bearings." With a deep breath Alice followed Ruby while Stone went to get some water. The pavilion was shady and cool, a nice respite from the sun. Ruby arranged some wooden Adirondack chairs so that they faced the green woods, and Alice took a seat with a grateful sigh.

Removing some tissues from her Michael Kors mini-backpack, Ruby dabbed at Alice's face, blotting up smeared mascara. Alice breathed steadily, calmly, and let herself be pampered.

Although Ruby was not the nurturing type, she knew

how to pull a look together. Perched on a chair across from her, Ruby looked ready for a cocktail party in her black cropped pants, cheetah print tee, and dangly gold earrings. Her hair was a simple auburn flip held back by a headband that seemed to be a natural twist of braids. Probably a wig from Ruby's collection, but every piece looked so good on her that Alice had trouble discerning fake from real. "Thank you. I haven't had a good cry for years."

"Feeling better, honey?"

"I think I got most of it out of my system. It just hit me, the act of searching. That sick feeling of not knowing whether someone you care about is safe. I remember when my girl went missing, how it felt to lose her and worry about her constantly. The sleepless nights. I lived and breathed for news of Lauren."

"I'm glad to hear you speaking her name again. How many years did you call her she-who-shall-not-be-named?"

"That was my defense. It was all too painful. You remember that she cut me off, and it broke me. I hate not being able to reach out to her. And you know how I hate a loss of control. But I was making progress. Accepting the distance, the separation. I was doing okay, until today."

"You've been through a lot with her," Ruby said. "Our kids certainly know how to push us to the brink sometimes. My Isaac had his run-ins with the police. He climbed the fence of someone's pool. Spray-painted the school one night and set trash cans on fire. That boy had a case of the stupids, no doubt. But he made it through. And the girls, they know how to push my buttons, but at least they didn't tangle with the cops."

"You've raised three wonderful people," Alice said.

"It takes a lot of prayers and a lot of luck," Ruby said. "But honestly, my kids put together were nothing compared to what you went through with Lauren."

Settling back in the chair, Alice thought of the early years when Lauren had been an infant, a toddler, a kindergartner. The age of innocence. Her affectionate daughter had been quick to make people laugh, eager to comfort friends. Smart, energetic, and obedient, she had been a natural athlete who could run like the wind.

The trouble had begun with normal teenage defiance. Breaking curfew. Parties with alcohol and marijuana. Alice had reeled Lauren in from time to time with curfews and stern talks. Overall she felt confident her daughter would learn her lessons and move on with adulting.

Then a soccer injury in Lauren's senior year of high school had led to painkillers from the doctor, a treatment that had continued long after Lauren's knee had healed. Tissue had been mended, but phantom pain had persisted.

Her girl had become hooked.

There'd been multiple attempts to get Lauren help... years of counseling and intervention. Alice and Jeff had paid for therapists and summer camps in the earlier years, then rehabs, personal coaches, and outpatient programs.

Some of the treatments had worked, at least for a time. Periods of sobriety. Lauren's sober pregnancy and the early years with the twins had been a hopeful time for Alice. Then a few occasional drinks had slipped into a few too many, then roaring nights of alcohol abuse. And slow-moving stretches on cannabis. And back to opioids after oral surgery.

Lauren's addiction had taken their family on a rollercoaster ride that never seemed to end. But Alice had tried to keep up, running alongside her girl, caring for the twins when their mother couldn't handle them, encouraging Lauren to get help. Keep getting help.

"A mother can't give up on her daughter," Alice said aloud. "You're not allowed to give up on someone you love. Even when they push you away."

"Sometimes being a mother sucks," Ruby said. "You never stop worrying."

"You never do."

"Well, I have something that might ease your mind. I know you usually don't want to talk about any of this, and I respect that. But I've heard some good news about Lauren lately. Seems she's been doing well with her recovery."

"Really?" Alice's heart lifted. "How do you know? Wait, no. Don't tell me. She doesn't want me in her life, and I need to respect that. Still . . . it's good news, isn't it? From a reliable source?"

"A rock-solid source."

Alice took a deep breath, soaking in fresh air and gratitude. "That is a relief. Thank you for sharing."

"Actually, there's more." Ruby leaned forward in the chair, garnering Alice's full attention. "And I'm telling you this part because she wanted you to have the message. She's hoping to make amends with you one day."

Alice's shoulders tingled, a sort of adrenaline shot, as the news filtered through her. Could it be true, after all this time? After the terrible breach? "I'm not sure what to do with that. It's hard to believe. I mean, I want it to be true, but . . ."

"You've been hurt before," Ruby said.

Many times, Alice thought. But that hadn't kept her from trying again.

It was the sort of news Alice had been hoping to hear

for years. Why, then, did the thought of seeing her daughter make her uneasy? Fear of rejection? Disappointment? Would she be able to believe in Lauren's recovery?

She hoped so. One thing Alice had learned through their long separation was that she could never give up on her daughter. Yes, she'd stayed away at Lauren's insistence, but she always dreamed of a reunion. "All I can say is, I hope she's doing well, and my door is always open."

Chapter Eleven

Stone stepped into the shade of the pavilion and delivered two bottles of cold water, along with the news that the drone operator had arrived. "Madison's bringing Eddie down from the parking lot, and we'll launch from somewhere in this field," he said. "Apparently, the other end of the park is thrumming with soccer players and parents. I forgot it was soccer season when we arranged the search. The parking lot's packed."

"It's always soccer season around here," Alice said. She'd followed Lauren through countless games and tournaments, and then, years later, the twins took the field.

"You might want to come on over and check out the drones," Stone said. "Once they're in the air, the view is pretty amazing."

They took Stone up on the offer, and within an hour, Eddie Redmond's nerdy fascination with flying objects consumed Alice. A thin, Black man with a neatly trimmed beard and thoughtful brown eyes, Eddie was a senior at Portland State, a math major who had founded a business using drones to capture video for Realtors and assist police operation in overhead searches.

"They look like four-legged spiders with propellers,"

Alice said as Eddie set the drones out in the clearing near the pavilion.

"You're looking at the Stealth Lark 2000 and the Iron Bird K-26," Eddie said. "They may look simple, but these birds can fly."

"I read an article about a drone that flew into a woman's face and cut her nose," Ruby said. "Should we have helmets or face guards or something?"

"You're good, ma'am." Eddie checked over each propeller as he spoke. "The drones I flew as a kid weren't always so responsive to navigation, but these models are much improved. Their anti-collision system uses built-in sensors to prevent collisions with objects or the ground. And they're wind resistant, so they don't get blown off course like previous models."

Watching the first drone launch, Alice felt like a girl witnessing the operation of a new toy on Christmas morning. Once the drone rose above the tree line and flew forward toward the river, Eddie showed them the multiple views that appeared on his iPad.

"The top window is the pilot's view for navigation," Eddie said. Below that was a close-up view that showed details, like stones and benches by the river. "And we can also switch to panoramic view," Eddie said, showing a broad picture of the riverfront.

"Amazing," Ruby said.

Alice stayed glued to the screen as Eddie handed it off to Stone to navigate, while Eddie launched the Iron Bird. It was fun to fly along. Swoop low over water. Out over little islands. Over trees.

"It gets so close," Alice marveled, "I can actually see through the water to the river mud. Look, there. It's something."

"Mmm. Looks like a tree trunk." Stone showed her

how to mark the video, so that it could be more closely examined later.

"Oh, this is fun," Ruby said. "Like playing video games with a purpose."

"Guilty." Eddie smiled. "I think you ladies are on to me. So now that Stone's got Lark on the riverfront, I'm going to have the Iron Bird come over the park. Lots of treetops to avoid, but there are a few clearings where I can swoop down and capture some detailed ground video."

Alice and Ruby squeezed in to watch his screen.

"Watch out for that bird!" Ruby warned.

Eddie pivoted the course of the drone quickly. "Yeah. We don't want to give old robin redbreast a haircut." Alice followed the drone's journey as it dipped low over the clearing where an old log cabin had been restored as a restroom. Then they rose high, over the treetops, to skim over the canopy of green until another opening came into view.

"Looks like a parking lot," Eddie said.

The rectangular lot was smallish, with only about a dozen or so cars parked there. "That's not the main lot," Alice said. "Probably overflow."

"You can see the little cars go in and out," Ruby said.

Alice watched as a cherry-red car with a black roof pulled into a spot. "Like a toy village." The driver emerged from the car and, leaving her door open, hurried over to a parked vehicle. "Weird."

"Do you see that woman?" Ruby asked. "I think we know her."

"Here. I can drop down lower," said Eddie.

"I think it's Emerald," Alice said.

Emerald was peeking into the car, knocking on the window.

"She's looking a bit frantic," Alice said.

Just then Emerald looked up at the drone, as if she'd just noticed. Immediately, she started waving her arms, gesturing wildly, indicating distress.

"She's trying to get help," Stone said. "Madison!" he called over to the pavilion, where Madison was talking with a group of searchers.

Alice was already hurrying over to the pavilion. "Emerald is in the overflow parking lot, signaling for help," Alice said. "We have to get there, fast."

Madison was on her feet, waving Alice up the trail. "The patrol car is right at the trailhead. You can show me the way."

Madison turned on the roof rack, and red and blue lights swirled around the vehicle, pale but visible in the sunshine. "I need to take it slow here, with all these pedestrians around."

"It's not too far. The cutoff is just ahead." She showed Madison where to turn on the narrow lane just before the soccer fields. Dust rose behind the vehicle as Madison picked up some speed, then slowed at the mouth of the lot.

Off to the left, Emerald danced about, still gesticulating toward the overhead drone. Spotting the police vehicle, Emerald waved her arms, and then came toward them barreling across the lot, curls bouncing, arms waving, eyes wild.

"I found her car!" Emerald shouted. "Michelle's Subaru! I found it!"

Chapter Twelve

"You mean we can't even get inside her car?" Emerald complained to the police, expressing the disappointment of the gals waiting a respectable three feet away from Michelle's Subaru Outback.

In the forty minutes it had taken Madison's backup police unit and a tow truck to arrive, Violet and Taylor had finished their morning search, and Ruby had brought them to the overflow lot to see what they could find out. Madison had notified the husband of the discovery, and was now over at the edge of the parking lot near a flatbed truck, going over paperwork with the driver. Alice was dying to ply the gals with questions about Santino, but at the moment the newly discovered car held everyone's attention.

"We don't want anyone touching the Subaru," Officer Daniel Zhao said. "Our forensic team will try to lift fingerprints."

"Well, I'm the one who found the car," Emerald said, raising her hand. "My name is Emerald Shanley, Emerald, like the gem, and I confess, I've touched the car already. You see, I couldn't be here earlier for the search because I had a Spanish lesson. And then by the time I arrived, the regular parking lot was jammed with all the soccer people. So I remembered the overflow lot, which is how I found Michelle's car. Anyway, I was knocking on the window to see if anyone was in there. The glass was dusty, and I couldn't see inside, so I gave it a swipe with my hands." She spread her arms wide in a gesture of appeal. "My fingerprints must be all over it."

Zhao seemed to be holding back a smile. "We'll keep that in mind, but it should be okay. As long as you weren't inside the car."

"I wasn't, but I'd like to take a look." Emerald stepped closer to the rear door and pointed. "You see, I think that's Michelle's handbag on the floor."

"Her purse was left behind?" Violet tapped her chin with a fingertip. "Is that a good sign or bad?"

"I'm not sure," Emerald said, "but I'm pretty sure it's hers. A Ralph Lauren." She leaned in and squinted into the darkened rear window. "Definitely a Ralph."

"That sounds like Michelle," Violet said, "exquisite taste, not too showy." She turned to the uniformed officer. "Can't we take a look?"

"Sorry, ladies, but this vehicle is going to be towed away." Officer Daniel Zhao pressed his palms together in prayer position, as if in apology. "I know you're concerned for your friend, and I assure you, we're doing everything we can to find her."

"As are we," Violet said, chin up in a stance of dignity and defiance. "I'll have you know, Officer . . ." She squinted at his name tag.

"Zhao," he said.

It sounded like "Jow" when he said it. Well, sort of, with a "Shh!" sound and a breathy "h" somewhere. Alice knew from Madison, who spoke fondly of him, that Daniel's grandparents had emigrated from China to California, though he was born here in Oregon. Alice appreciated his manners and winning smile, and she wondered how deep Madison's fondness ran for this young officer.

"Officer Zhao, we have spent the morning looking for our friend," Violet continued, "and we are engaged and determined to find her. Can't you pop the lock so we can look through her car? There are probably some clues there."

"The car will be unlocked eventually. And, honestly, if there was a concealed trunk, we would have opened it to make sure she wasn't trapped inside. But since it's a hatchback, we can see the back. No one inside. I'm sorry if that's too gruesome a detail."

"No apologies," Alice said. "We all want the truth."

"I appreciate your involvement, ladies, but right now we need to protect and preserve the chain of evidence. If your friend was abducted or injured, the interior of that car is a potential crime scene. We'll take it to the county lab, where they'll go over it carefully."

"Checking for hair, blood, fibers, chemicals, anything that seems out of the ordinary," Alice said, recalling the forensic procedure from crime novels.

Zhao's eyes opened wider for a moment. "That's exactly right. Do you have law enforcement experience?"

"I've read plenty of procedural mysteries," Alice admitted.

"And she watches reruns of *Law & Order*," Ruby said, as if that would score points with the cop. Ruby enjoyed harmless flirting, and age was no deterrent. "We all do."

"Great show," Zhao agreed, looking over toward the rig with a flatbed in the rear. "You ready to load it up?" he asked the driver, who gave him a thumbs-up. "Ladies, if you don't mind, we need to clear the area so the tow operator can take over here."

"You're giving us the boot?" Ruby asked.

"Afraid so." Officer Zhao gave a nod, stern but not mean. "Thanks for your cooperation. We'll take it from here."

Another disappointment, Alice thought, stepping back as the tow truck began to back toward the Subaru. But at least they'd found the car. She hoped it was a good sign.

Chapter Thirteen

Alice led the gals to a path at the edge of the overflow lot. "This should take us back to the main lot," she said. "But before we make a move, I'm wondering what you gals think about Michelle's car. What does it mean? Did she leave it here? Was she carjacked and then her vehicle was dumped here?"

Looking around the circle, she saw consternation and skepticism on the women's faces.

"My opinion—and this is strictly personal—I don't think a carjacker would leave a Ralph Lauren handbag behind," Madison said.

"Agreed." Emerald gave a brisk nod, curls bobbing. "And the car looked neat and tidy inside, the way Michelle kept it."

"So, if best-case scenario, Michelle escaped of her own volition, why leave her car here?" Alice asked.

"Well, if she expected us to put out an alert with the make, model, and description of her car, she wouldn't want to be caught driving it," Madison said.

"And maybe she needed to get closer to transit to make

her getaway," Violet said. "Dragonberry Lane is so isolated, a long walk from anywhere."

"That's right," Ruby said. "We may be surrounded by trees, but there are paths that lead out of the park, and it's a short walk up the hill to Church Circle. And if you stay on the main road, it's less than a mile to the State Street Shopping Center, and the beginning of the downtown shops."

"Excellent points," Alice said, still not sure what her next move should be. "I wonder what Lars is thinking. I've been invited to his press conference at Dragonberry Lane this afternoon," she said.

"I wanna go!" Taylor said. "I want to see his studio and new art and stuff."

"Then come with," Alice said. "It's at three."

"I can't. I volunteered to help set up the sound system for tomorrow's concert at Waterfront Park. You know, that end of sunshine fest they have every year? When you man the sound system, you get to work with the bands."

"Good experience," Alice said. "I'll be there, at least for a while."

"You will?" Taylor seemed surprised. Was it because Alice and her friends didn't usually attend outdoor concerts? Ruby always said they were too buggy and loud, and evenings were often when they hung out at the house to chat over puzzles. "Who else is going?"

"Violet and I will be there to talk with the book club ladies," Alice said. "Gain more insight into the Michelle situation."

"Okay, cool. Maybe I'll see you there." Taylor was not enthused at the prospect.

"We'll leave you alone, if you have a date," Violet said.

"No, no date. Just helping out."

Normally Alice would have pressed her, but she didn't want to push in front of the group. "So, what's next for the afternoon? Anyone returning to the search?"

"I'll be here, of course," said Madison. "Now that we've found Michelle's car, we'll refocus our search to the area around this overflow parking lot."

"You've done a thorough job, honey," Alice said. "Those drones were quite impressive."

"But still no sign of Michelle," Violet said.

"Well, she did leave her car here," Madison said. "That's a sign."

"But I feel like she left it here, and then she took off." Violet closed her eyes and lifted her hands, fingers splayed, as if they were mini-satellites. "She's not here. I don't feel her vibe at all."

Madison crossed her arms across her chest but pursed her lips tightly. The debate between scientific and psychic knowledge was an ongoing riff in their sphere.

Alice wanted to point out that Violet had picked up the wrong vibes on more than one occasion, but she decided to let her sister be soothed by her beliefs. Michelle was, after all, her friend. And Alice knew how a missing person could hurt the heart.

"I've got to throw some cards on her," Violet said, referring to the tarot cards that she tried to interpret. "I should have done it before, but I was scared, and fear is such a strong emotion, it can block out the truth."

"Sounds good," Alice said, supporting her sister. She was not sure if she believed the predictions of tarot cards, but she had seen Violet formulate sound advice from those illustrations of cups and thick wands, kings and queens, a star card, and a naughty devil. It was as if the cards helped her hear a message in the wind or read the future from the way the earth was spinning that day. "Maybe tonight?"

Violet nodded. "For now, I'll keep searching. I'll team up with you, Emerald, if you want. Taylor is off to do her volunteer thing, and Santino had to head out."

"Perfect," Emerald said. "I'm here to do my part."

"We could use your help. Anyone who wants to continue searching, meet at the pavilion at one," Madison said. "I need to get back to our command center now. Let's check in later, Gran."

"Yes, and make sure you get some lunch," Alice called after her retreating granddaughter. "And stay hydrated." To the others, she said, "She works so hard."

"Come on, Alice," Ruby said in a low voice, "she's a full-grown woman."

"You're right. I know." Alice tugged on the neckline of her shirt. "You just never stop caring."

"What about my hydration?" Taylor reached for her throat, gasping. "I'm feeling kind of thirsty."

"There are water bottles back at the pavilion," Alice said. "Besides, you let Santino get away."

"He wasn't our captive," Taylor said with a laugh. "He had to get to the gallery. Apparently, buyers come through on Sunday afternoons, and they like the artists to be there to discuss their work."

"I see. So, was he forthcoming with information about Lars? What did you learn?"

"Not a whole lot," Taylor said. "He didn't want to talk about Lars, but I think he's into Aunt Vi, so they spent most of the time talking about art. Impressionists and the art in the Louvre and who's that artist you like? Shaggy?"

"Chagall. Marc Chagall. His painting, *Paris through the Window*..." Violet thumped a fist to her heart. "I love it so. Santino knows it, of course."

"Of course, but what does he know about Lars Olsen?" Alice pressed.

"He didn't want to talk about Lars. Bad memories, he said." Violet tipped her head to the side, sympathy in her eyes. "Though there were good times when he was in art school with Lars and that other guy, Sol, he called him. But Solomon's dead now, cancer. And when the three of them were striking out on their own, when they were sort of celebrated for the movement, Lars felt like he wasn't getting enough credit. He got jealous over every show, every sale that Santino and Sol had. And there was some situation with a woman, a model that Lars was dating. It didn't end well."

"Interesting. What was her name, this model?" Alice asked.

"Like I said, he didn't want to talk about it," Taylor said.

"*As* I said," Alice corrected.

Taylor rolled her eyes.

"He said that the dark vibrations block the spiritual channels, which I totally understand," Violet said. "Aggressive energy shuts me down, every time. After a heated parent-teacher conference, I can't do a tarot reading for weeks. Nothing comes to me."

"Difficult times," Alice agreed, unwilling to be drawn offtrack. "I'm sorry Santino's gone. He may be the key to really understanding Lars."

"Well, he did say he would be in town awhile," Ruby pointed out. "Let's track him down."

"You won't have to look too hard," Taylor said. "Just go to the gallery. It's open today from one to six."

A visit to an art gallery? "What a lovely way to spend a Sunday afternoon." Alice shot an inquisitive look at Ruby. "Are you in?"

Ruby smoothed back her hair and smiled. "Giddyup."

Chapter Fourteen

"Thank goodness I didn't dress in hardcore hiking gear today." Ruby finished applying her lipstick and pursed her lips in the mirror of the passenger-side visor. "This outfit has the flexibility to go from a morning in the park to an art gallery to a lakeside. If we are eventually going to get some sustenance?"

"As promised. Right after we talk with Santino," Alice said, driving with the flow of traffic on State Street.

She moved to the right-hand lane to avoid a turning truck, then noticed the signs for the shopping center looming ahead on the right.

"You know what? We have a few minutes until the gallery opens. Let's grab some eats now."

"Music to my ears. But I thought we were going to find a place in town center, near the gardens or the fountains, or splurge at Andre's?"

"There are a few places right here." Alice did a quick scan. "French Bistro? Or Buttery Bakery."

"I do love the eggs Benedict at Buttery," Ruby said. "But can we sit outside? That place is the size of a matchbox."

"Looks like outdoor dining is open." Once they found a

table under the shade of a charming red umbrella, and Alice checked out the view toward the back of the shopping complex, she wanted to clap her hands in glee. This would be perfect. From her spot at the table, she could take in the entire shopping complex, a few rows of stores situated around an L-shaped parking lot. An uninspired design, but the place made a splash decades ago when towns were giving up Main Street space for one-stop shopping in a plaza. The large Market of Choice at the corner of the L had gotten a facelift recently; it now resembled a Craftsman-style barn with fluorescent produce shining from the cornices. A welcoming anchor store, but not what Alice was looking for.

Sipping her decaf latte, Alice considered the nearby business with a new eye. If she wanted to get away, who here could help her? Probably not anyone at Sweet Dreams, the infant boutique, or Planet Love, the organic grocer and nursery. Stu Davis, owner of the hardware store, could sell her a wrench or a gazebo kit. The cleaners, the vape store, the liquor store, the gift shop with two statues of adorable hounds guarding the door . . . all useless to someone on the lam.

Ruby stopped talking abruptly and snapped her fingers in the air. "Hello? Alice. You haven't heard a word I've said."

"Guilty. I'm sorry, was it important?"

"Everything I say is substantial and relevant. But tell me what you're looking for." Ruby craned her neck to peer out around the edge of the red umbrella. "Is someone watching us? Is he handsome?"

"I'm just sitting here wondering if Michelle found an escape route through this shopping plaza. We know River

Bend is less than a mile away, and one of the park trails leads here. If Michelle deliberately left her car in River Bend Park, how long would it take her to walk here?"

Ruby's eyes opened wide. "So, this is why we're eating at Buttery Bakery instead of one of the grander places in town."

"Again, guilty. I can't stop thinking about Michelle, and I wanted to scope out the proximity of this place to the park."

"It is close." Ruby gripped her mug, calculating. "Twenty minutes, more or less, depending on pace. Quite doable."

"But where would she have gone from here?" Alice sat back in her chair, frowning. "No car rentals here. Maybe she had a rendezvous with someone?"

"Mmm. Such a public place for that." Ruby tilted her head to look down the line of shops past the hardware store. "There used to be a travel agent down there. Remember that? It was there for years. Now it's a cell phone place."

"A travel agent." Alice nodded. "The world has moved on." She looked up as the server brought their food—eggs and bacon on a croissant for Alice, eggs Benedict for Ruby.

"A special treat," Ruby said demurely. "But we've earned it with our morning hike."

From the parking lot to the pavilion? Not a big calorie burner there, but Alice kept the observation to herself.

"Bon appetit!"" their server said as they tucked in.

A few delicious minutes later, Alice was chewing on a crisp morsel of bacon when she heard the thrum of a heavy vehicle toward the back of the parking lot. A truck delivery, she suspected.

At the same time, two teenage girls let out a yelp and

started hurrying toward the rear of the brick building housing the grocery store. What was back there?

She leaned forward and saw that the girls were running to a green city bus waiting at the median strip there. She swallowed the bacon, savoring the flavor and the "Aha!" moment.

"A bus stop."

Chapter Fifteen

"Actually, it's a terminal," said Brianna, the young woman waiting on their table. "Not much to it, I know. But you can get the metro bus into Portland. In the other direction, it runs over to Oregon City, then turns around."

"A bus," Ruby hissed. "I should have remembered that. Celeste used to take it into Portland for her harp lessons."

"Oh, yes, the harp. Her symphonic phase." Alice looked up at Brianna. "I see a few different bus signs there. Do you know if any long-distance trips are available? San Francisco or Canada?"

"Not sure about that," Brianna said. "But there's probably a schedule posted there by the signs."

They thanked Brianna, left her a hefty tip, and strolled to the back of the parking lot to the cement island with old-time lampposts and hanging baskets of flowers—a West Hazel tradition—in the center.

"The petunias are getting a bit leggy," Ruby said. "But then we're in October. Next thing you know they'll be replaced with wreaths and Christmas lights."

Alice found the information on the signposts confusing.

"No schedules, but what's this? Just the final destination?"

"Looks that way," Ruby said as the Portland bus let out a blast of air with the brakes, and then rumbled off. "Over there. Does that one go to Idaho?"

Alice saw a sign for Boise. "It seems that way. I wish they had more details posted here. For more information, there's a barcode that takes you to a Web site."

"Oh, technology! What will we do when AI completely takes over?"

"I'll be in the library, clinging to some real books," Alice said absently. She didn't like gumming up her cell phone with data, but she turned on the camera and took a shot of the barcode. "Yes, Boise, Idaho." She clicked on another code. "And here's a bus that takes you to Las Vegas."

"Hell's bells, Michelle could do a lot of damage in Vegas, if she remembered to bring some cash." Ruby seemed cheered by the thought. "You know, Alice, we could hop a plane to Vegas to search for her there."

"We could, but these buses don't run very often. The Vegas bus leaves on Tuesday nights, and we know Michelle disappeared sometime after Friday morning."

"Goodbye, Vegas. I'm so disappointed."

"Don't be. We've also got San Francisco, Sacramento, by way of Ashland, home of the Oregon Shakespeare Festival."

"I'd love to catch a show, and I think their season runs for a few more weeks. Where else?"

"Also east to Black Butte, Bend, and Sunriver. Oh, my, there's a bus to Colorado. Another to Montana. Transit for folks with fear of flying." Excitement flickering in her chest, Alice lowered her cell phone and looked beyond the signposts to Ruby. "I have a strong suspicion we might be on to something here. If Michelle really wanted to get away without being tracked, it would have been smart to leave her car and purse and get on a bus."

"I feel it, too. This is a find." Ruby clapped her hands together. "So where are we going to search first? I know a wonderful restaurant in the RiNo district of Denver. They serve an authentic pozole that's to die for. Or I could score some 49ers tickets in San Francisco." As CEO and owner of a successful business, Ruby went first-class when she traveled.

"Tempting as all that sounds, I'm going to start by sharing this theory with Madison. She'll have better access to the transit information. She'll be able to see which buses would have aligned with Michelle's time of disappearance."

"Madison is good with details like that," Ruby agreed. "But you know I always have a go bag packed and ready. Denver or San Francisco, you just let me know."

"Of course." Alice didn't see herself jetting off anytime soon, but if it meant finding Michelle, who knew? "For now, I'll be happy if we can catch Santino at the gallery and extract a little background info on Lars."

Chapter Sixteen

"Is he there?" Alice asked, lingering outside the gallery situated on an exclusive block of real estate in West Hazel. Flanked by a members-only whiskey bar and a double-platinum Realtor that handled only multimillion-dollar properties, the gallery was too rich and sleek to appeal to Alice. Though the Coyote Jones sign, with a graphic of a fedora over the C, did tickle her interest.

Ruby lifted her head, striking a regal pose as she peered inside. "I see people in there."

"Why do I feel out of my league here?" Alice frowned into the glass window, her reflection softened by fuzzy landscape paintings in soft blue, gold, and green hues. At least she thought they were landscapes. Or were they just horizontal lines? She'd always had an interest in fine art, enjoyed visiting museums, but now, approaching a gallery, she felt awkward. "I could never afford anything, and I have this sinking feeling that I'll say something stupid and embarrassing about his paintings."

"Oh, honey, you are as welcome here as Warren Buffett, and you can let me make the stupid statements. I gave up being embarrassed years ago." Ruby reached for the curved gold handle of the door. "Besides, art is subjective. I'm sure the artist is hungry for attention, and we can give him plenty of that."

Inside, the entryway was a narrow bottleneck with room for just a handful of paintings. Welcoming paintings with more horizontal lines, but warmer colors. Alice breathed more easily, soaking them in for a moment before recognizing how the lines varied and included blotches and shapes of color. Clouds? A waterfront? Curved lines that resembled breaking waves. Pine trees. Dune grasses. They were indeed landscapes, she was sure of it now. And somehow that recognition made her feel as if she were in on a secret.

A handful of people milled through the adjoining room—a couple with a child, and two men who spoke to each other in a whisper as they paused at each painting. Santino stood toward the back of the gallery, talking with the man and woman while the little girl—nine or ten—made a game of leaping from one inlaid black square to another on the marble floor.

As the little girl hopped away from Alice, Santino noticed her and Alice nodded. He was still wearing the lovely suede blazer, and his mustache curled ever so slightly as he smiled. A man of subtlety, Alice thought. Quite different from the unfiltered emotiveness of his onetime colleague Lars Olsen.

Alice glanced at the card posted beside each painting, noting the titles: *Sandstorm. Asleep at Sea. Beach Palette. Solemnity Sea.* "So they're seascapes," she said quietly to Ruby. "What do the red dots mean on the cards?"

"That painting has been sold. And there's a lot of them. He's doing well."

Santino ended his conversation with the couple and came over to Alice and Ruby.

"You came! I'm flattered." His gaze darted to the doorway. "Where is Violet?"

"She's continuing the search down at the river." So, Taylor had been right about his interest in Violet. Brave, though how could he have realized that Violet hadn't dated for the past twenty years? Although various factors seemed to have led to her single lifestyle, it was something that had sort of evolved over time. As Violet seemed to have plenty of companionship through the book club, school events, colleagues, and families, Alice had never pursued the topic with her. "It was good of you to come this morning."

"I went for Michelle. I think you know that. Lars I have no use for, but Michelle, she is a good person. I knew her before Lars did. In a way, it's my fault they're together." He gave a half frown. "Shame on me. But I've moved on from Lars. As I told your sister, I can't fall into that hole. And I didn't want to complain to Violet. It's a bad look, I think, to be a crybaby."

"It's not a complaint, but a window to the past—your time back in art school, when you and Lars were both in your twenties. We've been having trouble filling in the missing pieces in Lars's background."

"A time I'd rather forget." He crossed his arms over his chest, as if locking up the memory.

Alice needed to change tack. "Did you stay in touch with Michelle?"

"I tried. We spoke, but rarely. I called her when I got the spots in the galleries here. She was encouraging, but she couldn't tell Lars." He lowered his arms and flashed a welcoming smile to three women who'd entered the gallery. "He's a jealous one. How do you say? Green with jealousy. That's how I would paint him."

"It's too bad you two have parted ways, after being close friends in art school. I imagine you must have shared some good times and intellectual exchanges. To come up with a new approach to art together, that's remarkable."

The wry smile on his face reached his brown eyes. "Not so new. A different portal, an innocent view, the primary shapes and colors of childhood. And actually, we were three. Sol, Laddy, and me. Unfortunately, we lost Sol." He touched the fingertips of his right hand to his forehead and made the sign of the cross.

"I'm sorry. That must had been a difficult loss. Did it strain your relationship with Lars?"

"It was already over. You see . . ." He checked the other patrons, who seemed content. Ruby was talking with the two men, leaning in to decipher their whispers. "He didn't know how to behave with women. He had quite an ego, even as a young man. The jealousy, it was a rage. There was a young student, a model for us, and—the poor girl. Laddy hurt her. The police were called. It was such an ordeal."

"Have you told the police about this?"

He waved off the notion. "It was twenty years ago. I think the charges were dropped and he cleaned up his act. I don't know enough to tell anyone anything."

"It does establish a behavior," Alice said.

"The police can dig it up, if they so choose. I don't think he ever laid a finger on Michelle, if that's what you're thinking. She wouldn't stand for it. But I know Laddy's a jealous, selfish man who doesn't deserve such a love."

"You call him Laddy. A nickname?"

"His given name. I say it wrong. Larr-ee. Laurence Ottermeyer. He hated it. Thought it sounded like a door-to-door salesman. So, he became Lars Olsen. Voilà, an artist with a hint of Scandinavia."

Lars had changed his name . . . no wonder there was no record of him attending the art school. Alice couldn't wait to do some digging on the young Larry Ottermeyer.

When the door opened again, admitting a new group, Santino clasped his hands together and gave a slight bow. "I must see to my guests, and I've probably already said too much." He stirred the air with one hand with a look of disdain. "The dark energy swirls around us. Please, give my best to Violet. And you should both drop in at Coyote's gallery in Portland. This is a small gallery, room for only a fraction of my work. You'll see a better range of my paintings there."

"I would love that," Alice said.

"It opens Thursday, and the weather promises a lovely evening. Have you done First Thursday? It's always a fun night out in any city. Free wine and snacks. You can stroll from one gallery to another, along with other art lovers." He smiled. "Violet will love it."

"I'm sure she will." Alice gave a friendly nod as he went on to address the newcomers.

"Did you get anything?" Ruby asked.

"I did. Though I'm struck by what a terrific salesman Santino is." Had he sold her an account of the past that painted him in a positive light? He'd seemed genuine. But then, there were two sides to every story, and Alice sensed there was more to learn about Lars Olsen Ottermeyer. She looked forward to the media briefing in—she checked her Fitbit—forty minutes.

Then she remembered her promise to Lars. "Oh, no!"

Ruby pressed a palm to her chest. "What is it, honey?"

"I need to whip up a casserole, pronto!"

Chapter Seventeen

"Looks like someone's having a party," Ruby said as Alice turned down onto the narrow strip of Dragonberry Lane, passing the occasional car wedged between shrubs and boulders on the grass shoulder.

"It's supposed to be a media conference to focus attention on a missing person," Alice said, "though it does look festive."

Two news trucks framed the parking area, one of them hazardously close to the overgrown ravine that ran along the yard's edge just inside the north fence. Satellite feeders towered into the sky, reminding Alice of those traveling amusement park rides. From the news vans in front of the house, Alice saw that the local TV stations were well represented, their reporters and producers clustered in groups, talking and joking like old friends at a class reunion.

"It's tight," Alice said. Even the narrow drive alongside the house was blocked by cars. "I'm going to double back to the lane and find a spot on the edge, by the bushes."

After finding a spot, Alice let Ruby out, squeezed her car into the vines of an overgrown honeysuckle shrub, and opened the back door. The foil tray of lasagna from a high-end grocer had cost a pretty penny, but Alice didn't dare try to pass off a frozen one as her own. "It's the price of admission," she'd told Ruby as she'd handed her credit card to the cashier. It had also made them ten minutes late, though the casual crowd made it clear that nothing had started yet.

Weaving around people and cars in the makeshift lawn parking area, Alice and Ruby came across an interview in progress. Perky and smart Emma Suzuki, whom Alice recognized from *Portland Live at Five,* was questioning a portly Black man dressed in a fedora, buttery leather jacket, black jeans, and designer athletic shoes. Emma was her usual inquisitive self, but her subject, a man with personality plus, had her laughing.

"Who's that?" Alice mouthed to Ruby.

Ruby leaned in close. "Coyote Jones. I've never met him, but I've seen pictures. And that hat—his trademark."

So this was the art dealer, Coyote Jones. With the face of a cherub and the body of a linebacker, the man had a presence.

"You think I'm fooling with you, but I speak the truth." Coyote removed his sunglasses, revealing solemn amber eyes. "Scandal breeds interest in the art world. So something like this, the artist's wife disappearing, could stir up a lot of interest for Lars Olsen's art."

"Then you see this as an opportunity for Mr. Olsen?"

"It's a facet of the art world. But I don't wish any ill will on anyone, you know what I'm saying? I hope Michelle turns up safe and sound. And soon. No amount of money is worth the anguish my friend Lars is going through right now."

"Have you noticed increased interest in your client's art since the disappearance?" Emma asked.

"Whoa, Emma, I'm going to correct you on that. Lars Olsen isn't included in my stable of artists. He established himself long ago and doesn't need me to nurture or promote him. Yes, he has shown in my gallery in the past. And who knows . . . maybe again in the future."

Wrapping up the interview, Coyote glanced at his cell and told the interested bystanders that he was needed inside. Most eyes were on the art dealer as he headed up onto the wooden porch and into the house.

"Me likey Coyote." Ruby watched him walk away, fleet of foot for a man of his stature.

"But what he just said, it's despicable," Alice said. "Cashing in on tragedy?"

"I know. I would have to rehabilitate that part of him. But you know how the bad boys always steal our hearts."

"Steal and trample," Alice said, regretting it immediately. She had been no shrinking violet, and her husband, Jeff, had hardly been a bad boy. A cool dude who loved to spin tales and had no aptitude or cares for budgeting—that was Jeff Kowalski. Now that they were divorced, Alice had forgiven him for pursuing his singular goals and pleasures without involving her in the journey. She could forgive, but, like a cautionary tale, his deeds would not be forgotten.

"Let's take the casserole inside," Alice said, starting up the porch steps.

"I wouldn't go in if I were you." A young man in a baseball hat with a press badge dangling from around his neck summoned them back with the curl of his fingers. "No one but art people are allowed inside until Lars gives the go-ahead. And I don't know about you, but I don't want to see Lars lose his temper. The guy's a regular Mount St. Helens."

"We're friends, with a casserole." Alice held up the tray. "But you're right; I don't want to poke the bear, Mr.—?"

"Ted Bilicki. Call me Ted. With Sunrise Media." He extended his hand, a firm handshake that said he was not a man to waste time. "We do all the local publications, *West Hazel Gazette* included."

"Thank you for covering this," Alice said. "With a missing person, public awareness is vital."

"Happy to help, but I don't need to be here to get the story. We take our hard information from the police department. I'm here out of courtesy, though it's not too courteous to make us wait around."

"What's the holdup?" Ruby asked.

"The *artist* isn't ready for the *cameras* yet. Word has it that he's setting up all his paintings, making us take a tour if we want to hear his statement about the missing woman. Pretty cheesy, right? I think he's pushing to sell his work."

"Disheartening," Alice agreed.

"Are you going to write that part in your article?" Ruby asked.

"I dunno." Ted shrugged. "Honestly, most of our readers will pay attention to the missing person story, but the stuff about the artist will seem like a fluff piece."

"We do have an arts society downtown," Ruby said. "Plenty of patrons."

Ted shook his head. "Your art patrons aren't reading the *Gazette*." He craned his neck toward the windowed wall of the dining room. "I have half a mind to leave."

"We'll go see what's keeping them," Alice said. "We come bearing gifts. No one's going to turn us away."

Ruby headed to the front door, but Alice grabbed her arm and guided her to the side door, which she recalled led to a mudroom. "Let's slip in the side."

Entering to a loud argument, Alice and Ruby hugged the wall and moved to the side of the room, escaping anyone's attention. Invisibility was a superpower that came with age, Alice had learned, as she'd approached her sixties and found that many folks failed to acknowledge the gray-haired lady as an active player in the room.

Lars's voice boomed with indignation. Something about doing it his way or the highway. How he'd been up most of the night preparing for this.

"He's in a good mood," Alice muttered, crossing the short space at the back of the house while no one was looking. It wasn't hard to find a place to hide, as the dining room, once a broad space with its half walls lined with paintings, was now a makeshift gallery, stuffed with rows of easels displaying canvases. Hovering behind a painting, Alice took the opportunity to take in the art while the men in the open-concept kitchen and living area hotly debated a plan. She noticed lots of red in the paintings . . . a color to match the tension between the two men.

Ruby scrunched her face at the painting, then moved on into the catacomb of canvases.

"After they walk through and have a chance to take in the paintings, they'll spill out onto the porch, where we'll conduct the press conference," Lars said. "Why is that so hard to grasp?"

"What's the point of bringing them in?" demanded the other man.

A familiar voice.

Peeking out, she recognized Detective Bedrosian, the lead investigator from the West Hazel Police. Brown eyes, bold chin, dark hair flecked with white, Bedrosian could be attractive when his face wasn't pinched with disdain or disapproval, which it often was. The man liked to argue. Today he looked a little like an unmade bed in his white shirt and paisley necktie, his sleeves rolled up. From the peeved tone in his voice and the wrinkles in his shirt, she sensed that he'd been going at it with Lars for some time.

"We've been over this a million times." Lars raked his wavy blond hair back. It hung wild and loose today, a cultivated look of artistic genius. Beside him a much younger, shorter woman looked up at him with a pouty expression, rubbing his shoulder as if to calm the beast within. "A glimpse of Michelle's home will help the public relate to her. We're building compassion, so they'll care and help find her."

"Not really buying it," Bedrosian admitted.

Lars threw his arms in the air. "Are you here to torture me?"

"Believe me, I'm just here to make a statement on behalf of the West Hazel PD." Bedrosian's mouth was puckered and sour, as he lifted his jacket from the back of a kitchen chair. "After that, you can throw a hootenanny in the barn, for all I care."

"All right then." Coyote Jones's low voice was like a salve over the room. "We good? Bring the reporters in here, weave them through the exhibit, and funnel them outside. Agreed?"

"Have at it." The detective swatted the air, annoyed.

"Open the doors! Do it now." Lars cued the two young people in the room—his assistants, perhaps?—and they hurried out of the kitchen to usher the waiting folks in.

The staff members seemed like kids. The young man was taller than Alice, a little gawky, with reddish-blond hair, a square jaw, and a smile that seemed too sweet for someone involved with Lars. The gal was petite but solid, with long, black hair and a sleeve tattooed on one forearm. Hard to put an age on her, but she seemed mid-twenties. Dressed in a black dress with black Doc Martens, she had a smile that reminded Alice of a shark. A hungry great white.

Ruby came round the corner of the aisle of paintings, where she'd wandered off, soaking in the art. "Sorry to say, but Lars is no Santino," she murmured, hand shielding her lips tactfully. "Was that Detective Bedrosian I heard complaining?"

"Yes, indeed. I'd rather he didn't know we were here."

"I'd rather not be here with him around." As the lead on the homicide investigation of Ruby's husband, George, Bedrosian had fingered Ruby as a prime murder suspect. He'd had his reasons, but Ruby wasn't a fan. Hard to shrug off being pinned for homicide.

"Remember, we're here for Michelle." Something Alice needed to remind herself, as she could think of a dozen better ways to spend a Sunday afternoon.

"And you're right about this house," Ruby said with a shudder. "An odd vibe."

"A claustrophobic nightmare," Alice said, glancing over the rows of paintings cluttered in the dining room space. "Let's get out of here before the audience files in." She was edging out past a painting of a flaming red apple on an arrow when her jacket caught on the edge of something. She turned to see the apple painting wobble and tip toward her.

"Oomph!" she gasped, hugging the darn lasagna to her chest with one hand to reach for the painting with another.

"Easy, there!" The tall kid swooped in, grabbing the canvas. "Close one." He looked over his shoulder and then smiled at Alice. "Good thing Lars didn't see."

"Such a delicate construction." Alice glared at the display. "Like rows of dominoes."

"Ready to fall," Ruby added.

"No kidding." The young man adjusted the leg of the easel, tested its stability, and backed away. "Lars had us buy every easel within twenty miles of here. We were up most of the night, trying to figure things out."

"It is a little tight in here," Ruby said. "Most galleries can manage to give each piece a bit of space."

"Yeah." The kid leaned down, lowered his voice. "We tried setting up in the barn. Plenty of space there. But it's old and damp. Lars says the damp is fatal for a canvas. And it's pretty dark in there. No way to bring in the right light."

"But here, you've got plenty of sunlight," Ruby said.

"Right? All these windows. This is usually Lars's studio." He spoke quickly, confiding in them as if they were the only friendly faces in sight. And maybe they were. "We had to do a quick cleanup and lug the artwork from the barn to set up in here. Took most of the night, but Lars said we had to get eyes on the art." The kid was earnest, bright, and imminently likable.

"And ready on a Sunday afternoon," Alice said. "That's very impressive. I'm Alice Pepper, by the way, and this is my friend, Ruby. We're friends of Michelle. Oh, and Lars asked us to bring him some dinner." How easily the little white lies floated from her lips and somersaulted through the air. She held up the aluminum tin, glamping like a fifties housewife.

"Henry Finley. I'm Lars's assistant. A student. Here to learn the craft."

"If you're lucky." The snide comment came from the petite shark girl, who had homed in on Henry. "I'm his protégé. Lars hired you to fetch and clean, dude. Everyone starts at the bottom." She turned to Alice and Ruby. "I'm Lars's apprentice, Rosie Suarez. Do you want to take my picture in front of the artist's paintings?" She squinted at them. "Wait, are you reporters?"

"Friends of Michelle."

"Oh." Rosie's interest plummeted with their apparent status.

"So you both must have met Michelle," Alice said.

"Plenty of times," Rosie said.

Henry gave a shrug. "I'm new, so not that much, but she was always real nice. Always made sure I had water or tea. She liked to brew tea. And she used to sneak me cookies, but Lars got mad at that."

"Stop talking about her in the past tense." Rosie sent Henry a searing look. "Lars wants you at the door. Nobody gets out of here until they go through the art gallery."

"Will do." Henry nodded. "Ladies? Did you tour the gallery?"

"Oh, it was lovely," Ruby said. "And we'd better deliver this meal to the kitchen before this place fills up."

Alice and Ruby moved away from the ersatz exhibit, stopping in the kitchen to put the lasagna in the fridge. Pausing at the door, Alice looked back at the space, now cluttered with makeshift art displays and buzzing with people who seemed to be going through the paces, aware of Lars's plan to get "eyes on his art."

Alice had wanted a chance to wander the house looking for clues about what had happened to Michelle, but that wasn't going to happen now. Then again, she was getting a peek into the "machine" that seemed to keep Lars Olsen's career in motion.

Sometimes, the best clues came from watching and listening. Eyes and ears.

Chapter Eighteen

Lars's statement to the media was inconsequential, and Alice found herself bored and fidgeting like a ten-year-old at the edge of the porch as the artist droned on about his dear wife.

Ted Bilicki covered a yawn and adjusted his cap. "My readers would have scrolled ahead five minutes ago," he muttered.

Aside from mentioning the discovery of Michelle's car and purse—"Which gives me hope!"—Lars provided little information about Michelle but delivered a lengthy opus on himself. Alice was offended, on Michelle's behalf, at how quickly Lars went from talking about his missing wife to slinging his artwork. The reporters gathered on the lawn seemed to be equally disappointed, as a few of them slunk off to their cars when Detective Bedrosian began to take questions.

Seeing that the press event would take a few more minutes, Alice signaled to Ruby, and then slipped around the house. The side door was still unlocked, the house empty of people, it seemed.

"Hello?" She strode in through the mudroom, paused

to groan at the old splatter of crimson in Lars's paintings, and turned back to the rest of the house.

No time, she told herself. *Move quickly. What's the most important place to search?*

The fireplace.

Madison had said it was clean when the police swept through the house, but now it was full of flaky bits of ash. Someone had been burning papers, and a few large chunks sat on the charred bricks.

Leaning into the mouth of the beast, Alice picked up a fragment of parchment paper. It seemed to be a corner of a page of illustrations from Michelle's manuscript. There were also burnt scraps of thinner papers, probably printer paper. On one piece she could make out a few handwritten words: ". . . why I need to get . . ."

Get where? Get away? Get back at you? Get a dog?

There were a few more legible lines, as well as other half-charred paper scraps, but Alice couldn't examine them now. Nor did she have time to focus on the bits of illustrations that had been tossed into the fire. Michelle's creations? She hoped not.

Unable to find a ziplock bag in the kitchen, she settled for a large Ball canning jar and used the ashen wrought iron shovel from the hearth tools to scoop up the biggest chunks of paper. What a mess. She screwed the lid on and slapped dust from her jeans. The fat jar was like a bowling ball in her handbag, but at least it didn't stick out.

Where to look next?

When Michelle showed the book club her illustrations, she had retrieved them from a credenza behind the couch. Alice edged over to the area near the front of the house, daring a glance out the window. Fortunately, the press conference had wrapped up and people were no longer on the porch. She ducked down anyway, opened the doors on the dark walnut piece. There were photo albums, old music CDs, and a CD player. A second door held art supplies, but no sign of her illustrations. Her manuscript seemed to be gone.

Knowing that someone would walk in at any minute, Alice moved to the bedroom at the back of the house. The door was open, but still, she called inside, not wanting to intrude.

First impression: the room was a mess. The bed was unmade, the comforter falling off one side, the pillows dented and smashed. Clothing was scattered on the bed and floor. Alice nearly stepped onto a tangle of lingerie. Thongs, it seemed. She touched a small, pink woman's bathrobe slung on the bench and recoiled, realizing it was damp. Recently used.

Who's been sleeping in my bed?

Alice had a strong suspicion of who might have taken over Michelle's side of the bed.

A dozen or so books sat in two stacks on Michelle's nightstand, and Alice went to check them out, half expecting to find a copy of *Gone Girl* or *The Invisible Man*. A book could provide a blueprint for an escape plan. But the books were a potpourri of mysteries, popular novels, and literature.

She turned to leave and saw Rosie Suarez standing in the doorway. Suspicion confirmed.

"What are you doing in here?" Rosie's eyes narrowed with distaste.

Right back at you, Alice thought, but she didn't want a confrontation. She turned away and went to the stack of books on the nightstand. "I was just looking for a book I lent Michelle. We're in a book club together, you know, and I need to read it next." Rosie wouldn't know that was a lie. She sifted through the books for show.

Rosie pushed the tangle of thong lingerie under the bed with one Doc Martens as she picked up a few items from the bed. "Oh, yeah? What's it called?"

"*The Mysterious Affair at Styles.*"

"Never heard of it. Is it about Harry Styles?"

"Not at all. It's an Agatha Christie mystery, her first."

"Yeah. I have heard of her."

Alice put the books down. "Unfortunately, I don't see it here. I'll keep looking, but thanks for your help." Alice exited the room, but Rosie called after her, following her into the hall.

"Wait. I know you're friends with Michelle, and I just want to say, she's a great person. Lars has told her everything and she's fine with us being together. Their divorce is in the works. She's giving Lars a big chunk of money, and we're going to open our own gallery somewhere else. Maybe Seattle, to give everyone some space."

Now this was a new twist. Alice pasted on an interested smile to hide the feeling of disbelief. "Seattle is . . . it's a great place for young people like you."

"And their art scene is more international than Portland. Down here, we're the redheaded stepchild." She cocked her head and gave a laugh at her own joke.

Under different circumstances, Rosie could be likable. But with Michelle missing, it seemed cavalier of her to boast about these plans.

"Let's hope we find Michelle soon so you can get on with your plans," Alice said.

"Yeah, definitely." Rosie gave a thumbs-up

Chapter Nineteen

Was it true that a divorce was in the works for Michelle and Lars? If so, it was a well-kept secret. Did Michelle know someone had been sleeping in her bed? Probably, Alice thought, conscious of the heft and bulk of her purse as she moved through the house. Time to stash it in the car before someone noticed she was lifting some of the glassware.

Outside, Alice was surprised to see Ruby chatting with Detective Bedrosian. Thank goodness it looked friendly, so far. She deposited her acquisition in the car and noticed a few honeybees bouncing on the far side of the roof. They did love the honeysuckle.

After she slammed the car door she noticed a bit of commotion over by the ravine. The remaining people seemed to be focused on something there—a car stuck on the edge of the gulley. The chasm also functioned as a rain swale, a drainage ditch used to channel the water of downpours and excessive storms away from structures on the property.

As someone gunned a car engine, Alice joined Ruby and the detective, who were watching with skepticism.

"I am so afraid that car is going to roll right back and fall in the ravine, I can barely watch," said Ruby.

"I don't think so." Bedrosian frowned. "But I guarantee someone's going to end up in the mud." He cast a glance at Alice. "Ruby tells me you're friends with Michelle."

Alice gave a nod. "She's well-liked in our community. Any new leads?"

"You know I can't say," he said. "But I don't know if you've noticed, but the only person who's mentioned kidnapping is the husband."

"So you don't think she was kidnapped?" Ruby asked.

He shrugged. "Not for me to say."

But the subtext was clear. Alice and Ruby exchanged a hopeful look.

Lars gave a holler, and all eyes turned to the ravine, where Henry stood awkwardly trying to avoid the sticker vines. "Ready? When the engine revs, you push!" Lars ordered.

The driver hit the gas, and the spin of the tires sent weeds and mud flying. Everyone watched as the rear of the car sank an inch into the ground, shimmied, then caught traction and moved forward onto the gravel.

Applause and some lukewarm cheers scattered through the parking lot. Lars let the car roll a few yards ahead, and then put it in park and emerged victorious, taking a bow.

Down in the rain swale, a grimy Henry swatted with one hand while covering his eyes with his forearm. He was speckled in mud, his neat shirt and khakis a mess. "Bees! Hornets. Something . . . something stung me."

Alice and Ruby went to help the kid. Coyote was already there, extending a hand down to Henry. "Come on out of there, son." Henry was tall, but Coyote had height and heft. Soon, Henry was on solid ground again, and Coyote was plucking the last vine from his shirt.

"It smarts." Henry held out his arm, scowling at a swelling red welt.

"Just a bee sting," Lars hissed. "You'll be fine."

Witnessing that snapshot of cruelty, Alice wondered how Michelle could tolerate this man. Maybe Lars was the reason for her disappearance.

"You allergic?" Coyote asked.

Henry's face was beginning to scrunch up in pain. "I don't think so, but it sure stings." Wincing, he shielded his left arm, where two angry red welts had already erupted.

"Come inside and wash up with soap and water." Alice put a hand on his shoulder and guided him toward the house. "I understand a good rinse might help remove the venom. Come along."

He didn't argue, respectful boy that he was, and she hustled him inside, squelching a desire to lash out at Lars. It wasn't the right time.

Inside, a handful of people were milling around, looking at the paintings. Leftovers from the press conference, or newcomers? Alice couldn't tell. She directed the kid to the sink. As he folded his sleeve nearly up to the shoulder, she turned to the fire-engine-red fridge. "I'll see if they've got a cold pack; that should help with the sting and swelling. And pain medication. Have you taken ibuprofen before? Are you okay with it?"

Henry nodded as he spread foam onto his biceps. "That would be great. Thank you."

"And vinegar," Alice said, wrapping ice cubes in a kitchen towel. "I don't want to root through a stranger's kitchen, but when you get home you might want to try vinegar to reduce the sting."

"I will. Thanks." He patted his arm dry and took the ice. "How do you know all these remedies?"

"Experience. Reading. First aid."

"Do you have kids?"

"All grown. A daughter and two granddaughters, not much older than you. How old are you?"

"Seventeen. I'd be starting college now, but this is my gap year, learning art."

"From Lars?" Alice couldn't imagine Lars had much to teach a duckling like Henry Finley, but then she was no art expert. "What I mean to say is, I'd think you'd start with an art school."

"I wanted to. But tuition is expensive, and my mom says this is a once-in-a-lifetime chance. He's an amazing artist."

Alice did not find Lars's talents to be *amazing*, but this was no time to argue vocabulary with a young man still feeling the sting of a bee's wrath.

He looked down as he sat on a stool at the counter. "My mom's gonna be mad. This is my good shirt." The kid was a wounded puppy, far more innocent than her granddaughters at seventeen. That year Taylor had been vaping and playing Roxie Hart in the school musical version of *Chicago*, and Madison had been hosting international students from Japan and setting up a nonprofit agency that paid tutors for floundering grade school students.

"Get Lars to pay for your shirt," said Alice. "Are you done with your shift here?"

He nodded. "I just had to stay till most of the people were gone. My mom's on her way."

"You stay put until she gets here." Alice turned away from him, scoped out the living area and the dining room art show, and wondered if her work was done here. She'd gotten a good look at the workings of Lars Olsen's art studio, and more than enough of his cantankerous ways. But before she left, she wanted to make sure she got credit for the meal she'd brought; it might help to stay in Lars's good graces.

Just then Lars, Rosie, and an attractive man in a blue blazer breezed in the front door on a tinkle of laughter. Alice recognized the man as a TV reporter for a Portland station.

"It's always hard for me to part with a painting," Lars said. "They're like my children, all special to me, but I know it will be in good hands with you. Which one are you interested in?"

"It's sort of a crimson jungle? My partner will love it." The reporter led them into the catacomb of paintings to point out which one he wanted to purchase. Lucky Lars. He'd gotten a sale out of the day.

As Alice waited for the negotiation, she browsed through some of the aisles, taking it all in. It seemed that Lars still clung to the childlike, primal approach he'd pioneered, with brash splatches of color and rough lines. "Stick drawings," she observed in front of one painting in which five stick people seemed to be dancing around a fire. Some aspects of his childlike approach were cheerful, though too many pieces were splashed with red that reminded her of blood. Hints of violence in childlike scenes; it was unsettling.

"I'm psyched!" The reporter emerged and headed to the door. "Let me just get my checkbook." And he was outside again.

"There you are." Alice found Lars and Rosie in the twisted gallery. "Just wanted to let you know that Henry is in the kitchen, nursing his welts with ibuprofen and ice. It appears that he's not allergic, thank goodness."

"That is a good thing," Lars agreed.

"Next time, cut the kid a break," Alice said.

Rosie smirked, but Lars pressed his hands into prayer position and bowed. "Sage advice." His mood had shifted. Was it the glory of the sale?

"I'm heading out," Alice said, "but I wanted to make sure you get the dinner I brought for you. The lasagna's in the fridge. Heat it at three fifty until the cheese bubbles."

"That's so kind of you." Sensitive Lars had taken possession of the artist's body. Was he psychotic, or simply a convincing actor? "I love lasagna. We'll have it for dinner."

"That was the plan." Before Alice could tell him it would go well with a green salad, Lars's face brightened and a voice boomed behind her.

"Here we go. Now who should I make the check out to?"

And just like that, Alice was invisible once again as Lars moved aside, enthralled with his buyer. Sometimes invisibility was a gift, like a superpower. Other times, it was a consequence of age and class bias.

Over at the kitchen counter, Henry nodded. He'd been observing the rest of the room while looking at something on his phone.

Alice nodded back. The language of invisibility.

Chapter Twenty

Before Alice left, there was one more part of Dragonberry Lane she needed to check out. As the path out to the pond was more dried mud than gravel, it was fortunate that Alice was still wearing her walking shoes from the morning's search in the park.

What was she looking for back here? She wasn't quite sure. But it seemed negligent to leave without getting the lay of the land.

As she rounded the slight rise, the path before her narrowed from a lane to a foot rail. Below her, the land sloped down abruptly to a mucky water's edge. "A mud beach."

Off to her right, the jungle of brambles that had taken over the ravine extended to the water's edge, resembling the unfriendly watering hole of a horror film. A weathered rowboat lay overturned and partially covered by plants with fat leaves. Surrendering to the earth.

To her left was a mud bank, which probably flooded after heavy rains.

Alice eased down the slope to study the boat. It didn't seem to have been moved recently, but she had to check. She felt her entire body grimace as she edged into the weeds and looked for a clean spot to lift the vessel. If only she had gloves. Bracing herself for water rats and slithery things, she gripped one edge and lifted with a grunt.

It was a heavy lift, with the plants clamping down on the boat. But as sunlight seeped into the darkness under the hull, she saw dried grass but no body, and no snakes.

"Thank you, God." The boat settled back onto its fat green salad, sending a small legion of insects skittering.

Brushing her hands, she turned to the pond. The water had a brownish tinge, enlivened only by the surreal green of algae. A stagnant pool, lacking the fresh water of an underground spring.

The dead pond summed up the property with one quick look.

Could something be hidden in the murky waters? Absolutely. Had the police considered that possibility? Alice would ask Madison, but she didn't think Michelle was here. Her spirit, her abandoned car, her excitement over the new possibilities in her life—all of those things suggested that Michelle had escaped this place.

It was a short walk back to the house. As Alice approached the backyard, a field of foot-high grass and dandelions in need of mowing, a car appeared from beyond the house. It navigated the narrow side driveway and pulled around to park on the gravel patch that scarred the backyard. Alice moved quickly across the open space to a row of somewhat warped arborvitae. The trees provided cover, while the spaces between gave her a look at the car and one rear corner of the house.

The sedan was a dark color—gray or green—a nondescript vehicle, though the driver, when she emerged, caught Alice's eye. She was a willowy woman, maybe as tall as Alice, but younger, thinner, draped in a black, classic raincoat that was oversized for her and yet elegant. Much of her face was hidden by sunglasses. Her blond hair was pushed back with a red band that looked like something fashioned from a scarf on a whim. A look that said "this was effortless" when it really had taken some time. The fact that her red leather gloves matched the scarf confirmed that it was all part of the grand fashion scheme.

Alice didn't need to look down at her hiking clothes to confirm that fashion was never part of her personal scheme. Well, bushes could be convenient.

The sleek woman went around to the side door and knocked. Waited. Opened the door and called inside.

When Lars appeared at the door, the woman abruptly turned and strode back toward the car. Not happy with him. She complained about a "waste of time" and he barked back something Alice couldn't hear.

Too far away. Alice hurried to the end of the arborvitae. A better vantage point, and close enough to catch most of the conversation.

Lars was now at the side door, yelling into the house, "Boy? Henry! Your ride is here."

Such rude behavior. If any potential art buyers were left in the house, they were probably at this moment flying out the front door.

When Henry emerged and faced the woman, Alice surmised that she was his mother. Both were blond and tall. And beneath those sunglasses, the woman's face probably mirrored Henry's.

"I got stung." Henry lifted the ice pack to reveal his arm, and from the bits of conversation Alice could catch, it was clear that the boss was not happy. She pointed Henry to get into the car, and then stormed over to Lars.

"You had him in the ravine? Are you kidding me?" The

annoyance in her voice made it loud enough for Alice to hear every word. "He could have been crushed by that car!"

"It wasn't as bad as it sounds. Someone had to help that reporter. How was I supposed to know there was a bee's nest down there?"

"Next time call Triple A. Henry isn't here to be your pit crew. He's a talented young man and you've got him in the thickets trying to lift a truck?"

"My staff members have to juggle some menial tasks."

"Not my son." She pointed to the young man in the car. "We have a deal, *Lars*." She said his name with disdain, as if it had a bad taste. "Look, I'm sorry about your wife, but that doesn't change the terms of our arrangement. Either take Henry under your wing and give him the attention he deserves or pay the bill."

Bill? Alice squinted, maintaining her hiding place behind the tree. *What bill?*

"You think you'll get that money out of me? Good luck trying."

"I've got a lawyer. The courts don't care that you're a big-shot artist. A debt is a debt."

"You're being ridiculous," he groused. "Chasing that money after all these years. You know I don't have it."

"You have an out, Lars. You are going to mentor Henry. You are going to do it cheerfully. Full-heartedly reveal your genius. Well, with as much enthusiasm as an old sourpuss like you can muster. You're going to share your vast knowledge, sweetened by the tiny nugget of joy in your withered heart."

"And what if I don't?"

"I'll see you in court."

Chapter Twenty-one

The green herbs in the deck pots bobbed and sprang beneath her fingertips as Alice plucked basil for dinner. How wonderful it felt to be home in joggers, a sweatshirt, and thick socks after a long, adventurous day! She clipped three large basil leaves, carried them into the kitchen, and dropped them into a simmering pan of homemade marinara sauce. In thirty minutes the basil leaves would suffuse the sauce with flavor as they shrank to withered strings that she would toss out before serving. After a long day, spaghetti with marinara sauce was a quick and easy crowd pleaser.

And she would have a full table. She'd set six places at the dining room table. Stone and Madison would be here soon, and Taylor would be home from her run-through any minute.

While Alice had thrown together the sauce, Violet had sat quietly on a barstool setting up a tarot card spread on the peninsula. Ruby was in the laundry room, trying to piece together scorched scraps of paper from the Dragonberry fireplace.

Alice was glad to be surrounded by people she loved,

and her large, modified Craftsman home, affectionately called Alice's Palace, certainly had space to accommodate everyone. Violet had moved in after Jeff got the boot, and Ruby had asked to rent some space downstairs after the home she'd shared with her departed husband no longer seemed welcoming. After losing money on the restaurant she'd opened with Jeff, Alice was relieved to have rent money to offset the mortgage. But the greatest joy was having family and her best friend under her roof but out of her hair. They were women with very full days, but there was always time in the evenings to share a puzzle, a coffee or a glass of wine, a laugh, or a worry.

Setting the sauce to simmer, Alice opened her laptop on the coffee table and leaned forward to start a search. Last night she had searched for information regarding Lars Olsen's tenure at the Bridgeport School of Art—and had found nothing.

Now she tapped in his real name, Larry Ottermeyer, and searched for him in Connecticut. This time, she got a few hits. Some of them were obviously the wrong person—the curator of a small seafarer's museum in Mystic, and a plumber in Hartford. But his name came up in the Bridgeport College of Art database, and she printed a photo of him working on a sculpture, as well as his graduation pedigree. Then she searched for crimes on the Bridgeport campus that year and found a few mentions of assault, one in which an art student had been accused of holding a female student against her will.

One of them might be a match. The articles were printing when she heard her name.

"Alice!" Ruby called from the laundry room. "Honey, I hope you know this is a colossal mess."

"Just paper and ash," Alice replied as she went to the laundry room off the kitchen. Wrapped in an apron, Ruby stood at the tiled counter beside the sink. As she pinched a pair of tweezers to lift a charred scrap of paper, the edge brushed against the mouth of the jar and fine black ash exploded through the air, showering the countertop and sink.

"Whatever you do, don't sneeze," Alice said.

"And don't you get me started laughing. We're liable to send a black cloud gusting through the house."

Alice turned her head away to let out a deep breath. "I wish we could clown around in the dust, but what I'm seeing here scares me. See these scraps of illustrations you've pulled out?"

"Yes, there's a cute little dark-haired girl in most of them. Is it a comic strip?"

"I think they're Michelle's illustrations for a graphic novel she's working on. The main character is a girl named Jing, which means 'clear and shining' in Chinese. Jing is a character who has visions of what is in a person's heart, and she helps them find what they need."

"What a lovely sentiment," Ruby said. "And now, it's been reduced to ash. Such a shame. And over on this side of the sink I've put together the bits and pieces that seem to be part of a letter."

"Smells good in here, and I'm starving," Taylor called from down the hall, and Alice heard the garage door go down. "She's talking about the tomato sauce, not this ash," Alice told Ruby. A moment later, Taylor said hello to Violet, then peeked into the laundry room. "What's going on?"

Alice explained that she'd pilfered the scorched fragments of paper from the Dragonberry fireplace. "It looks like one of the pages was a handwritten note. I'm thinking it was from Michelle to Lars."

"Of course it was," Ruby said. "And that grouchy bear threw it into the fireplace to spite her."

"I knew it!" Violet pushed into the laundry room, indignant. Vi must have been listening to their musings. "I knew Michelle wouldn't leave town without telling someone. And Lars has been lying all along!"

"We don't know that," Alice said. "But I like the theory. From the phrases I can make out, it seems like a farewell note. See how it says, 'Don't come looking for me'? That's substantial."

"And look here," Ruby said. "She says something about 'time and space.' I bet she needed to be alone to think things over. And this scrap here says, 'This is why I need to get away.'"

"It doesn't say that," Taylor said. "Some of the words were burned off."

"But we get the gist, don't we, girls?" Ruby insisted. "Michelle left hubby a farewell note—maybe considering a breakup—and he tossed it into the fire."

"Plus, he's trying to cash in on her 'disappearance' to sell some of his art," Taylor said.

Just then the doorbell rang, and Alice held a finger in the air. "Hold that thought."

She scurried to the door, her fluffy socks skidding on the floor like a teenager. Maybe it wasn't romantic to greet Stone in her sweatshirt and joggers, but she'd had a long day, and had made the decision that if he wanted to get to know her, he'd need to see the slumming, no-makeup version. If that didn't scare him away, he was a true man of character.

"Good evening." His ruggedly handsome face exuded

warmth when he smiled. Damned if his eyes weren't twinkling.

"Hey, you." Her pulse quickened. Was she blushing? How adolescent. She didn't want to be involved with a man right now, but here he was, and oh, he was all that.

"I brought some red wine."

"Love it." She took the bottle. "Come in. We're in the laundry room. I found some ashes at Dragonberry, and we're doing our forensic best to decipher them."

"Ashes? As in a body? Hell, do you think it's—"

"Oh, God no. At least I hope not. Just scorched papers. But here's what we're thinking...." She gave him the thumbnail version of the theory, and then they pressed into the laundry room behind the other women.

"Ladies." Stone nodded. "We've got to stop meeting this way."

"Why is everyone in the laundry room?" Madison asked from the doorway. She must have been off-duty, as she wore faded blue jeans, her black Cons, and a black T-shirt topped by a coral V-neck sweater. Madison was so different from Taylor, and yet Alice loved them both so stinking much. Yes, Alice often fought to keep them on track, but the once-removed feature of grandchildren had given her the joy of relishing their talents and personalities. A consolation prize for her failures the first time around? Whatever the reason, Alice was grateful to have been in their lives over the years. Raising them part of the time, loving them always.

"What's with the charred scraps of paper?" Madison asked, pulling Alice back to the moment.

"Ruby will go over our newfound evidence one more time, while I cook the pasta," Alice said, taking charge of the situation.

"Wait, Gran." Madison held up one hand. "How did you get your hands on evidence?"

"Totally legal." Or so Alice assumed. "Ruby will explain. I've got to get dinner on the table." She headed back to the kitchen.

"Gran, wait..." called one of the twins. "What are we having?"

Alice smiled. "Murder with marinara sauce."

Chapter Twenty-two

The group decided it would be a social dinner, free of crime discussion. "Better for digestion," Ruby said, twirling spaghetti on her fork. It was nice to take a break, but Alice couldn't remove herself completely from the Michelle situation. Thinking over her day, she saw the evidence pointing in a specific direction.

"That was delicious, as always," Ruby said, rising to start clearing the table. When Alice stood up, everyone insisted that she stay out of the kitchen for cleanup, since she'd done the cooking.

"That's the rule," Madison said, opening the dishwasher.

"All right then." Alice got up from the table and went to grab the printouts about Larry Ottermeyer. On the way, she found a puzzle box sitting on the coffee table.

"A new puzzle! Perfect timing." They had finished the cursed blue-sky puzzle late last night. "Seven hundred fifty pieces, and it's custom-made. But the illustration is delightful." It was a childlike illustration of a girl in a garden with a man and a woman. Simple, but chockful of colorful flowers, yellow stars, and fireflies in a sky full of blue swirls reminiscent of Van Gogh's *The Starry Night* painting.

"Where's this from?"

"I brought it," Taylor said. "Someone at rehearsal asked me to give it to you. They said you'd know who it was from."

"Really? Well, it looks like an early Lars Olsen." And Lars would be vain enough to merchandise his art in puzzle form. "Is it from him?"

Taylor shook her head. "He wasn't there, but rehearsal was crazy. Jammed with people, and kind of disorganized. Turns out there are two backup bands, and one of them is missing their lead singer. Allergies or strep. Anyway, it just got handed to me in the chaos."

"Someone knows the perfect gift for me." Alice hated to think that Lars was trying to butter her up; impossible. In fact, he was the sticking point of today's investigation.

She went to the large granite peninsula and positioned herself where she could see all the worker bees in the kitchen. "I have a few general observations from today, with the booby prize going to Lars Olsen. That man doesn't even pretend to be worried about his wife's disappearance. He didn't search for her. He turned the press conference about her disappearance into a market to peddle his art. And he seemed happy as a clam to have dinner with his apprentice, Rosie, who seems to be keeping Michelle's side of the bed warm."

"And you know this how?" Madison asked.

"Trust me, they're not being discreet," Alice said.

"Those two have sex written all over them," Ruby said, forking leftover pasta into a container.

"That would be an interesting tattoo," Taylor said.

"Rosie told me Michelle and Lars are getting a divorce. She says Michelle has agreed to pay Lars a large settlement so Rosie and Lars can start over and open a gallery in a new city."

"That poor girl sounds deluded," Violet said. "But I wouldn't put it past Lars to lie to her. I think we can all agree Lars is a big pile of poo." Violet's hair was coiled in a loose bun, and she paused a moment to blow the strays away from her eyes. "He's not trying to find Michelle, and that letter you found might explain why. She told him she was leaving. Probably just temporarily. Sounds like she expected him to leave her alone and maybe cover her absence at work. But instead, he reported her missing to make a whole incident out of it."

"And cash in on it," Alice added.

"I believe it's a crime to file a fake police report," Stone said.

"It could be a felony," Madison said, "but we'd have to prove he knowingly filed incorrect information. And right now, our priority is finding Michelle, making sure she's safe."

"Of course, Michelle is numero uno." Ruby handed Taylor a dripping pot to dry. "Just saying, jail would serve Lars right," Ruby said. "Liars and blowhards are so unattractive."

In the pause, over the sounds of pot scrubbing and running water, everyone cast a curious look at Ruby, who had recently lost her husband because of his cheating, swindling ways. Alice had to hope that the experience of seeing George's dishonest character after his death had given Ruby new insight in men.

"A man without integrity is no man at all," Violet announced with a firm nod.

Had her sister seen that on an Amish sampler? Though it did sound like an adage a vice principal would share with a twelve-year-old boy with chronic behavior issues.

"I agree that Lars is treading in criminal territory,"

Madison said. "But I need to point out, Gran, that the scraps you picked out of the Dragonberry fireplace would never be admissible as evidence."

"Of course they won't." Alice nodded. "I understand the rules of evidence. However, for those of us who are not representing law and order, the fireplace letter is proof enough. I think Lars burned her precious drawings, her ticket to a new creative pursuit and perhaps career. That part makes me so mad."

"Remember when Michelle showed us the illustrations at book club?" Alice asked her sister. "She'd had interest from a publisher and was working to put together a complete illustrated novel to submit. But even there, among Michelle's friends, Lars had been jealous. He'd made some comment about being the only artist in the family."

"He tried to crush her creativity," Violet said sadly.

"He drove her away," Alice said. "So she decided to take a breather. She wrote him the note, and left town."

"And she left her car in the parking lot, purse and credit cards inside, so that Lars couldn't find her and pester her if he hired someone to track her down," Taylor said, pointing the dried ladle for emphasis.

"Michelle must have known the park was a short distance to the shopping center where all the buses come through. Alice and I scoped it out today. I bet Michelle walked from River Bend Park right over to the bus terminal and jumped on a bus to . . ." She looked up at Alice. "Where'd she go?"

Alice turned to Madison. "Did you check those bus schedules?"

"I haven't had time. The search ran long, and then I had the paperwork on the impounded car. But I did get to search a few databases on Larry Ottermeyer."

"I found Larry, too!" Alice waved the printouts. "At least I was able to confirm that he was a student at the art school."

"Who is Larry Ottermeyer?" Taylor asked.

When Alice explained that the artist had changed his name for marketing purposes, Stone chuckled. "Even back then, he thought he was a superstar," he said. "Note that he kept the same initials, LO."

"That superstar was charged with assault while he was a student at the college," Madison said. "The victim, whose name is redacted in the report, claimed that Larry O held her against her will and caused her physical injury."

"He's a known abuser?" Taylor paled. "I wonder if Michelle even knew that."

"It's a worry for her," Madison said, "but it was around twenty years ago, and he was charged but not convicted. The charges were dropped."

"I wonder if people know? I mean, should we warn Rosie, the art apprentice?" Violet asked.

"It was twenty years ago," Madison said, "but it would be good for her to know, in case the abusive behavior has persisted. I plan to speak to her tomorrow."

"I can't believe you're actually sharing confidential police information with us," Ruby said, eyebrows wiggling.

Madison rolled her eyes. "It's not confidential. These arrest reports are public records, though they don't show up in every database."

"Come on, now," Ruby said. "Admit it. You give us preferential treatment."

"I'm doing my job," Madison insisted.

"Of course you are, honey," Alice said. "And I, for one, am so grateful to have your shared insights and expertise."

"Me too," Taylor said. "Oh, yang to my yin. You get the facts straight and I put a creative spin on them."

Madison's nose wrinkled. "Wait, I'm yang? Isn't that the male side?"

"Depends on how you look at it," Violet instructed. "There's a complex richness to any archetype. Which brings me to my reading on Michelle. The cards I pulled for her indicate that there is indeed turmoil, though it's not so much physical danger as an existential crisis."

"I want to see the cards." Taylor tossed the towel onto the counter and came over to the peninsula for a look. "I always feel like the visual conveys its own message."

"I always get goose bumps." Ruby crossed her arms, a defensive gesture. "Some people say tarot cards are dangerous."

"How are they a threat, Ruby?" Alice shifted to peer at the three cards. "Are the cards going to come alive and take over your life?"

"I just don't want to hear bad news, doom and gloom."

"But the cards don't curse anyone." Violet left her station at the dishwasher and came to the counter to look down on the tarot card spread. "They simply represent the atmosphere in a person's life. Sort of like a karmic weather report. As usual, I've pulled three cards—past, present, and future—with Michelle in mind."

"The Devil card?" Ruby frowned. "That can't be good."

"Always a stinker in the mix," Alice said. The card was creepy. The Devil had huge Batman wings attached to the naked torso of a healthy man with the head and lower extremities of a beast.

"The Devil can represent entrapment and emptiness," Violet said. "A lifestyle leading you down a rabbit hole. Here in the position of Michelle's past, I have to believe that she felt trapped and oppressed in her marriage with Lars. The thing about a card like this, is that the awareness of a bad situation can push you to make a change."

"So, Aunt Violet, you think Michelle left town to escape Lars?" asked Taylor.

"Honey, I'm sure of it now." Violet tapped the middle card. "Now here in the present is the Magician. It's a powerful card. See how he's holding a wand up to the sky? Some people think he connects heaven and earth."

"What does it mean?" asked Madison.

"The Magician says, 'You have the power to create your own reality.' "

"I've never cared for magic, but that's a good power to have," Stone said.

Taylor nodded. "Cool. Things are looking up for Michelle." She tapped the third card, a cheerful graphic that showed a boy handing a goblet to a girl in front of a village square. In the foreground were five other cups, all of them topped with a white flower. "And how about this one, Aunt Vi? Her future."

"That's the Six of Cups. It's the card of reunions and memories, kindness and creativity. It often means that someone who's been gone awhile is returning."

"Really? Someone like Michelle?" Ruby asked.

"That's my reading of it." The hairs that had sprung loose from Violet's bun now framed her face, emphasizing the light in her eyes. "I'm feeling good about this, folks. I think Michelle's going to be fine."

Violet's buoyant hope sparked small smiles around the room, a sweet moment. Vi's enthusiasm was usually contagious, and everyone wished the best for Michelle.

There were a few other loose ends, questions to be answered, theories to debate, but Alice hated to tug down the banner of hope. Tomorrow and tomorrow and tomorrow, as the Bard had put it. Or perhaps that was the work of his fledgling assistant.

"Ladies, I'm going to skedaddle before I turn into a pumpkin." Stone thanked Alice for dinner and saw himself out. She watched him leave, marveling at his perfect instincts to stay just long enough.

"I guess I should go, too," Madison said.

"Stay! We have a new puzzle, and it's gloriously colorful." Alice was already lifting the lid of the box. "This illustration is adorable, so full of color. Like something you'd see a child draw. Though now that I've been exposed to the art of Olsen and Santino, I've learned about the Unfiltered approach to art." She grabbed a handful of pieces to start searching for borders and sorting by color. "I'm digging in."

Ruby yawned. "I'm going to put my jammies on, but I'll be back to help."

"I'm so tired, but the beginning is always exciting." Taylor started to turn over and sort pieces. "So much potential and discovery."

"I like the end," Violet said. "That satisfying snap when the last piece goes in its place."

Alice loved the entire journey . . . the curiosity, the tedium that organized thoughts and calmed the mind, the camaraderie of building a picture together with the gals.

How she loved them! Alice Pepper's Lonely Hearts Puzzle Club.

Chapter Twenty-three

Monday morning, Alice attacked her league of e-mails, and then returned a few phone calls. Board members required quick responses, and Friends of the Library, the fundraising group that operated independently of the county system, couldn't be kept waiting. Wanting to stretch her legs, she found Julia wheeling out a cart of books and joined her in the fiction section. She gave Julia an update on the search for Michelle as they worked side by side shelving books.

"So, you're thinking that Michelle left her purse, ID, and car behind and jumped on a bus so she wouldn't be tracked?" Julia asked.

"That's the consensus among friends at the moment."

"And the husband drove her away?"

"That's the popular theory, though our best indications of his spite are the ashes from the fireplace, which are not admissible as evidence."

"Yeah, well, this isn't a court of law," Julia said, reaching up to slide a book onto the shelf. "And if the husband is fooling around, it doesn't look so good for him. But I'll say this, sounds like you learned a lot about the art scene, meeting Lars Olsen and Santino."

Alice nodded as she tucked away the last volume. "Yesterday was a lesson in Contemporary Art Appreciation 101, from both the artists' perspective and the business end. Coyote Jones, the art dealer, gave us a rundown on the varying value of paintings. Apparently, some artists are *dying* to get famous."

"Terrible joke, but sadly true," Julia said. "I like your theory, but I've been trying to think outside the box, and there are some other scenarios you might want to consider. Like, maybe Michelle has gone into the witness protection program, and not even the police can find her."

Alice squinted at her friend and smiled. "*Hide and Don't Seek.* I read that one years ago."

"The book popped into my head last night. Or it could be a double agent situation, and she's been undercover all along. I mean, she's fluent in a few languages, right?"

Alice wagged a finger. "I know a novel with that plot, too. What was the title?"

"It's on my desk. Just started rereading it. But the point is, this could be huge. More than just a domestic thing or a discontent woman."

"You're right. I need to keep an open mind."

"And watch your back," Julia said.

"Should I beware of spiked tea and poisoned darts?" Alice teased.

"I'm serious. I'd hate for you to go missing, too."

"Point well taken. I'll be careful."

With the cart now emptied, Alice checked her Fitbit. "I'm going to take an early lunch and head over to Michelle's studio. I have an appointment to chat with Kamaria. And then I'll check in at the martial arts academy. Do you know anyone there?"

Julia waved her off as they wheeled the cart to the check

area and workroom beyond. "We're a soccer family. No room on the calendar for anything else."

As they approached the counter, Beto looked up and waved Alice over.

"Someone was here asking about you," Beto said. "A woman. She was very nice. But when she didn't want to leave her name, I got a funny feeling."

"Suspicion?" Alice trusted Beto's instincts. With neatly clipped dark hair and warm brown eyes magnified by square black glasses, Beto was their greeter—that first person you saw when you walked into the library. He read folks well and had a knack for making people comfortable. "Did she seem unstable? Menacing?"

"I didn't sense that she posed a threat. Just that she was hiding something. Maybe she wanted to surprise you."

"An old friend from college? From the neighborhood in Queens?"

"She's not that old," Beto said, and then blanched. "Not that you're old, or anything."

"Lucky for you I'm comfortable with my age," Alice teased.

"I hope I'm not blowing things out of proportion. I'd hate to be judgy."

"You're right to mention it. I appreciate having a heads-up." It was probably nothing, but after Julia's talk of double agents and high crimes, Alice wanted to proceed with caution.

Noting gray skies, she grabbed an umbrella and her purse before heading outside. A soft rain drizzled in the air, just passing precipitation, according to the forecast. For the sake of tonight's outdoor concert, Alice hoped the weather prediction was correct.

It was a short walk to the main avenue of West Hazel,

where she passed Andre's, noting that the lime and yellow umbrellas on the outdoor patio had been folded up for the rain. No outdoor dining today.

The rain had subdued traffic on the avenue. The occasional car pulled up to park, and folks darted in and out of shops, but it was a quiet Monday. She felt a pang as she passed the Sweet and Savory Ice Cream Shop. Maybe she'd stop in for a grilled sandwich on the way back.

Although the umbrella cut off her view, she focused on Tatiana's Flower Shop ahead. The tiered rows of vases held blooms that formed a wall of brilliant colors: garnet red, deep purple, lavender, raspberry, orange, and lemon yellow. Approaching the shop, she smiled at the way the flowers reveled in the misting rain. Beautiful.

But something seemed a bit off. She sensed that someone was watching her; that chill sensation between the shoulder blades. She stopped under the flower shop awning, lowered the umbrella, and looked around. Two doors down a woman in a trench coat and rain hat ducked into a pottery shop, as if dodging Alice's view.

"Did I just frighten the Morton Salt Girl?" Alice said aloud.

Glancing in the other direction, she saw three teenage boys dash across the avenue and jog into the ice cream shop. An ice cream emergency, or just trying to stay dry? Shouldn't they be in school? Or maybe they were seniors on early release.

It was one thing to be on alert about an unknown stranger; quite another to be a busybody. Maybe Beto's warning had gotten to her. In the stillness near the flowers, she took a second glance at the street. A man walking his dog passed by with a nod, and a few cars passed. Nothing out of the ordinary. She must have been imagining things.

The dance studio was a few blocks away, off on a side street. Alice stepped inside, grateful to be out of the cool drizzle as she stashed her umbrella in a stand.

She had stepped into a waiting room full of moms and dads, grandparents and nannies. Folks scrolled on their phones in the waiting room or watched their kiddos through a glass window that ran along the left-hand wall. Walking toward the office in the back, Alice glanced at the class of preschoolers in leotards. Most were prancing and swaying along with their teacher. A few students were dancing to their own tune or pouting in a lumpy stance.

In the rear office, Kamaria paced with the door open as she spoke on the phone. Noticing Alice, she motioned her inside and ended her call.

"I'm so glad you're here," Kamaria said. "I'm freaking out. So worried about Michelle." Tall and graceful, with her dark hair scraped into a bun, Kamaria's stress was masked by the grace of a ballerina. "The police came by yesterday. That detective . . . Bedrosian. He really scared me. I wanted to help, but I have no idea where she might be. She's a great boss, and we work well together, but our relationship is friendly and professional. We don't hang out or share gossip outside the studio."

"Understandable. So, you haven't heard from her since she disappeared," Alice said, taking a seat in the small but tidy office.

"Not a word. I was kind of floored when she didn't show up at your fair on Saturday. That was a fluke for Michelle. Yesterday I spent the whole day keeping all the classes going here and putting together next week's schedule." Kamaria leaned back against the windowsill, her lips pressed together, tears shining in her eyes. "I've stayed calm, but now the panic is setting in."

"Calm is good," Alice said gently. "The thing with panic is, it's really hard to peel back once it wraps around you. And you know Michelle. She's a capable woman. I hear she knows quite a few defensive moves."

"She's a black belt." Kamaria grabbed a tissue and swiped at her eyes with a deep breath. "Michelle's amazing. And it's just not like her to be irresponsible. Not answering calls or texts."

"She's not getting your messages," Alice pointed out. "We found her cell phone yesterday, though she may have left it behind to make a getaway."

"Get away from what?"

"We're not sure, but there's speculation that she disappeared deliberately." Alice held the younger woman's frightened gaze. "Did she give any indication that she might be leaving town?"

To her surprise, Kamaria nodded. "Now that I look back at the last few weeks, I think she knew something was going to happen. She was preparing me to take over the studio. She started training me to do the scheduling here, the billing, the advertising. She had me start sending out the monthly bulletin to the parents and students. Do you think she knew she was in danger?"

"Maybe she planned a secret trip and she knew you could handle the business while she was gone."

"But I can't...."

"You're doing a good job, Kamaria." Alice rose and gestured toward the hall. "I passed a large class of children and contented caretakers out there who would argue otherwise. Things seem to be in control here."

The young woman straightened. Such exquisite posture, though she was a good five inches shorter than Alice's six feet.

"I always thought ballerinas were tall," Alice said.

"It's the toe shoes. Dancing on pointe adds a few inches. Have you ever danced?"

"Only at weddings and bar mitzvahs." Alice smiled. "That was a joke."

"You're trying so hard to make me relax. I appreciate that, but I'm a bundle of worry." Kamaria sighed. "I just hate to think of Michelle out there alone. No one looking out for her. Michelle is capable, but we all need someone."

A wise insight from one so young. "What about Lars? Has he checked in with you?" Alice asked.

Kamaria shook her head. "He has nothing to do with the studio. Michelle and Lars have kept their businesses separate. Makes sense. They both had established careers when they got married."

"Still, he could lend some support."

Grabbing her clipboard, Kamaria glanced out at the little dancers now streaming out of the studio space into the waiting room. "Let's just say I'm not holding my breath."

Chapter Twenty-four

Waterfront Park was on the west end of Gooseneck Lake, the part that stretched a few fingers into the downtown region of West Hazel with boat docks and launches on the lake, paddleboat and kayak rentals, a food truck court and the city park. The east end was quieter, more suburban, ringed by trees and private homes. It was there that Alice built her restaurant a few years ago. Her dream business, her pride and joy, until she learned that they were losing money and her husband had cashed in most of her savings to subsidize the place.

Her ex-husband now. And her former business. Jeff owned it now, the rascal, though she tried to keep the peace with him for the sake of their granddaughters. He wasn't a terrible person, just toxic in her life.

She'd come early enough to find a parking spot without fuss. The plan was to meet the book club gals in the west pavilion at six, a good hour before the concert, which would give her some time to chat as they began their concert picnic.

The forecast had been correct. Any signs of precipitation had dried in the mellow sunlight, which now cast a golden glow over the park lawns and trees. Walking along the path in the light breeze that smelled of clover, Alice was reminded of the things she liked about outdoor concerts. When music rolled over a beautiful landscape, the world seemed right.

Though the euphoria could quickly fizzle with rain, humidity, wet grass, ants, flying insects, broken glass, sticky foods... too many hazards.

Less than a dozen spectators had taken spots on the grassy meadow and berm surrounding the stage. Alice shielded her eyes from the sun to see if she could spot Taylor out there. No sign of her among the sparse concertgoers, but a minute later Alice spotted her walking over to the stage, accompanied by a youngish woman in big round sunglasses, with a baseball cap plunked over her long golden hair.

"Taylor?" Alice called lightly, realizing that if she raised her voice she'd be the shrill granny calling her granddaughter over. She couldn't let that happen.

Instead, she followed Taylor and the blonde along the path toward the big concert stage, which had a white tented ceiling in the back that resembled mounds of shaving cream. The two women went to the staircase along the side and climbed the stairs, chatting the whole time.

Down on the path, Alice paused. What was up there? Did she dare? She wasn't an employee or volunteer. She reached for the handrail, looked up, and started climbing. After all, who was going to question a sixty-five-year-old woman who pretended to know what she was doing?

Alice climbed to the landing, a backstage area loaded up with amplifiers, speakers, and equipment. She spotted Taylor in a group of people off to the side, near an electronic board. Either lights or audio—Alice wasn't sure—

but it all looked professional and technical. She headed over but paused a few feet away, not wanting to interrupt what seemed like a meeting.

As she waited, her eyes went over the group there. A diverse group of young people, most not of her generation. A few had partially shaved heads, bright colored highlights, piercings. One young woman in Jackie O sunglasses and a navy baseball cap had stunning shiny hair, the color of a copper penny, that hung down beneath the cap. Sensing the mood of creativity and nonconformity, Alice was glad to see Taylor involved with like-minded people.

One dark-haired man in the group caught her eye. It took just a moment to place the strong jaw, dimpled chin, dark eyes and warm smile. Nick Zika, now in his forties, now a rock star, had been a neighborhood kid here in West Hazel. A good kid, if a little wild at times. There was a time when Alice was sure he'd had a crush on Lauren, who had found him cute in that pesky brother sort of way. Had Lauren's opinion of him changed once he'd become famous? Well, he'd grown up, too. Time had transformed many things.

He must have felt her stare, as he looked over and flinched. He bowed his head and said something, and a moment later the group dispersed, Taylor heading over to the sound board.

Nick approached her. "Alice. It's been a minute. How are you?"

"Just fine, Nick. I hope I didn't disrupt the meeting."

He waved the notion off. "We were done. How's it going?"

"I wasn't expecting to see you here. Will you be performing tonight?" Alice asked.

"Me? No, I wish. It's a beautiful venue, but . . . no."

"He's beyond playing places this small," said a guy with spiky hair and low-hanging jeans. He handed Nick a cowboy hat and flashed a broad smile. "He can't even walk around here without some kind of disguise. Besides, West Hazel can't afford him."

Nick took the hat and gave Alice a wry look. "Guess I've gotten too big for my britches."

"That's my line," she teased. "How are your parents?"

"Good. Still over on Eighth Street. Dad retired but Mom is hanging in there. And you look well. I hear you're still at the library."

Alice found it hard to believe anyone would be talking about her to Nick Zika, but then again, she did know his parents. "Still there. In fact, I noticed you have a book checked out that's long overdue."

His smile broke and he paled. "I do?"

"Nick." She touched his arm. "It's an old librarian joke."

"Aw, man." He pinched the bridge of his nose. "I was imagining the fines from two decades."

Alice hoped it hadn't been that long since he'd read a book, but she wasn't going to preach. "I came up here to say hello to my granddaughter." She nodded toward the sound equipment. "You probably don't recognize her over there working on the audio? That's Taylor."

"Is that so?" He turned his head, looking over his shoulder. "Oh, yeah, I see the resemblance. Taylor," he called, "come on over."

Taylor extracted herself from the work and joined them. "Hey, Gran."

Alice was surprised Taylor wasn't annoyed at her meddling. "I was just early for my meeting with the book club gals. Saw you walking by."

"Cool." To Zika, she said, "We've tested all the mikes. One of the amps is crackling. Pooch is working on it." When Nick nodded, Taylor explained that he was one of the producers of the concert.

"Good for you," Alice said. "Giving back to the community."

"So says Gloria Zika."

"Tell your mother I said hello. I'll leave you to your work. I've got somewhere to be."

She headed out, Nick following to call after her, "Careful on those stairs."

Good grief, did she look that old?

Over at the pavilion, the ladies had begun to arrive and set up their picnic table. Rachel brought Alice a can of seltzer while Emerald worked at uncorking a bottle of wine. Someone had brought a cooler of wine and seltzers, and various platters of cheese, crackers, dips, nuts, veggies, and grapes were arrayed on the table.

"I brought Killer Cupcakes!" Violet announced, striding in with a pink box held high, as if it were a crown on coronation day.

The women oohed and cheered. "My favorites," Emerald said. "Did you get the lavender tea flavor?"

"And chocolate cherry?" Rachel inquired.

"Yes, indeed." Violet put the box down on the table and unbuttoned her wool jacket. "It's getting crowded out there. People are all whipped up over something."

"Someone said Zika is here," one of the women said, a breathlessness in her voice. Was that cool, calm Juanita with a schoolgirl crush?

"I believe it. His parents live here," said Holly, archive of information. "Maybe he's visiting."

"Really? How I'd love to run into him." Juanita pretended to swoon. "Excuse me, but haven't we met in a previous life?"

"You would never say that."

"I would! I would definitely flirt with a gorgeous rock star like Zika."

Alice would have agreed that Zika was adorable; the decades had not robbed him of cuteness. Still, she kept mum, sensing that her admission of a connection to him would seem like a betrayal of his privacy.

"So ladies." Alice caught their attention as the women gathered round the table. "You know I'm not a detective—"

"Disclaimer!" Violet chimed in.

"But I want to share my theory about Michelle's disappearance. I don't think she was kidnapped, as her husband has insisted."

"Oh, thank goodness!" Merrilee said. "We love her so much and we've all been sick about it."

"Here's how I see it. . . ." Alice quickly explained the goodbye letter to Lars she'd found in the fireplace. Her theory that Michelle left her car and ID and credit cards in the park so she couldn't be easily tracked down. "We're thinking she walked from the park to the bus station." She shrugged. "It's possible. But where would she go? Any ideas?" Alice felt like she could see the path now. Find Michelle and make sure she was safe. And if she wanted to be left alone, so be it.

"Did you check with her relatives in California?" Holly asked. "Her aunties?"

"The police have been in touch with the family, but they haven't heard from her."

"You have to wonder, what was the final straw?"

Juanita plucked off a grape. "The thing that made her leave Lars."

Merrilee snorted. "Besides the fact that he's a narcissistic lump of—"

"Merrilee," Violet, ever the vice principal, cut in, "let's keep this PG-13."

"Money problems are often at the heart of relationship conflicts," Rachel said.

"I've seen Lars shamelessly shilling for cash, but it's hard to know if it's out of desperation or greed," Alice said. "Any sense of their finances—Michelle and Lars?"

"I know that Michelle was disappointed with Lars," Merrilee offered. "His business seemed to be going south, and she was upset about it."

"Actually, she was mad." A frown hardened her expression as Merrilee poured herself a glass of wine. "That Lars, he always acts like he's rolling in money, but . . . I shouldn't say anything." She shook her head. "She told me in confidence."

"Michelle was mad at Lars?" Alice pressed her. "An argument over money?"

Merrilee nodded, but her lips remained pinched together.

"You can tell us," Holly said evenly. "We're her friends."

Merrilee let out a heavy breath. "Recently she found out his business account was overdrawn. She said his finances were worse than she expected, and she would have to delay her retirement."

"And she pulled out of our Europe trip, remember?" Rachel pointed out. "We're all going to the South of France together next year. Michelle was really jazzed about it, but she had to cancel. Money is tight."

"That's Lars for you," Emerald said. "Gosh, you guys, I

completely forgot about Michelle missing out on France. She was so disappointed. I promised her I'd make it up to her with a few trips to the cabin." She turned to Alice. "My husband and I have a place at Sunriver, which we don't have occasion to use much now that the kids are grown. Our club goes there for occasional retreats."

"Michelle loves Sunriver," Holly said. "Hiking and biking and spending time outdoors under the trees. Soaking in the hot tub and looking up at the night sky."

"It's a very nice getaway," Juanita agreed. "Michelle told me it's like heaven on earth."

"She loves it there," Violet agreed.

"You should come with us sometime, Alice," Rachel said. "It's so easy and relaxing. There's time to curl up and read. We cook for each other or go out to eat. And sometimes, after the dishes are loaded and the kitchen clean, we crank up the music and have a dance party."

Alice was nodding, imagining this cabin in the trees. Something about Sunriver was resonating in her thoughts. Heaven on earth.

"That's it." Alice stood up, banging her can on the table with a bit too much force. Liquid shot out the top, followed by a foamy overflow. At least it was just seltzer. "I know where to find Michelle."

Chapter Twenty-five

"Sunriver?" Madison asked, later that night, as she joined the gals in the puzzle nook. "You think you'll find her there?"

"It's worth a try," Alice said, searching the puzzle for a place to fit in the piece in her hand—a white background with a green blob, which might have been a leaf or a treetop or a corner of grass beneath the family's feet. They were working on yesterday's puzzle, which they'd all been too tired to finish last night. "Ruby and I are heading out in the morning. Takes around three and a half hours, depending on traffic. Emerald has offered to drive us, and we can stay at her place if we decide to stay the night."

"I'd like to go to Sunriver," Taylor said.

"Don't you work tomorrow?" Alice squinted at her granddaughter, hoping that she wasn't losing interest in her job at the restaurant after only a month or so.

"Well, sure, but I could get off for something important like this."

"I'd go with you," Violet said, trying to fit two pieces together, "but it would be irresponsible to duck out of school at the last minute."

"All those little kids who need detention," Taylor said. "They'd miss you for sure."

"Detention is a thing of the past," Violet said with a smile. "I have new and improved methods."

"It's probably just a wild goose chase, but I'm happy to take a day off. Imani can handle things just fine." Ruby didn't look up as she spoke; she was piecing together the large apple tree beside the sun.

Taylor stuck out her lower lip, pouting. "The FOMO is killing me."

"Nothing exciting to miss out on," Alice said. "We're going to talk with some local merchants and rental agents, ask if anyone has seen Michelle. And there are a few campgrounds we can check out."

"Such a nippy time of year to be camping." Violet shivered. "She needs a roof over her head. I hope you find her and help her."

"Michelle is a smart woman. I bet she has strong survival skills," Alice said, snapping in her green blob and searching for another piece. "I love a brightly colored puzzle, but this one haunts me somehow. There's something so familiar about the art."

"That's because we spent half of yesterday afternoon stuck staring at his paintings," Ruby said. "This is definitely a photo of a Lars Olsen."

"I think you're right, Ruby." Violet twirled a piece of blue squiggles until it snapped into place in the sky. "The childlike rendering, and there's so much red, with the flowers and apple tree. Just like Lars's heavy use of red. Isn't that symbolic of violence or bloodshed?"

"We're not art critics," Taylor said, "and I'm not so sure this is his work."

"We'll find out after it's done," Alice said. "Which may

be tonight." She looked up at Madison. "So, any advice for how to search central Oregon for a missing woman?"

"Sounds like you're going about it efficiently." Madison ran her thumb over a bit of condensation on her water glass. "But I'm not sure you'll find Michelle there. Something's come up in the investigation; something that points to Lars trying to do away with his wife."

Progress on the puzzle stopped abruptly as everyone looked up at her.

"Tell us!" Taylor demanded.

Madison looked up from her phone. "I can only tell you this because Bedrosian just released information to the media. Maybe it's nothing, but Michelle and Lars had a revocable living trust drawn up a few months ago. It gives Lars control of Michelle's savings and successful businesses immediately upon her death."

"Really? That does seem fishy." Alice turned a puzzle piece in her fingers. "And what if Lars dies?"

"Michelle inherits his money and property, but there doesn't seem to be much there."

"Mmm. At least it's equitable," Alice said.

"But highly suspicious, given the circumstances." Violet sighed. "What if the cards were wrong? Maybe she's not okay."

Alice held up her hand, stopping the doubt. "Let's stay positive right now and proceed as if we'll soon find her safe and happy." It would do them no good to slip into a quagmire of doubt at this point. Forward motion was the thing.

"I wish I could go to Sunriver." Taylor mooned over the puzzle. "I need a vacation."

"We're not going for fun!" Alice insisted, though any road trip with Ruby was bound to have a few laughs.

"We're almost finished. This adorable puzzle is coming together." Ruby counted the pieces left on the table and then looked back at the puzzle. "Oh, no. No, no."

Alice plunked a piece in to complete the little girl at the center of the picture. "What's wrong?"

"We have six pieces left, and seven spots." Ruby frowned. "We're one piece short. Ladies, check your sleeves and elbows."

The pat-down began.

Alice didn't want the night to end this way. A missing piece? The puzzle was brand-new, so bright and cute, and to lose the satisfaction of plunking that last piece into place . . .

"Check the box," she said, scooting back from the table. "Maybe a piece fell on the floor." Using the flashlight on her cell, she got down on one knee and searched under the table, bracing herself to find crumbs and menacing dust bunnies. Fortunately, the house cleaner had come through a few days ago with a Swiffer. She did find a few pine needles and a piece of breakfast cereal. "No puzzle pieces," she said, before straining to get up. Her muscles were strong, but lately she'd had some twinges in the knees.

"There's nothing else in the box." Regret filled Violet's eyes. "We're missing a piece."

Chapter Twenty-six

"Good news, ladies," Emerald announced as she jangled her keys in Alice's kitchen Tuesday morning. "It's a gloriously sunny day, so I brought the convertible."

"Nice." Alice took a sip of coffee, wondering why anyone would want a car without a roof. It was barely nine, too early for deep thinking, too chilly outside for a windy ride, and she was only halfway through her second latte. Things weren't really computing yet. "Let me get my jacket." Alice grabbed a quilted gray jacket from the closet, then tugged out a purple scarf at the last minute. It might help to dress up her comfortably washed-out jeans and V-neck black sweater if they decided to go out to eat. Jeans were her outfit of choice when she wasn't appearing in a professional capacity. She found them comfortable and nostalgic, reminding her of the seventies when she and Ruby had fancied themselves hippies, sewing patches onto their jeans and altering the waistband to make them hip-huggers.

Ruby, who disparaged denim, had emerged from her downstairs en suite dressed in black slacks, a silky brown-and-white-striped blouse topped by a cocoa-colored suede duster. Her hair was a cascade of mocha curls with glimmering gold streaks catching the light. Stunning. But many years ago Alice had learned not to compare herself to other women. One of those liberating lessons of turning fifty.

"Are we ready?" Emerald asked.

"All set." Alice grabbed her overnight duffel bag.

"If we're driving with the top down, I'm sitting up front," Ruby said, toting her leather satchel out the door. "Otherwise, I'll be holding on to my hair from here to Idaho."

"But we don't drive to the border," Emerald said, popping open the trunk of the cherry-red car.

"Point is, I'm not getting my wig blown off."

"Oh, I see." Emerald gave a thumbs-up. "Gotcha."

Their trip began, top down in the neighborhood, cruising in the crisp, autumn air. Ruby tied a scarf over her hair, an insurance policy, as she called it, that made her look like a sixties movie star. Emerald was equally glamorous in her big, round sunglasses, her hot pink scarf trailing in the wind behind her.

Quite a contrast to Alice, who felt like a giant in a doll's house as she angled her body on the bench seat in the back.

But the sky was blue, the sun bright, and Alice had a day off for her mission, maybe two. She stretched her legs out and decided to enjoy the ride as Emerald upped the volume on ABBA's "Dancing Queen," and all three women sang along.

Somewhere between "Fernando" and "Mamma Mia" they entered the freeway, and the high speed turned the wind into a mighty force. Hurricane winds. The tip of Emerald's long pink muffler kept dancing into the back seat as Alice braced herself against the blast of wind. She steeled herself, tried to be a good sport, and then leaned forward.

"Can we pull over?" she yelled.

"What?"

"Land the plane!" Alice shouted.

Emerald took the next exit and pulled into the parking lot of a Burgerville. With the car in park, she turned to the back and gasped. "Oh, Alice, your hair! I'm so sorry."

"That's nothing compared to the insects I've been picking out of my teeth."

"Bugs in your teeth!" Emerald exclaimed. "We can't have that."

"It was just a squadron of gnats, I think."

"I won't hear of it." Emerald pushed a button on the dashboard. "Up goes the roof!"

To make up for the wind effect, Emerald got in line at the drive-through and bought three breakfast sandwiches with coffees. "Got to keep our energy up," she said cheerily, reminding Alice how much she admired this woman's ability to stay positive in strained circumstances.

The drive went smoothly from then on, the quiet in the car giving them a chance to line up the people and places that Emerald thought they should check in Sunriver.

They skirted the sparkling surface of Detroit Lake, which fortunately had water after a very dry year. The terrain grew thick with trees as they looped over and around the mountains and headed east. In just over three hours they were taking the exit for Sunriver Resort, entering a woodsy community of cabins and trails sprinkled with log-cabin-style shopping centers.

"We can stop at the house and wash up, drop off our bags, and then head to one of the little restaurants for some lunch." Emerald turned off the main road, then turned again onto a circular street called Ponderosa Pine. "This is us," she said, turning into the gravel driveway of a large house of wood and glass. A small wooden porch on the side provided a spot to sit under the tall trees, which covered the entire area like a protective canopy of forest.

"What a lovely retreat," Ruby said. "I see why your book club gals enjoy coming here."

As they were removing their bags from the trunk, someone across the circle gave a shout. "Emerald!"

Alice turned to see a couple emerging from a cabin across the way. The dumpling of a woman in a colorful knit sweater gave a wave and prodded the man as he passed by, carrying a suitcase to the car.

"My neighbors!" Emerald waved enthusiastically. "Hey, you guys!" She turned to hand the keys to Alice. "Let yourself in. The front door sticks, but just give it a shove. I have to say hi. Jill and Scott have been gone for the last year. Amsterdam! Be right there." Emerald ran off, crunching over dried leaves to give the neighbors big hugs.

Alice managed her bag and Emerald's, as Ruby had two of her own to tote to the porch. "I'm so hungry, and it's barely noon," Alice said. "Let's get in and out." She turned the key in the lock and pushed in the door. It didn't budge.

"Give it some muscle," Ruby said. "It's just a little sticky." She squeezed past Alice to give it a shove. A robust push. A hefty heave with her hips. The door squeaked and groaned, but it seemed sealed shut.

"Do we have the right house?" Alice turned the knob and banged her shoulder into the door.

"Let's do it together," Ruby directed. "One, two, three!" On cue, they tackled the door at the same time, to the sounds of splintering and squeaking wood.

At last, the door squealed and popped open with a wretched bang.

"That was painful," Alice admitted, reaching for the luggage as Ruby stepped inside.

"Charming," Ruby said.

Alice stepped into a tiled entryway, the open living room to the left with leather furniture and a stone fireplace, the staircase directly ahead. The fresh, lemony smell indicated a recent cleaning. Lugging her duffel bag into a welcoming space that reminded her of a mountain lodge, Alice thought she saw a shadow shift at the top of the stairs. Or did it? Was it just the sun reflected on the hall mirror? The small living area and stairway were shadowed by the waning golden sunlight that slanted through the windows. Still and quiet.

But then, another movement, a flash on the stairs.

A dark object swept along the banister.

A huge bat? A giant bird?

A person.

A figure in black leaped over the upstairs railing, latched onto the handrail a few steps up, and then swung toward Alice and Ruby.

Frozen in shock and disbelief, the two women grabbed each other as the wild person leapt toward them with a shriek.

A battle cry.

An attack!

Chapter Twenty-seven

Fear thundered in Alice's heart. The bags fell from her grip as she and Ruby stumbled back toward the front door.

"What is it?" Ruby was pressed against Alice with only one eye open and squinting toward the assailant.

Alice didn't have an answer. "We need to get out." As she yanked Ruby upright and fumbled for the door behind her, the energy in the room changed.

"Oh, no! Ladies!" came a low voice. "I'm sorry. So sorry. Alice? Is that you?"

Alice looked over to see a trim woman dressed in black yoga pants and a long-sleeved black hoodie. She pushed the hood back to reveal . . .

"Michelle?" Alice gaped.

"I thought the house was under siege. What are you doing here?" Michelle asked.

"Looking for you."

"Really? And for this you blow up the front door?"

"Apparently, it's a little sticky," Ruby said, recovering her cool. "But your response was straight out of a Hollywood movie! Swinging down the staircase and flying through the air. Please tell me how you keep yourself so fit?"

"Kung fu." Michelle swiped a strand of hair behind one ear. "And other martial arts."

"Exactly what I need," Ruby said.

"Come to my studio and I'll teach you." Michelle extended her hand, introducing herself, and Ruby reciprocated, babbling on about how finding Michelle was an answered prayer, in more ways than one.

"Do you do personal training?" Ruby asked.

"Whoa, wait. First things first. Michelle, we came here to Sunriver looking for you. Everyone's been concerned since you were reported missing. It's been days with no word. We've been so worried."

Michelle still seemed confused. "Missing? I told Lars I was leaving. And I left him a letter with no uncertain terms."

Alice and Ruby exchanged a look.

"I knew it," Alice said.

"You were right," Ruby agreed. "Fireplace ashes don't lie."

"I don't know what you're talking about, but I'm sorry for the dubious greeting. I heard such a terrible noise, I was sure someone was breaking in, and I've been alone here, trespassing."

"You didn't know the door sticks?"

"I haven't opened it. I've been using the back door. The key's under a rock sculpture in the back." Michelle tilted her head, her eyes sympathetic. "Are you all right?"

Alice did a quick mental head-to-toe inventory to see if she'd been hurt. Shaken, yes, but jumbled nerves and a racing pulse didn't qualify as an injury. "I'm okay." She looked at Ruby.

"Just scared out of my gourd." Ruby smoothed back her hair. "But that was pretty darned exciting."

The footsteps on the porch made Alice turn. The door swung open with a shrill squeak, and Emerald's face went from smiling to stunned to euphoric. "Oh, by gosh, by golly! They found you!" Her arms opened wide and Michelle moved gracefully into her embrace.

"They found me, but I was never lost," Michelle said, stepping back to gesture at the house. "I was always here, sorting myself. I used the key under the mat to get in, and I've kept things tidy. I'm sorry for any worry or trouble, truly. Lars must answer for this. He knew I was safe. He should have told the police."

"He's the one who's been stirring the pot," Ruby said.

Michelle frowned. "What a stinker. Em, I'm sorry I invaded your house. I wanted to ask you, but I couldn't have anyone knowing my whereabouts. Lars can be such a bully when he needs information. I'll reimburse you rental fees, of course."

"Don't be silly. I'm just so glad you're safe. This has become a glorious day." Emerald picked up her bag and tossed back her curls. "We have much to discuss, but first, a visit to the ladies'. Let's refresh, then we'll find a lovely café and sit round a table and catch up over lunch."

It was a plan. The ladies dispersed.

With a lightened heart, Alice scrolled to Madison's number on her phone as she walked out onto the deck. Breathing in the traces of fir and pine and turning leaves, she typed out a message.

We found her. Michelle is alive and well in Sunriver.

She considered adding a little barb like "Told you!" but reminded herself that she was the grandmother in this relationship, and it wouldn't hurt to model good behavior.

Instead, she smiled and pressed send.

* * *

Seated on the outdoor patio of the resort lodge, the women were surrounded by scenic views: acres of golf greens, reflective ponds, and wild grasslands, all rimmed by hills and mountains, purple and mauve against the graying sky. It was chilly and rain seemed to be on the way, but Emerald had insisted they sit outside, cozy under the warmth of some heat lamps. Emerald had a thing for fresh air.

"This all started with me wanting to get away and have some space," Michelle said. She seemed content and peaceful, her hair shiny and dark against the ivory cardigan Emerald had loaned her.

Alice was all ears. It wasn't every day that you heard how a person made herself disappear.

"I wish you'd told me," Emerald said. "You can use the house anytime."

"But I couldn't trust Lars. I booked a trip for myself in Ashland, but Lars threw a fit. Maybe it's the financial strain, but he went over the edge, crisis mode. Told me I could never leave. Well, that did it. After that, I plotted my getaway, all in secret. Withdrew some cash from the ATM. Left my car and belongings behind so I couldn't be traced. I wasn't trying to fake my death or fool anyone. I just had to break free of him for a while."

"And your mission was successful," Alice said. "It took us days to track you down, and that was all based on conjecture."

"And we wouldn't have been looking so diligently if we knew you were okay," Ruby pointed out. "But Lars had to go and scare the cops and the media."

"And us." Emerald reached over the table to touch Michelle's arm. "We were so worried."

Michelle rolled her eyes. "I left him a note. All in writing."

"And we found that note, half-burned in the fireplace," Alice said. "Honestly, it gave us hope that you were okay. I'm afraid we also found the remnants of some of your illustrations that had been tossed into the fire. Beyond saving."

"No doubt Lars trying to get back at me. He can be spiteful."

Alice seized the moment to broach some difficult topics. "I hate to pry, but has he ever been violent? I only ask because there's a police record dating back to his college days. He was charged with assault, and he may have kept a woman against her will, but the charges were eventually dropped."

"Lars mentioned that episode. I have seen him throw some hot tantrums, but he hasn't threatened physical violence against me. Psychological tension is his game."

"Promise me you'll contact the police if that ever changes," Alice said. "And I'm sorry about your ruined illustrations."

"Not to worry. Everything that's going in the graphic novel came here with me. My sketchbook, some teabags and protein bars. I lived like a little nun. The solitude was lovely." Michelle unfolded the cloth napkin and set it on her lap. "But right about now, I'm ready for a juicy steak."

"There's one more thing . . . about divorce?" Alice winced. "This is total gossip, but you should know that Rosie Suarez thinks you and Lars are divorcing. And you've agreed to pay him a significant sum to make it all happen. Any of this ringing a bell?"

"That lying weasel . . ." Michelle heaved a sigh. "And I suppose this payment is financing his new life with Rosie?"

"That's the version I heard."

"Not true, but I suppose I could easily make that happen."

"Before you make any hasty decisions"—Alice looked up and caught the attention of a server—"let's get some lunch on the table."

Soon after their order had been taken, Alice's phone rang. "It's the police," she said, "my granddaughter Madison."

As the outdoor dining area was nearly empty, Alice put Madison on speakerphone, so that she could confirm Michelle's safety. The conversation went round and round for a few minutes, with Madison wanting to send local law enforcement to do an in-person safety check.

"No need," Michelle insisted. "I'll be returning to West Hazel tonight." She turned to Emerald, adding, "If that's all right with you? Now that I've found the answers, I want to square things with Lars."

"Well, sure," Emerald said, pushing away a glass of red wine. "If that's what you want."

Michelle nodded. "I'm ready."

"Then we'll meet with you in the morning," Madison said. "In the meantime, we'll be notifying Lars, your next of kin, that you've been found and you're safe."

"Fine." Michelle nodded.

"Let's hope he doesn't throw an impromptu press conference," Ruby muttered.

"Does anyone else need to be notified?"

"I'll call my auntie Jean in Los Angeles," Michelle said. "She'll let the family know."

"I've taken the liberty of letting the lovely ladies in our book club know, via our text thread." Emerald lifted her water goblet, her face aglow with joy.

Alice held up her wineglass, and a moment later four glasses clinked in a toast.

"Everyone is overjoyed that you're safe," said Emerald. "Here's to you, my friend. A wonderful end to our search."

Over the cell, Madison added: "Cheers."

Chapter Twenty-eight

"This rain is going to slow us down a bit." Emerald flicked on the windshield wipers as heavy rains spattered the car and danced in the street. "We probably won't get home until closer to eight."

"Don't rush." Michelle seemed small and delicate, like a fuzzy ivory creature retracted and curled into the back seat of the car. "I'm going back to face a temperamental man who's bound to be angry and disappointed. Take as long as you need."

"I feel bad that I got things so wrong," Emerald said. "Of course, I realized Lars was temperamental at times, but I thought you two made a good couple. I got the sense that he brings excitement to your life, and you keep his feet on the ground when he's about to fly too close to the sun."

"It was that way, once. Once upon a time. Despite the age difference, we were good together. But he's become so jaded. Discontent. Interest in his art has slowed, and I know he owes his dealer big-time. Coyote advanced him tens of thousands of dollars before this dry spell. And now Lars is envious of my success in business. Jealous of my new pursuits. I lost the ability to reach him," Michelle admitted, shadows masking her face. "One morning I woke up and saw the hollow shell of an old woman in the mirror. My essence, my spirit, had been chased away. Gone."

The image brought back memories for Alice. "If it's any consolation, I've been there, too." After she'd taken a sabbatical from the library, after they'd used most of their savings to open the beautiful restaurant on the lake, she'd found herself trapped in the drudgery of endless work. To market each morning, then waiting for deliveries at the restaurant, then prep, then the meal rush, then cleaning and scrubbing until the early hours of the next morning. All while Jeff played host under the twinkling lights at the front of house, comping drinks and upping his popularity.

"The restaurant business solidified the separation in my relationship with my husband, Jeff," Alice said. "We had different goals. He got what he wanted, and I got lost along the way."

Michelle reached over and squeezed Alice's arm, reassuring. "But you found yourself again, and began an exciting new chapter, didn't you?"

"I did," Alice said. "I returned to the library, a job that fits like a glove. I've got people I love at home." She ran a hand through her hair, feeling lighter. "All I need is a new hairstyle, and I'll be a brand-new me."

The conversation veered off to different looks that might suit Alice. Ruby offered to let her try a few wigs—a way to check out a hairstyle without committing.

At one point the conversation turned to finances, and Michelle revealed that her husband had recently asked for a huge loan. "One hundred thousand dollars. A lot of money, and he wouldn't tell me what it was for. Now, with what Rosie told you, I have a sense of his plan."

"Wow. That's hard to imagine," Emerald said, her gaze intent on the darkening, rain-slick highway. Driving through the storm had to be challenging.

"Money matters often cause friction in a relationship," Alice said, her shoulders tensing as she recalled her fiscal issues with Jeff. "We sank our savings into the restaurant, but it wasn't enough." She did a stretch, opening her chest, reminding herself that the failing business was Jeff's burden now.

"I bought my husband a Maserati," Ruby said. "He loved that car, but it didn't end well."

It ended when George was murdered, but Alice figured that was a story to tell Michelle another time.

"Bad, bad husbands." Ruby clucked her tongue. "Why do we want them so much?"

"Just for the record, I want to say that my husband, Paul, is a wonderful man," Emerald said. "He's a hard worker, a great provider. We laugh and share stories, and he loves my cooking, and we take trips together and . . . I just love him, I really do! So not every man is a bad guy."

"Paul is a good man," Michelle agreed, leaning forward to pat Emerald's shoulder. "Never feel guilty about having a good marriage. But if Paul asks for a million dollars, think twice."

Alice and Ruby chuckled at that, and Michelle let out a heavy sigh.

"You know, I think I'll give Lars the money, after all." Michelle nodded. "Our divorce settlement. A hundred thousand dollars, and I'm free."

The price of freedom, Alice thought as they drove on through the rain.

* * *

Night had swallowed the air and sky, and rain slashed through the beams of the headlights as Emerald pulled onto the back road leading to Dragonberry Lane.

"Do you think Lars will be mad, now that the publicity gig is up?" Emerald asked.

"The moods and reactions of Lars are always a mystery."

"What if he blames you?" Emerald's protective instincts had emerged. "Maybe we should go in with you. You know, protection."

"From Lars? He has a temper, but he wouldn't hurt me physically. Besides, he's probably not even home. Probably at Rosie's place. He can't stand to be alone."

So, Michelle knew about the affair. Alice supposed it was not the first time. "Still, you don't have to return tonight," Alice said. "There's a guest suite available at my house. You're welcome to it."

"Did you hear that? Your own room. Come with us to Alice's Palace." Ruby coaxed Michelle. "We can have a girls' night, watch a movie or work on a puzzle. Right now you need to be surrounded by friends."

"I'm grateful for your help, but I need to deal with this now. Finish things off with Lars. I hate procrastinating. And once he hears he's getting his money, his mood will improve." Michelle peered ahead, squinting through the streaks on the window as the silhouette of the dragon-head building came into view. "The lights are on, a sign that he's home."

"And maybe he's hosting a party," Alice said. In truth, the house glowed starkly in the night, probably a drain on the electrical grid. The yellow light that beamed from the main windows was about as welcoming as fiery dragon breath.

Funny that lights in the windows were usually a welcoming sign. Alice's thoughts fell gently on "Bye Bye Blackbird," an old song her grandfather used to sing to her. In the song, the light in the house was a beacon of belonging. Grandad's voice was slow and mournful as he sang of being lonely and misunderstood, longing to return to the security and comfort of home.

Perhaps Michelle longed to be home, but from where she sat, Alice saw nothing hospitable about the well-lit house at the end of Dragonberry Lane.

"I'll text you to check in as soon as I get home," Emerald said, slowing the car as it edged closer to the front porch. As they rolled to a stop, all eyes were on the oddball house.

"Are you sure you don't want to wait till tomorrow?" Alice asked.

"I can see the fire blazing inside," Ruby said. "I wouldn't go in there if I were you."

"Lars is such a firebug, and he loves that giant fireplace." Michelle gave a sigh. "It's okay, really. He knows I'm on my way back. Maybe Rosie's with him. I would welcome the distraction." She opened the door to a cool gust of damp air and the sound of rain hitting the porch. "Thank you, ladies, old friends and new. You brought me back to the world. I owe you all a delicious meal."

There were waves and goodbyes as Michelle retrieved her small satchel from the trunk and bounded up the few steps onto the porch. They watched as she disappeared inside the door.

There was silence in the car as they pulled away and plunged back into the darkness of Dragonberry Lane.

"Doesn't feel right," Alice said.

"Oh, well, I'm sure she's going to be fine." Emerald's voice held a positive but unconvincing lilt.

"And Lars will head off into the sunset, with his sassy younger apprentice." Ruby yawned. "Those two deserve each other."

"I hope it works out for everyone. But Madison should get the credit." Alice took out her cell and tapped to call Madison's number. "Hi, honey. Got you on speaker with Ruby and Emerald." Two gems! That hadn't occurred to her before. "Just wanted to let you know we dropped Michelle off, safe and sound, on Dragonberry Lane." The car bounced over two ruts in the road. Alice would be relieved to get out of this back seat. "So another case solved and closed, with excellent results."

"Actually, it's kind of weird . . . I mean . . ." There was the sound of shifting, a scurry on the line, and Madison seemed stressed. "You just dropped her off at the Dragonberry house?"

"Yes, Officer." Alice was so proud of that girl. "What's going on?"

"I'm not sure, but we just got a nine-one-one call, someone's been attacked there."

"Where? Back there?" Emerald bellowed.

"That can't be," Ruby said. "We just left there."

"Turn the car around," Alice said. "We've got to go back."

Emerald white-knuckled the steering wheel and hit the brakes. The car skidded on wet gravel but came to a halt, rain falling through the beams of the headlights for a second. Then Emerald looped to the left, stopping short of two fat trees on the roadside, before spinning back in reverse, a jolt of brakes, and then back in drive. Emerald braced herself against the wheel as the car sped ahead down the lane, back toward the house.

"We're close," Ruby said. "We can help."

What were they rocketing into? Alice wondered, holding on to the door handle. She kept her eyes on the meandering lane, as if that would help Emerald stay on track. At least it helped Alice feel in control as the car bumped and jogged over the rutted driveway.

Just as the lights of the house came into view, two white lights seemed to split away from the house and cruise onto the driveway. "What the hell?" Emerald winced.

"It's a car . . . coming this way."

"There was no car in the driveway," Ruby said.

"Well, something with lights and a roaring engine is headed our way!"

"Okay, okay." Emerald slowed the car and moved to the right, trying to stay on the dirt and gravel track. "I can't move over too far. There are stumps and boulders and such. Lars is not handy with home maintenance."

"You're good," Alice encouraged her. "Slow and steady. We'll be fine." She hoped she was right.

The vehicle lights grew more intense, loomed large, and then, with a whoosh and a growl of a racing engine, zoomed past them.

"That is one crazy driver," Ruby said.

"Good job, Em." Alice turned to watch the shrinking red taillights. The car veered off the road to the right, but it seemed to bounce out of the shrubs before speeding off.

"Moving like a bat out of hell." Ruby was clutching the armrest on the door. "The rudest driver ever."

Alice turned back to peer through the windshield as they closed in on the house, its windows still ablaze with light. If ever there was a facade that had the face of a monster . . . "I don't like the looks of this." As she stared ahead, the front door opened, more light streaming out, as someone staggered out onto the porch.

"It's Michelle." Alice could make out her features as the headlights washed over her. Her face was fierce, almost crazed, and her white sweater was soiled with dark splotches. Blood.

She'd been attacked.

"She's bleeding!" Emerald gasped. "Oh my gosh... Lars tried to kill her."

Chapter Twenty-nine

Michelle paused a few steps from the front door, staring warily into the darkness. "Are you the police?" Her ivory sweater was smeared with blood.

"Just us, your friends," Alice said, sensing that Michelle was in shock. "We heard you need help."

Ruby was the first to reach the porch steps. "Honey, are you hurt?"

"You're bleeding," Alice said, "and we're here to help you."

There was a vacant pallor in Michelle's eyes as she pointed one bloody arm toward the house. "Lars!" She gasped, as if it were all she could manage in her breathless state.

Emerald drew close to her. "Did Lars stab you?"

"No. Lars is stabbed. Dead."

Dead? That seemed impossible to Alice. How could things have gone so wrong so quickly?

"I called the police. Where did I leave my phone?" As Michelle lifted her right hand to shield her eyes from the rain, the gesture caused a new smear of blood across the front of the pale sweater. A gruesome contrast. From her fluid movements, Alice suspected she hadn't been injured at all. The blood had come from someone else.

Lars.

Expectations always slowed the processing of true facts.

"And what happened to Lars?" Emerald asked gently.

"Stabbed in the back. With this." She lifted her left arm, and a bloody blade glinted silver.

As if in unison, Alice and her friends bellowed and stumbled back at the sight of the butcher knife.

"Jumping Jiminy!" Ruby exclaimed. "Is that a knife?"

Eyes wide with bald shock, Michelle waved the black-handled kitchen carving knife in the air. "I pulled it out! I had to! I didn't want him to die, but this was stuck in his back. I had to take it out," Michelle said plaintively. "He can't have a knife in his heart!"

Emerald winced, stepping back until her bottom rested against the porch railing. "I don't do well with blood."

Ruby put her hands up and stood her ground. "It's okay, honey."

"You're probably in shock," Alice said gently, though she sensed that Michelle was struggling to process things at this point. "Put the knife down. Can you do that? Put it down."

Michelle's face contorted as she glared at Alice. "Knife?" She looked up, suddenly seemed to recognize the weapon, then let it drop from her hand. It clattered to the wooden boards of the porch and slid under an Adirondack chair.

"We'll leave that there." Alice pointed to Ruby. "The police are on their way, but please call and make sure there's an ambulance, too."

Emerald moved to console her friend as Alice peered in the open door. "Let's see if we can help Lars." She inched inside, leaving the door open behind her in case she needed to escape quickly. Her pulse was thumping wildly in her ears but she tried to ignore it. She told herself that the attacker had probably left in that speeding car, and maybe Lars was still alive. Maybe she could save him.

At first, she just saw fire. The flames of the fireplace roared. Over the burning logs there were the remains of something squarish. A box? No, a frame—maybe just the wood upon which a canvas had been stretched. If it had been a painting, it had burned beyond recognition.

The tall screen had been pulled aside, leaving the ashes to pop menacingly toward the room. Chunks of dusty ash had spread past the apron of the hearth. The fireplace tools lay in disarray on the floor, scattered amid chunks and shards of broken pottery, and something golden yellow and crumbly that Alice couldn't identify. When she came closer and saw a bowl of salsa that had spilled onto the table, she realized the gold crumbs were smashed corn tortilla chips.

Which seemed to indicate that someone—maybe Lars—was relaxing with a snack when all hell broke loose. Over in the dining area, many of the canvases that had been lined up in rows had fallen into odd heaps, as if a wild animal had bucked and paced through the room. Some of the paintings that had landed in a heap may have been damaged.

"Looks like there was a terrible brawl in here," Alice called, feeling somehow safer if her friends could hear her.

The sofa, which faced the fireplace, blocked her view of the seating area. When she stepped around the end table, she saw him. Lars Olsen lay face down in a pool of blood.

Alice was relieved that his cheek was against the wood floor, sparing her the expression on his face. Although she could hear Detective Bedrosian scolding in her head about "trampling a crime scene," she knew she had to try medical intervention if he was hanging on.

Avoiding the puddle, she moved closer. She squatted beside him, a difficult but necessary pose, and pressed her fingers to his neck. Although she was no expert, she couldn't find a pulse at his carotid artery.

She let out the breath she'd been holding and called, "He's dead."

Did anyone hear her? It was creepy being alone with a body, especially someone she'd known. Looking down, she noted bits of gray frizzies growing just over his ear, and that unfortunately meager little skinny tail at the nape of his neck. One of those idiosyncrasies that made him human.

She felt sorry he was dead, worried for Michelle and anyone else in Lars's sphere. Lars had stepped on toes, offended people. But snarky behavior usually didn't evoke murder.

Her knees cracked as she rose and stepped back gingerly. She'd stayed away from the puddle, and now she needed to get out of here. Protect the crime scene for Detective Bedrosian. Without moving, she scanned the room once again.

Why the massive fire? Was it Lars's obsession, as Michelle had said, or had someone lit it to cover something up? Or had there been a plan to burn even more of the paintings? Destroy Lars's legacy after he was dead, except that Michelle had come home and interrupted that plan?

Something popped on the hearth, and sparks flew out toward the body, which was now unprotected by the screen. One fireplace poker lay on the floor, its handle near Lars's right hand. Had he been reaching for it? Or maybe he'd dropped it. Hard to say.

She was curious about the back of the house, but she didn't want to traipse through in case there were forensic traces that could lead to the killer.

But she had to remember the placement of everything in this room. Better yet... She took out her cell phone and snapped some pictures, careful to avoid getting poor Lars in any shot.

Shattered dishes. Laundry in the fire. Artwork toppled as if horses had galloped through. Some canvases were torn, the wood broken.

There had definitely been a scuffle here.

The rain had stopped, making it possible to huddle outside until the police came. Emerald and Michelle huddled together on the porch steps, Emerald cooing and offering small bits of comfort as Michelle sobbed quietly. Alice had to give Emerald credit; she had a gift for soothing meditations.

Alice and Ruby stood near the open door, occasionally peering inside as if they expected the furniture to be rearranged or Lars to be resurrected, plodding toward them like a zombie.

"This is not how I expected the day to end," Ruby said under her breath. "You're sure he's dead?"

Alice nodded. "There's a lot of blood."

"Well, these Michael Kors boots are not stepping foot inside that door."

As if it could be as simple as keeping the soles of your shoes clean, Alice thought as the trees of Dragonberry Lane began to throb, red and blue. The police were here.

Alice went to the rail of the porch and waved people toward the front door. "He's inside."

She was glad to see the paramedics rushing in with their

heavy plastic boxes of equipment. If she'd been wrong, if there was still a chance, they had the tools to help him.

Two other police vehicles had pulled up, uniformed cops emerged. Alice was relieved to see Madison in the group.

"Gran." Madison shook her head. "Why am I not surprised."

"We had to turn back. We'd just dropped Michelle off, alone and . . ."

"I get it." Madison scanned the scene, spotted Michelle. "Ms. Chong? Michelle." Madison went to the steps, leaning down to speak quietly. "I'm Madison Denham, with the West Hazel Police. We talked earlier on the phone. Can you tell me what happened?"

"They stabbed him." The words emerged softly from Michelle's huddled form. "Someone killed my husband. I came home and found him that way."

"That sounds terrifying," Madison said. "I'm so sorry. Did you see the attack?"

"No." Michelle didn't lift her head. "But I saw the killer leaving."

"Who was it?" Ruby asked.

"I didn't catch the face. I heard footsteps, then saw a dark blur by the laundry room. They must have ducked out the side door. And then I heard a car and they were gone."

"We saw that car," Emerald said. "It was shooting down the lane, in a hurry to get out. It almost hit us."

"The killer," Michelle murmured.

"I saw that car, too. We're all witnesses," Alice told Madison. She kept her voice calm, though she wanted to make sure Madison was getting all this. Proof of Michelle's innocence. "But we didn't see a car here when we dropped you off, Michelle."

"It must have been parked behind the house, by the side door. You can't see it from the front."

Alice recalled seeing that unpaved area the day of the press conference. "Did you and Lars park there?"

"Lars keeps his van there. And Rosie, his apprentice, she always parks there."

"Rosie," Alice said pointedly, looking at Madison. Would she remember that Lars had been involved with his art apprentice? Alice would be sure to bring it up later. Even as they were driving here, Michelle had thought she would find Lars with Rosie.

Which begged the question: Had Rosie killed Lars?

"Do you have any idea who might have wanted to kill him?" Madison asked.

"Who kills a man because they don't like him?" Michelle finally lifted her head, but she didn't look up. "Yes, people had issues with Lars. He's been lying to Rosie for months. He treats his assistants like dirt. He tries to cheat his art dealer, and he would sell out a friend in a heartbeat." Michelle let out a huff of breath, touching her brow. "Maybe that's too mean. He wasn't all bad but . . . he was selfish, sometimes cruel."

The details of Lars's treachery would have made a fine tombstone engraving in a Dickens novel.

**HERE LIE THE BONES OF LARS OLSEN
BACK-STABBING SCOUNDREL, CHEATER, LIAR
HE'LL NEVER BE COLD IN HELL'S BRIMSTONE
AND FIRE**

Chapter Thirty

The night became a blur of raw emotions and dark images for Alice. A shiver seemed to grip her, though she wasn't actually cold, and she had a keen desire to get home to a hot shower, an attempt to cleanse her mind of sordid memories: the body, the blood, the gaping house with its fierce monster-mouth fireplace.

Lars was pronounced dead, and Alice's mind was swimming with scenarios that placed the butcher knife in Rosie Suarez's hands. Maybe she was sick of his lies. Maybe Michelle's return had set her off, making her see that Lars would never leave his wife. Or maybe it was about art. Could he have stolen her ideas? Or did he criticize her talent, refusing to acknowledge her gifts?

Yellow crime-scene tape was stretched across the posts of the front deck, making the dragon house even more eerie.

And though Rosie was prime in Alice's mind, she had a strong sense that the police weren't happy with Michelle. Of course she didn't want to talk. She was probably in shock, too stunned to defend herself or put the pieces together. It seemed cruel for the police to hint that she was a possible suspect, but Detective Bedrosian kept insisting there was more to Michelle's story.

"No one leaves until we get statements," Bedrosian bellowed.

Alice went first, then Ruby. It bothered Alice that she couldn't listen in on the other interviews, but Detective Bedrosian stood firm. "This investigation is confidential police business," he said gruffly.

"Of course it is," Alice agreed, "please forget I even asked." She didn't want to annoy him; the last thing she needed was for Bedrosian to pressure Madison, worried that she might be discussing the case with Alice.

Which she would, of course. Though Alice didn't expect her granddaughter to compromise the case by giving her confidential information.

As Emerald was being interviewed, Alice was hallucinating about a cushy pillow beneath her head, and her white marshmallow comforter surrounding her with softness.

Alice was talking quietly with Ruby when a giant motor home roared slowly past the house toward the side driveway. Madison ran over to stop the driver before it rolled in too far, shouting something about taking casts of tire treads. "Look at that," Ruby said. "A camper for the cops." She summoned a young officer who'd been walking by. Alice recognized the dark hair and smooth face with high cheekbones. Officer Zhao.

"Officer, we're wondering, are there any beds inside your police camper?" Ruby asked him. "Bunks, maybe? My friends and I are ready to hit the hay."

"No beds, ma'am." He smiled. "That's our portable crime lab and mobile headquarters."

Ruby sighed. "We're so tired."

"We'll try to get you on your way as soon as possible."

"Thank you, Officer Zhao." Alice summoned a weary smile. "I've noticed that your schedule seems to overlap with Madison's." Was that intentional? Had something sparked between them?

"Sometimes we're partners. But in answer to your question, the trailer is the police chief's baby. A way to process crime investigations at the scene."

Alice thanked him. At least someone on the police force was accommodating, and handsome, too.

By the time Emerald had finished talking with Bedrosian and Madison, Ruby's patience had worn thin. "Madison, come on now." Ruby's voice was stern when she pulled Madison aside. "When is Detective Crankypants going to let Michelle leave?" Ruby had a rocky relationship with West Hazel's chief detective, ever since he'd targeted her as a suspect in her husband's murder. "Now, listen to me. That poor woman is traumatized. She's covered with blood, which you all won't let her wash off. Plus, it's getting late, and I don't need to tell you, some of us here are not spring chickens. People need sleep. Hear me now, enough is enough."

Madison had tilted her head, her eyes warm with sympathy. "I hear you, but Detective Bedrosian is in charge."

Ruby turned up her collar against the cool night air. "Well, you can tell him I'm lodging a formal complaint."

"Will do, Aunt Ruby."

To give Madison credit, she did act with kindness. Alice saw her apologize to Michelle for taking the ivory sweater. "Forensics will analyze the bloodstains, and hold it as possible evidence," Madison said, gently placing one of those space-age foil blankets on Michelle's shoulders.

"Your sweater," Michelle said, taking Emerald's hand. "Forensics is taking it."

"It's theirs to keep," Emerald said. "It's replaceable, but you're not. I'm glad you're okay."

And soon after Ruby's tirade Madison brought a woman in a white coverall over to Michelle. "This is Gina. She's going to swab the blood on your hands and arms... and anywhere else," Madison said. "Sorry you had to wait for forensics. After this, you're free to wash up."

"So, you're checking to see if the blood on her hands belonged to Lars?" Alice asked. When the women nodded, Alice felt the situation sinking to a new low. Were they trying to pin the murder on Michelle?

"But of course it's his blood," Alice said. "She pulled the knife from his back. And when she went to check on him, there was a puddle of blood and she—"

"We've got this, Gran." Madison patted her shoulder. "Trust me on this. You're the librarian, I'm the cop." And before Alice had a chance to argue that roles could be so stifling, Madison disappeared in the fray of investigators.

"That was a bit dismissive," Ruby said. "Sorry, honey. It feels awful to have your input ignored. As if you're invisible."

"It does sting a bit," Alice admitted. "But in the past, invisibility has worked for me. It's much easier to eavesdrop and squeeze information from a crowd that way."

"I like it." Ruby nodded. "You get to hear and see all, and people forget that you're there."

"Exactly." As Alice scanned the dragon house, the yard strewn with police vehicles, she realized she'd absorbed important information just by being here tonight. "Sometimes, I think of it as a superpower."

It was after ten when Alice and Ruby pulled into the garage. With each step along the garage floor to the hallway to the kitchen Alice felt the comfort of home begin to relax her weary muscles and bones.

"Murder is an exhausting business," Ruby said when they reached the kitchen.

"Murder?" Taylor popped into the kitchen from the living room, where the TV was still chattering. "Oh, no, not Michelle!"

"Michelle is fine," Alice said. "Or at least, she's alive. She was going to spend the night here, but the paramedics brought her to the hospital to be safe, since she's spiked a fever and is feeling a little dizzy."

"Oh, okay then." Taylor picked up an oatmeal chip cookie from the baking sheet on the counter and broke it in half. "Then what's the deal with murder?"

"What's the deal with my kitchen?" Alice was distracted by the sheet of cookies, a cardboard pizza box, a pot on the stove, and a pool of brown liquid on the countertop. She gave it a dab with a paper towel. "Soy sauce?"

"I had a friend over for dinner. She made the dumplings, and I did the cookies. But did someone get—"

"Lars Olsen." Ruby was sitting in a chair in the nook, removing her boots with grateful sighs. "He was dead when we dropped Michelle at her house."

"What? What happened?"

Ruby and Alice took turns filling in the blanks—the condensed version. "The police suspect Michelle, who was caught holding the knife. But your grandmother thinks he was offed by Rosie, the painter's apprentice."

"She's definitely a suspect. The cops told her not to

leave town." Alice sat down at the nook table with a glass of water. "But there will be others. Lars stepped on a lot of toes. For now, I need to get horizontal and let my brain encode the information of the day."

"Ditto, except I'm going to soak in the tub and turn on some Bach and wash away the sadness." Ruby grabbed her boots and opened the door to the basement stairs. "My en suite awaits. Good night."

"Thanks for coming along," Alice called after her.

"Wow." Taylor poured herself a glass of milk. "I knew I should have gone to Sunriver."

"Sunriver was great, but I don't think you would have done well at Dragonberry tonight." Death scenes gave Taylor a panic attack. Which kind of made sense, when Alice thought about the body she'd seen on the floor tonight. She would need an engrossing book to chase the cold image out of her head. Maybe she'd slip under the covers and listen to a few chapters of an old favorite. She noticed Taylor staring into the open fridge. "Sorry I missed your friend."

"She had to go."

"The kitchen?"

"I'll do it now, but for the record, you guys weren't supposed to be back until tomorrow."

"True." Alice looked down at the completed puzzle on the table. Well, nearly completed.

The rendering of a happy family surrounded by flowers, trees, sun, stars, and clouds was missing one piece. The lack of completion and closure had annoyed Alice, but now she viewed it with a new sense of curiosity.

The piece existed, somewhere. She simply needed to find it.

A puzzle piece, a killer . . . anything could be found if you looked in the right places.

Chapter Thirty-one

The next morning, Alice was on her second cup of coffee, setting up a colorful new puzzle and plotting ways to find out more about Lars Olsen's last hours, when the door from the lower level opened and Taylor appeared in flannel pants, fluffy slippers, and a gray U of O hoodie that was long enough to serve as a dress.

Alice was pleased to see that Taylor had gotten out of bed for her; she had to turn away to hide her smile.

"Gran?" Little smudges of yesterday's mascara underlined her eyes as she squinted around the room. "What's the emergency?"

"I need your help."

"Putting out a fire? Your text sounded urgent."

"I need your youthful insight and tech savvy." Alice laid out the challenge: how to find and approach Rosie Suarez in a place where she could feel comfortable enough to talk. A public place.

"You mean, like stalking her?" Taylor asked.

"More like a stakeout."

"But she's not a criminal."

"She is a suspect. Please. The police will be putting Michelle under a microscope, and that's not fair."

"Gran, Michelle could have killed her husband. She had opportunity."

"But a woman plotting murder doesn't spend days on the lam, inconvenienced and uprooted. I would have killed him right off the bat, save myself a trip."

"Remind me to stay on your good side." Taylor smirked as she started scrolling through her phone. "All right, fine, I'll see if I can find her on X or Insta or the old people platform, formerly known as the Book."

While Taylor searched for information on Rosie Suarez, Alice whipped up scrambled eggs with light sour cream and scallions, bacon and toast on the side.

"There are photos of her at the gym—Total Tone, which is in Portland. Looks like she's a regular there, but hard to know when she'd be there."

"Not the sort of place I'd like to drop in on." Alice couldn't see herself getting a trial membership just to sweat through an exercise class beside Rosie. While she enjoyed regular walking, sweat was not on her list of fun things to do.

"Wow, she's got a cool sleeve." Taylor looked up. "A tattoo on her arm?"

"I know what it is." Alice was having some trouble keeping up with popular body art. When she was a kid her mother had told her tattoos were for sailors, and it was taking some time for her brain to reclassify the ink as body art.

Taylor found pictures of Rosie at some of the local galleries and art shows. "There she is with Lars, and this guy is the art dealer Coyote Jones. You met him, right?"

Alice nodded. "And I've been to his gallery in West Hazel."

"Santino has a show there, this week, I think. He invited us. But he especially wanted Aunt Violet to come. Remember his crush? So cute. We should go for First Thursday, when all the galleries are open and you can breeze in and out, get wine and appetizers, meet people." Taylor straightened, looking up in a moment of recognition. "That's this Thursday—tomorrow! I'm definitely going. Santino was a cool guy." Taylor went into the nook to sit at the puzzle table and let out a yelp at the sight of a new jigsaw puzzle. Most of it was still in the box, but a few border pieces were set out on the table. "Gran! Did you find the missing piece?"

"I did not. But I double-checked the corners of the box, then packed it away. Next chance I get I'll do a thorough sweep and mop and search every corner of the room. I know it's here, somewhere."

"Wow. Okay."

"Now I'm more confident than ever that the puzzle came from Lars. It's his simplistic art."

"I don't think so," Taylor said. "I'd remember him giving it to me. Actually, I don't even think he attended the rehearsal or the concert."

"Well, I can't ask him about it now, but I can show it to people who know his art. Which brings us back to Rosie." Alice placed two plates on the counter, the eggs still steaming and the bacon smelling glorious. "How can we find her?"

"There's a mention that she teaches at Cold Spring Community College." Back at the counter, Taylor swooped up some eggs and seemed to savor them as she ate and searched on her iPad.

Thank goodness she'd moved on from that vegan phase.

"Okay, here we go. She's in the art department, and according to their fall term schedule, Suarez teaches Drawing I Tuesday and Thursday nights, and today from ten to eleven fifty."

"Perfect. I'll leave work early and meet you on the campus outside her classroom at eleven forty."

"Meet me?" Taylor shook her head as she bit off half a strip of bacon. "I was just getting information for you."

"Look, she just lost a man she was planning to run away with. The last person she'll want to talk to is a woman of my generation who's friendly with her lover's wife."

"Ew." Taylor crinkled her nose. "You are not allowed to use the word 'lover,' ever again."

"Will you just try to get her to open up? You're the perfect antidote to her pain."

"This is not what I want to do on my day off," Taylor moaned.

"I appreciate your help. You're the only one I can turn to with this." Yes, Alice was trying to flatter Taylor, but the truth was the youth connection was the best way to reach an isolated young woman like Rosie.

"Fine, but after that you'll owe me lunch."

"Of course," Alice said. They would feast on the finest Cold Spring Community College had to offer.

"You take the stairs; I'll cover the main entrance," Alice told Taylor. Rosie Suarez's classroom had been easy to find on the main floor of a stately three-story brick building with patches of ivy on the facade that looked as if it had been plucked from a New England campus back east. Through the small window they could see Rosie mingling with the class, tucking her long dark hair behind her ears as she walked among students who had tacked their sketches to the wall for critique.

Their waiting game paid off a few minutes later, as dozens of students streamed past Alice. After the crowd thinned and fizzled to a handful, Rosie emerged from the classroom wearing a backpack and carrying a large sketch pad.

Alice fell into step beside her, heading toward the main

doors. "Rosie? I'm Alice Pepper. Not sure if you remember me from Dragonberry Lane. I'm hoping you'll talk to me about Lars."

Rosie flinched as she shot a look at Alice. Today she wore gray tinted round glasses that had a googly-eyed effect, though they were nearly successful in hiding the red rims around her eyes. "Really? You jump out and confront a person on the worst day of her life?"

"I'm sorry," Alice said. "But in situations like yours, a sympathetic ear might help."

"Why would I want to talk to you? I've already been put through the wringer by the police."

"The police can be relentless," Taylor said, having moved with quick steps to catch up.

"Who are you?" Rosie squinted at her.

"My granddaughter Taylor. She's trying to help me figure out who killed Lars Olsen."

"I didn't kill Lars."

"I didn't say you did, dear." Alice wanted to say more, but she sensed Rosie was near the edge. She seemed to be wincing, but when she took a deep breath, Alice could see that she was trying to keep herself from crying.

"I was teaching a class when he died, okay? A seven-thirty class, so I was out of there before . . . you know. And the police know that." She sniffed. "I can't believe this has happened. A few days ago Lars sold some paintings after the press conference—the first money he'd made in a long time—and he was sure Michelle would come through with more. He was so happy. And now . . ." Tears filled her eyes, and one rolled down her cheek. She lifted her glasses, shoved them into her dark hair, then swiped the tears away. "I can't. I can't do this."

"Take a breath," Taylor said.

"You need a break, a moment." Alice looked out to the campus, rolling green hills and paths punctuated with a few plazas and stone structures where students hung out. "Can we buy you a coffee? Or maybe a quiet bench."

Rosie lowered the glasses to her face, cast a cautious look over her shoulder, and seemed relieved the volume of students streaming by had been reduced. "Over there." She nodded toward a cluster of trees, and they headed that way. "This is so embarrassing. I can't be falling apart in front of my students. I need this teaching job, now that I'm losing everything I put into Lars."

"You've suffered a huge loss," Alice said, surprised by the surge of sympathy she felt for this young woman. "I know it's upsetting, but I'm trying to understand what happened to Lars before Michelle found him last night."

"I was there when he got the call that Michelle was coming back." Rosie sat down on the end of a bench. Alice sat beside her. Taylor hovered beyond Alice, observing but allowing distance. "I thought he was going to freak, but he said it was a good thing, moving forward. He was going to push her to give him the money and make the split."

"So he was upbeat?" Alice asked.

"Pretty much. There was some hitch about Henry Finley, something I didn't get. I mean, Henry's just an intern, a new hire. I told Lars he should just fire him, but he said he couldn't."

"Why not?" Alice asked.

"I don't know," Rosie said impatiently. "It's not like he let me in on his bank accounts or his history. But I always figured it had something to do with Claudia, Henry's mother. She's always acting like she owns Lars."

Alice had noticed a tension between Lars and Claudia

when she'd seen them together. "Are they related? Maybe brother and sister?"

"I think they went to school together, a hundred years ago."

"Art school?" Alice asked. With Larry Ottermeyer.

"Whatever." Rosie shrugged. "I just . . . I can't believe he's gone, you know? I was just with him, hours before he was killed. I had to leave to teach my night class, but—"

"What time did you leave Dragonberry?"

"Around six, I guess. I had to go home and finish grading student projects. I didn't want to leave him. Now I wish I'd stayed. Maybe he wouldn't be dead."

"That's a heavy lift," Taylor said. "But you can't undo the past. And it's not your fault that he's gone."

"I feel so guilty. I wish I could have saved him."

"So you went home around six," Alice said. "And then off to school for a seven-thirty class. Did anyone see you at home? Chat with any neighbors?"

"I live in that crappy apartment complex by the railroad tracks. The neighbors won't look you in the eye, let alone talk."

"Do you remember if there was a fire burning in the fireplace at Dragonberry? A huge blaze?" Alice asked.

"There probably was. Lars liked to have a fire going. But usually normal size. He stoked up a big fire last year around Christmas, and he worried that the house was going to burn down."

Alice nodded. If Rosie had her facts right, either Lars or the killer had added fuel to the fire after she'd left. A small detail, but sometimes details added up. "Do you have any idea who might have wanted to kill Lars?"

"Not really." She winced, then sighed. "Except, maybe . . . look, I know you're friends with Michelle, but you'd better watch yourself. From talking to the police, it looks like she killed him." Tears began to flow again. "I didn't think she was that kind of person, a killer, but you never really know a person."

"You never know," Alice agreed, though Rosie's comment reminded her to call Madison and see if she could get a "public information" update on the homicide case. Her gut told her that Michelle didn't possess a killer instinct any more than Rosie did, but her impressions could be wrong. Either woman could be a convincing actress, though Alice had spent enough time with Michelle to feel like she'd connected, and the woman possessed an authentic moral compass.

Rosie, on the other hand, was a jumble of drama and emotion. And for good reason. Alice wasn't passing judgment, but it was hard to get a bead on the mercurial young woman. There was time to watch and wait.

On the way back to the parking lot, Alice gave Taylor props for responding well to the situation. "She tolerated me, but I think she connected with you," Alice told her.

"Hell to the yeah. I kind of feel sorry for her. Do you think she killed him?"

"I was suspicious, but now I don't think so. We'll have to see how it shakes out after the police check her alibi. I'd also like to see the timeframe forensics derives."

"Listen to you, all *Law & Order*."

"Well, I tend to see the good in people. Ruby says I'm just a sucker for a sob story." Checking her phone, Alice saw that she had a text from Emerald, reporting that Michelle was still weak and dizzy, but she was being checked out of the hospital. Could Alice accommodate her until her house was cleared as a crime scene?

The thought of returning to Dragonberry Lane made Alice shudder.

She texted back: **Of course. Happy to host her at my place until she can find new lodgings.**

"I'm heading back to work," Alice told Taylor. "But I need your help getting Michelle set up in one of the en suites downstairs. Emerald will be dropping her off, and she's still a bit under the weather."

"Isn't that weird? I mean, she's Aunt Vi's friend, but you barely know her. Can't she stay with Sapphire?"

"You mean Emerald? No. Emerald is off to Mexico with her husband, and Michelle's been through so much. She needs some TLC. Can you make sure she's comfortable?"

Taylor clasped her hands together. "Clean sheets and towels for the suspected murderer checking into the widow's suite? Killer service is our middle name."

Alice couldn't help but laugh. "Honey, your talents are wasted in the kitchen."

"Exactly what I keep saying to Gramps."

Chapter Thirty-two

Wednesday night's dinner was a small, simple affair—grilled BLTs and chicken noodle soup for Alice, Taylor, and Madison. Violet was out at a school function, Ruby was having dinner with a friend, and Michelle was napping downstairs. "I'm starting to feel better, now that I had your special cure," Michelle had told Alice earlier. The homemade chicken stock had been in the freezer; Alice had just added noodles and carrots.

"I'm glad the soup helped," Alice said, "but the cure for grief is elusive."

"You think I'm sick with grief?" Michelle frowned. "I'm a pretty tough cookie."

"But anyone in your situation is likely to go through grief. Shock. And a boatload of disappointment."

"Dr. Angelino says it's viral. That I should rest."

Isabella Angelino was Alice's primary care provider, too. "She's the doctor; I'm sure she knows best," Alice said. Sending Michelle back downstairs with a small Japanese teapot full of rooibos tea, Alice watched her go, mouthing, "Definitely grief."

Over their sandwiches, Madison shared what she could of the murder investigation.

"We checked with the closest neighbors to Dragonberry Lane, but no one saw anything out of the ordinary the night of the murder," Madison reported.

"Which is not surprising," Alice said, "since those properties are spread out, kind of isolated."

Madison nodded. "The central lab in Salem is processing the forensic evidence our team collected. They found Michelle's prints on the handle of the knife."

"Of course," Alice said. "She was handling the bloody knife that night." She looked down at her sandwich, snapping off a piece of bacon. "Is this getting too gruesome?"

"It is when I've just downed a BLT." Taylor slid the plate of sliced cucumber closer, alongside a bowl of ranch dressing. She was dipping and crunching as if she'd been sequestered on the international space station for weeks with only applesauce and Tang. "Gross things like that make me want to go vegan again."

"Sorry." Madison pressed a napkin to her mouth. "To keep it clean, we also found a second set of latent prints on the knife. They belong to Rosie Suarez."

"Oh, no! We talked to her today, and she seemed genuinely sad." Taylor wagged a cucumber stick at her sister. "I think that girl is innocent."

"Maybe." Madison shrugged a shoulder. "It's possible that her prints were on the knife before the murder, considering that Rosie was staying in the house while Michelle was missing."

"And what about Rosie's alibi?" Alice asked. "That class she teaches at the community college?"

"You know about that?" Madison squinted.

"Yes, ma'am, Officer," Taylor teased. "We got the suspect to reveal all."

Alice shot Taylor a withering look that told her to knock it off. The twin rivalry was tired.

"The security cameras at Cold Spring show her coming through the doors of Main Hall at seven thirty-five, which is in the window of time when the coroner believes the murder occurred. Michelle's call to the nine-one-one dispatcher came in at seven twenty-five."

"So, it's inconclusive, but it could have been Rosie Suarez speeding away from the Dragonberry House." Alice pushed her plate back. "Rosie could have killed him."

"What?" Taylor threw up her arms. "I thought you believed her?"

"I did. But she may be lying. We need to keep an open mind." Alice turned back to Madison. "What else do you have?"

"We'll have to wait a few days at least for other forensic results. The TV shows get that part wrong; test results are not instantaneous. We've got a forensic accountant going through Lars Olsen's bank accounts and records."

"Rumor has it he had some outstanding debts," Alice said. One hundred thousand dollars—that had been the amount that Michelle had described as the breaking point in their marriage.

Madison wiggled her butter knife on the table. "So far, I can't confirm or deny those rumors."

"Fair enough," Alice said. "So, we know you're looking at his apprentice. I'm thinking you'll want to talk to his other close business associate, Coyote Jones. And since his old friend Santino is in town, he's worth interviewing. Did I miss anyone?"

"Just the suspect sleeping downstairs," Madison said.

"I told you, Gran," Taylor said, slapping her sister a high five.

"I don't think Michelle killed him," Alice said. "But if she was involved, she wasn't alone. Remember, someone was in that vehicle that fled the scene."

"I wonder who?" Taylor licked the last bit of ranch from her finger and noticed the others staring at her. "I wasn't being obnoxious. I really want to know who did it."

"Licking your finger is kind of obnoxious," Madison said.

At the moment, Alice would have put her money on Rosie Suarez, but the evidence was still tentative. "Okay, kiddos." Alice rose, plates in hand. "Dishes in the dishwasher and I'm moving to the puzzle table."

As expected, Madison and Taylor joined her to work a puzzle she'd brought home from the trade table at the library: a colorful array of art supplies. Tubes of paint, pastel sticks, crayons, a rainbow of pencils . . . all surrounded by doodles and illustrations. Five hundred pieces. Bright and pleasant. Easy-peasy.

"Oh, one thing I forgot to mention." Madison was collecting puzzle pieces that belonged among the paint tubes. "The art assistant, Henry Finley? He showed up for work this morning at the crime scene. Apparently he hadn't seen or heard anything about the murder. He's not a social media person. And he was scheduled to work, so he got a shock when he came walking up Dragonberry Lane. He actually started crying."

"That sounds awkward," Taylor said.

"It was sad. So hard to tell the guy his boss was dead. Murdered. He's just a kid."

"Seventeen," Alice said. "Right on the cusp."

"After the way Lars treated him, I was surprised the kid was so broken up," Madison said.

"Lars was hard on the people around him," Alice said,

searching through the pile of puzzle pieces to find the last bits of the border. "It makes for plenty of suspects when someone like that is killed." Sifting through the box, Alice found one more border piece before noticing that her granddaughters had stopped puzzling and were staring at her with pinched expressions.

"What's wrong?"

Madison's brows were arched in that authoritative demeanor that ticked her sister off. "Look, Gran, there's something else we need to talk about."

Her serious tone made Alice's heart sink. "Tell me."

"It's not that bad," Taylor said. "It's just that . . . don't get mad. Promise me."

"I never stay mad at you, sweetie. Tell me this minute."

"The last puzzle we did, the one with the missing piece? It's not from Lars Olsen," Taylor said. "It's actually from . . . she-who-shall-not-be-named."

"Lauren?" Years ago, Alice had assigned Lauren the nickname of "she-who-shall-not-be-named" as a way to bring some levity to a difficult situation. Hearing the name now, Alice was relieved . . . and gobsmacked. "Why would she give me a puzzle?"

"It's sort of an olive branch." Madison's eyes had softened to a fuzzy look. "Mom wanted to reach out to you, open the door."

"But with a puzzle?"

"She's trying to speak your language," Taylor said. "She had the puzzle made from some artwork she did when she was little. I chose a few pieces from a bin of old drawings and school projects that are stored up in the attic. Mom said this drawing was one of your favorites, probably because it shows little Lauren and you and Gramps."

"I can't believe I didn't recognize it." Alice got up from

the table and went to the cabinet to find the box with Lauren's puzzle. One look at the photo brought a rush of memories. "Yes, of course. She made this for a school assignment; draw your family. I was so pleased with her work, sure she had artistic abilities. She was a talented child." Alice smiled at the sweet memory.

"So you're happy?" Madison asked.

"Of course. I . . . I never wanted this separation between your mother and me to carry on." How to explain that Alice never wanted it at all without casting the blame onto their mom? "So, what next? What does the puzzle really mean? And the missing piece?"

"That's something I think Mom should explain herself," said Taylor.

Alice peered through the kitchen, toward the open space of the living room. "What? Is she here now?"

"Oh my gosh, Taylor, don't be a tease." Madison frowned. "No, we're not hiding her in a closet, Gran. But she is in West Hazel. Visiting." She looked down at her hands a moment, her lips stretched in a downward turn. "We've been seeing her, meeting with her in the last few years. More often recently." She looked up, her face apologetic. "You probably knew that."

"How would I know?" Truthfully, there had been clues pointing to Lauren's occasional presence in town, but after the girls had turned eighteen, Alice had given them space to navigate certain things on their own. "Impressive as I may be, I'm not omniscient."

"You know everything," Taylor said. "When you saw me talking to her at the children's fair, I thought the jig was up." Seeing Alice's blank look, Taylor explained, "The blond woman? The Marilyn Monroe type?"

"That was Lauren? So she's blond now?"

"She's wearing wigs," Madison said. "Courtesy of Ruby's House of Wigs."

"Ruby is in on this?"

"We can always count on Ruby to help," Taylor said. "But I was sure you were on to us. And then at the concert, when you almost ran right into Mom . . . that was crazy."

"I did?" Alice's confidence plummeted. "What kind of sleuth am I? What kind of mother doesn't recognize her own daughter?"

Taylor rolled her eyes. "You would have totally pinned her if Zika hadn't stepped in that night. And then last night, when you guys came home from Sunriver a day early? That just about killed me. She had to sneak out through the back deck slider."

"Lauren was here? In my house?" How embarrassing to be so clueless.

"You know all my friends, Gran. I figured you'd be suspicious when I didn't mention a name."

"Enough with the lies," Madison said. "We're sorry. Anyway, if you want to meet with her, we'll set things up." Madison spelled out the plan with her usual efficiency. "If you don't, that's okay, too."

"Of course I want to see her." It was understandable that the twins might have doubted Alice's desire to reconnect with their mother. Over the years of Lauren's absence, she had pretended that she'd been the one to sever the relationship, claiming she needed a break from her unreliable daughter. Alice had acted as if the choice to separate had been hers, hoping to cover up the truth and save the girls from feeling abandoned.

When in fact, it had been Lauren who walked away.

Lauren who told Alice she was a toxic force in her life.

Lauren who had removed herself from the lives of her

bright, lively twin daughters, leaving them repeatedly in Alice's care.

Alice had been forced to let go of her daughter before Lauren could make her way back. In the meantime, the twins had found their way to her, reuniting on their own terms.

It was all good news—a breakthrough. A landmark had been reached.

And it all left Alice feeling frightened and worried.

The door to the basement suites opened, and Michelle emerged, teapot in one hand, cell phone in the other. "No, I don't belong to your church," she told the other party, who was apparently on speakerphone.

"Well, do you attend our services?"

"No, I don't attend. I'm Buddhist."

"I see. Have you looked into having a Buddhist funeral?"

"Why would I do that? My husband would want a church funeral. He wasn't Buddhist."

"I'm sorry, ma'am. We just can't help you."

Michelle placed the phone and teapot on the counter, ended the call, and sighed. "Funerals are hard. No church wants to bury a dead man of mediocre faith."

"Do they know he's a famous artist?" Taylor asked. "That might change some minds."

"I didn't think to mention it, but the coroner called me. Dr. Jane. Very nice. She thinks the body will be released sometime this weekend." Michelle held her hands up. "And then what? What do I do with a body? Lars needs a funeral and a place to go."

"I know just the person to help." Alice reached for her cell phone. "I'm going to call Stone."

"Is he a minister?" Michelle asked.

Knowing Stone, a jack-of-all-trades, Alice wouldn't have been surprised to learn he'd led a congregation at one time. "Stone will help you through the process. He's a fixer." And a wonderful man. Any excuse to have him dropping by the house was fine by Alice.

Chapter Thirty-three

"This is absolutely magical," Alice said as she zipped her car into a spot in Portland's Pearl District. A stellar parallel parking job, necessary on First Thursday, a celebration that attracted extra visitors to the downtown area.

The streets glistened from a recent rain, reflecting the illumination from streetlamps, shop fronts, traffic lights, and party lights strung playfully along the facade of the Coyote Downtown Gallery, which loomed on the next block. It had been a festive three-block walk, arm in arm with Taylor, with Violet and Ruby in the lead, and the art lovers they'd passed here and there seemed equally pleased to be out and about on this breezy October night.

Alice tried to keep up with the high spirits, tamping down her anxiety over meeting with Lauren. Taylor had told her that it would be a few days until Lauren would be back in town. "You need to be patient," Taylor had warned her.

As if Alice hadn't been waiting years to see her daughter.

For now, Alice was glad for the distraction of an outing. "I can't believe I've never attended First Thursday in Portland."

"It's great, but you're a little late to the party, Gran," said Taylor. "October is the last First Thursday gallery event this year. They'll start again in April."

"Well, I'm happy to be here now," Alice said. "Especially since I've met the artist."

"I'm interested in seeing Santino's work," Violet said, still walking ahead of them. "He seems like a lovely man."

"You're sure to connect with his work," Ruby said, turning back to wink at Alice and Taylor.

"Yeah, and if we have time, I want to stop in at the Flying Fish Gallery on Ninth Avenue." Taylor's boots clunked over a steel plate, and she gave an extra rhythmic stomp as they waited for a light. "My friend Olive has a piece in a group exhibit there."

"Sounds good." As they waited on the corner, Alice surveyed the street, checking for familiar faces in passersby. Her granddaughters had vowed that they wouldn't stage a surprise meeting with Lauren. "We wouldn't spring that on you," Madison had promised. Still, Alice was on alert, afraid of being foisted into a vulnerable position in a very public place. The reunion would happen, but it required emotional preparation. Planning. Inner peace. Nothing important came easy.

Opening the door to the Coyote Gallery, Alice was met with warmth, laughter, vibrant colors, and cheerful patrons. The building was older than the modern West Hazel gallery, but there was a certain charm in the brick walls, smaller nooks that held only a handful of pieces, and scarred wide-plank pine floors. This was a space that had seen things: people and art, ever changing but still resonating with creation, passion, pain.

Santino left a small group standing at one of his paintings and came to greet them by the door. "Ladies! You made it." Dressed in a crisp white shirt and gray pants in a textured fabric, he looked elegant and minimalist. A blank canvas, Alice thought. He tapped a palm against his heart and gave a little bow. "I'm so happy to see you."

"This is exciting." Taylor flashed her fingers, as if shining blinking lights. "How's it going? Any celebrities?"

"Two very tall men who I'm told play for the Blazers team, and a charming grand dame of theater who has retired here in Portland." He raised one brow. "I don't name names, but I will tell you later, when people are not earsdropping."

"Eavesdropping," Alice said. She couldn't help herself. "Congratulations on the show. And I'm sorry about Lars. I know you had your differences, but you used to be friends. I have some questions for you."

"Please!" He held up one hand. "Let's not talk of him until later. He's made this a difficult night for me. Just this afternoon Coyote removed four of my pieces from a wall in the rear of the gallery to make room for his handful of paintings by Lars. Mediocre pieces, to be totally honest. But death is good for business. If you look now, you'll see red dots on all the placards for his art. Sold out, and at inflated prices." He pressed his lips into a stern line as he gestured around him. "Even in death, Lars tries to steal the show from me."

"How disheartening." Violet's lips formed a pout.

"It is a shame when tonight should be about celebrating your art," Alice said, though she was itching to ask him a few questions about Lars.

"Nothing you can do but push forward, right?" said Violet. "Don't let us keep you from your patrons. We're here to see your art, and I assure you we won't be lingering at the rear wall. Where do you recommend we begin?"

"Here on the left-hand wall." He gestured, taking a few steps back. "If I may guide you, perhaps?"

"A personal tour?" Alice said quietly to Ruby. "He really is into Violet."

And so began the guided journey through selected art by Santino. Alice, Ruby, and Taylor followed along, but the tour group seemed to encapsulate Santino and Violet, who pointed out themes and techniques she noticed and asked questions—such smart questions—that seemed to move and delight the artist.

By the time they reached the back of the room, where tables of appetizers and wine awaited them, Vi and Santino had a steady, exclusive patter going.

"Our little Violet has a beau," Ruby whispered. "It's a first."

"Not quite, but the first in decades." Violet and Santino had moved to another wall of paintings, while the others shifted toward the appetizer table. Decades ago, there'd been a young man in Violet's life, a steady, congenial guy who had treated her with respect and admiration. "Remember Bill?" Alice asked.

"Oh, that's right." Ruby nodded, seizing the toothpick skewering a date wrapped in bacon.

"Who's Bill?" Taylor's eyes opened wide, and she lowered her wineglass. "The legendary fiancé?"

"He was before your time, and I don't know if they were officially engaged, but—"

"Might as well have been." Ruby dabbed at her lips with a cocktail napkin. "They seemed so happy, but then they split up, and within months he was getting married to someone else."

Alice nodded. "When I asked Violet what happened, she said she just couldn't see herself in a boring life, waking up with a Bill every morning."

"The girl had a point," Ruby said.

"After that, there was no one." There'd been a few close

friends, of course, but Violet seemed to have closed the door on intimacy. Had that been a lifetime choice? Was she still closed off?

The question hung in the air over the couple as they joined the gals near the refreshments. Seeing the way Santino seemed to buoy Violet with his conversation, Alice felt a new attachment to him. This wasn't the demeanor of a killer. It couldn't be. Could it?

"The irony, for me, is your vision of a piece. You see things in the painting that no one else can articulate."

"I do?" Violet stood up straighter, her expression softening.

"I believe you're in touch with things that are not... tactile? Is that the word? Perhaps you pick up the vibration of colors."

Violet gasped, her eyes round with wonder. "It's true. How did you know?"

"I could feel it. I see auras."

"Auras? I do, too, and you... you're turquoise and tangerine and white. Clear and bright."

Alice watched the exchange, trying not to stare in wonder as her normally reticent sister formed an immediate bond with this man. Ruby reached over and squeezed her arm so hard it was sure to leave a bruise.

"Ouch." Alice pushed her away and rubbed the sore spot.

"Did you hear that?" Ruby demanded. "Did you?"

"I can't tell if they're into each other, or getting ready to read each other's tea leaves," Taylor said, plucking a deviled egg from a platter.

"Either way, it could be good for Violet." Ruby sipped her wine, then added, "She deserves to be happy."

But she's already got a happy life, Alice thought. Or at least that was the way she'd always seen her sister. If Violet was falling for Santino, Alice would have her back, of course. But she had to remember that this man had a complicated relationship with his old friend, the artist who had just been murdered.

Was Violet falling blindly for the dead man's fiercest rival? There were still questions to be answered on that front.

Chapter Thirty-four

Wineglass in hand, Alice and her friends wove through the increasing clusters of patrons in the gallery, revisiting paintings, pointing out things they liked and choosing the ones they would buy if they had a few thousand dollars to spare.

Although the childhood approach of the art movement was still evident in Santino's work, he had developed a certain style of depicting people. Moving beyond stick figures, his people had hunched, expressive bodies, more like bumpy potatoes with sleepy eyed, expressive faces. There was a heightened emotion in his work, perhaps because of his reliance on red tones—rose, orange, amber, and copper. "There's an earthy sadness here," Alice observed, "but I like the way that he depicts the little potato people together in groups and families. As if to emphasis the importance of human interaction and connection."

Violet nodded. "Love. It's the foundation of his work."

While pointing at Violet behind her back, Ruby mouthed: "She *loves* him!"

But Alice was unfazed. Violet was simply discussing the artist's work. Moving on to another painting, Alice stepped back and accidentally bumped into someone behind her. "I'm so sorry." Being careful not to spill her wine, she turned to find a familiar young woman scowling up at her, short dark hair sculpted against her scalp, round, amber glasses shielding her eyes.

"You again!" Rosie Suarez let out a huff of a breath. "Seriously? Are you stalking me, Alice Pepper?"

Alice pressed a "Who me?" hand to her chest but answered, "Not today."

Taylor sidled over with a friendly smile. "Hey, Rosie. We came for the show," Taylor said. "We know Santino. Wait, that sounds really snobby."

"No, it's okay. Maybe you can introduce me."

Taylor shrugged. "Sure. What do you think of his work?"

"His use of color is interesting." Rosie shrugged. "He's done a lot to advance the movement, but Lars wouldn't want to hear that."

"I could see that," Taylor agreed.

As they chatted, Alice tuned them out and scanned the gallery for the owner. You would think Coyote Jones would be present at a major show like this, especially on First Thursday. Ruby had come along tonight in the off chance that she might run into him. "I just can't resist a man who exudes that much self-assurance," Ruby had said. "Anyone with that kind of power and control had to work to get there."

Ruby checked with one of the gallery attendants, who assured her that Jones would make an appearance. "He's coming. Right now he's out to dinner with an investor." Ruby wiggled her shoulders. "I told you he was a big deal."

Alice wanted to see him, but for a different reason. Michelle had revealed that Lars had been in deep with

Coyote Jones, owing him tens of thousands of dollars. And in a sudden reversal, when Lars had been killed, the dealer was recouping his losses, with a chance to make more on Lars's extensive collection.

That put Coyote on the top of the suspect list for Lars Olsen's murder. Well, at least the top of Alice's list. Ruby argued that a big deal like Coyote Jones wouldn't need to stoop so low as to kill a client. But Alice held firm, contending that money was a huge motivator, and if a client was worth more dead than alive, the dealer had reason to kill.

"Let's go over to the Flying Fish Gallery," Taylor announced, explaining that her friend had a piece in the show. "It's just a few blocks away, and the rain stopped."

Violet and Rosie were game, but Ruby and Alice decided to stay behind.

"Text us if the show is irresistible, and we might head over in a bit," Ruby said, positioning herself at the door to greet Coyote when he arrived.

Having studied the paintings, Alice transitioned to the next level, surveying the patrons. She positioned herself near a pillar at the back of the front room—the perfect spot to monitor visitors. She chatted with folks who recognized her from the library, and spent a few minutes with Frederika Jenson, one of the Friends of the Library who was known for tooling around town in her electric-blue Miata, and encouraged a charming couple as they considered purchasing Santino's paintings entitled *A Day in the Park*.

Otherwise, Alice was happy to blend in, semi-invisible, so that she could observe and soak it all in.

When Santino strolled over, buoyed by his recent sale, Alice caught his attention. "Do you have a minute to talk?"

"So sorry, Alice. But I will get to you later, I promise you, my friend." His smile exuded warmth, his eyes respect. It was no wonder that his commercial success exceeded Lars Olsen's. He paused to laugh at a joke from two men who claimed to have a spot for a Santino original in a beach house they didn't yet own.

"It's still a dream," said the bearded man in a washed-out denim jacket. "But dreams do come true."

"They do!" Santino laughed, turning toward the door, and then freezing in place when he caught sight of someone there. "Claudia?"

Alice followed his gaze to a tall strawberry-blond woman who had just walked in. Dressed in black gloves and trench coat with one of those fancy but spare hats on the side of her head, she moved with the grace and swagger of a model. Alice searched her memory for the name of the hat. A terminator? A fascinator! Red, with beaded netting, ribbons, and a fake satin rose in the center, she wore it perched on the side of her head like a member of some royal wedding.

She seemed familiar.

But Santino definitely knew her. "Claudia?"

Henry's mother? Alice recalled that she'd been wearing red gloves that day at Dragonberry Lane.

"Claudia, I can't believe it. What are you doing here?" Santino held out his arms and she came to him.

Although there were at least a dozen people in the front room, no one beside Alice paid much attention to the surprising reunion. Alice stood nearby, blending into the walls, and yet close enough to hear every word. She took her cell phone from her pocket and pretended to stare at the screen for a moment, but the scene in front of her was irresistible.

"My dear friend." Smiling demurely, Claudia closed her eyes as he took her gloved hands and then placed a kiss on each cheek. "It's been too long."

"Years." He shook his head. "Nothing I could say or do got through to you, and now, here you are. Did you come for him? For the funeral?"

"I've been here for weeks," she said. "But you're correct. I did come for Lars." When he squinted in confusion, she added, "Not romantically. I came to settle a score."

Santino drew in a slow breath, his gaze pinning her, as if he needed to make sure she didn't escape. "Oh, dear Claudia, don't tell me you finally did it." His voice was soft and sad as he added, "It was you, wasn't it? You killed him."

Chapter Thirty-five

Were those tears in her eyes? Alice watched, riveted, as Claudia and Santino stood in silence for a moment, the other sights and sounds in the room having faded. The question hung heavy in the air, and Claudia didn't deny the claim.

She pressed a leather-gloved finger to her face, swiping at a tear before answering, "I wish I did."

"You would have had every right." Relief seemed to ease the tension between them as Santino drew her close into a hug, patted her back, and then let go. "Lars was so cruel to you. You should have pressed charges. You know, today that sort of violence would have landed him in jail."

"Precisely why I couldn't pursue charges. I didn't want to ruin him. But it was so long ago." Claudia nodded. "I was young. I thought I loved him. Maybe I did."

He shook his head. "Nearly twenty years ago. I hope he treated you with respect this time."

Two decades ago, Lars had been in art school. Alice surmised that Claudia had known him then, had suffered by his hand. Had she been the victim mentioned in the reports, the woman who had been kept captive and injured by Lars?

"This time I stood my ground. He was the same old Lars, though his wife seems to have softened some of the edges."

"Michelle. She was good for him. A saint."

"She would have to be to last with him for a few years." Claudia drew in a deep breath as one hand went up to smooth down her hair and check the position of her hat.

Don't worry, it's Audrey Hepburn perfect! Alice thought, somewhat admiringly.

"So here you are, with this fabulous show." Claudia spread her gloved hands to encompass the gallery. "You've been very successful. Critical acclaim and commercial success."

Santino touched a crisp white point of his open collar and shrugged. "Art has brought me a rich life."

"You're a success, and Lars is dead." She smiled. "It took nearly twenty years, but you won, my friend. The real question is, how hard did you have to fight for your victory? Did *you* kill him to get him off your back?"

From her position by the pillar, Alice couldn't see his face, couldn't gauge his reaction, though the silence between them was loaded.

"It's really not that dramatic," he finally said. "Bastard that he was, I always loved him. But you know how that is. You could have had just about any young man at art school. Most girls, too. But you chose Larry."

"Don't remind me," she said. "You're infuriating!"

"Some things never change. So, you're coming to the funeral, then?" Santino asked. "It's bound to be an event, the dead celebrity artist. And the beauty of it is, he can't hurt us anymore."

"But I can still hurt him." Claudia unbuttoned and removed her coat, but left the gloves on as she laid the garment over one arm. "I've filed some legal documents. As they say, revenge is a dish best served cold."

"Like ice cream or chocotorta?" He turned around and took her arm, and from this angle Alice could see him beaming with delight. "Well, I will be happy if you can finally get something out of Lars. Do you have a good lawyer?"

"I do. It's all in the works. But I didn't come to talk about business. Tonight is the night to celebrate you, your show. Congratulations, Santi."

"Come." He reached a hand behind her, and she moved closer. "Let me show you my masterpieces."

Alice's thoughts were brimming with news and questions about Lars's past when she found Ruby in front of the gallery waiting to talk with Coyote Jones. The big man was emerging from the back of a shiny black SUV, and while Ruby was impressed with the fact that he had a hired car, Coyote couldn't take his eyes off Ruby, clearly smitten with her.

Good news: the feeling was mutual. He was the reason Ruby had come out tonight.

Bad news? It was hard to know just how trustworthy Mr. Jones, the entrepreneur, would prove himself to be. Alice wasn't about to share her new information about Coyote's two clients, Lars and Santino, and the woman who seemed to be interwoven in their college art scene.

Alice and Ruby waited as Coyote released his driver, telling him to grab some dinner and be back in an hour or so. The driver closed the back door and hustled around the large vehicle to take the wheel.

"My driver, Kevin," Coyote said. "We grew up together."

"And now he works for you," Ruby said.

Coyote nodded. "Yeah, it's good to have him around. Most of my staff are people from the old neighborhood back in California. I like to pay it forward and work with people I trust."

"Did you trust Lars?" Alice asked. "Not to speak ill of the dead, but I'm sure you know he had a reputation for cutting people out of deals."

"Sometimes you have to work with artistic types who aren't completely transparent. It's a hazard of being an art dealer." He cracked a sardonic smile, which quickly faded. "But it's tragic, what happened to Lars. Shocking." As usual Coyote Jones was dressed to kill—in fashion terminology. He wore a tailored tweed jacket with a black shirt underneath. The shirt had a crisp collar, open at the neck. His jeans were slightly washed out, but probably pressed. Taller than Alice and broad in the shoulders and chest, he must have paid a fortune for alterations. Worth every penny.

"Do you have an inkling who might have killed him?" Alice asked.

"Everyone and no one," he said quietly. "Much as Lars alienated a lot of folks, it's hard to imagine someone working up the lather to kill the man. I mean, a knife in the back?"

"It's telling, isn't it?" Alice said. "I've been wondering if it's symbolic. A backstabber? Or if it was simply a convenient method in the moment."

"Either way, it's cold, and against the man code. Where I grew up, that'd be the coward's way out. Can't even face up to the man you're killing?" He shook his head. "Uh-uh. Man was a chicken."

An interesting point, something Alice hadn't considered. The ethics of a killer. Was the murderer actually a wimp? Or maybe a woman.

"Were you friends with Lars?" Ruby asked.

"I've known the man for five, six years, but I wouldn't say we were friends. It's hard to trust a person who's always trying to squeeze more money out of you. When I first signed him on, I gave him a break on the commission. After a year, he wanted to cut my percentage in half." Coyote rolled his eyes. "That's not okay. In any negotiation, each party should get something. There should be some give and take. Maybe you don't get the best deal, but you get a fair deal, right? Not so with Lars. He wanted to win, all the time."

"That's no way to do business," Ruby agreed, and she knew. As one of the country's top wig retailers, she understood the dynamics of negotiation.

"So we hadn't worked together for a while, even though he owed me. His terms were unreasonable. Then he shows up Tuesday with some paintings for me—art that he wants to go into Santino's show. Man, I knew he was just trying to burn Santino. But I took the four pieces, stored them in the back. Then I find out he was killed later that night." He shook his head. "Weird."

"We got to see Lars in action when his wife went missing," Alice said. "He amplified the incident, even suggested it was a kidnapping. I guess he figured the more publicity the better."

"What happened with that wife?" Coyote asked. "Michelle, right? I thought I saw on the news that she turned up and she was okay."

"She did," Ruby said. "Alice and I helped find her out in Sunriver."

"Did you really? You ladies must have some mad skills." He swept off his fedora, revealing a brown head, completely bald, that seemed to emphasis his warm brown eyes. "Thing is, I need to talk with her about representing more of Lars's work. You saw his paintings inside? All four of them sold immediately. Two went to people who called in before I could even hang them."

Alice held up a hand to interrupt. "So, you're profiting from the artist's death."

"I am, but the commission from those four paintings will barely make a dent in his outstanding loan. That cat was behind the eight ball. I didn't wish him dead, but now that he's gone, seems fair that his debts should be settled. I know Lars had a good-sized body of work, and right now a Lars Olsen is fetching a high price. I'd like to talk to Michelle about her plans for the collection."

The two women exchanged a hesitant look. "We could connect you," Ruby said.

"I'm not sure she's ready to make those decisions yet," Alice jumped in, knowing Michelle had barely been out of bed these past two days. Soup and tea and toast had seemed to sustain her. At least she was getting some use out of Alice's little jade-green cast-iron Japanese teapot that kept the tea hot for hours. It came in so handy when someone in the house didn't feel well. "Why don't you give us your card, and Michelle can reach out to you when she's ready."

"Of course." In a fluid motion he handed them each a business card with a little fedora on it. "I trust you'll put in a good word for me. Michelle doesn't know me well, but I do own one of the largest galleries in Portland, and I'm a straight shooter."

"We like that," Ruby said brightly as Coyote opened the door and held it while the women filed into the gallery.

"And you think *I* see the good in every suspect?" Alice murmured in her friend's ear. "You were about to give away the ranch."

"Guilty, I admit it. I melt like butter when that big man's around."

Alice smiled down at her friend, a bit tickled to see her so giddy about a man after what she'd gone through recently, losing her husband, George, under difficult circumstances. "Just pace yourself, honey. Slow and steady. Make sure you get a good sense of what's under that sexy fedora."

"I do love that hat!" Ruby sighed. "But yes, I promise to look before I leap. Girl Scout's honor."

Chapter Thirty-six

Inside the gallery Ruby continued talking with Coyote as Alice surveyed the growing number of patrons milling through the rooms. The evening had filled in some of the blanks regarding Lars's murder.

Santino was not grieving the loss of his rival.

Claudia had a grudge against Lars that would soon manifest, she claimed, as a lawsuit.

Coyote Jones was recouping his investment now that Lars was dead, and he stood to earn a lot more, potentially millions, if his estimates panned out.

And Lars had been, quite literally, stabbed in the back. Alice had known this, but she hadn't considered possible interpretations of the method of death until Coyote Jones had pointed it out. Something to talk through with the gals over their nightly puzzle.

Alice moved through the gallery, checking on Santino, who was now surrounded by a group of young people, individuals with notable tattoos and eyewear, denim, and leather. The gallery was thrumming with an aura of Portland cool—a success for Santino. There was a good chance she wouldn't get much of his time tonight.

But as she turned toward the rear of the gallery, she spotted Claudia Finley standing in front of Lars Olsen's quartet of paintings. Here was a new source of information.

Though she'd have to work to get Claudia to warm up to her, this was a prime chance. She had to snap it up. *Be direct, be friendly, talk about her son,* she told herself as she strolled over to join Claudia.

"Where's Henry tonight?" Alice posed the question in a pleasant tone, but it struck a nerve.

Claudia's spine straightened and she reared back, like a cat preparing to strike. "He's taking a night off."

"Well deserved. He's a hard worker."

"He is." Claudia stared a moment, eyes searching behind the fake smile. "And how do you know him?"

"We met on Dragonberry Lane. The day of the press conference. I helped him tend to that bee sting."

"Oh, yes, he mentioned that an older . . . a kind woman helped him that day."

"I'm Alice Pepper." *The old lady.* Alice would have extended her hand, but it seemed rude to foist it upon on a woman who kept her gloved hands tucked away in the loose pockets of her dress. Most likely she was a germaphobe.

Claudia introduced herself, but she didn't seem to see Alice; it was as if the younger woman's spirit had left the room.

"That was a nasty welt on his arm." Alice tried to engage her. "I hope he didn't prove to be allergic."

"He's not, but I thank you. That was a hard day for him."

"Yes, I heard Lars had pushed his assistants to work through the previous night. He was quite a taskmaster."

Claudia gave a quick smile. Polite but not interested. "I'm sorry, did you say you were a friend of Lars?"

"No, but I was his librarian. Head of the West Hazel branch."

"How nice." Again, Claudia kept looking toward the back of the room.

What was back there? Alice scanned the people milling past the four paintings by Lars Olsen. Those paintings—Claudia seemed fixated on them.

Alice pressed on. "So Henry tells me you've known Lars for decades." A lie, but Claudia wouldn't know that. "Did you go to art school together?"

Squinting, Claudia gave Alice a second look. "Actually, we did. I'm sorry, what did you say your name was?"

"Alice Pepper. So, are you an artist, too?"

"I went on to pursue a different career, but Lars and I had some memorable years together."

"Did you continue your modeling? I know you had some success with it in art school."

"Modeling..." Claudia pressed one black hand to her chest. "I can't believe Henry told you that. No, my modeling career ended in art school."

After Lars tortured and injured you? Alice had to pinch her lips together to keep from asking the probing question.

"I'm a nurse now," Claudia said. "Well, I was back in Connecticut. I guess I'm taking a hiatus here."

"During Henry's gap year." Alice nodded.

"That was the plan till... well. Now that Henry's mentor is gone, we're scrambling for a new plan."

"Heading back to Connecticut?"

"You sure do have a lot of questions, Alice." Claudia adjusted the coat in her left arm, all the while assessing Alice.

I'm not a danger, Alice wanted to say. If anything, she'd be the person to champion the comeback of an abused woman and her kind, polite son. "If you think I have a lot of questions for you, talk to Santino. But I was just curious about Connecticut. I'm from back east, too. Born and raised in Queens, New York."

"Henry used to love going to Manhattan on the train." Claudia softened.

"I have an aunt in Connecticut. She lives in a lovely town with an adorable Main Street. A gazebo in the town square . . ." Alice was thinking of a TV show the twins used to watch.

"Connecticut was our fallback plan at first, but we've reconsidered. Looks like we'll be staying here for the time being."

Alice asked about their accommodations, and Claudia described their bed-and-breakfast in downtown West Hazel. "Old and charming and close to everything, but I think the real relic there is the landlady, Posie Underwood. She's a dear thing, always trying to serve us tea."

"I know the place. Posie is a regular patron at the library." Legal name Patricia, mid-eighties, Alice knew. Certain things just stuck in the memory banks.

"I'm going to mingle some more," Claudia said, gloved fingers touching Alice's wrist lightly. "Nice to meet you, Alice."

"I'm sure I'll see you around West Hazel, Claudia." Alice smiled, then caught her attention once again. "There's just one thing, a difficult subject. Since you knew Lars, I'm wondering if you have any insight into who might have had reason to take his life."

"That's a heavy one." Claudia looked queasy for a second. "Honestly, when I first heard about it, I figured it was the wife. She supposedly found him, right? Maybe they argued, she had enough, she killed him."

"Maybe," Alice said, though the theory had holes. There'd been barely enough time for an argument from the time Michelle had been dropped off, let alone the physical struggle that had caused the mess in the room. Add to that the speeding car escaping down the lane, information that hadn't been released to the general public. "People who know Michelle well don't believe she killed Lars."

"What do I know?" Claudia lifted a gloved hand to the ceiling and looked up, as if the answer were about to descend upon them. "You know, I knew Lars like, twenty years ago, and he pissed a lot of people off back then. I can only imagine the damage he did here in Oregon over the past few years." She gestured to patrons milling in front of the nearby paintings. "Talk to a few people who knew him recently, and I'm sure you'll find a handful of discontents with motive."

Alice watched as Claudia gave a nod and turned away.

Turning to Lars's paintings, Alice wondered just how large the field of suspects might be. Could Lars have ticked off everyone in this room? The two young women who walked arm in arm and leaned close to talk quietly when they paused before each painting? The handful of schoolteachers who glided through the gallery in a small wobbly cloud? The couples. The business types. The bubbly women who enjoyed laughing.

Alice turned to the source of the laughter and smiled. That laughing group was hers, Violet and Taylor, back from the other gallery tour.

"Gran, there's something down the block you need to

see!" They had come upon an outdoor sculpture display that Taylor found ingenious. "It's after eight. Come see it before they close." Nine o'clock was the end of the First Thursday showings.

Violet fetched Ruby and their group headed out into the cool air, passing through the spots of light and shadow that mottled the damp pavement. The conversation was giddy, as Taylor expressed her love for a snail made out of an old electric fan. Skeptical, Alice remained silent until they came upon the sculpture garden, a small courtyard decorated with animals and flowers made of old appliances, kitchen utensils, and stained glass. The exhibit lighting made the mirrored glass neck of the snail sparkle, even as it caught the stained glass of tall flowers and the metal of their kitchen spoon petals.

"Delightful!" Alice agreed. The artist had used dozens of common household items—scissors, colanders, whisks, tire rims, doorknobs—to create the whimsical garden. "I need to get more information on the artist," she said, heading into the gallery. The whole crew followed her inside, where they were warmly received by two gallery attendants.

"We were just about to close up," said a petite young woman wearing a red apron. "But I've got some bags of popcorn left. And anyone want a little more wine?"

While the others gathered around the snack table, Alice talked with Jason, one of the gallery attendants, about the garden sculptures.

"Aw, man, you just missed the artist," Jason said. "But here's her card, Sparrow Lightfoot."

Alice told him that there was an odd space outside the windows of the library basement. "A cement drainage area. It's unsightly now, and we're trying to come up with a way to transform it."

"I'm sure Sparrow would love to hear from you." As they were talking the door opened and closed a few times, and a few other late stragglers entered the gallery. Jason excused himself to go talk with a newcomer, and Taylor came over to Alice holding out a folded piece of paper.

"A message for you."

"For me? From . . . ?"

Taylor shrugged. "Santino. I peeked."

Alice read the message:

> Sorry to put you off. If you have more questions, meet me at the gallery after closing. Back door.
> Yours, Santino

"Well, that's good." Alice shot a look at Taylor. "Where did you get this?"

"One of the Coyote Gallery staff brought it over. Someone heard us say we were coming here, and the kid was told to give it to a tall woman named Alice who looks like a female George Washington. Isn't that a riot?"

"Really?" Alice touched her hair, which she'd bothered to curl into ringlets that evening for the special occasion. "I've been called worse, though I wouldn't want that description to catch on."

"Well, it worked. He found you."

"Mmm." Alice reserved further comment as she shoved the note in a pocket. "All right, I'm going to head back over there. Do you gals want to stay here?"

"We're coming with you," Violet said with a slightly tipsy wave. "Everyone's closing up."

They headed back down the block, still buoyed by the excitement of the evening. In the midst of a terrible murder, it occurred to Alice that art had the ability to lift spirits, and she appreciated that her friends and family were open to new experiences.

The Coyote Gallery was dark, but that was no surprise, considering it was after nine. Alice stood back to assess the building, then saw that the back door had to be on the right, at the end of the little alleyway between the gallery and the bar next door.

"This way!" She motioned the group to follow past the gallery windows, then hooked left into the walkway. Not a true alley as it wasn't wide enough for a car.

Also not a very hospitable entrance; the door was covered by a rusty steel gate, and two large plastic garbage bins stood like sentinels beside the door. Still... he'd directed her to the back door.

"Let's see if Santino is true to his word," Alice said, reaching through the brown bars to knock on the door.

Violet moved close and wagged one finger with a little smile. "Honey, you've got to knock with authority. Like you mean business." She pounded away, her small white fist creating a decent racket.

"That should get his attention," Ruby said from a few paces down the path.

"It's hard to ignore a vice principal," Violet said, knocking again.

But no one was answering.

"It's dead in there." Alice knocked again, shaking her head. "I think everyone's gone."

She was knocking again when she heard the scrape and creak of a metal door opening. But the gallery door hadn't moved.

"What was that?" She turned and saw that the back door of the building across the walkway had been opened. "Hi," she said, presuming the person might help.

Instead, the dark nose of a pistol jutted out through the opening.

A gun?

Yes.

And it was pointed at them.

Chapter Thirty-seven

"Get down!" Alice yelled, pulling Violet away from the door and yanking her down against the wall.

There was a scramble of shoes on the pavement as someone screamed. Ruby?

Alice lost sight of the weapon as she and Violet landed hard on the cement, the brick wall at their backs. The trash cans grumbled as they were pushed aside. The fabric of Alice's jacket snagged against the brick as she hunched against the wall.

Alice looked up in time to see the flash as a loud crack split the air. A shot fired.

She sucked in a breath, still as a stone, despite her racing heart. She wasn't hurt. But Violet?

"You okay?" she whispered, squeezing Violet's arm, still in her grasp.

"Yes," Violet said quickly, unmoving. Watching.

Staring up at the gun, still there in the crack of the doorway.

And then, the loud pop of another shot. Alice flinched at the noise of the blast, amplified by the tight alley. This time, she saw that the shooter lifted the gun, aiming up toward the roof.

Her ears were still ringing as the pistol was retracted. The door closed.

"Everyone okay?" Alice called, springing onto her feet faster than she'd thought possible at her age.

"We're good." Taylor was helping Ruby to her feet.

"Nothing says the night is over like a couple of gunshots," Ruby said.

Alice turned back to her sister, who was still on the ground, fumbling with her phone. "Violet, honey, do you need a hand up?"

"I'm calling nine-one-one. That was unacceptable behavior."

"Damn tooting," Ruby agreed. "What was that about?"

As the sound of sirens flared in the distance, Alice wiped cinders from her bottom and tried to fit the pieces together. She'd gotten so much information at the show. But then, the dark gallery. The odd note. Gunshots into the sky. "I think someone is trying to scare me off."

"From what? Art galleries?" Taylor demanded as sirens grew louder.

Alice folded her arms and looked toward the beam of red light sweeping the street at the end of the alley. "They want me to stop digging into Lars Olsen's murder."

"It was a revolver. I could see the rotating cylinder," Taylor told the officer, a middle-aged man with a shiny bald head and a warm smile.

"You mean the little fat round part?" Ruby asked.

Taylor nodded. "Definitely not a semi-auto or a derringer."

"How do you know these things?" Alice asked.

"My friend Brandon took me out shooting a few times. His father has a gun collection. You just learn stuff when you're around it."

"Thank God I didn't know about this." Alice didn't own a gun, and she advocated gun safety. "More sleepless nights."

"We practiced safe protocol." Taylor shook her head. "I'm not an idiot."

"Okay, so we have identified a black pistol that was shot in the air, twice." Sergeant Bristol had a trace of a British accent that gave an official-sounding ring to the information he was jotting down.

Within an hour, the four cops from the Portland Police had pulled together the narrative of the shooting. They had contacted Coyote, who expressed alarm that the women had been in danger. He told them the gallery had been closed and locked by 9:05. He was at a restaurant on the Eastside with several friends, including Santino, who demanded that he speak to Alice.

"Alice, my dear, I'm devastated that someone tried to hurt you. Tell me you're okay, and your beautiful sister Violet."

"We're okay," Alice assured him. Santino insisted he knew nothing about the note. He had the dinner commitment, and couldn't have stuck around, anyway.

Two officers had gone into Mackie's, the bar next door, to ask about the gunshots and any suspicious patrons who might have been carrying a weapon. Two patrons seated in the back reported hearing the pops, but assumed it was firecrackers. The bar had enough of a crowd that night that someone trying to slip through to the front door could escape notice. The bartender complained that the back door had to remain unlocked—fire code. Sometimes patrons slipped out that way for a smoke. Or slipped out on their tab. He couldn't be everywhere at once.

"Unable to identify suspected shooter in the pub," Sgt. Bristol said succinctly as he added the information to his report.

"Aren't you going to dust the door of the bar for fingerprints?" Ruby asked.

Bristol shrugged. "Unlikely anything will come of that, with the sort of traffic they get through that joint. Besides, our crime here is illegal discharge of a firearm. Maybe, it could be pushed to attempted assault. Either way, we're not going to shake down the city to find our suspect tonight."

A special unit was called in for assistance in getting on the roof of the single-story gallery. Their search uncovered one bullet that had taken a chunk out of the brick chimney but remained intact. Alice felt vindicated, somehow, that the bullets had been real. Officer Bristol showed them a photo of the bullet, next to a placard to identify it.

"Looks like a nine millimeter," Bristol said. "That's the most common revolver. But then again, you probably know that, don't you, young Taylor?"

Taylor flipped her hair over one shoulder with casual confidence. "I'm not a buff, or anything, but yeah, I know."

"Here's what I think." Bristol tucked a thumb in the yoke of his bulletproof vest. "I think someone pulled a really rotten prank on you ladies. Very traumatic, being in a shooting. But it seems clear the shooter wasn't aiming for you. Not even close."

"Thank goodness we have strong hearts," Alice said. "It was a vicious prank. You'll let us know if you manage to identify the culprit?"

"Absolutely." Bristol tapped his clipboard. "I've got all your contact information. And we have one bullet, if you ever find the gun to match."

A frightening prospect, Alice thought as she led the way back to her car for a subdued trip home.

Chapter Thirty-eight

The car ride home was quiet as the women fell into thought, chatted about the night's exhibits, or dozed off.

Alice didn't sleep, of course, but kept her eyes on the road, a shiny black slick of water in the gathering rain. Twenty minutes to West Hazel, and she'd go straight to bed. A good night's sleep would help her sort things through.

At home everyone said good night and headed off to bed. Alice changed into long pajamas and dug her slippers out from deep in the closet. The barefoot days of summer were over, and at the moment her toes felt a little icy. She sat in the puffy leather chair by the window, cracked open her book, and read the same line a few times without comprehending.

When she closed her eyes, she heard the gunshots.

When she tried to think of something else, she felt a tug of worry over Lauren. Where had she gone? Would she change her mind about their meeting?

And when she took a deep breath and tried to move beyond anxiety over her daughter, she was back on Lars. Murdered. By whom?

Too much traffic in the head.

She headed downstairs for some herbal tea and a bit of

puzzling to distract her tired brain. She was halfway down the stairs when she heard the voices. Michelle sat at the kitchen counter with a steaming mug of tea. Ruby, Taylor, and Violet sat in the puzzle nook, jigsaw pieces in hand.

"You couldn't sleep either?" Violet asked.

"What took you so long?" Ruby quipped without looking up from the puzzle.

"Tonight, I'm only going to work with blue pieces," Taylor announced. "Blue is a calming color. Turquoise, teal, navy, royal blue—but not purple."

"Don't forget cerulean and electric blue," Alice called. She plugged in the electric teapot, picked out a bag of Sleepytime tea, and then leaned over the counter to face Michelle. "You okay, honey?"

"Much better, thank you. I've been texting with my aunties in Taipei—it's tomorrow afternoon there. And I want to thank you. Your friend Stone has been a huge help. Already he has found a church that will host Lars's funeral, and a funeral director who is handling every little detail." She lifted the warm mug under her chin. "Stone is quite a gem. He's going to help with Dragonberry, too. The crime scene has been dismantled, so the police will allow me to return." She looked down into her tea. "Stone is sending a cleanup crew in the morning. The house needs work, so much to sort through, but I can't bear to go back. Not just yet."

"It might be best to stay away for now." Alice touched Michelle's wrist gently. "You're welcome to stay here."

"I'm grateful to have a place to stay." Michelle's gaze went to the women at the puzzle table. "You have good women here. A little odd, but good and kind."

Alice chuckled as she poured hot water in a mug to steep. "Our lonely hearts puzzle club."

"Is it a club?" Michelle nodded. "I could teach you ladies mahjong."

"Not a club, but I've wanted to learn that game for the longest time!" Alice kept signing up for the mahjong group at the senior center, every Friday, but there was always something that kept her from attending. "Please, stay here as long as you like. One of the reasons I fought to hold on to this house was to have a place for friends and family. My granddaughters were in and out over the last decade or so. It was important for them to have a place to call home."

"I appreciate the space... and the privacy." Michelle pursed her lips to one side. "You were right about grief. I've had some good cries in the last few days." She shook her head. "Lars was a lot to deal with, but he did have some good qualities. We had some happy years together. I had given up on him, but it hurts to know how his life ended."

Alice nodded sympathetically. "It's hard." She straightened, pushing away from the counter. "Come sit in the puzzle nook with us. There were some interesting developments tonight that might lead us closer to finding Lars's killer. If you're ready to hear this stuff."

"I am ready to engage." Michelle rose, gripping her cup of tea. "My time as the suffering widow is over. I want to uncover Lars's killer and set things right with the estate. I even sat for an hour-long discussion with the police tonight."

"Really?" Taylor's mouth opened wide. "The cops came here?"

Michelle nodded. "They said people often remember important details of an incident after the shock wears off."

"And did you have sharper recall?" Ruby asked.

"I told them what I remember. I hope it helps."

"A busy night for all," Alice said.

"We told her about the shooter," Ruby called from the nook. "Michelle said we did everything right. Defensive moves and all that."

"You can't win against a gun. You must have been so frightened," Michelle told Alice.

"Petrified."

"I hope that dangerous encounter didn't have anything to do with my Lars. I don't want to put you and the other ladies in any danger."

It's definitely related to Lars, Alice thought, but she didn't want to further amp up Michelle's anxiety. "Come join us. This is a fun puzzle with lots of color."

"I'm not a puzzle person. It makes me too nervous to worry about finding the right piece. But I want to hear about the mystery you're piecing together." Michelle followed Alice over to the nook, but she took a seat on the built-in bench away from the table.

"And it might help to hear your insights on these people." Alice brought her cup of tea and squeezed in at the puzzle table.

"All right, ladies"—Alice put her mug down on the table—"tell me what you think about our friend with the gun."

"It could have been some random bozo," Violet said. "Sergeant Bristol said the police encounter that sort of thing a lot."

"I don't think Bristol said 'bozo,' " Taylor mused.

"Well, one thing we know is that it wasn't Santino or Coyote," Ruby pointed out. "They were both out to dinner with witnesses."

"Although I see Coyote Jones as the sort of man who might pay a gunman to scare us off," Alice said. "In the same way he might have hired someone to kill Lars. He has the resources to pay someone to do his dirty work. The man is surrounded by support staff. His driver, his personal trainer, chef... Lars owed him money, and he could bank on the value of Lars's work going up after his death. Money is a big motivator."

"Yes, indeed," Violet said. "Money, fear, and love drive most plots."

"And we know that Coyote grew up in a poor town, a rough and tumble childhood. He's got the edge to do away with a man to get a leg up in the world."

"Alice!" Ruby sat back against the banquette and slapped her hands to her heart. "You are ruining a potentially hot romance for me!"

"Sorry, but I have to speak the truth." Alice folded her arms. "Don't you see him as capable of pulling this thing off?"

"Maybe I do," Ruby admitted. "Ticks me off, but you've got his profile nailed."

"I'm not so sure," Michelle said. "I've known Coyote for a few years now. He likes to spend money, that's true, but deep inside, I think he has a good moral compass. His own North Star."

"That matters," Alice said. Michelle's opinion was important, especially since she couldn't get an instant gauge on a person's moral character. "Would you say that Coyote and Lars were friends?"

Michelle was thoughtful for a moment, then pressed her eyes closed for a second. "Lars didn't have friends. Not since his art college days. But Coyote was good to him. He was the only dealer in Portland who would take Lars on when we moved here. And when sales dipped, he loaned Lars money to help buy our house."

Were those actions acts of kindness or business transactions? Alice didn't know enough about the art world to get a clear picture.

"It sounds like some of that loan was paid back last night," Violet said. "Coyote had four of Lars's paintings in his possession, and he sold them with a huge markup."

"He wants to talk to you about getting access to more of Lars's art," Ruby said. "He says there's a huge profit to be made if you move quickly."

"Mmm, I'm not surprised." Michelle raked back her shiny dark hair with one hand. "Trends in the art world can be like tornados; you have to bob and weave quickly. But the work involved..." She pressed a palm to her cheek. "His paintings will need to be inventoried and catalogued. Lars was not a good record keeper. And I'll need to delve into his financial records. We kept that part of our lives separate."

"I could help organize his paintings," Taylor offered. "I can be pretty efficient, and I'd be interested in seeing his art."

"Thank you, Taylor." Michelle came over to the table and stood behind Taylor. "I'll probably take you up on that. But this business with Coyote Jones could topple everything. I have to know if he can be trusted. He's Lars's dealer. If he tried to kill him..."

"It's one theory," Alice said. "But I can probe a bit more. The best test of a person's character is the people they surround themselves with."

"I can probe, too." Michelle smiled. "I'm not afraid to ask the hard questions."

Alice swallowed a sip of tea, nodding. "That may come in handy. Right now we have a handful of suspects, and so far I've been unable to winnow them down."

"Who else do you have a theory about?" Michelle asked.

"There's Rosie. She was with Lars that night, and her alibi doesn't really cover her." Alice explained how they had seen the young woman at the gallery, how Rosie didn't like Alice, how she had peeled off. "She could have returned with a gun to scare us off."

"That could have been Rosie," Taylor agreed. "But when she left us, she was just heading over to a gallery on the Eastside. And the big point with her is, why would she kill Lars? She wanted to run away with him. And now she seems lost without him."

"No, I don't see Rosie killing him," Michelle agreed. "She's a little parasite who gloms on and stays attached and is happy for the ride."

Alice could visualize the image.

"And are there more?" Michelle pressed. "More people you know that might be the killer?"

"A woman named Claudia Finley," Alice said, handing Taylor two puzzle pieces with blue streaks. "The mother of Henry, the new art assistant? It seems that she was friends with Lars back in art school, and it didn't end well. It's possible she was the woman he was charged with kidnapping and assaulting." She told them how Santino had prompted Claudia to admit that she had killed Lars.

Violet looked up, holding a puzzle piece aloft. "And what was her answer?"

"That she wished she had."

Taylor whistled through her teeth. "That's a hot scoop."

"I don't know this woman," Michelle said, "but Henry is a polite boy, no problem."

"He and his mother came here from Connecticut to work with Lars," Alice said. "She seems to be in her forties, reddish blond. Both times I saw her, she was wearing gloves. I guess it's a look. Henry seemed less than thrilled, but Claudia is now intent on revenge against Lars. Maybe some sort of lawsuit against the estate?"

Michelle dismissed the matter with a quick wave of one hand. "She can talk to my lawyer. With Lars's prickly personality, I anticipate there will be claims filed against him. Those things don't worry me. I figure his estate will need to rectify the mistakes he made in life."

"Michelle, you sound like a wise sage," Violet said. "But I have an eight o'clock meeting, and I don't want to show up with jigsaw marks on my cheek."

"I have work, too." Alice rose, slowed by a surge of weariness. She would be able to sleep now. "We'll circle back to our suspects tomorrow with a plan."

"Tomorrow," Michelle agreed as everyone headed off to their rooms, tired but calmer now.

Chapter Thirty-nine

"It's hideous." Julia winced, holding her hands up to shield her eyes from the sight.

"It's ugly, all right," Alice agreed.

They were glaring at the mottled, discolored concrete wall that started below the windows and jutted fifteen feet above the glass of the subterranean children's section of the library. Over coffee Friday morning Alice had shown Julia some of Sparrow's art on her Web site with the intention of sprucing up the pit, and Julia had sprung to action, traipsing downstairs to check out the problem spot.

Behind them, the children's section chirped with activity. Caretakers and toddlers arrived for story time. Little ones were parked on the carpet of the story theater in the corner of the room, while moms and dads and grammies caught up on the latest gab. A mom helped her children select books in the picture book area. A little boy chased his sister through the aisles.

Viewing the activity as a sign of a healthy library, Alice tuned it out to focus on the new project.

"The question is," Alice said, staring at the shadowed box of a space adorned with a smashed juice box and a furring of moss, "how much would an art installation cost, and can we get the library council to approve the expense? The board members tend to favor book acquisitions and community programs over facility improvements."

"We'll never know if we don't ask," Julia said, reaching up to close the heavy blue velvet curtains that normally shielded patrons down on this level from the depressing sight of the drainage and airflow pit. "Let's start with the artist, since you were so jazzed by her creations. Sparrow . . . I *love* that name. I'll reach out to her about availability and pricing. Maybe she can come check out our pit. In the meantime, we can send an e-mail to the members of the library council, describing our excitement over the possibilities and inviting the members to check out the artist's sculpture garden." Julia pushed her glasses up on her nose as she stared off. "Gee, I hope her show in the Pearl is open for a few more weeks. I'll check."

"That's a marvelous plan," Alice said. "Let's include the Friends in the scheme." The Friends of the Library could be quite helpful on budding projects. "I've seen them make miracles happen."

"Done, done, and done," Julia said. One of the many reasons Julia was indispensable to the library and to Alice: she was a doer.

As Alice was thanking her associate, she saw a familiar face bobbing down the stairs. Long dark hair falling over the shoulders of a brown leather jacket, funky checkered black-and-white-frame glasses over a toothy grimace.

The shark girl, Rosie. It suddenly occurred to Alice that the shark look might have been the result of an orthodontic problem. Bad on her to assume.

But what was Rosie doing here?

Alice was about to find out, as the young woman had spotted her and was heading her way.

"Taylor told me I'd find you here," Rosie said. "I hope it's okay. Do you have a minute to talk?"

"Of course. Let's go upstairs." Leading the way, Alice wondered what had caused the sudden shift in dynamic. Today, Rosie wanted to talk to her. She needed something from Alice. Somehow, Alice had the upper hand. She brought Rosie into her small office but left the door open. Not that she thought the girl was going to pull out a butcher knife, but Alice liked the transparency of the open door, the fact that anyone could walk in at any time.

"I need your help." Rosie removed the checkered glasses and folded them up. "I have to get my stuff from Dragonberry Lane, but the police say I need Michelle Chong's permission."

Alice nodded. "That would make sense. She's the owner of the home."

"She'll never let me in." Sudden tears formed in Rosie's eyes. "Why should she? I'm the other woman. Probably an embarrassment. But I need my things. Most of my clothes are there, and I can't afford to buy new. This jacket and dress are borrowed. All my paints, my art supplies, canvases..." She pressed a fist to her mouth and nose, as if that would stem the tears. "I can't even tell you how much those materials cost."

"That does sound like a dilemma." Alice handed the young woman a box of tissues and gave her a moment to catch her breath. "I can ask Michelle about your clothes. I see no reason why she wouldn't release your possessions." In fact, Alice planned to leave work in the early afternoon to accompany Michelle for a visit at the Coyote Gallery. Michelle wanted an update on the contract between Lars and Coyote, and Alice wanted to return to the scene of the shooting in search of answers.

Rosie pressed a tissue to her nose and sniffed. "And I need my paintings, too."

"Your paintings?"

"The work I did under his guidance. It's the whole purpose of assisting an artist—to make your own work better. There are seven paintings that I did. A few of them got stuck in Lars's collection when some art critic said he liked the style, but they're mine, and I need them. They're probably worth a lot now, and I'm so broke. But I might be able to sell a few of them and get out of this hole."

A financial hole—or the emotional black hole of a woman who'd lost her lover? Alice wasn't sure, but this was no time to probe the vulnerable young artist. "I'm so sorry you're going through this. The issue of your paintings is beyond my scope of knowledge, but I'll talk to Michelle."

"Thanks." Rosie dried her eyes, then threw the balled-up tissues in the bin. "All I'm asking for is what's mine." She thumped a fist against her chest, a warrior's determination shining in her eyes.

"I understand." Alice walked Rosie to the door. "I know Taylor has your info. I'll be in touch after I speak with Michelle."

"Soon, right?"

Alice held back a sigh. "Yes, sometime today."

Watching Rosie go, Alice wondered if she was telling the truth about the ownership of those paintings—artwork that now had substantial value.

She had to appreciate Rosie's genuine qualities. Young and fierce and heartbroken and broke. Alice couldn't imagine going through the trauma Rosie had experienced at her young age. She thought of Lauren and knew that there'd probably been strangers who'd helped her girl along the way. Likewise, Alice wanted to help Rosie. She felt for her, she really did.

But...

The young woman had the ability to turn tears on and off like a faucet, and she was quick to play the victim card. There was something that kept Alice from trusting her. Some missing puzzle piece that kept Alice from seeing the whole picture clearly.

Best to proceed with caution.

Chapter Forty

"We're early," Michelle said, peering through the glass of the gallery, "which is good. I want to get a look at the recent sales that belonged to Lars. I feel like I need to rein in control of his business. Those paintings that Rosie wants are another example. Her request may be legitimate; I just don't know what I'm dealing with yet."

"You'll sort it out," Alice said, holding the door open for her. "I'm sure there's a lot of work ahead, but Stone will help you get organized."

Inside, an attendant greeted them and offered help. They learned that Coyote hadn't arrived yet. The gallery wasn't officially open yet, but they were free to browse. The gallery was empty but for two men who were walking from one painting to another. Michelle marched straight to the Lars Olsen paintings on the back wall. Alice gave her a minute with them before joining her.

"Unremarkable. This is not Lars's best work." Michelle leaned closer to read the placard beside one painting after another. "All of these sold? I can't believe the prices. Fifty thousand dollars for four paintings? Lars wasn't even getting half that."

"His estate is quite valuable since his death," Alice said.

"Poor Lars. This is the sort of success he wanted. Too late." Michelle turned away from the back wall. "I know he would want me to sell his work now. Build interest. But I have my own successful business. It's all bittersweet, as I don't need his money. I must sound so entitled. A first-world problem."

"And yet, still a problem," Alice said. "Maybe you'll find a charity that seems appropriate."

"Maybe." She sighed. "Well, since we're here, we might as well soak up Santino's art. He was always the greater talent of the two rivals."

Someone entered the gallery, and Alice looked over, assuming it was Coyote. Instead, Santino strode across the floor dressed in all black but for a long duster made of a patchwork of brightly hued materials. Ruby, sapphire, gold, turquoise, purple . . . a coat of many colors that flounced gracefully around his knees as he walked.

Michelle caught sight of him and smiled. Alice was surprised to see that something akin to joy reached her eyes. "Don't you look splendid."

Santino looked up, wide-eyed with shock. "My angel, Michelle!" He swept across the room and took her hands, much in the way he had greeted Claudia. "I went searching for you when you were lost, but I always knew you were fine. A strong warrior woman."

This was the drama of Santino; as Violet had said, he fell into the passion of a moment.

"I was never lost," Michelle said, "just hiding for a time."

"But here you are now! It's been too long," he said. "I had hoped to see you while I was in town for the shows, and then, the terrible business with Lars. I'm so sorry, but I won't lie. You were always too good for him."

"And you were always a charmer," Michelle said as he kissed her hand. "I was just telling Alice, here, that Lars was jealous of your talent."

"He was wise to recognize my superior gifts." He flashed a sly smile and gave Alice a nod. "Good to see you again, especially after your brush with death. Have you returned to buy a painting?"

"I'd love to, but I'm afraid your art is beyond the budget of a librarian. I do see a lot of red dots, though. Last night was a success?"

"A very nice attendance. It went well, but for your unfortunate assault."

Alice waved it off. "It was nothing." Not true, but she wasn't here to earn sympathy. "We're actually meeting with Coyote. Before he gets here, I hope you don't mind my asking if you think he's dealt fairly with you through the duration of this show."

"Coyote? He's more than fair, in this show and all the others. For me, his commission is lower than the standard." He looked around, adding, "And there've been times, like back when Lars tried to blackball me, and Coyote was the only gallery willing to give me a show. Coyote is the rare dealer who supports artists. Don't you agree, Michelle? You must have seen how he boosted Lars's career, as well."

"I know he helped Lars out from time to time, but I wasn't involved in Lars's business transactions. We tried to keep our work lives separate. Well, except for the paints and brushes and canvases littering our dining room. Lars wanted the Dragonberry house so that he could set up a studio in the barn, but somehow it all crept into our home."

Alice detected a certain fondness in Michelle's voice as she shared the memory, and it reminded her how grief sometimes came in waves. Bits and pieces that washed ashore, and then receded beyond our reach.

"So now I'll be taking a crash course in the art business," Michelle said. "But enough sadness. I'm here at a spectacular show standing with the artist himself. Do you have a moment to show me your work?"

"It would be my pleasure." Santino extended his arm and Michelle attached herself to the graceful man in the gem-tone coat. "Let me show you my latest work, inspired by diamond drops of rain on a blade of grass."

As the two friends glided to a group of paintings, Alice went to the front of the gallery and stepped outside. The pub next door was open, its RUSTY NAIL sign lit. Not her sort of joint, but she wanted to ask around about the shooting. She was about to head over when Coyote's hulking black SUV pulled up.

Alice waited in front of the gallery as the driver hopped out and opened the back door. Coyote emerged, slowly but gracefully for a man of his stature. He was dressed in black today, with a buttery leather blazer and a black Stetson.

"Cowboy Coyote?" Alice called as he crossed the pavement.

He grinned. "A fantasy of mine, though I've never been on a horse." He nodded toward the building. "Is Michelle inside?" When she nodded, he thanked her for arranging the meeting.

"She wanted to see you," Alice said.

"You joining us?"

"I'm going to do some errands."

"Seriously?" He gave her a hard look. "You're going to wander alone after what happened last night?" He pointed a thumb at the gallery. "You know, you pay top dollar for Pearl District real estate. You establish a nice business. But there's no guarantee that some thugs won't come along and hurt someone. Alice, please, come inside."

He had a point. "I won't go far." Though the shooting had been in the alley, a few yards away.

He tipped his hat back, considering. "I'm gonna worry."

"I'll be back in twenty minutes."

He handed her his card. "This time you call me directly if you need help. Anything."

She nodded and thanked him as he went inside.

Once the door closed, Alice turned to the street, glad to see the SUV still waiting at the curb. She went to the passenger side and waved to get the driver's attention.

"Kevin, right? I'm Alice Pepper, and I was hoping to ask you a few questions. Could I buy you a cup of coffee?"

Turned out that Kevin didn't feel comfortable grabbing a coffee while he was on the clock, but he was happy to talk in the car.

While Alice was not one to climb into a car with a stranger, this was Coyote Jones's driver. She felt at ease when he popped out of the vehicle to help Alice into the passenger seat. There, she found an otherworldly quiet behind the tinted glass.

"Do you want some heat? It was chilly this morning, right?" Kevin spoke quickly, offering climate control, water, a printed copy of the *New York Times*. Alice declined, though it was nice to be pampered. She understood why Coyote wanted Kevin around.

"So you drive him around?"

"Yeah, I drive him everywhere. But I'm more like a personal assistant. I maintain the vehicle, run his errands, fix things at his condo, stuff like that. I'm pretty handy."

She asked about other employees, and he mentioned that the boss's personal chef was Kevin's wife, Jenna. He also had a bookkeeper and secretary from back home, who'd relocated to Portland.

"And everyone came here willingly?" Alice asked.

Kevin laughed. "Yeah. When you grow up in a town like Goldwyn, you don't want to stay."

"Goldwyn, California. Sounds beautiful."

"It's not. It's an old mining town near the Nevada border. Some guy found gold in the 1800s, built a town around it. But it was all tapped out a hundred years later. Now, if you don't get out before you turn twenty-one, you'll be addicted or dead before you hit thirty."

"Oh. That's awful." He explained it in such a cavalier way. "You make it sound like a running joke."

"It's one of those things in life, you either laugh or cry about it." Kevin shrugged. "My wife and I, we try to stay positive. Glad to have survived. We got kids now, and we're hoping they're better off. We're trying our best."

"I can understand that." Staring out through the windshield, Alice thought of the decisions she'd made to keep Lauren safe over the years. As a parent, you tried to do your best. She turned to Kevin, trying to be tactful. "This will sound like a weird question, but I have to ask. Do you think there's any way your boss was involved in Lars Olsen's death?"

"Lars Olsen, the artist? It's not so strange; the police asked about him, too." He looked toward the gallery and shook his head. "Coyote wouldn't hurt anybody that way.

We ran with some tough guys when we were growing up, but even if some illegal stuff was going on, there was a moral code. You weren't out to kill anybody."

"But accidents happen. People argue, lose their temper..."

"Not Coyote. But anyway, the police backed off when they heard we were up in Seattle on Tuesday. I drove him up for some business meetings, and we stayed at a hotel up there for the night. He's thinking of opening a gallery up there, and I hope he does. Ever been up there? Elliott Bay? It's beautiful. I wouldn't mind moving up there."

An alibi. Alice should have known. She should have asked Madison, though her granddaughter couldn't always divulge details of an investigation.

But as Alice chatted on with Kevin, the truth about Coyote hit her hard.

She'd been wrong about him, thinking he was a ruthless entrepreneur, willing to hire someone to kill off a client or scare a bunch of curious women. Coyote Jones was a man in touch with his past, who had found a way to share his success with childhood friends. Much as Alice hated being wrong, she was humbled to admit her mistake and inspired by the true details of Coyote's character.

"I know Coyote might look like a big scary dude," said Kevin. "Sometimes he plays the part, black hat and all. But the guy has a heart of gold. Look at what he did. He got himself out of Dodge, built up a company, and then he went back and rescued a few more of us. That's a hero, in my eyes."

"A good man, and a good friend," Alice agreed. She thanked Kevin for his time, and waited a bit awkwardly as he rushed around the vehicle to open the door for her. When he offered to walk her to the door of the gallery, she wondered if she looked older than her years.

"No, thank you," she told him, smoothing down her buttonless blue cashmere cardigan and hitching her bag onto her shoulder. "I've got other plans." With the verve of a woman on a mission, she strode across the sidewalk and flung open the door of the Rusty Nail.

Time to belly up to the bar.

Chapter Forty-one

Alice stood in the doorway of the dark, sour-smelling pub and told herself not to freeze.

It was just a bar, mostly empty on a mediocre Friday afternoon.

You can do this.

She forced herself to take a step, then another. If only Ruby were here to take command of the place, chat with strangers, make this fun. Trying to penetrate the room on her own, Alice was reminded of the times when she'd cruised through strange bars searching for Lauren. Drinking had been part of Lauren's addiction, mostly a fallback when drugs had been scarce, and alcohol had been cheaper and readily available. A bar scene could be alienating when you were afraid of what you might find there.

But that's over, Alice reminded herself. *Lauren is doing well. Snap out of it!*

There was no music, but two televisions flashed from either end of the bar. The volume was cranked up on one, and a male voice espoused the benefits of a supplement powder for prolonged health. A man and woman sat at the table at the front of the room, by the single window, and another table was occupied with four men who had plates of food in front of them.

Three men sat spaced apart on stools at the bar. Where was the bartender? No one in sight.

She thought about sitting at the bar, and then changed her mind. She would go straight to the side door.

Go now. After a pause, her nerves responded and her legs began to move. She had passed through most of the room and was staring into the dark corridor when a voice called: "Restrooms are for patrons only."

She froze. Was that directed to her?

Yes. There was now a heavyset young man in an apron standing behind the bar. He was rinsing glasses and sliding them onto the overhead rack to drip dry.

"I'm not using the restroom. I just wanted to check the side door." She scanned the room, checking if anyone reacted to her mention of the door. It was possible that the bar had a few regular customers who might have noticed some of the commotion yesterday. No one flinched.

"Come here." The bartender motioned to her, not buying her excuse.

She hitched her bag onto her shoulder and went to the end of the bar, as far from the gray-glazed patron on the end who was staring blankly at one of the TVs. "Sorry to bother you, but I have a few questions. Were you working here last night, around nine, nine thirty?"

"Nope."

"Do you know who was working? Or maybe some of these patrons were here at that time?"

"I think Andrew was bartending last night. Yeah, Andrew. Are you a reporter or something?"

"I'm a librarian. But I'll be honest with you. I suppose

you heard about the shooting last night in the alley at your back door? I was one of the women under fire."

"No way?" The bartender's face came alive as he looked up for the first time. "If that's true, then you're a kickass librarian."

Coming from the bland bartender, Alice deemed it a huge compliment.

"Have a seat, Superwoman. I'm buying."

"You can call me Alice."

"What, you don't want to be a superhero?" He smiled. "I'm Glen. So what you drinking?"

It was early for a drink, but it seemed rude to refuse the gesture. "I'd love a tonic water with lime."

"You got it." He stepped away from the sink, wiped his hands, and reached for a clean glass.

She sat on the lumpy barstool, trying to appear comfortable. "Have you heard anything about the incident?"

"Just something from a text Andrew sent out. Sounds like the police were here for a while. Was it some gang retaliation?"

"I don't think so. Most of the women with me were my age." Alice leaned closer and added, "Sixtyish." She surveyed the bar again, but the space was dead. "I came back here hoping to find out more about the person using us for target practice. I was with three other women, but none of us have any idea about the shooter's identity."

Glen placed a tall glass in front of her. "Why would anyone here know who it was?"

"Because the shooter was here, in this pub." She extended her arm over the bar, her fingers pointing like a gun. "He reached one hand out through the slightly opened door and took two shots."

"Whoa. I didn't know that." He stepped to the side,

closer to the gray man. "Did you hear that, McGill? There was a gunman in here last night."

The man lifted his head, his hooded eyes glancing left at Alice. "I didn't see anything. Except the cops, when they came in, asking lots of questions."

"Too bad." Glen shrugged.

"I appreciate anything you can remember, Mr. McGill. Do the police come in here often?"

"We try to keep things copacetic here," Glen said.

"Do you get many patrons here from the gallery next door?"

"Sometimes. But a lot of times when they have a show, they throw in wine and appetizers. They don't need us."

Alice took a sip. "Refreshing," she said, thanking him. "My friends and I attended a show next door last night. That's what brought us to town. So I'm thinking it was someone from the gallery—or one of the places we visited—that shot at us." She took another sip, then added, "I just don't know what we did to tick them off."

"Did you know the artist that got killed this week?" asked Glen.

"Lars Olsen. I'd met him."

"He's been in here. In fact, he was sitting right here"— Glen tapped the bar with his fingertips—"the night he was murdered."

"Really? Did you tell the police?"

"No one asked, but it was definitely him," Glen insisted. "He stops in occasionally for a drink. That day it was earlier in the afternoon, three, four o'clock, and it was an ugly scene, with him arguing with his date."

"Those two were going at it," McGill added. "Snapping at each other like an old married couple."

"It wasn't pretty. She wasn't drinking, but he was downing whisky. Shots, I think."

"Bourbon neat," McGill corrected.

So Lars had visited the gallery that day? She recalled Coyote saying that Lars was there, that he brought his paintings in to agitate Santino. "Do you know who the woman was? What was she like?"

"Most times he came in alone, but that day, I remember she seemed to be younger than him. Brunette, I think, or was it a redhead?"

"A right fair lass," McGill said, sporting an accent that seemed honed for effect.

"Did she wear glasses?"

McGill shook his head. "Can't say I remember much more, except the bickering and the insolence of the artist. No one should treat a woman that way. And it's rude to destroy the sanctity of a pub with your dirty laundry."

Alice appreciated McGill's turn of phrase. "I wonder what they were arguing about."

"Money." Glen shrugged. "Typical, but pretty serious. Basically? She threatened to kill him if he didn't come through with some money."

"Told him if he didn't get her the money, he'd regret it."

"Did he take her seriously?" Alice asked.

"Hard to say. But I thought she was pretty scary, decked out in black like an angel of death."

So now McGill remembered that she wore black? Alice doubted the integrity of his recall. "How long did they stay?"

"Too long," McGill grumbled.

"First, the woman got upset. Told him off and dipped." Glen folded up a towel as he described helping Lars arrange a ride home. "The dude couldn't even call an Uber."

"Ah, but she had a car," McGill said. "I remember the jingling of keys."

"Really?" Glen buffed the edge of the bar with a towel. "I don't remember."

Alice stayed a few more minutes, trying to squeeze more details out of the men. A description of the woman? The topic of their argument? They tried to remember, but the drama of the event was the salient memory. "This has been helpful." Alice tipped Glen and bought McGill a drink. The fellas had earned it. She couldn't wait to talk to Madison.

Chapter Forty-two

On the drive to West Hazel, Alice was able to reach Madison on her cell. "You're on speaker," Alice said. "I need you to put your detective cap on for a minute. I'm in the car with Michelle Chong, heading back to West Hazel. We were at Coyote's downtown gallery and I got a hot scoop. Did you know that Lars Olsen was drinking in the bar next to the gallery, the Rusty Nail, the afternoon of his murder?"

"I don't think that's in the timeline. No, it's not. Though we have Lars at the gallery between two and three. He brought Coyote four paintings to rep."

"The salient point is that Lars came into the bar with a female companion, and after he started drinking, they argued bitterly. She was demanding money, threatening him. A public spectacle, apparently. The bartender Glen and a patron saw it all."

"Did they identify the woman?"

"No, but my money is on Rosie Suarez, who had moved her possessions into Dragonberry while Michelle was gone."

"But Rosie didn't mention the argument," Madison said.

"Exactly. Something to hide. But beyond the identity of

the woman, the bar argument shows that Lars was in turmoil that afternoon. Agitated and drinking heavily." It was an ego boost to be able to deliver a bit of evidence to the police, even if it might not prove to be important. They chatted about Rosie's account of that night, which already had inconsistencies. Madison suspected that Bedrosian would bring Rosie Suarez in for further questioning.

"Also, we've got some question about Coyote Jones," Alice said.

"I need to know if he's a good guy," Michelle added.

Alice explained that Michelle was starting to settle the estate, and there was a question whether she should continue using Coyote as an agent. "You know I had my suspicions about Coyote, but I've come around. Looks to me like the man's an American hero."

"He's looking good in our profile," Madison reported. "We've confirmed that he was in Seattle the night of Olsen's murder. People have good things to say about him. Personally? I think he's a trustworthy man."

"I had the same take on him." Michelle nodded. "Thank you, Madison."

"We're doing a taco night at the house," Alice said, "discussing some ways for Michelle to organize Lars's collection. Stone will be there. You're welcome to join us, honey."

"I'll try," Madison said before signing off.

At home, Michelle went downstairs to her suite and Alice went upstairs to change into joggers, thick socks, and a black T-shirt with a gray Oregon State zip-up hoodie over it. After splashing water on her face, she paused for a moment to brush her hair, trying to imagine how she would look with a silver tint. Would it be elegant, or crass as Christmas tinsel?

Bounding out of her room to head down to the kitchen, Alice encountered Violet in the hallway. Their en suites were the only two on the top floor, and they were ideally situated on opposite ends to maximize privacy.

"There you are." Violet seemed overjoyed to see Alice. She had changed into yoga pants and a long, cabled cotton sweater in a deep peacock blue. Even in casual clothes, she exuded a smooth, professional demeanor. "I was hoping to snag you for a private sister moment." Violet glanced around with fake caution, as if they were sophomores sneaking out of the house to meet boyfriends after midnight.

"And here we are." Alice loved her sister's sweetness; that certain unfiltered affection that Violet tried to channel only in appropriate moments. Scheduled, on task, and methodical—that was the public Violet.

"I want you to know that I know about Lauren." Violet frowned. "That sounds redundant, but I heard Lauren wants to mend ways with you, and honey, I'm thrilled for you. I know this is speaking to a need deep down in your heart." She thumped a fist to her chest a few times as she drew in a breath. Sweet, sentimental Violet. She was so corny; she could say "Aw shucks!" and get away with it. "I just had to say, I'm here for you. I support you! Anything you need, anything at all, just give a holler." She nodded toward her bedroom suite. "You know where to find me."

Alice blinked back the tears in her eyes. "Thank you." Alice spent so much time chasing answers for other people, she forgot that people who loved her were running alongside her. "That means a lot to me. And to be honest, I'm scared. What if I screw this up again? I could say the wrong thing and she'll be gone forever."

"What? You did nothing wrong in the first place." Violet swatted away the pesky notion with one hand. "Don't think, even for a minute, that any of this is your fault. But... oh, of course, you're feeling confusion, aren't you? I saw it in the cards. The Moon card covers your present state of mind. Yes, it all makes sense."

"You did a tarot card reading for me?" Alice didn't really go for magic and woo-woo, but she respected her sister's knowledge and intuition for those things, and more than once, Violet's tarot card readings had proved to be not simply accurate but also therapeutic.

"Yes. I did it in private, because I know you don't always want to partake, and the story of the cards is a story of motherhood. I did the three-card spread, past, present, and future, and as I said, the Moon came up in the present situation. The Moon represents confusion and the psychological aspects of parenting. This comes up when parents question whether they are doing right by their kiddos. Which is precisely the concern you just relayed to me." Violet let out a sigh and lifted her eyes to the heavens. "Time after time, the cards don't lie."

"I'm glad the cards feel my pain and confusion," Alice said. "And the past? How bad was that? All my mistakes?"

"Oh, no, the Six of Cups card came up for the past. You know cups represent emotions and matters of the heart, and the Six of Cups is a card of childhood innocence and nostalgia for the activities and traditions of youth. It's so clear that you and Jeff gave Lauren a wonderful foundation. You had wonderful rituals at home, cooking and baking. Puzzles and family game night. Jeff was an engaged father when she had a million questions a day, and you both supported her through her love of sports and... oh I could go on and on. You were a happy little family, as

Lauren showed in her drawings." Violet tilted her head and tapped her chin. "I confess, I recognized Lauren's art in that puzzle. Not right away, but when I gave it the old educator's professional analysis, it came to me. She was a happy child. The problems started later."

A sense of relief washed over Alice as she absorbed her sister's reassurance. She'd heard similar feedback from counselors before, but somehow, hearing it from Violet made it real.

They had been a happy family. Whatever happened later was not because she and Jeff hadn't cared. Not a result of their mistakes or choices.

Vindication was not a magical spell to eat away guilt, but it sure helped ease the weight.

"You're processing, I can tell," Violet said, putting her hands together in prayer position. "That's good. I don't want to overwhelm you. Should we leave it at that?"

"No." Alice waved it on. "Hit me, Cassandra." In Greek mythology, Apollo's high priestess Cassandra had the gift of prophecy, but the curse of not being believed.

"Very funny, Apollo," Violet quipped, in on the joke. "Well, it shouldn't be hard to grasp, because the card of your future is the Empress." She pressed a palm to her chest and smiled. "It's the ultimate card of motherhood, Alice. And a heavy hitter, being in the Major Arcana."

"Sort of like Major League Baseball?" Alice was a fan. She hoped to visit every major league stadium in the country.

"A card with significance, a nurturing mother, full of feminine creativity."

"Doesn't really sound like me."

"Oh, but you have it in you." Violet's smile was wry now. "I know you're worried, but relationships are complicated organisms with molecules and auras and souls we can't begin to understand. You just need to be present. Show up for that meeting and let Lauren know that you care. The past is gone, and a wonderful future shines ahead."

"Not sure I believe you on this one, Cassandra."

"You're a good mother, Alice," Violet said emphatically. "And right now the cards, my intuition, and the universe are telling me that Lauren has finally figured that out."

Alice hoped her sister was right.

Chapter Forty-three

Dinner was a casual affair. Alice was happy to chop and prep so that she could lay out bowls of taco fixings on the kitchen counter. Cheese, onion, beans, sour cream, tomatoes, cabbage, shredded chicken, avocado, salsa, and cilantro, and a cast-iron griddle for heating tortillas.

"We have to make our own?" Taylor lamented. "That's just like being at work." Though she threw a few flour tortillas on the fire and offered to toast them for Violet, Michelle, and Alice.

"How is work going?" Alice asked, having restrained herself for weeks. "Is your grandfather treating you right?"

"He's fine, but it gets monotonous in the kitchen. I've realized that I like cooking, a lot, but when you do it all day for strangers, it sucks out most of the fun."

"My experience, exactly," Alice said as she set half a dozen bottles of hot sauce on the counter. "After all the excitement and preparation of opening my own restaurant, there was a day when I realized that my joy screeched to a halt in the kitchen." If only she had figured it all out before she had poured her savings and energy into opening her own business.

"Yeah." Taylor's eyes were thoughtful as she flipped the tortillas. "It kinda sucks, but I'm sticking with it for now. But it'll be a nice break to take some time off to help catalog the collection."

Seems like a responsible move, Alice thought as she accepted a tortilla and sprinkled on cheese and onions.

As the women concocted tacos, Michelle recounted her meeting with Coyote Jones. "He's been getting inquiries from collectors and dealers around the world. Interest in Lars's work is high."

"I think the word he used was 'frantic,'" Alice said, having attended that part of the meeting.

"He thinks the collection will be worth millions," Michelle said quietly.

"And does that make you sad?" asked Violet.

"A little shocked, and sad that Lars isn't here to enjoy the money, his flash of fame."

As they were eating, Ruby came in from work, looking smart in a raspberry double-breasted blazer and matching skirt, and an A-line wig with shiny, jet-black hair.

"Good evening, ladies," Ruby said. "Is it the weekend yet?"

"I love that on you," Alice said. "Purple is your color. Grab a plate and join us."

"Looks delicious. Let me get out of this CEO suit and change into fun Ruby."

"Yay," Taylor said. "We love fun Ruby."

While Ruby was upstairs, Stone arrived with a six-pack of Modelo and news of progress for Michelle. "The funeral is set for next Friday, and we got the Dragonberry house cleaned up." He twisted open a beer. "I think I've earned this."

Michelle thanked him as Alice toasted a few more tortillas.

"Am I going to the funeral?" Taylor asked. "I didn't really know Lars."

"You're welcome to come," Michelle said. "It might be nice to have a few familiar faces there, as I don't expect anyone else to attend. He didn't have friends."

"I think we should all attend," Ruby said, returning in jeans and a peasant blouse with shiny gold threads woven through the fabric. "Solidarity for Michelle."

"I'll be there." Alice handed Stone a plate of tortillas and threw a few more on the griddle for Ruby.

"Well, it's two o'clock at the Unitarian church on Willow and Main," Stone said.

Madison came in and pushed Alice away from the stove with a gesture that said: "I got this." Alice sat back on one of the sofas, happy to put her feet up.

"So back to Dragonberry." Stone rolled one tortilla until it resembled a burrito. Impressive. "We've tried to make the house a bearable place to be. The cleaning crew worked wonders. It's habitable, but it won't be comfortable." He took a bite and turned to Michelle, who waved him off.

"I have no intention of ever residing there again," she said emphatically.

"No need to reside there," he said, "though you've got a good amount of work to do there. We located three boxes of Lars's files and papers. Sent them off to the lawyers and accountants this morning. But you're going to need to be at the house when the art is catalogued. We can bring in an expert to help date and confirm titles of some of the work, but no one will know Lars Olsen's work with the context you can bring."

"His art doesn't bother me." Michelle pressed her palms

to her face. "I don't want to see Dragonberry again . . . the rug, the sofa, the chair with the dent in it where he always sat."

"The rug is gone, unsalvageable," Stone said. "And the furniture can be removed. Would you want it stored or donated?"

Michelle lifted one hand. "Donate, please."

"Everything?" Stone asked.

"You'll need a place to sit," Alice said.

"It's a shame that you can't borrow a sofa and rug for a few weeks." Violet turned to Alice. "Do you have anything in the attic?"

Alice laughed. "After furnishing a seven-bedroom house?"

"Ladies, I think a shopping spree is in order." Michelle smiled. "I'm buying."

"I volunteer for that assignment," Violet said. "I like to think I've got a good eye for design, and shopping can be fun, when you're spending someone else's money."

After some discussion it was decided that the large dining room table and chairs would remain. A few pieces of furniture would be purchased for a small seating area.

"I can't thank you enough for handling all this, Stone. But while you're getting rid of furniture, please clear out the bedroom, too. Just leave me my clothes."

"What about Rosie's things?" Alice asked.

"How could I forget the girlfriend?" Michelle's head rolled back against the couch. "Of course. Let her come in and pick up her belongings."

"And the paintings she worked on?" Alice persisted. "Sorry to stick on that point, but Rosie is going to persist until she has an answer."

"Though legally, Rosie's in murky territory," Stone pointed out. "You don't owe her any of the contents of Lars's collection."

"And some of those paintings are worth tens of thousands of dollars now," Violet pointed out. "Maybe more."

Michelle's eyes were closed for a moment, a quiet meditation, Alice suspected. "Money is not an issue now. I want Rosie Suarez to have her canvases. But I also would like a way to keep her honest. Just a way to check that she's only taking what's hers."

"A tricky task, since Lars is no longer around," Violet said.

"What about Henry?" Alice said. "He hasn't been around for long, but he was studying with Lars long enough to know what pieces Rosie was working on. He might be able to clarify or confirm Rosie's work."

"Henry... I probably owe him a phone call, and two weeks' pay. I haven't reached out to him, or to Rosie, since Lars died." Michelle nodded. "I'll ask Henry to help us. He can be our mediator. I can pay him. And Rosie can be there, too. She can see that no one is trying to cheat her in any way."

With the plan set, conversation turned to lighter matters.

Sales were up at Ruby's House of Wigs after a celebrity had mentioned them on a late-night talk show.

Madison was going out to dinner with her colleague Daniel Zhao.

Alice blinked in wonder. "Officer Zhao?" Surprising that Madison was venturing on a date, but shocking that she would share that with this crew.

"You mean that tall, dark, and handsome cop I see you working with?" Ruby asked. "I always knew he was digging you."

"Yuck, please don't say that." Madison winced. "I'm so sorry you had to hear that," she told Stone.

He chuckled. "I can dig it. They're from my generation." He rose and stretched his long arms out. "Which reminds me, I'm old. Better hit the hay if I'm going to keep chasing the ghosts out of Dragonberry."

"Ain't that the truth," Alice muttered. She walked him to the door, trying to push back the blues. She was grateful that he was helping Michelle, but it made him unavailable. "Someday, soon, when this all settles down, we'll do something fun."

He leaned against the jamb of the open door, his face half shadowed by night, his eyes glimmering with mirth and contentment and . . . love? Maybe that was pushing it.

"Yes, we will, darlin'."

He called me darling.

Her heart squeezed with joy, and she felt sure she would never breathe again as he leaned forward and pressed his lips to hers. A kiss to seal the deal.

Chapter Forty-four

Back inside, the women were relaxing on the overstuffed sectionals, chatting and chuckling over one of Taylor's stories. Alice went into the empty kitchen nook. Sitting at the puzzle table, she texted Rosie Suarez, inviting her to pick up her clothes and meet with Michelle regarding her paintings. The phone made a whooshing sound as the text flew off.

Staring at the table, she noticed a puzzle piece that belonged next to the border. She picked it up and tried it. A perfect fit. For now, this was the therapy she needed. As she sat searching for pieces to complete the colorful rows of pastel crayons in the art puzzle, Madison came over behind her and put her arms around her. "I love you, Gran."

"I love you too, honey." Alice seized on a puzzle piece that showed black wrapper and yellow crayon. "Everything okay?"

"Just what I was going to ask you." Madison came around to sit beside her. "Are you discouraged about the investigation? Or still in shock over that gruesome murder scene."

"I'm putting Lars's unfortunate demise behind me. But I

feel stuck, you know? Waiting for some clue to pan out, some suspect to slip and incriminate himself." Alice looked up from the puzzle and faced Madison. "And waiting to see my daughter. It's torture, honey."

"Oh, yeah, Mom. I think she'll be here Monday or Tuesday."

Stretching through the weekend. "Let me know when you have something more specific."

"And don't be discouraged." Madison slipped a piece of a pencil cup in place. "That was a good tip you caught today. I'm in the process of tracking that bartender down, but apparently Glen is off camping in New Mexico. We need to know who Lars was spending time with that afternoon. An argument—and some heavy drinking—that spells major conflict. A possible motive for murder."

"It might be significant." Alice turned a puzzle piece around in her hands. "We need to find the woman. But being in that bar, I got a clear sense of Lars Olsen's situation on the afternoon of the murder. Maybe I should stop thinking of suspects and their possible motives and focus on Lars's state of mind that day. What might he have done to provoke the murderer?"

"I get it. From the timeline, we know that he came into the gallery that afternoon to drop off his paintings. Coyote remembers that it was after lunch, and Lars was alone. But the mystery woman might have been waiting in the bar or the car. Coyote was worried about a possible confrontation between Lars and Santino, so he whisked Lars out and stashed the paintings in the back."

"Okay, so I'm Lars," Alice said. "Two days earlier I had a fake press conference at my home, an attempt to sell some paintings. He sold two or three that day. So maybe by Tuesday he was getting impatient. He knew Michelle wouldn't be officially missing forever, so he brought the paintings into the gallery, thinking the scandal of his missing wife might stimulate more sales."

"Right. But you left the gallery in a bad mood, because it seems you went straight to the bar next door to tie one on and argue with your female friend." Madison shrugged. "I'm guessing that was Rosie."

"Sounds about right. So maybe Lars is angry that Coyote didn't fawn over the paintings. Or maybe the argument is about a situation with Rosie. She admitted she and Lars had plans to run off somewhere together."

"Maybe she wants to get married and have kids," Madison said. "She's a young woman."

"Or it could have been about respect. She's an artist, too, but Lars didn't bring her into the gallery with him. Either way, Lars is pissed, drinking heavily, surly. The woman storms out, and the bartender ends up helping Lars call a car to get home. He actually remembered that the address had a 'dragon' in it."

"So an inebriated Lars gets a ride home around what, four?"

"Four or five, according to the boys at the bar. But wait . . . sometime in there, Lars would have gotten the call from you that Michelle had been found. His wife was coming home. Time to face the music." Alice squinted at Madison. "What time did you reach him?"

Madison frowned. "I'd have to check the police log for the actual time, but I remember that it took hours for me to reach him. Hours. His wife was missing, and he couldn't take a minute to respond to the police? I was so annoyed, I mentioned it to Bedrosian. I knew I couldn't leave an important notification like that in a voice mail. So, we were ready to take a patrol car out to Dragonberry when he finally answered my call. It must have been five by then."

"We were already on our way back from Sunriver." Alice

put down the puzzle pieces she'd been holding. "Rosie said she was with Lars when he got the call, so maybe she was at Dragonberry. She drove there to make up after their spat?"

"Possible. So now Lars knows the jig is up. His wife is safely recovered, so he's not an artist in scandal anymore. His paintings aren't going to get a sales boost."

"And he's going to need to borrow big money from Michelle," Alice said. "He'd already requested a hundred thousand dollars, according to Michelle. If he gets the money, he can pay back Coyote and run off with Rosie. And live happily ever after."

"If that was the plan, something foiled it." Madison let out a sad groan. "I hate to point the finger at Rosie. I feel sorry for her, and she's the only person in this scenario who's financially disadvantaged and working to dig herself out. But what if Lars decided to stay with his wife? Maybe he wanted to live under the wing of Michelle's financial protection and just keep Rosie as an assistant and a girlfriend."

"Dash her dreams," Alice said. "And if he was obnoxious about it, which is likely considering what he'd had to drink, it might have pushed her over the edge. Infuriated her enough to stab him in the back, when he wasn't looking."

"Such a tragic story," Madison said.

"Murder usually is."

Madison checked her phone. "It's late. I'd better get going. After our talk, I've got a few investigative trails to pursue. Time to take a deeper dive on Rosie Suarez."

"She's a hot mess on the surface. Poor kid. I'm a little afraid of what you might find when you dig deeper."

"It's okay to feel empathy, but if she killed Lars, she needs to be behind bars."

"Agreed." Alice turned her focus back to the puzzle, smoothing a palm over the areas that had been pieced together. Maybe she could finish tonight? Pull a late night? Nah. Just a few more pieces... "Should I be worried about setting up a meeting between Rosie and Michelle?"

"For now, no one should be in a room with Rosie alone. But I wouldn't profile Rosie as the type to go on a killing spree."

"That's some consolation, I guess?"

Madison chuckled. "Just be your usual socially aware self. Thanks for dinner. I think you 'unstuck' the investigation for both of us." She swiped a mini carton of coconut water from the fridge, and grabbed her jacket from the back of a chair. "And when you're feeling down, remember these words of wisdom: things always look bad before they get better."

Alice frowned. "That's a lame bit of advice. Who said that?"

"Detective Bedrosian."

"It figures," Alice muttered, snapping a piece in place.

Chapter Forty-five

The meeting with Rosie Suarez was set for Sunday at Dragonberry Lane. Henry would be attending at the same time, and Alice hoped that the young man would act as a buffer in the situation. Alice would attend, too, having warned Michelle that Rosie was still a prime suspect in Lars's murder.

Although Alice had spent most of Saturday at the library, the other ladies had spent the day conducting a spiritual cleansing and a facelift of Dragonberry.

Alice had attended the smudging, the process of burning sage to purify the house. Under Violet's direction windows were opened to let the bad vibrations escape the rooms, and give the good vibes a chance to enter. Then Violet and Taylor lit the end of a sage stick and snubbed it in sand until it was quenched to ash.

"Now we move through the house and let the sage cleanse and purify," Violet explained to the small group following her through the room, fanning the ribbon of smoke toward the walls with a feather. "A beautiful cleansing of negative energy." She waved the feather and smoke wafted toward the tall fireplace, which had been swept clean. A tall house plant and a garden statue of a fawn had been placed into the gaping brick space, making the mouth of the fireplace appear less voracious.

Violet paused by the front door, wafting smoke here and there, opening the door to wave the stick over the porch. "We want to make sure to guard this house from bad vibrations." Violet paused a few feet from the fireplace. The wood floor was shiny and clean now, but she knew the evil that had transpired there. She lingered there, chasing off negative energy and "making room for light and positivity."

Alice followed along, noticing the sense of relief that sifted in as they made their way through the house. Was it a placebo effect? Maybe. It certainly helped her chase away the memory of the terrible night, and Michelle was absorbed in the process. Seeing the tension eased for Taylor, who had an occasional phobia about death and spirits, Alice knew it was all worth it.

Then came the shopping trip. While Alice was at the library catching up on e-mails and acquisition requests, Michelle had led the women on a foray for furnishings.

"Just wait until you see," Taylor said Sunday morning as they pulled onto a semi-mucky patch of dirt in front of the house's big, angled windows, the eyes of the beast. "Aunt Violet found this really fun rug, full of color and kind of sixties mod. And then, when we realized most furniture would have to be ordered and delivered, Michelle negotiated with one of the sales clerks to let her buy the floor samples. She got cool chairs and lamps and a couch that . . . well, come see."

Taylor opened the door and Alice followed her into a transformed space. The high-backed sofa looked smart and inviting in a loden-green shade of brushed velvet. Two upholstered chairs with wooden arms flanked the couch, along with matching end tables. Brushed silver lamps gave intimate light, making the cavernous ceiling less cold. But the rug... with its teal waves, purple ovals, and splashes of orange and yellow, it was its own work of art.

"It's wonderful. So comfortable, yet bright and smart." Alice went to the edge of the rug. "What a fun area rug. Leave it to Violet to find just the right pop of color."

"The rug is called 'Fruit Bowl,'" Michelle said from the back of the room, where she had been standing beside a silver-haired man who seemed to be dusting off a tall painting with a dry paintbrush. "We decided that those purple circles are grapes, along with bananas and oranges."

Alice laughed. "Now that you've mentioned it, I won't be able to unsee it." She glanced toward the leagues of paintings that still slumped in awkward rows. "That clutter of canvases is the last vestige of the old house, but that'll change soon, too."

"We're here to make it happen. Here to help evaluate and catalog the paintings." The brush man gave a nervous smile and introduced himself as Drake Giardino. He was graying, but chipper and eager to work. The blue eyes magnified by his spectacles gave a sense that he was keenly observant.

Michelle introduced Taylor and Alice.

"Our friend Stone says you're well-regarded in the field of art restoration and appraisal," Alice said.

"Fortunately, most of Mr. Olsen's art seems to be in good condition. There was one piece found in the fire, *The Dodo*. At least we think that was it. Most of the canvas burned. But we've got a lot left to catalog and appraise. Coyote Jones will be here later today to assist in pricing."

"Where should we start?" Taylor pushed back the sleeves of her oversized black sweater as she ventured into one aisle.

"I brought some tools." Drake had brought tags and coordinating placards, as well as clipboards and inventory sheets to be filled out. Taylor would use her cell to photograph each painting and caption it to align with the inventory.

"We'll leave you to it," Michelle said, slipping on a thin black cardigan. "Alice, if you don't mind getting some fresh air, I have something to show you."

As they walked on the dirt road behind the house, up the rise toward the wretched pond, Michelle spread her arms and took in a deep breath. "Isn't this wonderful? When this time of year comes around, each day without rain is a gift."

"The fresh air is nice." Alice reserved comment on the mucky body of water and slime they were approaching.

Michelle told Alice how grateful she was for her help. "Violet has been a good friend, and the women in your home have closed around me like family. They remind me of my aunties and cousins. Many of my aunties have passed, but their daughters take over as the family caretakers. When all this business is settled here, this dragon over my shoulder slain, I'm going to Los Angeles to be with my family. Kamaria has agreed to run the studio for me, and I have a friend who's interested in the academy. A break from West Hazel would be good, don't you think?"

"We'll miss you," Alice said, "but you deserve to get away. Los Angeles is perfect. You can hole up there or spread your wings and find a different social event every day."

"It will be a new life. And right now, I need to get away from Lars. His ghost, his checkered legacy."

Alice turned to Michelle. Was she talking about his paintings?

"Here's what I wanted to show you." She stopped walking, pulled out her phone, and scrolled a few times. "Here's a document the accountants found." She handed Alice the phone.

CHILD SUPPORT UNIT, STATE OF CONNECTICUT was stamped across the top of the paper. The page seemed to be a ledger of money paid on an account in Lars Olsen's name.

"Lars was paying child support?" Alice said. "And the overdue balance is . . . in the neighborhood of one hundred grand."

"That's a figure that I kept hearing from Lars," Michelle said. "What he didn't tell me was that he fathered a child and was sued for child support more than a decade ago. My lawyers investigated the matter with the state agency in Connecticut, and it's legit. Lars didn't deny the claim in family court, and the child's mother had a DNA test done."

"Michelle, I'm so sorry. You must feel like the bottom is falling out."

"The existence of a child isn't a betrayal. Apparently, this kid was born seventeen years ago. I hadn't even heard of Lars back then. It's the lies that kill me. My husband has a son, and he's been evading child support all these years. More than a hundred thousand dollars in payments are overdue."

"That's a big nut." Alice frowned. "You okay?"

"Just feeling . . . stung. Don't get me wrong, it's not a financial hardship. The money can come out of the estate." Michelle raked her hair back with one hand. "Or else I can pay it from my savings. It's not the money. It's the sneaking around me and the fact that he dodged a huge responsibility. That part is mortifying."

"I get that."

"So the kid is seventeen or so? You know that kind of money can change the path of a young person's life. Maybe the down payment on a condo? Or college."

Michelle nodded. "That's a good thought."

The breeze picked up, scuttling across the pond, blowing ripples on the surface. "Do you think you'll sell this place?" Alice asked.

"Absolutely." She turned to Alice. "You in the market?"

Alice chuckled. "I've got more rooms than I can fill at the palace."

As they turned away from the wind and headed back to the house, the familiar pieces came to mind. A seventeen-year-old kid. A lawsuit against the estate.

Strawberry-blond hair. Some height. And a big jaw that had a horsey look at times.

"I know who he is," she said. "Lars's son. Henry! Henry is his boy."

Chapter Forty-six

It made perfect sense that Henry arrived with his mother. The boy was not his usual cheerful self. In fact, this goth version, pale with red-rimmed eyes, hiding in the recesses of his black hoodie, seemed more like the moody teens Alice encountered at the library. Behind deadline on a paper. Struggling to write a book report. Anxious about failure and brimming with wild emotions.

His mother guided him in the front door, though the arm at his back seemed more stern than comforting.

"Please, have a seat," Michelle offered, gesturing toward the couch.

Alice took a peek and noted that Claudia was wearing gloves, as usual—a fawn-brown suede pair that matched the plaid in her blazer. She was somewhat casual in black boots and blue jeans, but Claudia's casual was a notch above. *Once a model, always a model,* thought Alice. They sat together, mother and son, though Henry had the look of a man sitting on a bed of nails, and Claudia sat with her arms crossed, cold and defensive as she watched the activity around the paintings.

Taylor and Drake worked quietly, tagging canvases and

logging them in, already in a rhythm of independent work, with the occasional question and answer. Rosie cruised among the paintings, shark girl on the move, on the hunt, for what? Alice wondered. She had already picked out her four creations and set them aside, giving Taylor a chance to photograph them for Michelle's record-keeping.

A sage-green cast-iron teapot sat on the new coffee table between Alice and the newcomers. *No tea for you two*, she thought. A few minutes ago, Michelle had made a pot of herbal tea, offering a cup to everyone, including Rosie, who had declined. Alice realized that tea was Michelle's soother, but also a way to invite people into her circle. Alice still sipped from her mug.

"Thank you for coming." Speaking directly to Henry, Michelle went over the task at hand. "I know you weren't with Lars long, but I'm hoping you were aware enough to confirm which paintings Rosie worked on."

Hunkered down inside his hoodie, Henry nodded. "I'll try."

"Did you find your paintings?" Michelle asked, as everyone shifted toward the big, windowed room of canvases.

Henry and Claudia lagged behind, and Alice noticed Mom glaring at her son, who moved stiffly, as if in pain. Did the poor kid have the flu?

"Right here. These four." Rosie had stacked them against the writing desk, where she had previously placed three shopping bags full of clothing and personal items collected from the bedroom. She now stood defending her treasures with her hands on her hips. Gloved hands, though her fingers and thumbs were exposed. Were gloves going to be a new fashion trend? Alice hoped not. They made her own hands look gargantuan. "I focused on capturing the pond with a moon or sun reflected. Lars said I was good at depicting water, the motion and reflections."

Henry moved close to study the paintings one at a time, nodding silently. "Yeah," he finally said. "These three, at least. This second piece, with the branch of leaves in the foreground, I don't know. I just don't remember it." He turned to Rosie, his eyes wide with apology. "Maybe you painted it before I got here?"

"Are you kidding me?" Rosie's dark eyes flared with impatience. "How could you not remember?"

"I just don't, okay?" Henry stared at the floor. "I'm not saying it's not yours."

"This is ridiculous!" Rosie restacked the paintings, as if Henry couldn't be trusted to touch them. "They're mine!"

"Take them," Michelle said quietly. "All four of them."

Rosie's head snapped around to face her. "What?"

"I said take them. All four paintings clearly have a similar style, and your attachment to them is palpable. Please . . ." Michelle gestured toward the canvases. "You should have them. You invested much time and energy working with Lars. If these paintings can make you happy in any way, then something good came out of his life."

"Oh, okay," Rosie said, not so quick with a comeback. "Yeah, thanks." She gathered her three bags, juggling them so that she could grab one painting. "Can somebody help me with this stuff?"

Drake came to her aid, wheeling the four paintings on a small dolly so Rosie could focus on the overstuffed bags.

As the door closed behind them, Michelle turned to Henry. "Thanks for your help. As I mentioned, you're getting a bonus for coming in today, along with your two weeks' worth of pay." She handed him an envelope, his name written on it in a jaunty slanted print.

"Cool." He gave a nervous nod.

"While you're here, let me ask: Are there any paintings here that you worked on? I know you haven't studied under Lars for long, but if there's something you're attached to, I won't stand in your way."

"Well, there's one . . ." Henry tugged on the string of his hoodie and cast a nervous glance at his mother.

"No. Hold on." Pressing her eyes closed, Claudia held up a hand to silence him. "We're here on more pressing matters than a souvenir canvas and a few weeks' salary." Her eyes were afire as she reached into her purse and pulled out some papers, stapled together at the top. "This is the reason we came to West Hazel in the first place." She waved the documents in the air. "It's a child support agreement, signed by Lars. Meaning he acknowledged Henry as his son and agreed to pay monthly child support. Oh, and if you think this is some money grab, we had the DNA testing done. A kick in the pants for Lars, though he still withheld the money."

The topic seemed to shrink Henry, as he shoved his hands into the pocket of his hoodie and hunched over to stare at the floor.

Alice held her breath through the awkward moment. Over by the stockpile of canvases, Taylor stood still, a tag in hand, watching the loaded exchange.

When Michelle spoke, her voice was calm, even-toned. "I have recently suspected that Lars was Henry's father. I don't know why I didn't see the resemblance earlier."

"Well, you know it now. Lars fathered a child, though he never tried to be a father. I raised Henry alone, changing career paths to pay the bills, while Lars played in the art world and paid less than ten grand on a hundred-thousand-dollar-plus debt. We came here to shame Lars into paying up so that Henry could finance college or art school. Lars said he was going to get the money, but somehow I let him sweet-talk me into reducing the debt if he tutored Henry." She scoffed, the light catching the reddish tint of her hair as she lifted her chin. "My mistake. Lars was his usual prickly self. The tutoring was not going well. And before my son received anything approaching constructive training, Lars went and got himself killed."

Recalling the argument she had overheard between Claudia and Lars, Alice saw the pieces coming together now. A single mom, trying to collect child support for her son. Perhaps his only chance at attending college. But Mom put that plan on hold for a once-in-a-lifetime opportunity: her son would be tutored by an artist, a famous figure in the art world. Despite Claudia's hot, brusque manner, Alice felt for her: a mother defending her child.

Michelle raked her hair back with one hand, a nervous gesture Alice had come to recognize. "I'm so sorry for the way Lars treated you."

"Sorry doesn't cut it. Henry is here for the financial support he should have had as a kid, and don't think we're backing down just because Lars is gone. So, these"—Claudia extended the papers toward Michelle—"are for you."

Michelle's face was expressionless as she took the documents and began reading. "Twelve thousand dollars a year for ten years." She looked up. "That's barely half of his life. So you didn't file for support until Henry was older. You let Lars off the hook."

"Whatever," Claudia retorted. "We need the money, and we need it now."

Michelle turned to the next page, and then the next. "Of course." She turned and placed the papers atop the writing desk. "It appears he owes you a hundred and fourteen thousand, but we'll round up to one-fifteen. Would a personal check suffice, or do you want to wait until tomorrow for a bank check?"

Henry straightened, his eyes round with awe. Claudia squinted at Michelle as if she were speaking a different language.

Well played, Michelle, Alice thought, waiting for the next move on the chessboard. *Well played.*

Chapter Forty-seven

"Is this a trick?" Claudia's gaze darted around the room suspiciously. "Because if you're going to try to write me off with some bogus check, you should know I have a very good lawyer and that's a legal document. You can send us off today, but we're not backing down. Not ever. If we have to take you to court—"

"You will get the money Lars owed to you," Michelle said. "I insist on it. Lars was unreliable, but I've never shirked a debt or a business arrangement. And yours is a worthy cause." She spared Henry a smile. "But you should know that I have some very good lawyers, too, so consider that we're well-matched. But not opponents. I support your cause."

"I don't know what to say. We've been fighting for this so long . . ." Claudia shook her head. "It seemed like it would never happen."

"You have my word. Now, if it's all right with you, I'll have a bank check ready by tomorrow afternoon. You can pick it up here if you like. We'll be here, cataloging paintings until we get through Lars's collection." Michelle paused. "I take it you'll be attending the ceremony at the church on Friday?"

"We're planning to go," Henry answered, standing tall now.

Claudia nodded, blinking back tears.

"I'll reserve a place for you at the ceremony. Oh, and if you like you're welcome to join a reception in the church hall afterwards."

"Thank you," Claudia said quietly, eyes down. Without another word, she summoned her son and led him out the door, though he flinched at her touch. Definite friction between mother and son.

Alice watched as the door closed.

"Wow! You guys!" Taylor flicked her fingers in a "Blow My Mind!" expression. "That was wild."

Drake Giardino kept working in the stacks, refraining from comment. A true professional, Alice thought. She hadn't even heard him return from helping Rosie.

"Poor Henry didn't get to take the painting he wanted," Taylor pointed out.

"Poor Henry isn't so poor anymore," Alice said. "You know, when we set up this meeting, I fully expected Rosie to be the problematic participant. But it was Claudia who got really fired up."

"Claudia was defending her truth," Michelle said. "Watching out for her child. I appreciate that."

"Well, it all went better than I expected," Alice said. "Probably because you were generous with both Rosie and Claudia."

"It's important for Lars's money to go to the right places. You know, when you take fruit from someone else's tree, it can sour the stomach. Bad karma." Michelle shook her head. "Violet chased the bad vibrations out of this place. From now on, only positive energy."

* * *

Alice's positive energy began to wear thin when, over dinner Monday night, Taylor told her that the meeting with Lauren would be delayed again. "Something came up with work," Taylor said. "She needs to go to the East Coast. She's sorry."

"What kind of work does she do?" Alice asked, intrigued. "An airline attendant?"

Taylor laughed. "No, but not a bad guess."

"Am I close?"

"You can ask her about her work. Mom doesn't want Madison and me to have to mediate and stuff."

"You're already brokering a meeting." Alice felt her impatience seeping through.

"I know, I know. She wants to know if Saturday morning works for you?"

"Fine," Alice said, pushing hope back once again. Well, she'd waited this long.

Rather than complain to the granddaughters, she'd taken her annoyance to Stone, who had stopped by a few times this week, and had taken to answering her text messages with phone calls.

"I don't like texts," he said on the phone one night. "Too impersonal."

"But efficient at times," Alice said, stretching out on her bed and gazing off through the balcony door as they chatted. "You're right, it's hard to connect on an emotional level with text messages."

"So have you thought about the message you want to get across to Lauren?" he asked. "It might be good to have that clear in your head, since it's pretty important, this thing."

"Good point." These heart-to-hearts with Stone brought her back to junior high when she would light candles in the club basement, bring down the lights, and put a record on the turntable so that her parents wouldn't know she was on the phone for hours.

On Tuesday, Alice thought of a new avenue of investigation into Claudia Finley, who had begun a career as a nurse years ago. She called the Connecticut State Nursing Board. A soft-spoken associate told her that Claudia's Connecticut license would not directly transfer to Oregon. Alice requested Claudia's nursing personnel files, but complaints were a matter of public record. "If you fill out our form, we'll e-mail you a response listing any of Ms. Finley's complaints." Alice sent the request, annoyed that she would have to delay gratification.

After a relatively uneventful week, Alice's Friday morning schedule was so jam-packed, she wasn't sure she'd even make it to Lars Olsen's funeral.

At ten there was a session of Music and Motion in Mandarin in the children's section, a lovely half hour in which native speakers and beginners spoke in Mandarin and sang songs or played music as a way to wrap children and families in Mandarin language and culture. Alice looked forward to the meetings—always a learning treat for her—but today she needed to play host, as they were down one children's librarian, and her usual substitute Julia was out, tending to a soccer injury that had taken her daughter out of yesterday's game. Thank goodness for Mae Tan, an outspoken patron, who enjoyed stepping in as host.

At eleven, there was a meeting of the Friends of the Library, where one member suggested a statue or plaque honoring their town's artist Lars Olsen. *Let that idea fizzle and fade,* Alice thought, though she did talk up the garden sculptor Sparrow, and encouraged folks to read the proposal for the "window garden" outside the children's section.

The Poets' Society meeting at twelve thirty would have

been a piece of cake if they didn't also have the Pop-Up Library to pack for an afternoon visit to a local elementary school. So much to do! She snagged their two youngest employees and assigned them the task of loading the mobile library based on age-appropriate reading lists. "And throw in a few of your favorites from grade school."

It was a day to lead and delegate, and Alice embraced the quick pace like a veteran ballplayer brought into the game to pitch a few innings. When the poetry group said their goodbyes, Alice had just enough time to splash water on her face, touch up her makeup, and head over to the church a few blocks away.

The sky was threatening to spit, a menacing layer of gray, but she walked, quickly coming upon cars trying to parallel park and circling the blocks slowly. As she neared the church she noticed two uniformed officers directing traffic, while other pedestrians hustled along to the swarm of people on the steps.

A crowd for Lars? Was this the right funeral?

Chatting with a few people outside, she learned that the somber ceremony had captured the interest of the good people of West Hazel. A famous artist . . . a tragic death . . . West Hazel's own . . .

The man had only lived in West Hazel for a handful of years, and those who knew Lars might have preferred to describe him as *infamous*, but who was she to burst their bubble.

Inside the church, organ music rolled through the air along with the familiar scent of candle wax and floor cleaner. The volume of people made Alice pause. Although she had planned to sit with Taylor and Ruby, it would be an impossible task in the packed church, where people were squeezing into tight rows. A league of mourners stood along the back wall. The standing-room-only crowd.

What a hot ticket.

A man with salt-and-pepper hair and a dour expression came up the aisle, his black jacket stark against his clerical collar.

"If some of you would like to follow me," the minister said, "I can offer you seats in the choir section. Up to forty people, as today's service doesn't have a choir."

One woman raised her hand, and a few people lined up.

"Thank you," Alice told him, taking a place in line. The choir loft would be perfect for looking down over the congregation—simple observation.

But as the group filed to the back of the church, the brief steps didn't lead to an upstairs loft but to the back of the transept, the area just behind the pulpit. As Alice took her seat in the choir section, she realized that her view of the congregation was spectacular, indeed. But the milling crowd in the pews had an even better view of her. Just beyond the minister, everyone would see the gray-haired visage of that familiar face, the lady librarian.

She would have to maintain a somber, interested expression. She settled in, taking in the faces, tension mounting as the hour approached. In the first row, Michelle was flanked by her book club gals. She wore a retro black hat, a velvet wedge with netting that covered her face. Mysterious and lovely.

Emerald sat beside her, her curls giving way as she leaned close to whisper in Michelle's ear. Something reassuring, Alice was sure. Good friend that she was, Emerald had cut her vacation short to be back for the funeral.

Violet was there, whispering to Holly, who nodded. Juanita, in her million-dollar suit, looked ready to lead a business seminar. Rachel hugged Merrilee, who was crying already.

Here and there, Alice recognized shop clerks and teachers, neighbors and library regulars. One area with shortened pews was now filled with folks in wheelchairs; the contingent from the Hazel Gardens, an adult community that Alice contended was run by her aunt Gildy. There she was in her sequined black top, good for a funeral or a night of disco dancing. Her head was bent, probably napping, though her friend Mitzy was talking to her. Alice was due to meet Gildy for dinner this week.

Alice found Stone there, in the heart of the group, chatting with a smiling man. He'd brought a van of folks from the senior center.

Young and old had turned out for this one.

Well, Lars, you may have been snubbed during your lifetime, but the town of West Hazel has turned out in droves to see their famous artist.

A hand rose in the back, a tasteful wave, and Alice saw that it was Taylor, sitting with Ruby and Jeff, Alice's ex. Silent groan. Of course Jeff would want to be in on the "send-off for that moody artist who was a cool cat." Jeff loved a party, even one with a darker theme.

And who was Taylor talking to? A short woman, dark hair . . . Rosie Suarez. They seemed to be talking rapid-fire. About what? Alice was glad the young woman trusted Taylor, but a little concerned about dangling her granddaughter so close to the lion's den. Although Rosie was probably harmless. Emotional, dramatic, self-centered, brokenhearted, but a killer? Most likely, the girl was just a pain in the neck.

Just one of the many people Alice had come to know from Lars Olsen's world, faces and personalities with shades and dimensions that might have been a collage of the artist's life. Looking over the brimming crowd, Alice searched for the others. Where was Santino? She didn't see him out there.

Scanning the faces, she was surprised to see Claudia and Henry Finley sitting on the aisle in the row right behind Michelle. Was that planned? Most likely Michelle had invited them to sit up front, the artist's son. Whew, Michelle was a better person than Alice.

Or maybe Alice was just put off by Claudia's grit, her desperation to get her son's money. Alice didn't have details on the tortured relationship that had transpired between Lars and Claudia long ago, but it must have hurt her. Bad enough that Santino had thought she'd returned to kill him.

But it turned out that Claudia didn't want him dead.

In fact, Claudia must have spun into a full-fledged panic when she learned that Lars had been killed. If she had a decent attorney, she would have known Lars's financial obligations died with him.

On a recent night, as Alice had been working a puzzle with Violet and Ruby, Michelle had come upstairs to make a pot of tea, and the conversation had gone to Claudia, and the revelation that Lars had a son.

"Nice of you to pay off Lars's debt to the boy," Ruby said. "But I don't think you're legally bound to do that. My understanding is that a wife isn't responsible for a husband's debt, unless it was a shared debt." Ruby tapped a puzzle piece on the table. "And Mr. Husband's child support, due before you were married, is not your debt."

"How do you know these things?" Violet's face was scrunched up, and then she gasped. "Oh, of course, George. Sorry."

Ruby had gotten a quick overview of a widow's fiscal responsibilities after her husband George had died recently.

"Is that correct?" Alice asked.

"It is." Michelle poured steaming water into the cast-iron pot. "My lawyer tells me I'm not responsible to pay off Claudia and Henry, but I know it's the right thing to do. As I said, good karma."

So, Michelle's good karma became Claudia's good fortune. Alice imagined Claudia's desperation when she'd learned of Lars's death. She must have made the decision to persist, press on with the child support agreement, try to strong-arm Michelle into paying.

In the end, Claudia and Henry had gotten what they were owed without a fight.

The organist was now holding on a few chords, as if waiting to switch to an opening hymn. The standing crowd in the back of the church parted like the Red Sea, and the murmurs died out. A large man walked through. The congregation held its collective breath for him.

He wore a smooth black coat, cashmere, and he held his brown fedora over his heart.

His brown head was shiny, but it suited him well.

Alice appreciated his gesture of respect as he walked to the front of the church and moved into a pew with a spot, apparently reserved for him.

The artist's dealer. A celebrity for a celebrity.

Lars would have liked that.

Chapter Forty-eight

"Santino is at the gallery, my place down the street," Coyote told Alice and Ruby as they gathered in the church hall after the ceremony. The fedora was back on his head, restoring his trademark look. "His show is open today, so he's hosting."

"Really?" Ruby squinted in doubt. "You'd think he could close the show for an hour or so to attend his old friend's funeral."

"He could," Coyote said, turning to help himself to some cheese from one of the tempting spreads. "He chose not to."

Throughout the church hall there were sodas and water on ice, as well as three tables laden with nuts, cheese, crackers, dried fruits, dips, and fresh vegetables. Servers circulated with sliders, mini eggrolls, and warm cheese tarts. Michelle's caterer had produced a lovely spread.

Alice used the moment to fill a small plate with snacks, as she'd powered through lunch. "I think the question is," she said as she plopped a limb of grapes onto the plate, "*why* did Santino skip the funeral?"

"Between you and me, he's hurting," Coyote said.

"Doesn't want to admit it, but Lars's death hit him hard. The old friend that backstabbed you and destroyed the relationship. I think we all have someone like that in our lives. In the Hallmark scenario, you come to terms with them and get back in the groove later in life." He popped a crumbly slice of cheddar in his mouth, smiled, and swallowed. "But now that Lars is dead, Santino can't get closure. It's killing him."

"Poor thing," Ruby said.

Lack of closure—Alice knew how that felt. Munching on walnuts and dried apricots, she wondered when her family would stop torturing her and make the meeting with Lauren happen. They were scheduled for tomorrow morning, but the can had been kicked down the road so many times, Alice had lost her enthusiasm for the chase.

"We should pay him a visit when we're through here," Alice said. "Cheer him up." In truth, she had a few questions to ask him.

"Well, if you come, please don't bring the gloved lady." Coyote shot a sardonic smile across the hall at Claudia Finley, who was talking with Michelle and Emerald.

"Why does she wear gloves everywhere?" Alice asked.

He shrugged. "Signature style, I guess. She's been in the gallery every day this week. Acts like she's visiting Santino, but she always corners me to pump me for information about the Lars Olsen paintings. When am I getting inventory from Michelle, what will the prices be, what's the estimated value of the collection." He rolled his eyes. "At first, I thought she was interested in acquiring his work. Now, she's making me nervous. I don't want to compromise my relationship with Michelle by giving Claudia information. Michelle is the legal owner of the collection now. I've seen the paperwork for the trust. All legit."

"I see what you're saying." Ruby nodded. "You're thinking Claudia might try to sue Michelle to get Henry a stake in his estate?"

Coyote put his hands up. "Pure speculation."

"But well founded." Alice nibbled a piece of apricot cheddar as she considered the problems a lawsuit might pose for Michelle. "That's concerning. I'll run it by Michelle." She pilfered two sliders from a passing server and decided to act. "I'm going to mosey over there and see what's cooking."

"Don't mention my name," Coyote warned.

"Mum's the word." Alice enjoyed the slider as she breezed over to Michelle's conversation circle, where Michelle was talking with a young couple, and Emerald and Claudia were discussing Portland's Saturday Market.

Henry stood apart, a few feet behind his mother, nervously pinching the button on his navy blazer.

Alice moved closer and touched his shoulder, surprised by the padding there. "How you holding up, buddy?"

The question seemed to bring tears to his eyes. "Okay," he lied.

She let her hand slip away. "These events are always challenging," she said. "I'm sorry you're going through a rough patch. Have you thought about what's next? Maybe art school?"

"I'd like to do that. I want to start in January back in Connecticut, but my Mom thinks we should stay here."

"Well, Portland State has the Schnitzer School of Art and Design."

He shrugged, eyes down. "I dunno. I just want to go home."

Poor Henry. He seemed to be suffering alone, set adrift.

"Henry," Michelle said, stepping closer. "You have to

come by to pick out a painting. Wasn't there something you worked on?"

"There was, but that's okay."

"Tell me, did your paintings depict clouds? Sort of ethereal and wispy, but if you look closely you can see a dragon?"

Henry's hands fell away from the button. "Yeah, that's mine. I wasn't finished but, how did you know?"

"It's different from Lars's work, but to be honest, our art restoration expert picked it out. He said it's a wonderful piece."

"Thanks."

"I want you to have it, but you must hurry now. We're almost finished with inventory and Monday we'll start moving pieces to storage or for display in galleries. My assistants have the weekend off, but I'll be finishing some work at the house tomorrow. Think you can stop by? Or have your mom text me. She has my number now."

He cast a worried look at Claudia. "I'll ask my mom." He nodded. "Tomorrow." He excused himself and went over to grab a soda.

"The ceremony went well. Anything I can get you?" Alice asked Michelle.

"I'm glad to have made it this far. Glad to have ordered extra platters from the caterer." Michelle scanned the room. "Who are all these people?"

"The good citizens of West Hazel." Alice smiled. "I think people long to be connected to a celebrity . . . even if he's no longer alive."

As they were talking, Taylor came to Alice's side and touched her arm. "Help?"

Both women turned to her.

"Rosie latched on to me in the church, and I don't know how to shake her loose."

"I saw you two talking."

Taylor flipped her hair over one shoulder as she checked Rosie's location across the room. "She's doing the talking and I can barely get a word in with her stories about Lars. How she feels so guilty that she couldn't save him. How he was competitive and selfish and obsessed with making a fortune."

"This is all sounding familiar, and not in a comforting way." Michelle pressed her hands together at her chest and gave a quick bow. "Excuse me."

"I feel bad for her," Taylor went on. "I really like Rosie, but right now she's melting down, spilling the beans, and I'm not the person to prop her up."

"What did she say?" Alice asked. "Did she admit that she was at the Rusty Nail with Lars the day of the murder?"

"Nope. She says she wasn't at the bar, but admits they did argue that day, after he found out Michelle was coming home. They were at Dragonberry, planning to run away together. He told her he owed a lot of money to a lot of people, but she didn't care. They were going to run away and hide from the world. And then he got the call about Michelle, and he changed his mind. Flipped on her. He was accustomed to the way Michelle took care of him, and in the end, he couldn't bear to leave his collection—his art."

"Just the thing a woman in love wants to hear," Alice muttered.

"She lied to the police about the timeline. She stayed later at Dragonberry. And she helped him build up the big fire. And then she was so pissed at him she threw one of his paintings into the fireplace."

"*The Dodo*," Alice said wistfully. "That solves part of the puzzle. Did the painting have a special significance?"

"Lars sometimes teased Rosie that she was a dodo,

stuck in the past. He said her style was too traditional, that she'd never make it in today's art world."

Alice frowned. "Such a mean man."

"A total turd." Taylor pressed her palms to her cheeks, inhaling deeply. "I'm so stressed. When people dump on me I just suck in all their trauma and freak out. Do you think I'm an empath?"

"I don't know much about it, but you know tricks for calming down. Deep breaths. Empty your mind. Press frozen tangerines to your eyes."

"Deep breaths." Taylor closed her eyes and breathed deeply.

"Oh, honey, I'm sorry I dragged you into this thing with Rosie." Alice rubbed Taylor's back between the shoulder blades. Usually that helped. "I didn't think it would be a problem for you."

"It's only a problem because I care about her, and it hurts to see her melting down. I told her she'd better tell the police the truth. She's going to be so screwed when they find out she's been lying to them."

"I know. The police are already watching her." Alice expected that Rosie would be facing murder charges soon. Her alibi and timeline were imploding. "Listen, we're going to head out, stop in at Coyote's gallery to see Santino. You should come with. No need to stay."

"I'm ready to go." Taylor nodded, letting out a breath as Rosie came barreling through a cluster of guests.

"There you are! I ran into Coyote Jones and guess what? I feel so much better. He's so sweet. He's heard about the paintings I did in Lars's studio and he wants to meet and talk about representing me. Isn't that the best thing ever!"

"That's pretty great," Taylor agreed.

"Good for you," Alice agreed. "You take care now. We're headed out." She had to gather Ruby and exchange a greeting with her ex-husband so she wouldn't be labeled as bitter. And she would have liked to spend some time with Stone, but it seemed that he had corralled his group to the exit a few minutes ago. The folks at Hazel Gardens had an early supper.

When Alice finally made it out of the building with Ruby and Taylor, someone called out to them when they hit the sidewalk by the firehouse.

"Guys! Hey, wait up!"

Alice turned back to see Rosie wave, then rush forward, cutting close to a woman with a stroller. Shark girl was on the prowl, following their scent.

As Rosie captured Ruby's sympathy over her dead boyfriend, Alice thought of accounts she'd read of sociopaths who told fluent, convincing lies, winning supporters and evoking sympathy.

Persuasive, personable at times.

Shaking off a chill, she hoped they weren't swimming with a shark.

Chapter Forty-nine

"I am so very moved that you have come to see me on this dark, sad day." Santino pressed his hands to his chest and swayed to one side. "There is nothing like the reassuring company of friends when your heart is breaking."

"We're here to offer comfort and joy," Ruby said, folding up her umbrella and stuffing it into a ceramic holder near the gallery's door.

"And a little bit of rain," Alice said, brushing the sleeves of her jacket. "The sky opened up on us while we were walking over."

Taylor patted him on the shoulder as she passed by, and Rosie stuck her hand out, baring her toothy grin.

"Rosie Suarez. We haven't met, but I'm an artist, too. Just tagging along with your friends."

"My pleasure, of course." He took her hand and gave a humble bow, but when she passed by, following Taylor to the back of the gallery, he gave Alice a cross-eyed look. "Was she the lover of Lars?" he whispered.

Alice could see why her granddaughters had banned that L-word. "Rumor has it."

"Coyote mentioned an interest in her work, but for me, everything associated with Lars is toxic. He was the pebble in my shoe, the rain on my parade, the knife in my back." He frowned. "Maybe that last is in poor taste."

"Don't hold back, now," Ruby said. "You've suffered a loss like everyone else, and you can tell us what's really in your heart. Sometimes we all need to vent."

"The tears have already fallen for the friend I used to have. I must move on with a scar over the wound." Santino shook his head. "This is my problem in life. I feel love so intensely, for a man or a woman, it's no different. I fall deeply in love, and then I'm hurt, and alone again. It's my destiny to be alone."

"That's the saddest thing I ever heard," Ruby said, taking his hand. "I wish Violet were here to give you a boost. Read your palm or your tarot cards."

"I know Violet." He smiled. "She has a beautiful aura. I love Violet intensely."

"Wow. You do fall in love fast," Ruby teased.

The door opened and a small group entered, laughing as they stowed their umbrellas. Santino went over to welcome them and chat. When he returned, Alice had a question for him.

"This might seem out of the blue, but I'm trying to understand her better. No one talks about it, but I'm curious about Claudia Finley's habit of wearing gloves. I've never seen her appear without them. Is she germophobic?"

"No, though that would be a good guess. Her hands are quite scarred." He looked around and lowered his voice. "This was a torture, little cuts done by Lars back when we were in college. She was a model, you know, and he was very jealous of the attention she received. Especially from men. So he cut her to end her career."

"Oh, how awful!" Ruby gasped. "And here we just sat through a ceremony honoring that monster."

Alice felt a flash of sympathy for young Claudia, and she remembered the woman mentioning how she'd had to change her career path. Lars Olsen had left her scarred, unable to continue with modeling for art classes, and with a son to raise on her own.

The door opened, catching Alice's eye. This time two uniformed police officers strode in, rain glistening on their shoulders, their black boots dripping on the floor by the door.

Funny, how you see the uniform first, thought Alice. Once she scanned past the gun and badges and paraphernalia, she saw Officers Denham and Zhao. "Madison? Everything okay?"

"We're here on official business." Madison cast a look toward the back of the gallery, curious but not alarmed. "Is Rosie Suarez here?"

Santino pointed to the back of the gallery, eyes open wide with alarm.

"Madison, what's going on?" Alice followed her through the gallery.

"We're trying to be discreet," Madison said, eyes straight ahead as she came upon Rosie and Taylor standing in front of the four Lars Olsen paintings.

"Rosie Suarez?" Officer Zhao asked. When Rosie turned around, blinking, he introduced himself and invited her to come along to the station to answer some questions.

"I already talked to the police." Rosie removed her round red glasses and squinted at him. "And I'm kind of tired. I just came from a funeral, and it's been really traumatic."

"We have some questions that can't wait." Madison glanced over at the group of visitors who were now watching intently. "And I don't think you want to run through it all here."

"This is fine." Rosie stuck her glasses back on and spread her arms wide. "Have at it."

"Did you take five knives from the kitchen of Lars Olsen's residence to a cutlery store to have them sharpened the weekend before Lars was killed?"

"Did I?" Rosie's arms dropped to her sides. "Well, yeah. I was doing Lars a favor. The knives were so blunt, it was dangerous. I was trying to make a stir-fry, and when I was chopping the blade slid off an onion and nearly took my finger off."

Madison and Zhao exchanged a concerned look.

"Okay, Rosie," Madison said, "you need to come with us."

"Don't be ridiculous. I didn't kill Lars. I was at class when he was killed, right?"

"The timeframe you gave us doesn't match the security video from the college." Zhao shook his head. "And your fingerprints were on the murder weapon. Which you had sharpened."

"I didn't kill Lars." Rosie's voice was tight now, her hands balled into fists. "I was so mad at him, I could've—"

"Rosie, maybe you should stop talking and take a minute to breathe," Alice said.

"I've got nothing to hide." Rosie waved her off. "Sure, I wanted to kill him, but just for a minute. He's boomeranged before, and I knew he'd come around again. But I had to get to class. I stomped out of there, figuring he'd come around by the next day and call me. We'd get back on track with our escape. We were going to get a little house with a yard, a place for kids and dogs. We were going to have a life together, two artists. Or, maybe the artist and the teacher. I could play second fiddle. I could have made him so happy."

"Just stop talking now, please." Madison pursed her lips. "Rosie Suarez, you're under arrest."

Alice put an arm over Taylor's shoulder and they watched in silence as Rosie's rights were read and her hands were cuffed.

"I loved him," she said, sniffing back tears. "I was going to take care of him."

The gallery was nearly silent as the officers led her out.

Santino let out a sigh. "Murder solved?"

No one answered. Alice looked at Taylor, who swiped back a tear, and muttered something about it all being unfair.

Would the people of West Hazel sleep a little more soundly tonight knowing Rosie Suarez was in jail?

Probably not.

Chapter Fifty

Most Saturdays, Alice enjoyed sleeping in, basking in smooth white sheets, stretching into another position and dozing off again for more luxurious rest.

But when her eyes opened just after seven this morning, she knew there would be no languorous relaxation. Today was Lauren. At last.

Still in her nightgown, she slid open the balcony door and breathed in the damp air. The sky was pale, a low ceiling of murky clouds obscuring the mountains, the rooftops, even the dark green spikes of evergreen treetops running down the hill below her.

Her daughter was out there now, somewhere close.

Please don't let me mess this up.

She dug into the back of her closet, searching for something with meaning. She made a pile of things that had to go to Goodwill. Golf shoes. Sequined heels. A wool sweater, the sight of which made her itch.

Finally, in a bin in the back, she found a bubblegum-pink T-shirt, still bright. Lauren had loved it back in high school, some twenty-five years ago. Alice had worn it to cheer her on at soccer games, and Lauren dubbed her the "bubblegum girl." She put the tee through a speed wash and went to grab a coffee.

Down in the kitchen, Michelle sat at the puzzle table sketching. Alice knew that drawing had brought her much solace during her time in Alice's home.

"Good morning. Looks like we're the only two up," Alice said.

"Ruby was up and took a cup of coffee for the road. She's off to Seattle with Coyote Jones."

"I forgot, he invited her along to scout locations." Alice wasn't sure what might come of that pairing, but they seemed to enjoy each other's company.

"Violet will be up soon. Our book club has a day trip to the Maryhill Museum in the gorge."

"Sounds good. Are you going?"

"I have other plans." Michelle's pen lifted from the pad. "Sorry to have taken up your puzzle table. I can move." She started to gather her markers, and something dropped to the floor with a clatter.

"No, stay. I'm just going to have coffee. Meeting Lauren today. No time to work a puzzle right now, and I wouldn't dream of chasing you away from this sunny view of Mount Hood." Alice leaned down to fetch the item that had fallen—a key chain with a pink tube on it that seemed to be a small flashlight. "Your keys?"

"Thanks, yes, at last, I got my car back from impound. It's nice to be back in my own wheels."

"I bet." Alice looked down at the sketch pad as Michelle's pen moved quickly, cross-hatching part of the illustration. "I never mastered art beyond doodling. Is that your graphic novel? Your zippy girl heroine with magical vision."

"Jing. Her special vision allows her to see what other people fear."

"That's a major superpower; fear is one of the strongest emotions." Alice lifted her mug from the quick brewer, adding, "I can vouch for that."

Michelle capped her pen. "I don't have magical vision, but I understand why this day would give you . . . trepidation. There's much at stake when you love someone."

"Exactly." Sipping her coffee, Alice marveled at the insight of this woman who had spent most of her career in very physical roles—dancing, acting, and martial arts. Brilliantly executed action roles that never hinted of the spirituality and wisdom within.

"You'll be fine, I can feel it." Michelle smiled. "I'm very happy for you, rediscovering your daughter. You both have an adventure ahead."

Alice cupped her warm mug, grateful to have Michelle here. Sometimes it helped to name your fears. "I sure hope so. What are you up to today?"

"I'll also spend time connecting." Michelle sipped her tea. "But while you are saying hello, I'll be saying goodbye."

"Enigmatic, but interesting. Tell me more, Yoda."

Michelle released a long breath. "I plan to spend time at Dragonberry, alone with Lars's work. The canvases will be sent off soon, and I need to decide if there are any paintings I want to keep."

"A thoughtful, yet difficult exercise. Are you sure you're ready?"

"I am ready to let the door close on Lars. It's happening quickly. The paintings will be removed from Dragonberry Monday, so I feel the need to take care of this task today, so that I don't get caught in the swinging door."

"An interesting image. I sense some fear on your part." Alice lifted her chin. "Maybe I have superpowers, too."

"The power of insight. You are an exquisite reader, not only of books, but of people and situations. It's Dragonberry." Michelle shuddered. "Don't tell Violet, but I still feel a sense of foreboding there. I hate being there alone, but I gave Taylor and Drake the weekend off. They've been working so hard. And my friends would help but I can't pull them away from their trip to the Gorge."

"Why don't you delay the shipping? Give yourself some time. There's no rush, is there?"

"Actually, there is. According to Coyote Jones, we may have a short window of time before buyers' interest in Lars's art wanes. We're paying rush fees to photographers and art movers, and I can't disrupt the process. Coyote has been so helpful; I don't want to disappoint him. For many reasons, it must happen today." She shook her head. "It doesn't feel right to go there alone, but what am I afraid of, the spirit of Lars, like *Casper the Friendly Ghost*? I'm being silly."

"You need to be mindful of your intuition. Of course you shouldn't be there alone." Alice checked her Fitbit. "If you can go later, I'd be happy to accompany you. In an hour or two?"

"I would be eternally grateful for your help. You've done so much for me already. Your investigation has cleared my name."

"Well, almost. I know the police have taken Rosie into custody, but . . ." But what? Alice had some doubts?

"Madison called me last night, and I'm no longer a suspect in my husband's murder. I'm free to leave town, and I've booked my flight to LA. There's a hole in my heart, and I need to be surrounded by family now. One can't underestimate the healing powers of my auntie June's dumplings."

Alice hated the feeling of loss, but she understood the need to move on. "We'll miss you."

"I'll miss you all, but I can't impose on your hospitality forever."

"On the contrary. If you haven't noticed, I have a penchant for surrounding myself with family and friends. And I have the house to accommodate that joy. You are always welcome here."

Michelle pressed a hand to her heart. "I have found great comfort here."

Endings and beginnings.

Upstairs, Alice pulled on the shirt and paired it with worn jeans, a white zip-up hoodie, and sneakers. This was a look from soccer days. Not to try to reclaim something that was over, but Alice wanted Lauren to know that she remembered. She may not have recognized Lauren's artwork on the puzzle, but she remembered the days and months, the mundane yet comforting events of Lauren's childhood. There was a place in her heart for the past, right alongside the space to etch new happenings.

Endings and beginnings.

Chapter Fifty-one

Lauren and the twins had settled on Waterfront Park as a meeting place. When Alice had pointed out that it might be rainy and cold, as October days tended to be, Madison had contacted Parks and Rec and booked a small pavilion overlooking the river. "It's neutral territory," Taylor had told her. "And more private than a coffee shop or sandwich place."

As if they were diplomats trying to negotiate their countries out of a cold war. Alice hoped that one day, down the road, Lauren would feel comfortable enough to spend time at the house that was once her home.

Moving quickly through the drizzle with her hood up, Alice spotted the small pavilion and noticed a fire burning in its built-in fireplace. Whoa. After Dragonberry, fires seemed to hold more threat than cozy appeal. But there was a young woman tending it with authority. Lauren? She wore Jackie O sunglasses, despite the gray, along with jeans and a retro satin baseball jacket. Her shiny copper hair was piled up on her head and staked with two chopsticks.

"Hello?" Alice said, dismayed when the woman turned to reveal a round face and wide nose. Not Lauren.

Jackie O smiled as she pulled the grate over the firebox. "You must be Mrs. Pepper." She pointed behind Alice. "There she is."

"Hi, Mom." Lauren rose from a boxy metal chair, one of two that had been pulled close to the fire. Her hair was completely blond, golden as blanched wheat, under a white baseball cap, but that smile, the pert nose, those eyes—this was her daughter. She wore a black trench coat and jeans and blue Converse shoes. A peacock-blue chambray scarf that dangled around her neck mirrored the sparkling blue in her eyes, her most stunning feature.

"Oh, honey!" Alice wanted to laugh and cry at the same time. "It's so good to see you! But, sorry, I promised myself I wouldn't gush."

"That's okay. I'm overwhelmed, too." Lauren extended her arms. "Can I get a hug?"

Alice stepped forward and folded her daughter in her arms and held her tight as the wave of relief and love washed over her. This was real. At least for now, in this moment, they were together again.

"I missed you," Lauren said.

Alice started breathing again. "I missed you too, honey."

Lauren patted her shoulder, then stepped back and thanked the woman, Scout, for setting things up.

"Text me when you're done," Scout said, heading off.

Was she a friend? A partner?

Lauren answered the unspoken question. "Scout is a friend from work. She agreed to set things up for us."

"And what is it you do for work?"

"We'll get to that. But first things first." She pointed to the chairs. "Take a seat. There's a blanket for you, since it's chilly here, and I know I'm always cold these days."

"Nice, thank you." Alice sat down, unfolded the blanket, and wrapped it around her shoulder.

"First, Mom, it's so good to see you, but I confess, I've been sort of spying on you these past few months."

Alice nodded, thinking of those times she'd sensed someone watching. At the children's festival. Walking through town.

Lauren wound her golden locks around one finger. "I'm sorry, but I needed to see you, and I was too chickenhearted to make it happen. Too scared."

"Scared of me? Oh, honey, I don't bite. You know that."

"I didn't have the guts to apologize, which is something every addict needs to do. I'm sorry, Mom. I know I've wronged you and hurt you, so many times. I cost you a fortune, in and out of rehab. I threatened to take the girls away from you, though I think you knew that was just a ploy to get money. I was kind of rotten."

"Well, your behavior was rotten at times." Alice wanted to stop her, tell her that it was okay, all in the past, but she sat with her lips pinched together and listened. She had learned in counseling that apologies were part of an addict's recovery, that apologies brought remorse, which could fuel positive action. At least, that was the theory. So, she let Lauren talk.

Lauren had been clean and sober for more than five years now. She owned a small condo in Seattle, where she worked for a music producer, recruiting and touring with new talent, hence the sporadic travel.

"And there's also this power you have over me, Mom. You're a smart, amazing woman, and you give great advice. But something inside me has always rebelled against that because . . . I'm just a defiant person. I think I've got it in hand now, but you know the mantra, one day at a time."

"We do know that one." When things were at their

worst, Jeff used to say, "One hour at a time." He'd meant it as a cold joke, but Alice had recognized the underpinning of truth. Alice maintained her quiet demeanor as Lauren kept talking about her recovery, her growing sense of responsibility, her guilt over leaving her girls.

"And then there's the whole me-first aspect of recovery," Lauren went on. "It's a selfish process, I understand that. And while I've been getting my act together, you've raised my beautiful girls to be . . . amazing women."

"You were there in the early days. In and out, at least. But the girls are pretty wonderful, aren't they?" Alice pulled the edges of the blanket closer and hugged herself, thinking of the twins.

"Madison has chosen a career that suits her need for order and fairness," Lauren said, "and Taylor is all over the place, I know, but she's a fascinating explorer, and one day I know she'll find her niche."

"No doubt," Alice agreed. "In the meantime, it's satisfying to see her trying on many different hats."

They talked about the twins for a while, and then about Alice's job at the library.

"I know about Alice's Restaurant," Lauren said. "And yes, I've seen Dad, but not often. His lack of motivation is . . ."

"Annoying? Disheartening? Maddening?" Alice put a hand to her mouth. "Sorry. Did I say that out loud?"

Lauren gave a wry smile. "I'm sorry the restaurant didn't work out for you, Mom. I know it was your dream."

"It was . . . until it wasn't anymore. I still love to cook for family and friends. I had to get out of that industrial kitchen before that passion was sucked out of me. And I'm lucky I was able to return to the library. The work consumes me sometimes, but I do love it there."

"I'm happy for you. You were always a cool librarian, letting kids talk there when other libraries shushed us. Hosting game nights and mystery Sundays."

"Good times," Alice agreed.

Lauren dropped her feet to the ground and leaned forward in her chair. "So, here's what I'm hoping. I sent you that puzzle, the picture I drew of our family way back when, because I wanted to open the door to a new relationship between us. If you're willing. I mean, after me putting you through the grinder a few dozen times."

They'd been at this juncture before, more than once.

Please let this be the last time. It felt hopeful, more solid than ever. Alice leaned forward so that she could look directly into Lauren's sparkly blue eyes. "The answer is yes. Yes, yes, yes."

Stress seemed to drain from Lauren; as if Alice could have ever said no!

Alice reached over and clasped her daughter's hand. "I was so moved when I realized you'd made your artwork into a puzzle. I felt like you were speaking my language."

"I was trying." Lauren opened her fisted hand and on her palm was a puzzle piece. "This is the missing piece to the art puzzle. Taylor said it drove you nuts, but I was making a statement. I've been missing in action, I know, but I'm back."

Throat tight with love and sorrow and joy, Alice fought back tears. "I should have known," she said. "It was so obvious; you were the missing piece."

Alice took the puzzle piece and turned it around in her hands, loving the simplicity of the symbol. You needed to visualize something to make it real. Lauren was back. Alice couldn't wait to snap this piece into place on the kitchen puzzle table.

"And what's all this about tracking down a killer?" Lauren folded her arms. "Isn't that Madison's job?"

"You know I've always been a puzzler," Alice said.

"I hope you're being careful, staying safe," Lauren said sternly.

The love Alice felt for her bossy daughter in that moment... She was tempted to tease Lauren, poke at her maternal instincts. "When someone needs help, I just can't say no."

Lauren nodded. "That's you in a nutshell, Mom."

It was a moment to bask in love and relief.

Chapter Fifty-two

After a few giddy goodbyes, Alice sat in her car and watched her daughter and Scout drive off. She could feel herself gently wafting back to earth after the joy and hope of reconnecting.

"Promise me you won't worry about me, and I'll keep doing my part to stay clean and sober," Lauren had said. "One day at a time, of course."

Alice texted Michelle that she was available after "a great meeting," and they agreed to head toward Dragonberry Lane. Although she was tempted to text Ruby and Taylor and Violet with happy updates, Alice decided to wait until that evening. It felt right to spend the afternoon sorting thoughts and settling her emotions.

There was one exception. Alice called Stone, but got his voice mail. "Just wanted to let you know that my chat with Lauren went well. Details later, if you're available this evening. I'm off to assist Michelle one last time at Dragonberry!"

She was about to tuck her phone away when she noticed that she had a few e-mails. One was from the Connecticut State Nursing Board. An answer about Claudia Finley.

She opened the e-mail and blinked. Claudia Finley had received three complaints, all regarding the overmedication of patients in a postsurgical unit of a hospital. Accused of administering lethal doses of pain meds to patients. All three patients had died. Finley contended that the patients were self-medicating in addition to prescription meds, which was possible. "But three identical cases?"

Was Claudia Finley an angel of death?

It didn't make her more likely to be Lars's killer, but the uncomfortable coincidence didn't make for a strong character reference.

She called Madison but got voice mail. Frustrated, she left a message about Claudia Finley's nursing record and started her car. She was halfway across town when her phone dinged with a missed voice mail. Of course, the ringer had been off since her meeting with Lauren.

Waiting at a red light with the colorful flower shop in view, she saw that the message wasn't from Stone, but from Madison.

"Gran, I'm working but had to let you know that we got the DNA results back from the homicide scene. The only DNA on the murder weapon, the knife, was matched with Rosie Suarez and Lars Olsen. The analysis doesn't necessarily put Rosie at the scene, since she'd been staying at the house, using the kitchen.

"But there was one surprise. The fireplace tool—the poker—contained Lars's DNA, along with DNA that was a close match, but not Lars. A family member."

"Who's that?" Alice said aloud.

"There were burnt skin cells found on the honed tip of the poker," Madison reported in the recording.

"Not Lars, but a blood relation," Alice muttered, then drew in a sharp breath.

In unison, she chimed in with Madison's voice, announcing: "Henry Finley."

Chapter Fifty-three

"We're bringing in Claudia and Henry Finley now," Madison's message went on. "We're just outside their bed-and-breakfast in downtown West Hazel, so I gotta go. Talk later."

Henry Finley... Her heart raced a bit as she moved slowly through the green light, thinking about turning the car around. She wasn't far from the quaint bed-and-breakfast where the Finleys were staying with the ancient tea lady. If she zipped over there now, she might be in time to see the arrests, hear the confessions, witness the wrap-up of Lars Olsen's murder.

But she'd promised to meet Michelle....

A honk behind her made her pick up speed. She certainly didn't want to be that old lady cruising along at five miles per hour in a thirty zone.

There was no turning back; she needed to help her friend and stay out of Madison's hair.

But the revelation tapped at her, pushing her mind to picture the way the crime had played out.

Why would Henry's DNA be on the honed tip of the fire poker?

Because someone had jabbed him with it. That would have hurt like hell, left a mark, possibly a burn or infection. And Henry had seemed stiff recently. A pat on the shoulder had brought tears to his eyes. She'd thought he was sick, but he'd been injured.

Injured with the fire poker at Dragonberry, probably at the scene of Lars's death.

As scenarios ran through her head, Alice could imagine Henry visiting that beastly house on that cold, rainy night. The fire raging. Lars acting just as hot and volatile.

Lars had attacked Henry with the poker.

Henry and Claudia had probably come to Dragonberry Lane to prod Lars about the child support agreement. It was apparent that the "mentorship" had not been going well. Or maybe Lars had asked them over to weasel his way out of paying child support. If Rosie was telling the truth about Lars's change of heart, he was going to stick with Michelle, and he wouldn't have wanted her to find out about his fiscal responsibility for his son.

She figured that Claudia had been there too, as mother and son were generally inseparable. But she didn't see Claudia striking her son, and she suspected that Henry had killed his father in self-defense. The Finleys had to know that the child support agreement would be voided upon Henry's death. They didn't want Lars dead; they wanted their money.

Maybe Lars had taken a jab at Claudia and Henry had stepped in to defend her? Possible.

The jab with the fire poker had then provoked the stabbing. But it would have been tricky for Henry to suffer the attack, and then come around behind Lars to stab him.

So it had been Claudia, with her gloved hands, grabbing

the kitchen knife in a panic, ramming Lars in the back to make him stop wounding her son with the poker.

Most likely a hot fire poker. Alice cringed at the thought.

The Finleys had gotten the money they came to town for, but at what cost?

A young man had participated in the killing of his own father, and the violence, pain, and trauma of that moment would certainly haunt him forever.

Chapter Fifty-four

The drive down the muddy, puddled lane to the Dragonberry house revitalized images of the roaring fire, her imaginings of poor Henry getting jabbed with a red-hot poker, and his mother wheeling around to stab Lars in the back.

A real-life nightmare.

But that was another day, another time. The house had been cleansed and Zen-decorated, and Michelle was here today saying her own spiritual goodbye to her husband's work. At the end of the lane, she pulled up in front of the house and parked beside Michelle's Subaru, freshly recovered from the county impound lot.

The ground in front of the porch steps was mucky and indented with footprints. Alice moved around it gingerly and went to the front door and rang the bell. When there was no answer, she knocked and waited a minute. Was Michelle in the bathroom? Taking a walk out back?

Alice tried the door. Unlocked. "Michelle?" she called, stepping in.

Inside, the redecorated house was quiet and orderly. The fireplace was cold, still blocked by a statue and plant.

The paintings were set up in a more orderly fashion, now labeled with bright yellow number cards.

"Michelle?" Alice called, walking around the sofa toward the fireplace and freezing in place.

Teapot on the floor. Spilled tea, mug on its side.

Body on the couch. "Michelle." Her body was folded sideways onto the sofa, as if she had collapsed to the right from a sitting position. It wasn't a sleeping position.

Panic thrummed in Alice's ears as she rushed to her friend. "Are you okay?" She pressed her fingers to the side of her neck, hoping and praying. "Yes!" There was a slow pulse. Still alive.

Struggling to tamp down her shrieking nerves, Alice pulled out her phone and called 911. Michelle looked pale, but Alice could see the rise and fall of her chest as the line rang. That was some relief. Alice wondered what had happened. A fainting spell or a . . .

"Don't move." The cold voice startled her as she caught a dark glimmer in her peripheral vision.

A shiny black gun held by Claudia Finley.

Alice's hopes slunk to the floor.

"Something's wrong with Michelle," she said, like a kid defending herself to a hall monitor. "I'm just calling for an—"

In that moment her phone was torn from her hands, a result of Henry coming in from the right with a hard slap. The phone clattered to the floor as a voice answered. Henry picked it up and cut off the call.

"That hurt." Alice massaged her hands.

"Sorry," Henry muttered, scuttling back toward the table and chairs.

"Michelle is fine." Claudia, dressed in black jeans, sweater, and gloves that could have placed her in a James Bond film, came around and moved closer. She held the gun with two hands, the way they taught you at the shooting range. "She's just resting."

"But I couldn't wake her up," Alice said, "and please, stop pointing that thing at me. Did you think I was a thief, come to make off with the paintings?" A stupid theory, but maybe Claudia would latch on to it, see it as a way out without getting in deeper.

"Over there." Claudia motioned her back with the gun. "Sit on the couch next to Michelle. You can pat her back and comfort her all you want. That's what you do, right? You're the fixer, sooo sympathetic to people's problems. Soothe a bee sting or defend a widow suspected of murdering her husband."

"I try," Alice said, taking a seat on the couch. Trying not to tick off Claudia, she put a hand on Michelle's shoulder, then pressed two fingers to her neck. A pulse was still beating. Some consolation.

"Well, you should have stayed out of all this business." Claudia waved the gun in a circle around the room, making Henry wince when it pointed his way. "I warned you to butt out. When you started dogging me with all those questions, I figured a few shots would have you running scared, though I didn't know you'd have your gaggle of geese following along."

So Claudia had been the shooter outside the art gallery that night. If only Alice had pieced that part together. "My friends and family are a great source of support." Alice tried to turn up the heat. "In fact, they should be here any minute. Taylor and Drake have been here every day this week, so you'd better—"

"They're not coming. I heard Michelle telling someone about how this would be her quiet day to spend with Lars's art."

Dang, Alice bit her lips together, her bluff called. Stone was the only person she'd told about her detour here, but there was no telling when he'd get that message. And her call to 911 had probably been cut off before the location registered.

"Michelle's a fool to think there's any decent quality in Lars's art," Claudia went on. "Good old Larry. Pathetic. He was a loser back when he tortured me in art school, and he never changed, not really."

"I'm sorry for the way he made you suffer. He should have been locked up for assault."

"Instead, he became an artistic genius. The wonder boy of a new movement. A star on the rise, while I got left out in the cold."

"Life kicks us around sometimes," Alice said. "Things are unfair, our hearts are broken. But Lars is dead now, and you're alive. And you have this loving, talented son, and enough money to begin anew."

"It was the bare minimum, that child support agreement. I could have gotten more with a better lawyer." Claudia flailed one arm toward the roomful of paintings. "And there's more to be had. Coyote is talking about millions of dollars in sales. Once I found out what people are willing to pay for Lars's work, now that he's gone, I couldn't let Henry miss out on that. He's Lars's son; he should be an heir."

"But Lars had a wife, and they'd set up a living trust. Michelle gets everything." Alice nodded. "And you think Henry should get a piece of that pie."

"He should! The laws are so unfair." Claudia removed one hand to push back a lock of hair that had fallen from her ponytail. Her face showed the strain of hard years.

Alice figured it hadn't been easy, but Claudia had lost her path, her moral compass.

"If you need more money, I'm sure—"

"That's not the point. Michelle didn't need any of Lars's money. She's rolling in her own stinking success. We came here to give her a chance to share it. Give Henry his half. But suddenly she got weird about it. Needs her lawyer, needs to think about it, what's the right thing to do. So I went into the bathroom and loaded up a syringe. I'm really good with figuring out meds."

That's not what I hear. Alice didn't dare say it. Claudia was already on the edge.

"I calculated Michelle's dosage. Not enough to kill her, just enough to put her out for a while."

"And you're planning to steal the paintings while she's unconscious?"

"Are you kidding? We'd definitely be caught trying to fence a bunch of canvases. No, Michelle is going to commit suicide. She'll be found in her car at the bottom of that murky pond. I guess she took Lars's death pretty hard, after all." There was a decadent glimmer in Claudia's eyes, as if it were a delicious thought. "Michelle will be dead, an apparent suicide, and the proceeds from Lars's estate will go to his only heir. My son, Henry."

"And you think you'll get away with that?" Alice asked, her voice laced with disapproval.

"Sure. No one's going to know we killed her."

"*I'll* know," Alice objected.

"Well, sure. That's why we need to kill you, too." Claudia lowered the gun beneath her sour smile. "You're going to ride along with your friend into the water. I guess you could say we're killing two birds with one pond."

Chapter Fifty-five

Pushing back the panic, tamping down the fear that tugged at her to shriek, Alice focused on deep breathing for a minute. She knew she needed to stall, in any way possible, before she, too, was also injected with a dose of knockout drops. She thought of enlisting Henry, though when she looked his way he had melted into his hoodie, hunched over on the edge of the chair, rubbing his shoulder. Probably the wound from the poker burn.

"You're looking stressed, Henry," Alice said, trying to sound supportive. "If this plan doesn't sit well with you, now is the time to speak up."

"Leave him alone," Claudia whined. "He's just a kid, doing as he's told."

"He's almost eighteen," Alice argued. "He'll probably be tried as an adult. No mercy."

"That's not a problem because there won't be any trial!" Claudia was losing patience. "And he's a good boy who does what his mother says."

Henry reached for the string on his hoodie, tugging at the cords. "She might be right, Mom. I mean, if you give Michelle a chance, she'll probably share the inheritance."

He was on his feet now, pacing. "You could make her sign a paper that says that, right? I bet she'd do it."

"That's the most ridiculous idea . . . hold a gun on the woman until she signs the papers? Any judge that hears that scenario is going to boot us off to jail."

"But there has to be a way," Alice said, egging him on. "I'm sure you can get your share out of this without killing anyone, Henry."

"Mom, can't we?"

"You're forgetting that we've already killed someone." Claudia's words sent Henry's spirit crashing to the ground. "One notch on your belt, son."

He paused, casting a woeful look at his mother as he started rubbing his shoulder again.

"But that was an accident, wasn't it?" Alice asked. "And you didn't kill him, Henry. It was you, Claudia. When Lars attacked Henry with the hot poker, you reacted immediately to protect your child. It's what any good mother would do. When Lars wouldn't stop hurting your son, you searched for the nearest, quickest way to stop him. A kitchen knife."

"How do you know this?" Claudia scowled at Alice, then wheeled on her son. "Did you tell her?"

He shook his head, a frantic fear in his eyes.

"The forensic lab results didn't show any trace of Henry's DNA on the kitchen knife," Alice said. "It didn't show yours, either, Claudia, because you were wearing gloves."

Claudia looked down at her gloved hands, trembling now with the weight of the gun. "Finally, these damned gloves were good for something."

"But Henry's DNA was found on the tip of the fireplace poker." Alice turned to Henry. "It places you at the scene, but also reveals that you were a victim in this scenario. If you go to the police now, I'm sure these circumstances, along with the past assaults in Lars's history, would provide an avenue for leniency." Alice knew this much was a stretch, but she had to win them over. "You'll probably get off with probation."

"Mom?" Henry looked up, a pained expression on his face as he rubbed his shoulder. "Maybe she's right. We could go to the police, just try to straighten everything out."

"And lose everything we've waited and worked for? No way. We're on the verge of something big, and I'm not going to let you throw it away because some nosy librarian is predicting gloom and doom."

"But Mom, what if she's right?"

"I speak the truth," Alice said. "You're not getting away with this. With those DNA results, the police are going to come after Henry soon. They're searching for you now."

"I don't believe you," Claudia snapped. "I think you're making it all up. And if they do come for Henry, he's just going to say that Lars attacked him and he stabbed back in self-defense."

"That doesn't make sense. The angles are all wrong."

"I don't want to hear from you anymore." Claudia raised the gun for emphasis. "Henry, get my meds kit. There's another full dose in there, maybe two. Enough to take care of Alice."

Henry rose and plodded toward one of the back rooms, his distress apparent.

"Then, you need to carry Michelle out to her car," Claudia barked orders after him. "Put her in the back, and we'll move her to the driver's seat when we get the car closer to the pond. I'm not pushing that car up the slope."

Claudia walked past Alice, assessing. "What are you, two hundred pounds or so?"

"Excuse me?" Alice shot her an indignant look.

"Just to calculate dosage. Don't worry, it's lorazepam. I think you'll like it."

"I think not."

"It'll calm you down and make you sleep. Of course, too much could kill you, if I don't get the dosage right."

"I thought that was your intention."

"I'd rather you drown. When they dredge the pond and find you in a day or two, most of it will be out of your system." She perched on the edge of a chair so that she could lean the gun on the armrest. "They don't tell you that these things get heavy."

"You mean it's not in the murderer's handbook?"

"And bring me a gag," Claudia called to her son. "This one's getting on my nerves."

It might be a bad idea to keep needling Claudia. Alice knew she'd lost the woman's sympathy, but Henry had potential. The kid lacked his mother's grit. But how could she get around Claudia?

Henry reappeared with a syringe in hand. "This is the last dose," he said.

"What? There should be two or three. What happened?"

"We must have left them back at the room." Henry shrugged. "Sorry. Unless you have them tucked in a secret place or something."

"Let me look." Claudia handed him the gun. "You watch her!" she ordered before stomping into the bathroom.

With a hypo in one hand and a gun in the other, Henry came close to Alice and leaned in. "This is mostly saline," he whispered. "So pretend to get sleepy and pass out in, like, two or three minutes."

Hope flared as Alice whispered, "Why don't we stop her? You have the gun. Or call nine-one-one. Just—"

"I can't." He jerked back, giving a fake cough.

"Nothing left in the kit. I guess that is the last dose." Claudia came breezing back into the room as Henry's face hardened, stern and cold.

"Please, don't do this." Alice made one last attempt to stop them. "It won't end well."

Henry turned pleading eyes to his mother.

But Claudia took the syringe and came closer. Alice turned away from the sight of the woman attacking her with a needle. "It sure won't end well for you, but you pushed me to this, Alice. If you'd just minded you own business, you wouldn't be here today, would you?"

"I came here for my friend." Alice felt a jab, and then the push under her skin.

"Well, then," Claudia said, "you just have to go down with the ship."

Mostly saline he'd said, though Alice felt some softness moving through her system. No need to pretend it was working.

Relaxation. Letting go. Facing death? It didn't matter anymore because she could go to the resting place.

"You lied to me," she murmured as she sank lower on the sofa. "Nine-one-one."

"What?" Claudia snapped. "What's she saying?"

Before Alice could repeat her words, she was carried off on a gentle wave.

Chapter Fifty-six

The smell was the first thing. Dank and earthy, like mushrooms that had gone bad. And then the cold water that soaked her feet and legs.

A cold bath? It sent a chill through her. Her legs were trembling and then her whole body shook. Things were spinning. *Make them stop.* But no, it was in her head. Dizzy and sick. She wanted to sleep but the water wouldn't let her.

When she opened her eyes, everything was fuzzy. A painful vision from the front seat of a car that was tipping hood down into dirty water. Had she driven off a bridge?

No, Michelle Chong was in the driver's seat. Her body limp, collapsed on the steering wheel. They were trapped in a car that was sinking quickly into a deserted pond, far enough from any neighbor or main road that no one would hear their screams.

Alice couldn't believe that Claudia and Henry had followed through on the plan, but there was no time for regrets. No time to panic. A cold calm resolve pushed her to make a move.

Water was swirling in, rising up over the leather seats.

She had to wake up fast and do something. Get them out of this watery tomb.

"Michelle?"

No answer, because Michelle was not awake.

Drugged, just like you.

And sinking fast in the Dragonberry pond.

Do something! Get out! Alice knew that people drowned in cars all the time. She pulled the door handle on her right and shoved and shoved, reminding herself, *You can't open the doors underwater. And the water is rising.*

Get out. There had to be a way. She looked for something heavy to bang on the glass. Inside the glove box she was hoping to find a wrench. Just tissues and paperwork.

But even a wrench wouldn't work. She knew these things. She needed one of those special little punchers, a glass breaker. Alice had one in her glove compartment, but this wasn't her car. She searched the glove box again, and then the compartment between the seats as the water rose, seeping over her jeans.

Beside her, Michelle moaned—a good sign.

"Can you wake up?" Alice pushed her back from the steering wheel and though she moaned again, she was still out of it, her head lolled to the side. Leaning across her, Alice felt into the door pocket of the car, looking for the mini-glass hammer. Hadn't she seen one recently?

Come on, come on! Water's rising. No time.

She pushed the button of the moon roof, then tried to push it up. Useless.

Sinking back into her seat, she snatched away a brochure floating by the dashboard controls. Something in the water caught her eye. Something pink. A cylinder dangling from the key chain in the ignition. It could be Mace or a pocket flashlight but . . .

Her heart leapt, water splashing as she reached forward to snatch the pink object. When the keys came out of the ignition and Alice saw the print on the side of the pink tube, her heart lifted. Gr8Escape was a familiar brand. It was a car escape tool.

She pressed the end of the tube to the corner of the windshield and pushed.

The window glass exploded in hundreds of small chunks. Half of the shattered glass stayed in place.

Water began rushing in from the new opening, but Alice didn't care. She pulled the sleeves of her hoodie over her hands to buffer the flying shards and pushed the glass out, trying to clear the way. "We got this," she told Michelle as she moved to smash out the two front windows, just to be safe.

It had worked.

They had a path of escape.

A glimmer of sunlight through the gray murk of the water now rushing into the vehicle.

Except they were going to have to swim out, and Michelle was still out of it. How did you get an unconscious person to hold her breath? Shimmy through a jagged opening? Swim to the shore?

The water had reached the top of the dashboard now, gushing just below Alice's chin.

"Wake up. Please, honey. Come on." Alice patted Michelle's cheek. "If ever there was a time for you to harness your inner warrior, it's now."

Chapter Fifty-seven

To Alice's surprise, Michelle's eyes slid open. "What's happening?"

"We need to get out." She gave Michelle a shake. "Okay?"

Michelle lifted her head, mumbled something about koi swimming in, and then sunk back onto the seat. Well, semiconscious was better than limp.

"Honey, you need to help me help you. Try to keep your head above the waterline, and don't swallow the pond water."

The exit was a graceless, awkward affair.

Michelle coughed as water slapped her face. Helped by gravity-defying water, Alice was able to dislodge her from the cockpit and pull her into the opening without much effort.

From there—not so easy. Fortunately, Michelle was a trim woman. Leaning against the edge for leverage, Alice lifted her through the windshield opening and let out a cry.

That move was a mistake.

A gasp escaped her as she eased her wounded midriff away from the jagged edge. The skin on her arm and side, near the lower rib cage, shrieked. Working through the pain, she kept pushing until Michelle was hoisted onto the sinking hood of the car. Michelle huddled there, dazed but finally coming alive.

A quick glance down revealed a red stain of blood in the water and on her hoodie, as well as a jagged ridge of cubed glass along the edge of the smashed windshield.

If only Alice had listened to her doctor about doing some light weight training.

Still trying to shield her body with the hoodie, Alice finally managed to lever herself out of the jagged opening to land on the hood near Michelle. From there, she convinced Michelle to trust her as she put her in a swimmer's hold and side-stroked out of the deep water.

It was only a few yards of swimming until they reached a spot where Alice could stand on the soggy pond bottom and pull Michelle along. A few deadly yards. So close.

Alice was sure that tears were streaming down her face, mixed with the foul water and slime, as she dragged Michelle through the shallows and over the muck, far enough up the slope to be safe. Michelle moaned—a good sign. Alice gently lowered her head and shoulders to the ground and fell onto the mud beside her to rest, just for a minute, before her next move.

She lay with one cheek on the mud so she could keep an eye on Michelle, who had stirred a few times during their escape. Could they make it up to the house? Could Alice make it up there alone to call for help? Was her cell phone still there, abandoned on the side table? Or had Claudia been smart enough to remove it?

Were Claudia and Henry still there, like the evil thing that wouldn't die? Perish the thought.

But she felt confident that they had moved on. Claudia

was so sure of her plan, and she wouldn't have stuck around to risk being caught. She would drag herself up to the house . . . in a minute.

Alice pressed her palm to the gritty mud, thankful to be here and breathing on planet Earth. A short time later, the mud seemed to be flashing red.

Weird. More side effects of the drug?

When the flashing persisted, she lifted her head just enough to look up the slope. There, at the top of the ridge, was a police car, its emergency lights flashing. A uniformed cop stepped out of the vehicle, stared down toward the pond, and then ran toward her.

Help.

At last.

She closed her eyes and collapsed against the muck.

Chapter Fifty-eight

"Ms. Pepper... Alice? Are you okay?"

The dark-haired man came in and out of focus as the gray clouds beyond his head seemed to billow into black puffs.

A cop. Zhao?

"Where's Madison?" Her voice was soft and hoarse.

"Madison's okay, but she's going to the hospital by ambulance." Zhao leaned in close, assessing her. "She took a hard hit when the other vehicle crashed into her patrol car, but she keeps saying she's fine."

"Crash?" Alice was struggling to piece the bits together. "Who crashed?"

"Claudia Finley was driving the other car, speeding down Dragonberry Lane. Apparently trying to escape this scene. A potential drowning, that's what the nine-one-one caller said. We had just given up on the Finleys' B and B, realizing they weren't there. We were roaring down the lane—two squad cars and an ambulance—when Finley and her son came barreling down the lane, lost control, and hit Madison's car."

"That's terrible." Alice's focus was sharpening, though

it was easier to listen than to talk. "But Madison's okay? Everyone's okay?"

"Madison looks okay to me. Michelle has a slow pulse, but she's breathing. Claudia Finley is unconscious. She's been loaded into another ambulance. Her son seems uninjured, and he's talking up a blue streak. He says he's the person who called nine-one-one about the potential drowning. Says that you made him feel awful; he couldn't let it happen."

"A jolt to the conscience doesn't feel good." Alice pressed her hands into the sand to lift her torso into a seated position. A supreme effort. "Neither does drowning in a pond of slime."

"Henry told us how they rolled the car into the pond. How did you escape?"

Alice took a deep, sustaining breath, and then she told him. Zhao nodded thoughtfully.

"Alice!"

She and Zhao glanced up the slope to a tall, long-limbed man silhouetted against the gray sky. He swept his battered fedora off, revealing thick silver hair.

Stone. Relief swept over her at the sight of him. Even in her muzzy, slimy haze, she was happy to have him here.

He ran down the incline, reaching Alice in seconds. "Alice! Geez Louise! Are you all right? I headed over as soon as I got your message. Something just didn't sit right with me about you and Michelle being here alone."

"I'm okay."

Stone shot at look at Michelle, who was being tended to by Zhao. "Is Michelle all right?"

Zhao gave a thumbs-up. "She's responding, but groggy."

"She was drugged," Alice said, "as was I. Though Michelle got a heavier dose."

Stone squatted beside her and gently touched her cheek. "You're bleeding, Alice. There's blood on your jacket, too."

"It's what happens when you swim out of a submerged car through an opening lined with broken glass. I don't think any of the cuts are serious."

"You're being glib, as usual, but that's a pretty brave feat." Stone's voice soothed her like warm honey. Or maybe that was the lingering drug.

"Alice is a hero," Zhao said. "She got Michelle out of the car, too, and that's not easy when the other person isn't cooperating."

"You are amazing." There was a golden light in Stone's hazel eyes as he nodded at her.

"Those eyes . . ." She wiped something from her cheek—a clump of muck. "Is there green slime in my hair, or is that just a fond look?"

"You know I'm crazy about you."

Her heart danced, a little flicker under the weight of recovery. Crazy! That was far beyond fond.

Stone extended a hand to her. "Can I help you up?"

"You might want to wait," Zhao said. "We have an ambulance coming for you, Alice."

"I don't need it," Alice insisted.

"You should get checked over by a doctor," Zhao advised.

"And after what you've been through, driving isn't a good idea. I'd be happy to drive you to Riverwood."

"That sounds like a better plan." Alice pulled her soggy jacket away from her skin and grimaced. "If you can stand the smell of a swamp thing in your car."

"We'll crack a window," Stone teased. He put his hat on, extended both arms, and suddenly, she was lifted onto her feet. Her body was wobbly, but he held her securely.

With one hand around her waist, his body pressed to her side, his eyes met hers. "You okay to walk?"

Well, she certainly couldn't let him carry her. "I think so."

"We'll see you at the hospital, Officer Zhao," Stone said as he guided Alice up the ridge.

And that was how she floated away from Dragonberry Lane in Stone's arms.

Chapter Fifty-nine

Hours later, Alice felt a strong sense of relief and an odd glow of well-being as she relaxed on a hospital gurney. Maybe that odd glow was from the IV line in her arm, but she was alive, as were the people she cared about. Wasn't that enough reason to proclaim it a good day in West Hazel?

The ER bay was shared by Madison, who lay beside her on a bed of her own, close enough so that they could hold hands from time to time. She had taken a hard hit when Claudia had floored it trying to escape the Dragonberry house, lost control of her car, and crashed into the approaching police vehicle driven by Madison.

Michelle Chong was being treated in another bay, and she was lucid enough to send Alice a message through Nurse Karen.

"She says she's fine. Just a small cut on her shoulder. She's starting to come around, and she's eternally grateful to Alice."

"Such good news!" Alice exclaimed.

The attempted pond drowning and the unfortunate accident caused by escaping suspects on the lane had brought in five patients—an overflow at Riverwood Hospital, where Saturday late mornings in the ER usually saw a fair share of hand injuries from brunch-loving bagel buffs, asthma attacks, and suspected heart attacks.

At first a trip to the hospital had seemed excessive, but then Alice had realized the extent of her injuries. A cut along the hairline of her cheek had been glued, and the wound in her side had been stitched. Shielded by her jacket, the cut on her arm had needed only a dressing. Now she was supposed to be resting while an IV line dripped revitalizing saline into her body, but the shrunken pillow at her neck was annoying.

Stone was off searching for food, as Alice was famished after only a light breakfast. She had made the necessary phone calls to her ladies, updating them and convincing them not to rush to the hospital.

"We just arrived at the museum, but I'll leave right now," Violet had said breathlessly. "I can be there in two, three hours!"

"Not necessary," Alice insisted, providing details on the treatment she and Madison were receiving. "We'll be released before you get back. Please, stay in the Gorge and enjoy your day. I'll see you tonight."

And so Violet continued her tour with the book club ladies, Taylor stayed to finish her shift at the restaurant, and Ruby continued her excursion with Coyote Jones, who was "truly a laugh a minute."

Officer Zhao had spent some time in the room, taking Alice's official statement. The words flowed easily once the medication wore off.

"So Claudia Finley admitted that she stabbed Lars Olsen?" Zhao asked.

Alice rubbed the bandage on her arm, where the numbness was wearing off. "Well, I believe I proposed that scenario, and she didn't argue. But she did lay out her plan for killing Michelle Chong. She assumed that, with Michelle gone, Lars Olsen's estate would go to Henry. And when she learned of the increased value of Lars's paintings after his death, she wanted a piece of the pie."

"Money and love." Zhao nodded as he typed into his laptop. "Those seem to be the big motivators for homicide."

"And here we've been following the theory that Lars was killed by a scorned love," Madison said from her cot. She turned to Alice, adding: "We released Rosie Suarez when the DNA analysis came in. She's still brokenhearted, but she told me she's bouncing back."

"You know, Rosie may be the only one who truly mourned Lars Olsen," Alice said. "Though theirs was a complicated relationship."

"Aren't they all?" Madison asked, glancing over at Zhao.

From the smile he gave her, Alice was certain there was something going on between them.

"What's going to happen to Henry?" Alice asked. "I mean, he did call nine-one-one."

"But a little too late to stop the drowning, if you hadn't acted so quickly." Zhao shook his head. "He's being charged as an accessory to two counts of attempted homicide. He probably won't be charged in Lars Olsen's murder, but his culpability in this second crime might be left up to a jury to decide."

There was a knock on the open door and a young man with fat curls pulled back into a ponytail entered.

"My name's Christopher. I'm here to take Madison Denham for an MRI."

"Your turn," Alice told Madison.

"I really do feel fine," Madison told the attendant.

"But you need to get checked," Zhao insisted.

"Honey, I won't let you leave without your doctor's say-so. And it's protocol."

"I know, Gran." Madison pulled the blanket up under her chin. "Ready to roll, Christopher."

A few seconds later the young attendant whisked Madison away. Zhao thanked Alice for her statement, and she was suddenly alone in the bay she'd been happy to share with her granddaughter.

At the moment, she had one lingering thought. *Food!*

When footsteps sounded in the hall, she scooched up on the gurney and straightened the blanket, eager to greet Stone.

Instead, a pretty woman with golden blond hair under a baseball cap whisked into the room.

"Mom!" She paused inside the doorway, then rushed to her bedside. "Taylor told me what happened. I'm beside myself. Thank God you're okay."

"Lauren..." Alice could barely summon a word as a mixture of emotions washed over her. Surprise to see her so soon. Comfort knowing that her daughter cared. And a surge of love for this woman, her beautiful daughter. "You came?"

"I rescheduled my flight out when I heard. Mom, it sounds like you had a really close call. How did that happen?"

Alice smiled. "How much time do you have?"

"As much as you need. Here." Lauren handed her a package of butterscotch candies, one of Alice's favorites.

Nothing could have been better in this moment—except maybe a cheeseburger.

"I still love butterscotch. It's a long story," Alice said.

"I want to hear it all." Lauren pulled a chair beside the bed and sat down, her pert nose and posture making her resemble a star pupil. "Now, tell me everything."

Chapter Sixty

That night at the house, Alice felt as if she'd stepped onto the set of the old show *This Is Your Life*. Maybe it was the pleasure of having two visits with Lauren. Maybe it was the aftermath of trauma, in which you look around at the people in your life and say, "Yes! This is precisely where I should be on this planet, with these kind, funny, smart, bighearted souls!"

Taylor wouldn't let Alice in the kitchen. Instead, she brought home catering trays of rice pilaf, broccoli with garlic, and Marry Me Chicken, a savory-sauced chicken filet dish from Alice's repertoire that made customers swoon at the restaurant.

"Help yourselves, guys," Taylor said, removing the lid from the chicken tray. "The dish is a crowd-pleaser, but I take issue with the name. Like when you love someone you ask them to marry you? As if. It's so in the box."

"Interesting perspective," Stone said, staring down at the golden cutlet on his plate blanketed in a creamy brown sauce. "Maybe it should be called Gotta Love Chicken."

"It's delicious," Violet said, sneaking a taste. "But I agree, politically incorrect."

"I do love a warm meal after a long day," said Emerald, who'd been convinced to stay for dinner when she'd dropped Violet off after the museum trip. They floated tidbits about the Maryhill Museum to anyone who would listen. Founded by American pioneer Sam Hill. Started as a mansion under construction along the Columbia River, which went bust for lack of irrigation.

"They have a replica of Stonehenge and some Rodin sculptures," Violet said.

"And traveling exhibits." Emerald added broccoli to her plate. "I can't wait to go back."

"I can't wait to feast my eyes on the Impressionist art I've always adored." Violet sighed over a mouthful of pilaf. "Marco is helping me make my dreams come true. Did you hear, we're going to Europe over Christmas break."

Alice blinked. Had she had a memory lapse from the submersion? "Who's Marco?"

"Santino," Emerald said. "Marco Santino. He's going to take Violet on a museum tour of Europe to see the great paintings of the Impressionist era."

"Really?" Ruby gave a squeal of delight. "How wonderful."

"I guess I assumed Santino had one name," Alice said, "like Madonna, or Beck. But a trip to Europe would be lovely, Vi." She wasn't sure if this meant they were going as a couple or just friends, but it was something Alice had never pried into. When Violet had broken up with her college sweetheart after graduation, she hadn't wanted to talk about it, and Alice had given her space. But the years of solitude after that had led Alice to worry a bit about her sister. For Alice, it didn't matter who Violet loved; her concern was that Violet spent so much time alone. Maybe she was just as old-fashioned as Marry Me Chicken, but Alice believed everyone should have someone to love.

And in Madison's case, Officer Zhao had stepped up. Daniel—she was supposed to call him Daniel when he was here in her home wearing a T-shirt and jeans and those fat-tongued sneakers young men favored. Madison had been given a few days' medical leave, just to be safe, and Zhao had finally relaxed the secrecy around their relationship and allowed himself to come for dinner.

"It's not against department policy," Daniel had explained, opening a beer. "We're permitted to have a relationship."

"But we both want to move forward with the utmost professionalism," Madison said firmly.

"Of course," Alice said, nearly sighing when he touched Madison's shoulder and she smiled at him. Proving her point; everyone should have someone.

When Michelle appeared wearing a long-sleeved emerald blouse over an embroidered sarong skirt, everyone applauded.

"Thank you, all. Thank you for embracing me and supporting me." Michelle clapped her hands together and then gestured toward Alice. "But this is the woman you should be cheering for. She saved my life, in more ways than one. I will never forget your heroism and generosity, Alice."

Alice thumped one hand to her heart and tipped her head to one side, touched and a little embarrassed to be put on a pedestal. "It's been wonderful getting to know you," she said. "We'll miss you, but we're excited to hear about your new journeys in LA and beyond."

"I wish *I* was going to Los Angeles," Taylor said.

"Come visit me." Michelle patted her shoulder as people turned back to their food and conversations.

"I can't believe you're going." A pouting Emerald gave Michelle a hug.

"I need my family now."

"I know, but this family will miss you," Emerald said.

"Well, you come visit me, too. And I think I'll return one day." There was a glimmer in Michelle's eyes as she smiled. "Sunriver still calls to me. I always find peace there."

Emerald linked her arm through Michelle's. "You are welcome anytime, sweetie."

Ruby appeared with a glass of lemonade for Alice. "I understand you're not imbibing tonight?"

"Trying to clear the fog from my brain." Alice toasted her with the glass and took a sip. "How was Seattle?"

"Beautiful as ever. Coyote is a joy to be around. But you gave us all quite the scare, honey. I never expected you to take your first scuba dive without me."

Alice's heart was warmed by her concern. "Believe me, slime swimming wasn't in the plans. But we sussed out the killer."

"Yes, indeed. And Lauren? How'd it go?"

"Wonderful. Details later, of course. But all good."

"I'm so happy for you, honey." Ruby gave Alice a quick hug, then went off to join the martial arts lesson in the sitting room.

Furniture had been cleared away so that Michelle could share some moves with Taylor, Emerald, and Violet.

"From the basic stance, let's begin to throw some punches, like so." Michelle demonstrated, her fists jutting out one at a time. After an impressive round, she paused, drawing her arms back to her sides. "It will be an abbreviated lesson today. I'm not as grounded as usual."

"No wonder!" Emerald said. "Let's reschedule for a day when you haven't been kidnapped and drugged."

Ruby chuckled, and Michelle rested her head on Emerald's shoulder for a sweet moment.

Then Taylor stepped forward and waved to get attention. "I got this! I took some classes with Michelle. Just follow what I do."

Leaving the ladies to their lesson, Alice found Stone out on the deck, staring out at the starry night sky.

"No kung fu lessons for you?" Alice asked. "Or are you already a martial arts expert?"

"Got my blue belt. Should have stayed with it after that, but life got in the way."

From inside, Taylor called out, "Maybe I should go for my black belt!"

"Oh, Taylor," Alice said quietly as she sat back on a chair beside Stone. "When are you going to settle on a career?"

"I see my younger self in Taylor," Stone said. "Trying dozens of jobs and careers, hoping that something bites you in the rear."

"And what was it that took the bite?"

"Never did find a strong calling. Closest I came was . . . I guess the ministry?"

Alice gulped on a sip of lemonade. "Don't tell me you were a priest."

"Working toward it. I spent two years in a Master of Divinity program."

"You are full of surprises." Alice couldn't help but chuckle. "What made you give it up?"

"I realized there are many ways to serve, and it seems that when you become a man of the cloth, a barrier separates you from your congregation." Head tipped back, Stone smiled up at the sky. "Let's be real. People clam up around ministers, act all weird and stiff. I decided I wanted to be on the other side, with the real folk."

"A fine choice, Reverend Stone," Alice teased. She rested her head back against the chair cushion and tried to calm the restlessness that had shimmered through her for much of the evening. She felt a certain loss at Michelle's imminent departure. A thrill at Lauren's reappearance. A wary guardianship over her granddaughters and their developing careers and relationships.

Why now? Was she at some unknown crossroads?

When she explained it to Stone, he mulled it over a moment.

"Probably the close call at the pond," Stone said when she described her feelings. "I've found that when you're staring in the face of death, that odd sense of calm summons the important things to the surface. Gives us a chance to check over the path we're on."

"Mmm. You're probably right." She shook her hands in the air.

"Trying to release negative energy?" Stone asked.

She nodded. "A trick Violet taught me."

She thought of the people inside, friends and family who were so dear to her. If her chosen paths had led her to a life surrounded by these folks, she was happy with the roads she'd taken. Right now, the fork in the road involved Stone.

"I have a question for you." Alice turned her head to face him. "Are we going to have a relationship?"

He didn't flinch. At least he wasn't shocked. "Isn't that what we're doing?"

"I consider myself to be an intelligent woman, but somehow you're always a step ahead of me."

He reached over and took her hand. "When all I want to be is right alongside you."

She pulled his hand close, pressing it to her heart. "And that . . . that is the right answer."

ACKNOWLEDGMENTS

One of the things that attracted me to the creation of Alice Pepper's Lonely Hearts Puzzle Club Mysteries was the chance to write about female friends, women supporting women. The process of writing and marketing these books has brought me so much support, joy, and connection to wonderful women—friends, family, and fans.

I am forever grateful for your love and encouragement.

To the ladies, women, sisters in our YaYa book group, I am grateful and honored to know you and share in the complex and sometimes comical conversations of our meetings. I've learned so much from you, and I treasure the experiences that have taken us beyond wine and conversation to art galleries, beaches, mountain resorts, and road trips from Sunriver to Vancouver, BC, to Spokane to New York City. I could never have imagined a club populated by women who are experts in their fields: teachers, artists, designers, construction experts, writers, medical technicians, and community leaders. I have to believe that it's part of the magic of books that brought us together.

To the women who have supported me and *Puzzle Me a Murder*, I can't thank you enough for the launch party, book club events, and your attendance at signings. My sister Denise gathered dozens of readers who welcomed me to St. Augustine. Robyn Doel Busch and Wendy Handwerger threw a smashing summer book launch party. You're the best!

Thanks to my family, I have the space and peace to create at home. And I'm always grateful to the talented, hardworking staff at Kensington Publishing. My editor John Scognamiglio sparks these golden ideas, and publicist Larissa Ackerman spins a web of wonderful publicity in such an enchanting way.